THE DRAGON'S REIGN

TIM MULLINS

The Dragon's Reign © Tim Mullins 2020
ISBN: 978-1-922460-01-1 (paperback)

Published in Australia by Tim Mullins and InHouse Publishing.
www.inhousepublishing.com.au

Printed in Australia by InHouse Print & Design.

A catalogue record for this book is available from the National Library of Australia

The Dragon's Reign is dedicated to my friend and brother,
Jamie "Jimmy" Barnes.

Thank you for never letting me off the hook when
I lost anything competitive to you.
Thank you for telling my mother every embarrassing thing
I have ever done.
Thank you for spending all my money in that bar at Hervey Bay.
Thank you for never taking no for an answer – even when I told you twice.
Thank you for losing our last $20 note in that tiny gap in
the escalator when we were kids.
Thank you for demonstrating how to superglue cracks in your radiator.
No, it's not "good as new."
Thank you for getting us stranded in the middle of a river during
a thunderstorm on our last fishing trip – that was quite impressive
considering we were not on a boat.
Thank you for giving me an endless list of great stories to tell the world
at your expense.
Thank you for making me laugh for over fifteen years.
But seriously.
Thank you for everything.
You are the inspiration for James.
Thank you for the unwavering support and advice.
Thank you for teaching me the true definition of friendship.
Thank you for holding me up when I could not stand on my own two feet.
Thank you for always telling me I was better than I really was.
Thank you for being there, even when I didn't deserve it.
Thank you for teaching me how to grow as a man.
Thank you for making my life utterly hilarious.
This book would not exist without you.
Thank you, brother.

ACKNOWLEDGMENTS

I would like to thank my mother, who was the first to get excited about this project. I still remember that 4:00 am email you sent me after you read the first chapter I had written.

I would like to thank my father, who picked me up on my lowest day. I am forever grateful for the laughs and guidance.

I would like to thank Alana and Tim, for your endless love and support, and for the inspiration for what became Will and Lila. You have been irreplaceable throughout this journey.

I would like to thank Craig Cassidy. Without your guidance and friendship, I never would have reached this moment. To many great years ahead, my friend.

I would like to thank Bob, for your raw honesty and advice. Thank you for believing in this book and for lighting the way ahead when I could not see the path myself.

I would like to thank my Aunty Karen and Uncle Paul, for your support and encouragement and for seeing me through some of the tougher times in life.

I would like to thank Cameron, my oldest friend. You were there eighteen years ago when *The Dragon's Reign* was a terrible science fiction story written in a .txt document.

And Chardea, my niece and first ever fan. Thank you for your encouragement and confidence. You never let me give up on this book and I promised you that I would finish it. I hope it does not disappoint.

To all the amazing people that have supported the development of this book over the years, I thank you all. Thank you for giving me the strength and belief to see this through to the end.

I love you all.

PROLOGUE

Under a blissful, postcard, summer sky, families, students, and employees ready for their daily commute to work gathered at the Southport platform, anxiously awaiting the next tram's arrival. As Lisa stood in line at the ticket machine, her left hand gripped the handle of a floral luggage case while her seven-year-old daughter, Bia, tugged on her right hand. "Bia, enough!" Lisa glared at her daughter with half a smile.

"I'm bored," Bia whined as she looked up with a cross expression on her face.

Her mother smirked at the little girl's pigtails which hung out of her oversized, pink, Gold Coast tourism cap. "Can you please entertain your sister?" Lisa asked, turning to Gracie. Gracie was thirteen years old, dressed in denim shorts, flip-flops, and a cropped T-shirt. Her long dark hair came from her father's side while Bia had her mother's strawberry blonde hair. Gracie stared at her phone, flicking her finger across the screen as she scrolled through various dresses that were on sale. "Gracie? Please?" Lisa asked again.

Gracie rolled her eyes and looked down at her little sister. "Do you have to be so annoying?"

"Yes." Bia smiled back.

"Here," Gracie said, as she reached over, grabbed a tourism brochure from the nearby stand, and handed it to her, "read this!" Bia snatched the brochure with a cheeky grin.

Lisa reached the ticket machine and opened her purse; her phone was vibrating inside. Quickly, she pulled the phone out, swiped the screen, and pinned it between her shoulder and her ear. "Hi, honey!" she answered, searching through her purse for a credit card. "Yeah, the girls are good; we are waiting for the tram now." Her fingers found the card and swiped it through the machine. The machine beeped, and three tickets printed out. "Oh, I know, we can't wait to see you, too!" Lisa grabbed the tickets and stuffed her credit card into her purse. "Girls, say hi to your father," she said, holding the phone up.

"Hi, Dad," Gracie mumbled, scrolling through her phone.

"Hi, Daddy! Hi, Daddy!" Bia excitedly jumped up and down before her mother pulled the phone away and put it back to her ear.

"Okay, so you're going to meet us on Monday?" Lisa continued, leading the two girls over to the platform. "And you're sure you can't just come now? You're a colonel. Just order someone else to do it!" Lisa watched amusingly as Bia began to read the brochure that Gracie had given her. "I know, I know, it's only a few more days. Well, don't work too hard. The girls and I are going to be at the beach every morning. You know, we might just sit by the pool, enjoy the sun… Well, Gracie would, if she ever put her phone down."

Gracie glared at her mother. "I'm standing right here, you know," she snapped, shaking her head as the screeching sound of tram brakes came down the tracks.

"Oh, honey, I've got to go. The tram is here! Okay, okay, I love you, too. I'll see you on Monday! Love you, too. Bye!" Lisa ended the call and slid her phone into her jeans pocket.

The large yellow tram came to a halt. The eager crowd began shuffling forward as the doors retracted. People bumped and shoved their way onboard, and Lisa grabbed Bia's hand before they stepped into the carriage. "Quick! Go get those seats!" Lisa pointed to a pair of vacant seats a few rows down. Bia took off, running past a pair of teenage boys holding surfboards, jumped up on the seat, and clapped her hands in excitement. Gracie pushed past her mother, smiling at the two boys before taking a seat next to her sister. "Really, Gracie? I could use a hand here!" Lisa barked as she struggled with the heavy luggage case. As the tram began to move, Bia stood up on her seat, her eyes glued to the window. Lisa sat opposite the two girls and dragged the case in front of her. "Bia, sit down, please," she told her enthusiastic daughter with a sigh of exhaustion.

"So how long until we get to the hotel?" Gracie pulled her eyes away from her phone for the moment.

"Not long, maybe ten minutes. I've got to pick up our rental car as soon as we get there," Lisa said. Bia sat down and turned her attention back to the brochure.

"I told Marcus I'd meet him at one-thirty." Gracie returned her attention to her phone.

"Gracie! This is supposed to be a family trip! No friends!"

"Mum, I haven't seen Marcus since I went to school here! Besides, it's not like Dad is here anyway."

Lisa raised an eyebrow at her rebellious daughter. "Okay, first, who is Marcus? Second, your father goes on leave next week; he will be here on Monday. Should I tell him that you ditched us for some boy? You know he won't be impressed!"

"Did you know that the Gold Coast has more than fifty-seven kilometres of beach?" Bia interrupted, flicking to the next page of the brochure.

"Who cares? It's not like Dad is ever around anyway," Gracie muttered, just loud enough for her mother to hear, then returned to scrolling down her screen again.

Lisa leaned over and snatched the phone from Gracie. "Your father works hard. What he does is important. Don't you think he'd rather be here with us? I will not have you speak about him that way!"

"Give me my phone!"

"No," Lisa said, and put the phone in her handbag, "no phone for the rest of the day. No Marcus either!"

"But…" Gracie protested.

"No buts! I suggest you learn to change your attitude, too. I won't let you ruin this weekend."

Gracie sat back in a huff and folded her arms. Bia reached up and tugged on her shirt. "What do you want?"

"Did you know that the Gold Coast has over thirteen million visitors every year?" Bia pointed to the words on the brochure's colourful page. "And that it has the largest professional lifeguard service in Australia?" Gracie didn't answer. Resting her head back on the seat, she looked out the window as the tram began to cross over the Sundale Bridge. The marina below was a glistening sea of white as hundreds of docked boats, yachts, and ferries played audience to the passing jet skis and speedboats. "Did you know that Surfers Paradise was once called Elston?"

"Okay, Bia, read quietly, sweetie," Lisa said softly, then closed her eyes for a moment.

Letting out a long yawn, Gracie watched palm tree after palm tree pass by. The tram left the bridge and entered the suburb of Surfers Paradise. Sports cars, motorcycles, and taxi cabs littered the main road with an array of bright colours.

"That's the Gold Coast Highway!" Bia pointed out. "It runs along the coast all the way to Coolangatta!" The tram crossed over the busy road and headed deeper into the city. Reflections of the nearby ocean shimmered off glass-laden skyscrapers, which were mostly hotels and office buildings though each one seemed taller than the next. A single-lane road, Surfers Paradise Boulevard, ran parallel to the tram, teasing passengers with a glimpse of the Gold Coast's famous beaches as it passed through each intersection.

Camera-wielding tourists, groups of teenagers, and holidaying families all walked the busy sidewalks. "The bell always rings at twelve!" Bia clapped her hands as the tram sped by a large clock tower in the heart of the city. Various amusement rides, bars, and shopping centres rushed by in a blur. "That's Cavill Mall!" Bia pressed her face to the window. The famous strip was the central hub of Surfers Paradise, full of restaurants, boutique shops, and live entertainment. The little girl absorbed it all with an enormous grin.

After several brief stops, the tram soon emerged from the city centre and rejoined the Gold Coast Highway where early morning congestion was building across all four lanes. "Broadbeach is the next stop," Bia informed her sister. Gracie cracked a less-than-enthused smile and flicked the little girl's pigtail.

"Mum, open your eyes. This will be our station!" Gracie nudged Lisa with her foot.

"I'm not sleeping, just resting them," Lisa muttered. In fact, she was beginning to nod off. A loud bell rang as the tram slowly came to a halt. Dozens of people stood up and began making their way to the exits.

"Yay, we're here!" Bia cheered.

"It's about time," Gracie moaned. A fresh ocean breeze blew through the crowded carriage as the tram doors retracted.

Prying her eyes open, Lisa jumped up and grabbed her luggage case. "Come on, girls. Let's go!"

Bia smiled at her older sister and clutched the brochure in her little hand. "Can you carry me?"

"Not a chance." Gracie flicked her sister's pigtail one more time.

1

ANOTHER DAY IN PARADISE

The red light shone through a haze of sweat and perspiration. Blake drew a deep breath, gripped the wheel tighter, and tapped the pedal. A gunshot fired from the exhaust, echoing through the half-empty grandstands with a resounding cheer from the spectators. The light faded from red to amber. He shifted into first. Green. Blake dropped the clutch and slammed the accelerator to the floor, sling-shotting the car off the starting line. The crowd erupted with excitement, but he couldn't hear anything over the roaring engine. Second gear, the tarmac blurred into a grey smear. Third gear, everything melted away. Clutch in – fourth gear. The chequered flag fluttered in the wind as the car rocketed over the finish line, and just like that, a week of preparation was over. Blake finally let out that breath.

A blue summer sky sizzled over the dragstrip as hundreds of local petrolheads lazed about the grandstands with nothing but hats and ice-cold drinks to combat the heat.

Blake turned into the pit lane and parked in garage 34. Gary was standing next to a pair of tattered, fold-out chairs with a beer in hand and a big grin on his face. "Ha! A new record! I told you! I told you she's faster now!" With a happy chuckle, he plonked into a chair and took a long sip of his favourite beverage. Blake slid the damp, sweaty helmet off his head and climbed out of the car, immediately noticing that Gary's big belly had snuck out from under his shirt. He couldn't help but smirk. "You know, if you quit drinking, those chairs might actually see the year through. You've broken two already, and it's only January."

Gary lowered the beer from his mouth. "Yeah? Well, kid, maybe you should start drinking! You might loosen up a bit. Become *fun*, even meet a girl maybe… an *ugly* one, but still."

Blake Daniels was twenty-four years old, with blond hair and brown eyes, and was a bit too skinny for his six-foot-four-inch frame. He removed his racing jacket and looked down at the large sweat patch in the middle of his white T-shirt. Blake hated wearing a jacket and jeans in the summer, but long-sleeved clothing was a racing regulation, even for the little leagues.

Gary was fifty-two years old and a little overweight. A former touring car mechanic from Houston, Texas, his thick American accent had managed to stick around, despite having lived in Australia for the last thirty years. His signature grey slicked-back hair and moustache always looked combed, and yet his clothes always appeared dirty. Blake had often thought that probably came with being a mechanic. Gary pulled a half-smoked cigar out of his grubby blue shirt pocket and looked around for his matches.

"Don't light that! You can't smoke that here!" The pair turned to see Andy, a young track marshal, waving his hands at them as he entered the garage. Andy was nineteen years old and had been working at the local raceway for almost a year. "The last time I let you smoke one of those, I almost lost my job."

Gary let out a loud sigh and drank his beer.

"Hey! You can't drink that either. This is a racetrack. No alcohol allowed."

Blake was enjoying the moment. "Don't worry, Andy. He wants to give them both up anyway."

"Like hell I do," Gary grumbled as he stood up from his chair and dropped the cigar into the beer bottle. "Pains in my ass – both of you."

Satisfied, Andy eagerly turned to Blake. "That was really fast today!"

"Thanks," Blake nodded as he and Gary began packing up their things.

"*Houdini* looks great! I've got over five thousand saved up. I'll be building one soon!"

Andy was talking about Blake's race car, Houdini. Gary had built the car from the ground up. A two-door Japanese coupe provided the white chassis, and a turbocharged, straight six-cylinder motor provided the horsepower. The coupe was low to the ground, had a custom body kit fitted, a vented bonnet to expel heat, and a large GT spoiler to improve the rear downforce. Gary nicknamed the car Houdini because, like the magician who performed unbelievable tricks, Blake always managed to win the race, even when victory seemed impossible.

"Can I take a photo? I know I snapped some last time, but it was cloudy then, and my frie—"

"Go ahead, take as many as you want," replied Blake, cutting Andy off. Andy whipped out his phone and began snapping away at his favourite car.

Gary dangled the keys to his truck. "Let's get this car on the trailer. We've got at least an hour's drive home, and I don't want to get stuck in traffic!"

"Move your ass!" An hour later, the old red truck sat idle, rattling loudly in the backed-up traffic as Gary pointlessly cursed at all four lanes of the M1 motorway. "I could have moved to LA for this."

"You say that every week," Blake muttered, sitting in the passenger's seat scrolling through his phone.

"Do you think that kid has got a girlfriend?" Gary asked.

"Who? That cab driver? You interested?"

"Shut up. I mean that Andy kid. He just seems so needy."

"I don't know; maybe he does. He's not *needy*. He's just a bit socially… you know…"

"Annoying?" Gary chuckled as he turned on the radio.

Blake wound down his window. "I was gonna say awkward."

The old truck had only one working speaker in the passenger's side door, and Gary, being partially deaf in his left ear, always turned it up all the way so he could hear it. Blake hated it; the stereo blared right into his ear instead. Sometimes he wondered if Gary became deaf before or after volume control was invented, but like the chicken and the egg, he figured he would never know for sure.

The local news broadcast came on. Blake rested his arm on the open window and caught a glimpse of a small hatchback in the next lane. Behind the wheel, an elderly lady was glaring straight at him through a pair of the thickest framed glasses he had ever laid eyes on. Blake realised the radio from Gary's truck must be annoying her. "Hey, can you turn it down? Your grandma over here looks really pissed." Gary didn't respond. "Hey, turn it down!" Again, Gary didn't acknowledge him. Realising that he was speaking into his deaf ear, Blake reached for the volume dial on the radio. Gary slapped his hand away and pointed to the speaker.

…And the small rural town of Bayagin has been left in ashes after a massive bushfire swept through the area. The total population of fifty-seven people is currently missing. No bodies have been located at this stage, making it difficult to confirm whether the residents of Bayagin are, in fact, alive or deceased. Police have started a full investigation and are staying unusually tight-lipped on the details. Some reports have indicated that the fire may have been deliberately lit. We will keep you updated throughout the evening…

"A whole town – just gone!" Gary finally turned the volume down. "It's that darn global warming thing, I tell ya! We never used to get so much rain up here, and now we have bushfires wiping towns off the map!" He started to ramble on. Blake quickly remembered the elderly lady in the car next to them. She was still staring, except now her frail hand was reaching out the window with the middle finger firmly raised.

Blake blinked twice in disbelief then casually wound his window up.

"What the hell did you do to that sweet old lady?" Gary asked, shaking his head with disapproval. Blake rolled his eyes and turned the radio back up as the traffic started to move again. "See, that's the problem with your generation. No respect for your elders. First, you upset the old lady, and now you give me the silent treatment." Blake closed his eyes and slumped back. Listening to Gary's weekly rant was, surprisingly, a soothing and somewhat relaxing part of the regular drive home.

~~~~~~~~~~~~

"Wake up! Rise and shine. You're home, kid." Blake opened his eyes to find Gary tapping him on the shoulder with a freshly lit cigar in his mouth. The sun had fallen behind the distant mountains, leaving a touch of pink across the clouds.

He unbuckled his seatbelt and sat up, realising that he must have dozed off during Gary's lecture.

Blake could barely contain his yawn as he dragged himself out of the truck and slammed the old rusty door shut. Gary was double-checking the chains holding Houdini on the trailer. It didn't take them long to notice the dark silhouette watching them from the upstairs window of the house across the street. It was Old Lady Margret, Blake's least favourite neighbour.

Old Lady Margret had lived in the brick house across the street since she was a little girl. Known for snooping on people from her window, she had recently waged a campaign against Blake for keeping his race car at home. "It was noisier than my late husband's snoring," she had told the council in her letter. Blake now kept Houdini at Gary's house, which made more sense anyway since Gary spent the most time working on it. Blake grabbed his backpack and pretended he didn't notice her.

"Your girlfriend is watching," Gary mumbled, cigar clenched between his teeth.

"Funny, she seems more your age."

"She's staring at you, kid." Gary walked around and got back in his truck. "Good job today. See you Monday."

"Monday."

Tall wooden lampposts bathed Ayles Court in a white glow. Blake could hear the racket of Gary's truck driving away as he approached the front door of his rented two-storey home. A quick jiggle and twist of the key and the door swung open. The house was pitch-black. Blake flicked the light switch, but the light didn't come on. He tried again – nothing.

"Damn, power outage." Blake felt his way through the hall, passing the staircase before entering the kitchen, which was so dark he could barely make out the counter as he put his backpack down. Suddenly, a loud crash shook the ceiling above him. He listened quietly; it was dead silent. "James?" Blake pulled out his phone and tapped the torch app; the room lit up.

"James, is that you?" He made his way to the stairs, ears perked. A moment later, a hurried scamper came from the top. "Who's there? I'm not messing around!" Blake held the phone's light high and, one creaking step at a time, climbed the stairs, heart pounding through the silence. Pausing at the top, he gazed around the open room: the dusty TV and cheap couch were all alone. However, a window beside the balcony sliding door revealed something odd about his neighbour's house: bright lights shining from their kitchen. They still had power. Blake walked over and pressed his face to the glass. As far down the street as he could see, all the houses had lights on.

Maybe I blew a fuse, he thought as he pulled his face away from the window, *or maybe someone* has *cut the power off.* A nervous shiver danced its way down his spine.

Blake tapped his phone, the screen went black, and the torch light flickered off. The battery had died. He heard another scurry behind him. Blake slowly turned, but with no light, endless dark filled the narrow hallway.

"Who's there?" No response. He wondered if he should run while he still could. Maybe the neighbours could help. But what if there was no one there? Maybe it was all in his mind. He didn't want to look stupid. After all, houses creaked, even newer ones.

Taking a deep breath, Blake sucked up his fear and headed into the hall toward his bedroom, the very place the sound had come from. He couldn't even see his own hands as he felt the walls. Searching for the handle to his bedroom door, his fingers eventually found it when a dozen horrible thoughts flashed through his mind: *Who could be on the other side? A home invader? A drug addict looking for a fix? What if they had a knife? A syringe? A gun, maybe?*

Blake was about to tell himself to toughen up when a high-pitched buzz sent cold air rushing down the back of his neck like an open fridge. He spun around. "Who's there? I'm warning you!" A vague shadow was hovering only a few feet from his face, no bigger than a basketball. Blake's courage fled, leaving him stranded.

Suddenly, a blinding light beamed from the object. Blake covered his eyes. "Arhhh! Take what you want. I haven't got much money. It's downstairs; just take it." A moment later, every light in the house flickered on, and the blinding light vanished. Blake opened his eyes. "What the hell?" His brain took a moment to comprehend what it was looking at. A small drone hovered in front of him. It was silver with four rotors on the top and a large LED spotlight attached to the bottom.

A burst of hysterical laughter came from behind the bedroom door. Fear quickly turned to anger as he realised what had taken place. Blake barged into his room. Sure enough, James was rolling on the floor, laughing uncontrollably.

"Dude! Your face when you turned around – priceless!" James was Blake's housemate and best friend; the pair had been inseparable since the third grade. He was twenty-three, skinny and short, with messy dark hair and a pimple or two.

"You dick! Seriously! What the hell?" Blake kneeled and punched his cackling friend in the arm. "That shit was not funny! I could have beaten the crap out of you!"

"I don't have much money!" James's laughter grew even louder. "Beat the crap out of me? Was that before or after you cleaned out the crap in your pants?" He got up from the ground, red-faced and still snickering.

Blake stared at him, clearly unimpressed. "You're an arsehole, you know that?"

"I can't remember... the last time... I laughed that hard," James stuttered, wiping a stray tear.

Blake glanced at the drone, still hovering outside his bedroom door. "Where did you get that thing?" he asked, as if curiosity had not got the better of him.

"I built it at uni." James Jost was in his final year at university, chasing masters' degrees in engineering and computer science. "Check it out. You control it with this," he said, as he handed over a large grey tablet. The screen showed the doorway with the pair standing inside.

Blake waved his hand around. "A live camera feed? That's awesome!" He quickly forgot how mad he was with James.

"Yep! It has night vision, records 4K video, and has one of the brightest LED lights I could fit it with!"

Blake punched his friend in the arm again, saying, "Yeah, I noticed. Feels like I looked straight into the sun."

"Ah, don't be a bitch." James snatched the tablet back. "How did the car run today?" he asked, switching off the drone.

Blake flopped onto his bed and buried his face under a pillow. "Got a new PB. Eleven seconds. Man, it was hot out there, though! Oh, and Andy told Gary off for drinking again."

James carried the drone over to the bedside cabinet. "Doesn't it scare you that he drinks all the time? Like, is he drunk when he drives you home?"

Blake sat up, his blond hair standing on end. "He's not drunk. Technically, he's under the limit." James stared at him doubtfully. "Okay, okay, he gets shit-faced when he gets home, I know, but that's after, so it doesn't matter. Can we not go through this again?"

James shrugged and replied, "Fine, if you're okay with your mechanic being drunk while he works on your car – the same car that *you* drive at over two hundred kilometres per hour in! Sure, let's drop it. No problem; consider the conversation dropped."

"Good." Blake ignored his sarcasm. "I stink. I really need a shower." Rolling to the end of the bed, he lazily dragged himself into his small ensuite and began to wash his face.

"What are you wearing tomorrow night?"

"Wearing? For what?" Blake asked, drying his face with a hand towel.

James leaned in at the doorway and replied, "Brooke's party! I told you last week, remember? Michelle is going to be there, and it's a good chance for me to talk to her, one-on-one!"

Blake turned his shower on and removed his shirt. "Dude, I told you last week. I'm not going."

"Yes, you are, dumb-arse! You're my wingman, and it's your duty to talk to all of her snobby friends while I make my move!" Blake pushed James out of the bathroom and closed the door in his face. "Hey, come on! Be a good friend!" James yelled through the door.

"I am a good friend. Doesn't mean I'm going to that stupid party. Besides, I don't even know these people, and you said that Brooke chick is a total bitch."

James paced in front of the door. "Hey, I barely know her. And yeah, she is a bitch. But she also put an open invite to anyone at uni. Michelle will be there, so we are going to take advantage of it!"

Blake stripped off his dirty clothes and stepped into the shower. As the cold water ran over him, an intriguing question sprung to mind. "Hey! How the hell did you turn all the lights off from my bedroom anyway? The switchboard is in the garage."

"Oh, it was easy, dude. I just installed a device on our switchboard that sends a signal to my phone. Now, I can turn our power off anytime I want. See?" James pulled out his phone and tapped the screen. Everything went black.

What sounded like an explosion of glass shattering quickly wiped James's smile away. He tapped the screen; the lights came on. "You okay in there?" An agonising moan came from inside. Hesitantly, he opened the door and peeked through the gap. Blake was lying naked on the floor, covered in the shards from the shower screen, with a half-squashed bar of soap under his foot. "Wow, I never thought people actually slipped on soap. That's like cartoon stuff!"

"James… I promise… I'm gonna kill you!" Blake glared at him, slowly turning the tap off as water trickled over his head.

"I'm gonna let you freshen up," James said, as he cowered away, shutting the door before his friend could fulfil his promise.

∞∞∞∞∞∞∞∞∞

Beep! Beep! Beep! Blake sat up with the bedspread half wrapped around his head. The alarm beeped and buzzed as his phone vibrated across the wooden bedside table. He picked it up and pushed the awake button. The screen read 4:01 am. He was exhausted, having spent most of the previous night cleaning up shower-screen glass. He groaned; it was time to get up for work. Frustrated, he lay back and pulled the covers over his head.

Beep! Beep! Beep! Blake sat up abruptly; his thoughts tangled. He quickly yanked the sheets off and grabbed his loud, annoying phone. 4:45 am. He had fallen back asleep. "I'm gonna be late. Crap, crap, crap!" Blake leapt out of bed and knocked a small wooden picture frame off the bedside table. The photo was of a dog – Ben. He picked it up and put it back on the table. "Oh no… No! Not again! She is going to kill me." He grabbed clothes from his wardrobe, whipped his boxers off, and got into the screen-less shower.

~~~~~~~~~~~

The cold morning air rushed through the window of Blake's old white sedan as he sped down the M1 motorway. A text message lit up his phone. *Where are you?* It was his boss, Kimmy. Blake had been making a habit of being late to work, and Kimmy had recently given him a very stern warning. He turned off the motorway and took the next exit ramp. There it was: a large sign that read Bright Heart Couriers. He hated that sign. The car bounced and scraped over the steep curb as he pulled in and found a park.

The old brick warehouse was falling apart. The faded yellow paint had almost completely peeled off its walls, the concrete driveway was riddled with weeds, and the iron roof had more holes than a block of Swiss cheese. Two large roller doors constantly jammed, and the small office seemed to always smell like detergent. Blake had been working as a courier driver for the last six months. Though he didn't care much for his boss, it was a job that let him do what he loved most – driving.

Kimmy, known for her temper, was a short Chinese lady with jet black hair who always wore expensive business suits and never forgot the matching high heels. She was standing outside the office door. Her fuse was burning. Blake knew she was waiting for him to get within the blast radius. With his backpack slung over his shoulder, he went in headfirst.

"It's eighteen minutes past five!" Kimmy detonated. "I don't know why you can't get here on time. You're useless. You race cars! How do you win? You're the last one here every day. You must be the worst racer in the world." Her cheeks turned pink. "I gave you a warning last time. If you are late again, you're fired! Understand me?" Her face was now full tomato.

"Yes, I understand. Sorry, it won't happen again."

Kimmy stared at him. Blake stared back, unsure if she was going to say anything else. "Go, Snail Boy. You are so late! Why are you just standing here?"

"Sorry." Blake quickly scurried off into the warehouse. Finding the closest van, he lobbed his backpack onto the passenger seat.

"Yo! Snail Boy!" Blake turned to see Luther walking towards him with an orange clipboard. The bold, six-foot-seven aboriginal man was Blake's only friend at work. He was also Kimmy's head mechanic, handyman, and pretty much whatever else she wanted him to be. His dark blue overalls were always covered in oil and ketchup stains – part of his charm, he would say. A huge grin made it clear that Luther had been laughing. "Mate, that had to be a new record. That's the reddest I've ever seen her face go. Seriously, we could shove a pole up her arse and use her as a stop sign." He chuckled, patting Blake on the back.

"Yeah, she is pretty mad at me this morning. She threatened to fire me next time."

Luther handed him the orange clipboard. "Here is your run sheet. It's a big one today so you better get moving. Don't worry, mate, she never fires anyone." He shut the van door and gave a friendly thumbs up.

"Luther! Get back to work right now!" Kimmy's screaming voice carried so loudly across the warehouse that it made the big man jump. "Yes, boss. Right away. Was just going over the delivery run." Luther quickly hurried towards the next van. "Crazy bitch," he muttered under his breath, "you wait till I find a nice pole, you little…"

~~~~~~~~~~~

A couple of hours into his route, Blake found himself in the gridlock of the Surfers Paradise rush hour. His coffee cup was empty, and the radio was cycling though boring ads. The driver of a silver station wagon in the next lane was a young woman, perhaps a few years older than him. She was too busy putting on her makeup in the rearview mirror to notice that her two small children had escaped from their seatbelts and were now waving at Blake through the window. Judging by their uniforms, the brother and sister act were clearly heading to school. The young mother lowered her mascara wand and yelled for them to get back in their seats. A sudden honk brought Blake's attention to the lights: they were green, and the traffic had moved forward. A bus driver was mouthing something rather angrily in the mirror.

"Okay, buddy, I'm going," Blake said, as he drove through the intersection and turned up the radio.

Police have confirmed that a family of four are lucky to be alive after their farm was destroyed by a wild bushfire. This is the latest in a series of bizarre fires sweeping the area, and local law enforcement is refusing to comment further. We have received conflicting reports from multiple local sources. Some more far-fetched reports claim that…

The radio cut out as a phone call came through the speakers. Blake pushed the answer button on the steering wheel.

"Good morning, ugly." It was James.

"Morning, dude."

"So, I need to know. What do you think I should wear tonight? I was thinking of like, fully suiting up, but then I thought no. Michelle probably likes chilled-out guys. I don't want to overdo it. But, when I walk in tonight, she has to be like, well, hello handsome! You know what I mean? Hey, you still there?"

"Yeah, man, I'm here. Just wear whatever you're comfortable in. I think a suit is too much, though. Maybe buy yourself a nice pink dress for tonight."

"Ha ha, very funny, but I'm serious. You need to help me."

"I'm serious, too. If you sound any more like a girl, you're going to have to get your nails done – French tips, is it?" Blake laughed, pleased with his own joke.

"You actually suck. Help me, damn it! You know I'm bad with girl stuff, so stop being a dick. What are you wearing tonight then?"

"Pyjamas. Because that's what you wear to bed."

"Don't even think about not coming!" James's frustration was turning to anger.

"I still don't see the point in going. You have liked Michelle for a year and haven't even spoken to her." The van's GPS informed Blake that he had arrived at his next drop.

"Hey, man, you haven't asked out any girls either, so shut up! Besides, tonight is my lucky night. I'm going to ask her out, then you're going to have to listen to me and my hot new girlfriend tell our steamy, dirty stories to you."

Blake smiled at his friend's delusional confidence and pulled the van over to the side of the road. "You have a great imagination, dude," he said, then looked at his clock and remembered that he was still running late. "Anyway, I've got to go. I'm at my next delivery."

"You *are* going to that party! You hear me!" James's voice crackled through the speakers. "Blake?"

"Enjoy your party, madame." Blake ended the call and caught himself pondering what James had just said: he hadn't asked a girl out in a long time. Should he have? Admittedly, he didn't feel the need to, nor did he want to. The girl in the silver station wagon was around his age and already had two children. He just couldn't picture that life for himself. Family wasn't for him. It never had been – too much responsibility. He reached for the parcel and quickly shook the thought out of his mind.

2

THE PRICE OF HAPPINESS

Waiting for a seemingly endless red light to change, several disgruntled motorists stared at a pink convertible as it blared loud music into the street. The owner of this top-down party-on-wheels was Emma who, as always, was completely oblivious to the annoyance of those around her. Instead, the twenty-one-year-old grooved to the beat, substituting the steering wheel for a drum as she mouthed the words to her favourite new song of the week. A loud whistle, however, quickly caught her attention.

Two gawking men winked from a white delivery truck in the next lane. "Smooth, boys," she said, as she turned away, eyes rolling behind designer sunglasses. The light was green. Emma flattened the accelerator, screeching her tyres before taking the party onto the Chevron Island Bridge. A pair of jet-ski riders bounced across the glittery Nerang River, chasing the wake of a passing ferry, and carelessly sprayed its camera-wielding tourists with each turn.

The Gold Coast was home to the rich, the poor, and every kind of person in between. From surfers to super geeks, rev heads to real estate kings, the coast had something for everyone. Surfers Paradise happened to be Emma's favourite place to drive through. It reminded her of the lifestyle she loved so much – money, beaches, popularity, and sunshine, in no particular order, of course.

Chevron Island was a quick bridge ride out of Surfers Paradise. Thomas Drive, a single-lane street that ran straight through the middle of the island, was home to various restaurants, cafes, clothing shops and, more importantly, the best spray-tan salon in town. The rest of the island featured houses, million-dollar waterfront mansions, and the odd backpacker hostel for passing travellers.

Emma parked outside the tanning salon. Her reflection in the window confirmed that her light-pink dress matched her car perfectly. She snapped several quick selfies, posted the "cute" one, then went inside, the aroma of fake tan whisking through the doorway.

The salon had been decorated by its owner, Sandra, a self-proclaimed interior designer. A white marble counter with a couple of brochures and business cards stood before Emma as she entered. To the right were several metal lockers for customers to put their clothes in, and to the left were half a dozen black leather chairs, only two of which were occupied by clients flicking through magazines as they waited. The "Glamour" spray booths were located at the back. Sandra was standing behind the counter, admiring her nails.

"Hey, hey!" Emma made herself known.

Sandra's face lit up. "Well, if it isn't my *favourite* girl!" She ran around the counter and gave Emma a warm hug. "How have you been, babe?"

"I'm good. Just been busy. How about you?"

Sandra had naturally dark skin, and black curly hair tied in a bun. She always wore a different pair of seashell earrings with a matching necklace, and almost every dress she owned had a floral pattern on it. Today's dress was blue with orange poppies. Emma had been coming to Sandra for the last five years for her regular spray tan. If there was one thing that she had learnt in that time, it was that Sandra loved to talk – mostly about herself. "Oh, my God, I have so much to tell you! So, you remember the guy that I was seeing?"

"Aiden?"

"Yeah, him. So, a few months before I met Aiden, I met this other guy at a bar in Surfers. We got to drinking and to talking… then one thing led to another…" Emma's mind had already begun to wander as Sandra's story continued. "So, it turns out he is Aiden's older brother! Anyway, Aiden found out and now he won't speak to me. I told him it didn't mean anything, and it was just a fling. Besides, it was before I met him. Why is he even mad?"

Emma noticed that the two girls waiting in the leather chairs had stopped reading their magazines and were eavesdropping on their conversation. "Well…" Emma tried to find the right words as Sandra grabbed her hands for support. "Sweetie, I think Aiden won't speak to you because you slept with his brother, you know? It's going to make Christmas dinners pretty awkward, don't you think?"

Sandra stared blankly and said, "Yeah, I guess you're right. I just really liked him."

"Oh, no, don't be sad." Emma hugged her tight, glaring at the two girls watching. They both snapped up their magazines and returned to flicking through the pages.

Sandra grabbed a tissue from a purple box on the counter. "Em, sweetie, don't get a boyfriend. Men suck," she said, patting the tissue around her eyes.

"I know they do. That's why I don't have time for them."

"Is my makeup running?" Sandra asked, as she scrunched up the tissue in her hand.

"No, you're fine."

"What time do you want, honey?"

"Can we make it twelve o'clock tomorrow? I have a photo shoot on Sunday, and my skin needs to be perfect!" Emma unzipped her handbag and found her phone. The screen lit up. *Two Missed Calls – Dad.* She ignored the notification and put the phone back in her bag.

"Okay. Twelve, tomorrow." Sandra made a note of the appointment at the counter.

"Great, thanks heaps. I'll see you then. Have a great day!"

Sandra was already staring into a pocket mirror to check her makeup. "You, too, honey. See you tomorrow."

Emma exited the salon and stepped onto the sidewalk. She passed a chemist and two stores before a black dress in the next window was "too cute" to walk any further. *Just a quick look*, she thought.

Excessively loud pop music played throughout the store. The shop assistant, whom Emma suspected was responsible for the horrible sound blaring from the ceiling, was swaying to the beat as she folded various clothes at the counter. Emma headed straight to the back of the store and began browsing through the racks. Her bag began to vibrate. She opened it and quickly pulled out her phone. *Dad Calling* flashed on the screen. Reluctantly, she answered it.

"Hello? Emma, are you there?" Her father sounded worried.

"Yeah, Dad, I'm here. But I'm a little busy right now." Emma spotted the black dress from the shop window hanging on the next rack. "Can I call you later?" She unhooked the dress and held it up in front of her.

"Em, you were supposed to come and visit your mother this morning. I waited for you for over an hour."

"Dad, it's fine. I'll go see her some other time. I had a lot to do today." Emma switched the phone to the other ear as she looked over the immaculate stitching.

"Look, Em, I know you don't like going to see her, but today is her birthday, and family still comes first. You need to get your priorities in line."

Emma lowered the dress and rolled her eyes. "Dad, did you clear the credit card like I asked you to yesterday?"

"Yes, but…" Her dad took a deep breath. "Yes, yes, I did. Why? Did you find a dress you like?"

Emma glanced over the black garment one more time and replied, "Yeah, I think so. Oh, and I'll be out a bit late tonight, so don't wait up for me."

Her dad paused again, then said, "Okay, just remember what we talked about. Don't spend too much! If the price is too high, don't buy it! We are *not* rich. Okay, miss? Do you understand me?"

Emma was already at the counter. "Dad, don't be so annoying. I've told you before, no price is too high for your daughter's happiness. Anyway, I've gotta go. Bye." She hung up before he could respond and placed the dress on the counter.

The ditzy shop assistant scanned the barcode. "That's four hundred and ninety dollars, thanks."

Emma reached into her handbag and pulled out her purse. Flicking through multiple credit cards, she quickly picked one and handed it over. The assistant swiped the card, folded the black dress, and put it inside a fancy carry bag. Emma couldn't help but notice her father's name on the credit card – Thomas Riley. An instant wave of guilt swept over her.

Realising that she had been a little too rude, Emma unzipped her handbag and took out her phone. She flicked through her contact list and found her dad's number when *Brooke Calling* began to flash on the screen.

"Hey, hey!" she answered. Brooke was Emma's best friend. The two had met in the eighth grade and were more like sisters than besties. Brooke, admittedly, was known for being a bit of a bitch and just a tad up herself. "So, I just bought the cutest black dress! It's short, backless, and splits down the front. You would love it!" Emma began walking back to her car.

"Cute! That's why I called. I can't find a dress for tonight. So I was wondering if I could borrow one of yours." Brooke sounded like she was walking, too.

"Yeah, I don't mind. Did you wanna borrow the short purple one or the white one you borrowed last time?"

Brooke hummed as she thought about it. "Can I borrow your light-blue one? You know, the one you got from Byron Bay on your date with Zack."

Emma cringed as she said, "Oh, don't bring him up – worst date ever. But yeah, you can borrow it. I don't even care if you wreck it. Bad memories."

"Sorry, I know he was a total dick. Don't think about it. There is going to be a heap of cute guys at my party tonight, so you better look hot! Oh, and Michelle is going to be late as usual. She has an essay to finish. That girl is such a bookworm! Anyway, I gotta go. Love ya. Thanks for the dress. I'll see you tonight." Brooke rushed the call and hung up the phone.

"Bye," Emma said to a *Call Ended* screen as she arrived at her car. Throwing her shopping bag on the passenger's seat, she checked her makeup in the mirror and started the engine. Sunglasses on. Radio on. Music loud.

~~~~~~~~~~

"This is the place!" James exclaimed, as he leaned over the taxi driver's shoulder and handed him a folded twenty-dollar note. "Keep the change." He winked before climbing out of the car.

"Keep the change?" Blake asked, as he got out on the other side of the taxi. "Dude, it was *five* cents."

James shrugged as he replied, "It all adds up."

The taxi drove away, leaving the two men standing in front of Brooke's house. It was white with a black tiled roof, two storeys high, with a four-car garage and an immaculately kept lawn – at least it would have been if not for the half dozen cars now parked on it. Several rowdy partygoers were smoking cigarettes and drinking booze on the bonnet of a sedan. James and Blake weaved through the vehicular maze, stepping over a minefield of empty plastic cups, before they arrived at the vibrating front doors.

"Ah, do we knock?" James asked. Just as Blake went to respond, one of the doors swung open, releasing the blaring music. A young blonde girl squinted at them before hunching over in the doorway. The boys looked at each other with confused faces. Suddenly, the girl lunged forward and vomited all over the doorstep. "Yuk! That's gross!" James jumped back as her bodily fluids sprayed his shoes.

A second girl came out of the house and shoved Blake out of the way. "Cassy! Are you okay?" the girl drunkenly slurred as she leaned over to help her sick friend.

"Here, let us help you." Blake moved to assist them.

"No, we're fine, thank you," the girl snapped at him.

Blake stepped back with raised hands as the intoxicated pair stumbled towards the lawn. James was busy scraping vomit chunks off his shoes and onto the wall of the house. "You comin', Casanova?" Blake asked with a smirk.

James frantically checked his shoes for any bits that he might have missed. "That chick glazed my shoes! I don't want to smell like puke when I talk to Michelle." Once he was satisfied that his shoes were cleansed of gooey chunks, he turned to Blake with a cheesy grin on his face and asked, "How do I look?"

Blake looked James up and down. He was wearing dark blue jeans and a black T-shirt with the words "Sun's Out" printed on the front. The words were mostly covered by a bright orange silk vest he wore over the shirt. "What's with the vest, dude? You look like you're late for clarinet practice."

"Ha ha, very funny, dick! I bought this Sun's Out shirt today. Look, chicks like it, okay? Yes, I could have just worn jeans and a boring shirt like you," James said, as he gestured to Blake's light-blue jeans and plain white T-shirt, "but, when I wear this vest over the top, it says that I am *cool*, but I am also *sophisticated*, you know?"

"Okay, *Classy*. Let's go get your trophy wife," Blake replied, as he shoved James through the open door and into the hallway. They navigated through the crowded house and made their way to the living room. There, on a wooden side table, sat a bucket full of beers and ice.

"Beer?" James yelled over the loud music. Blake nodded. James nabbed two beers from the bucket, popped the lids off, and handed one over.

"Dude, that's us! Right there!" Blake pointed to the other side of the room where a group had gathered around a long fold-out table. James smiled. About half a dozen, red plastic cups filled with beer were laid out in a triangle formation at each end of the table.

"Beer pong!" James blurted out in excitement.

Blake, who was just as eager, cried out, "Let's show them how it's done!"

James sipped his beer, wiped his mouth, and approved with a loud belch.

∽∾∽∾∽∾∽∾∽∾∽∾

A couple of hours later, in the next room, Emma struggled to keep everything concealed as she battled with the revealing split down the front of her new black dress. At least it was keeping her mind off the boring conversation that she had been trapped in for the last twenty minutes.

"So, you're like, internet famous. My sister follows you. That's so cool! You have like half a million followers, right?" Josh asked with an intense stare. Josh was a tall skinny boy with freckles and blond curly hair. He lived down the street from Brooke and had a huge crush on Emma. Today he was sporting a striped button-up shirt that was tucked into a pair of skinny jeans and a pair of oddly bright yellow runners. Emma found that his eyes kept wandering to the chest area of her revealing dress.

"Just over a million," she politely responded.

Josh's face lit up with a grin from ear to ear. He took a step closer and was now within the personal bubble area. Emma had seen Josh eating corn chips earlier and could smell them on his breath. "Would you like me to get you a drink?" he asked.

"No, I don't drink. Thank you anyway," she replied and smiled.

Josh seemed unsure of how to respond. Just as he started to speak, a voice yelled from across the room, "Em! You look stunning!"

Brooke and Michelle both had cocktails in their hands as they ran over and took turns giving Emma a hug. Wearing Emma's light-blue dress – which already had a spill on it – Brooke's long blonde hair shimmered like a shampoo commercial. Michelle wore a more relaxed pair of denim shorts under a white shirt and her curly black hair up in a bun.

Josh began to sweat. The girls made him quite uncomfortable.

Sizing up the nervous boy, Brooke screwed her face up in disgust and said, "Seriously? When will you get the hint? She's *not* interested, Josh!"

Josh began to stutter. "Sorry, I… was just talking… to her." He quickly moved away from Emma.

"He's fine," Emma said, as she stepped between them. "We were just talking!"

Brooke was known for turning bitchy after a few alcoholic beverages. "Piss off, freckles," she snapped. Josh quickly scurried off into the next room. "Oh-my-God! What a loser! Em, you're *too* nice, honey."

Emma and Michelle locked eyes for a second to acknowledge their disapproval of Brooke's mean behaviour. "Bee, that was so mean," Michelle said, stirring her cocktail with a straw.

"Yeah, it really was," Emma agreed. "If you don't like him, then why did you invite him?"

"I didn't. My parents are friends with his parents, so they invited him. But I did put an open invite out on social media. There a lot of people here I don't know," Brooke replied, as she slurped from her cocktail straw then pointed to the living room. "Like these two idiots, for example."

The girls looked over to see James and Blake having a beer-chugging contest in the doorway. "Who are they?" Emma asked.

Michelle quickly butted in, "Doesn't the short one go to our uni?"

Brooke nodded and replied, "Yeah, I think he does. I don't know who the other guy is though."

James let out a loud burp, then immediately realised the three girls were looking at them. "Shit, dude, there she is!" He smacked Blake on the chest and tried to discreetly point at the girls.

"Awkward! I think he saw us watching him," Brooke whispered, as she turned her back to the living room.

"Okay, Romeo, go over there and say hi," Blake said, as he shoved James forward.

"Okay then, I will." James straightened his vest, puffed out his chest, and began to stroll over to the girls. Blake followed, watching as his friend walked like a constipated bodybuilder towards the woman of his dreams. "Ladies! How are we tonight?" James raised his hands in the air, as if to give them all a hug, then quickly aborted.

Michelle and Emma smiled graciously. "We're good, thank you," Michelle said.

James's mind began to race. *Shit, she spoke to me! Quick, say something funny!* Nothing came out. Brooke seemed very unimpressed. "So…" James drew a blank. No sentence came to mind; no joke, no witty line – nothing. Blake and Emma just looked at each other with awkward smiles. "So, Blake here is a race-car driver. One of the best in his series. He's fast at pretty much *everything!*" Blake cringed with embarrassment as his friend desperately tried to create a conversation. "Well, wait. He's not fast at *everything*, if you get my meaning." Michelle and Emma began to laugh. Blake wasn't sure if they were laughing at James's joke or his failing conversation attempt. James wasn't sure either.

Brooke stamped her foot on the ground. "Listen here, you inbred loser. Whatever you think is going to happen here is *not* going to happen, okay? Look at us three. You have no chance. So just get lost and get out of my house," she yelled, straight in James's face.

The room fell silent. James took a step back, turned around, and began to walk away. Blake was about to give Brooke a piece of his mind when James stopped, spun back around, and walked right up to Michelle. "Look, I've been in a couple of your classes for the last few years, and we've never spoken. Well, today is your lucky day! Yes, I am slightly drunk, and I'm pretty sure I threw up in some dude's hat. But I just wanted to tell you that I think you are an awesome chick! Your friend here is a total cow, though," he said, as he nodded towards Brooke, "but I would love to take you out sometime." James finally exhaled.

Before a stunned Michelle could respond, an enraged Brooke stepped in. "Yeah, sure, dickhead! She will go out with a twat like you as soon as you can clear those disgusting pimples off your face. Do you seriously think she would kiss a puss-faced shrimp like you? And where did your mum get that vest from? You look like such a creep! So, keep dreaming and get out of my house!" she screamed again, pointing to the doorway.

James was hurt. Badly. But he wasn't about to let Brooke see it. He stepped back, unbuttoned his vest, and threw it at her feet. "Here, Mum said you can have it!"

Brooke looked down at the vest, then at the words printed on James's T-shirt. "Sun's Out?" she laughed at him. "Who wears stuff like that?" James turned around and began to walk away.

Blake politely nodded at Emma and Michelle. "Well, nice to meet you both," he said, as they uncomfortably smiled back at him. He turned to Brooke, then pointed to the orange silk vest by her feet. "Enjoy it," he said. "Goes great with the tan you painted on your face." Brooke's jaw dropped. "Say hi to Charlie for me."

Blake was following James through the doorway when something caught his eye. The words "Buns Out", with the image of a lady's bare backside, were printed on the back of James's new shirt. The three girls tilted their heads as they saw the image, too. Blake glanced over his shoulder and noticed them trying to read the words. He quickly stepped behind James to block them.

"Dude, have you seen the back of your shirt?" Blake asked, as they entered the living room.

"No. Why? Did someone spill a drink on me?" James stopped and reached for the back of his shirt.

Blake nudged him forward, saying, "Nah, dude. No drink. Don't worry about it. Let's just get out of here."

Since the early years of high school, James had waged a constant battle with acne. Whereas most kids had their skin clear up after their teenage years, James's face hadn't changed. He usually had several pimples at any given moment, and while his face wasn't covered in them, it remained a sensitive subject for him. Blake knew that Brooke had hit a very raw nerve. "Hey, don't listen to that chick. She's just a stuck-up brat. Don't let it get to you, dude."

"I don't wanna talk about it," James said quietly, as they exited the house. "Let's just walk home. I could use the thinking time."

After drinking beer for a few hours, the last thing Blake wanted was the forty-minute walk home, but James was already having a terrible night so he sucked it up. "Sounds good to me. It's a nice night anyway." James wandered across the car-filled lawn and onto the road. Blake followed, silently reading the words on James's shirt again. Sun's Out, Buns Out. He let out a small snicker as the image of the lady's bare-naked backside suddenly made sense to him.

"What are you laughing at back there?" a frustrated James barked.

"Nothing. Just something funny I remembered."

Neither of them said another word the entire way home.

3

AMY

Wearing a pair of khaki shorts, a blue T-shirt, and a pair of bright orange flip-flops, James waited in line at the Chevron Island chemist. In his hand was a small tub of pimple cream. Still angry at Brooke's comments from the night before, James had decided to take immediate action. After oversleeping till 11:00 am, he had cooked himself a bacon and egg sandwich, left the dirty pan in the sink, and driven his black SUV to the chemist on Chevron Island. Given that the Gold Coast was one of the most beautiful tourist destinations in the world, James had underestimated how busy the city would be during a summer weekend.

The storefront's double glass doors were wide open, but there was no breeze at all. Even though the building was rather modern, it seemed the air conditioning was either broken or not switched on. James rocked back and forth, swinging his arms in boredom. Behind him waited an elderly couple. The older gentleman had white hair and wore his pants up rather high, while his wife tightly clutched her handbag with one hand and held a prescription with the other. Next in line, judging by the black leather vest and denim jeans, the various tattoos and his greying beard, was a biker, discreetly holding a box of men's hair dye.

A red-haired woman in front of James was impatiently standing high on her toes, trying to see over the people in front of her for some sign of what was taking so long at the counter. The child with her was a young boy who had the same red hair, sported a couple of freckles on his face, and was clearly very bored. He must have been four, maybe five years old, James thought.

Glancing over his shoulder, the cheeky boy poked his tongue out. Amused, and slightly surprised, James returned the gesture. The boy giggled, let go of his mother's hand, and turned his eyes inwards. James saw this as a challenge, and he never walked away from a challenge, especially a childish one. He quickly checked the boy's mother: she was too busy nosing to pay any attention to their antics. The boy was grinning with anticipation. James went crossed-eyed and made his tongue touch the tip of his nose. The boy screwed up his face and retaliated with a finger in each ear and puffed-up cheeks.

"Oh, it's on now, little man," James whispered.

Smugly, the boy tapped his foot, waiting. James raised one eyebrow, warning the child that defeat was coming. Using his left hand, he shoved a finger deep into his nose, filled his cheeks like a balloon, then crossed his eyes and held the face until he was almost blue. The boy cracked and broke out in hysterics.

Eventually, James straightened out his eyes. When they came into focus, he found himself staring into the pupils of the boy's mother. She did not smile, nor did she speak; she just glared at him. Clearly, she was not as impressed as her son was. James slowly removed his finger from his nose. Yanking the young boy in front of her, the grumpy mother whispered something angrily before facing him towards the front of the line.

James exhaled with embarrassment and looked over his shoulder. The elderly couple were shaking their heads. The biker, however, leaned out from behind them and gave a hefty thumbs up of approval. It was then James decided he would stare at the ceiling for the rest of the wait.

∿∿∿∿∿∿∿∿

The air in the booth was thick with the musk of fake tan, which relentlessly teased Emma's nose. Scrunching her face up, she stood completely still with her arms out to the side as Sandra sprayed her body and indulged in girl talk. "Em, I loved the photo of your black dress! The one you posted last night. It was hot, babe."

"Thanks," Emma said, trying not to sneeze.

"I was reading some of the comments that people left. Wow, people really love you! Do you ever read them?"

Emma was asked this question often. "Not really. I don't read them anymore. Most of the comments are either guys hitting on you, guys being perverted, or girls being mean." She lowered her arms and opened her eyes. "Some are nice, but there are a lot of nasty ones. I just do it for fashion sponsors. I take photos with their clothes on, get paid for it, and most of the time, I get to keep the clothes they send me. It's a girl's dream!"

"Do you make much money?" Sandra asked, surveying Emma's body for runs and streaks.

"I do okay, although Dad wants me to get a job, too, or go to university. He thinks what I do isn't stable enough for my future," Emma said, as she rolled her eyes.

"Your dad is a police officer, isn't he?"

"Yeah, he is – Constable Caution."

"All parents are overprotective. I know it's been rough, but maybe you just need to spend some quality time together."

"I doubt it. Every time we talk, we just fight about Mum. She really screwed things up for us." Emma quickly regretted mentioning her mother.

Sandra turned away to adjust the nozzle on her spray gun. "You know, hun, maybe it's also time to... you know, forgive your mother. I know it's none of my business, but forgive—"

"You're right!" Emma quickly cut her off. "It's none of your business!"

Sandra quickly conceded and raised the spray gun. "Sorry... I shouldn't have. It's not my place." Emma immediately felt guilty for snapping but decided to not say another word. "Okay, hun, just one more coat to go," Sandra said quietly, and began to spray the last coat of tan over her silent client.

~~~~~~~~~~~

Blake's phone vibrated on the passenger's seat of the idling delivery van. His boss, Kimmy, was calling, probably to find out why he was running so late for his next delivery. He ignored the call and sipped his now cold coffee. Traffic had been at a complete stop for the last thirty-five minutes, and the last thing he needed was her screaming voice in his ear.

A silver station wagon sat in front of his van at the intersection. Two young children had climbed out of their seats and were now waving to him through the rear window. Blake quickly realised it was the same family he had seen yesterday. The little girl wore a pink dress with matching ribbons in her pigtailed brown hair. The little boy had his short brown hair spiked up at the front, and wore a grey T-shirt and denim shorts. Blake guessed the girl was around three or four years old, and the boy was maybe five or six. He watched as their mother leaned over and yelled at the children to get back in their seats. After a few minutes, they did as she said. Blake sipped his coffee and watched in amusement as the frustrated mother tried to buckle up their seatbelts.

Another ten minutes passed as the traffic lights went through their pointless cycle. Bored, Blake let out a sigh, leaned back into his seat, and turned up the radio. Watching the world through the dirty windshield, he let out a loud yawn as one boring advertisement played after the other. Pedestrians weaved between bumpers as green walking lights flashed from the sidewalks. Board shorts and bikinis were common attire as the beach was only a minute's stroll down the road. The clock tower was across the intersection – a beige building, five storeys high, with a popular restaurant on the ground floor with seating outside. As always on a Saturday morning, the restaurant was packed, with waitstaff barely able to tend to their tables. To Blake's left was the Gold Coast tram line, and behind that was the Golden Palm outdoor shopping centre.

Blake's phone vibrated again – three missed calls from Kimmy. He wasn't in the mood to try and explain his traffic issues to her, not that he had any idea what was causing the long delay. All he could see was a long line of glowing red brake lights. *Kimmy Calling* began to flash on the screen when something in the distance caught his eye – two men running between the rows of traffic towards his van. A third person followed them, then a fourth, a fifth, now a dozen, all rushing in his direction. Confusion swept over the street as car doors were flung open and more people joined the fleeing crowd.

What the hell is going on? Blake wondered as he slid his vibrating phone into his jeans pocket, unclipped his seatbelt, and opened his van door – narrowly missing three people.

A lady was crying hysterically as she ran by. "Hey, what's going on?" he shouted. She ignored him and kept running.

"Miss, are you okay?" Blake spun around; scattering in panic, people were leaving shops and restaurants in droves. He noticed the young mother with her two children. They were still sitting in the silver station wagon and seemed just as confused as he was. He walked up to her passenger door and hunched down to the window. The young mother, in her mid-twenties, wound it down.

"Do you know what's going on?" he asked, and was immediately struck by the girl's beauty. She had dark olive skin and long black hair, but it was her piercing blue eyes that made him stare. He thought she might be a waitress or something as her polo shirt had words stitched above a small pocket, though he couldn't make out what they were.

"I have no idea! People just started running past, yelling. Do you think there is a crash ahead? I'm really late for work!" She fought to overpower the voices of her two noisy children.

Before Blake could respond, a mob of terrified patrons began pouring out of the ground-floor exits of the clock tower. "Hey, I think you need to get out of the car," Blake urged, as more people began evacuating various restaurants and cafes across the street.

The young mother was clearly shaken but did her best to remain calm as she leaned over to unclip her son's seatbelt. "Okay, kids, we have to go for a quick walk."

"Mummy, I don't want to go for a walk," the little boy insisted and kicked his mother's hands away.

"Let me help you," Blake said, as he popped open the rear passenger door.

The little girl began to cry. "Mummy, I don't wanna go with the man."

Blake crouched by her side and said reassuringly, "It's okay; your mummy is coming, too!"

Suddenly, a ball of fire exploded in the clock tower's second and third floor windows, sending a downpour of hot glass into the street. A man fled the building, screaming in agony as flames consumed his body. He made it several feet before collapsing onto the road.

The young mother froze, and her children began to cry uncontrollably.

Blake couldn't take his eyes off the now motionless man burning on the ground. "Everyone, out of the car!" he ordered, finally turning his attention to the car and its passengers.

"I can't get the seatbelt undone!" The mother panicked as she attempted to get a better grip on her son's harness. "He kept getting out so I forced the buckle together and now it's stuck."

Blake quickly unclipped the little girl's belt and lifted her out. Just as he turned back to help the trapped boy, a chunk of concrete slammed into the roof of the silver station wagon.

"What was that?" the startled young woman shrieked from inside.

The ground began to tremble. Blake stared up in disbelief as cracks spread through the clock tower like a black vine. "The building is coming down! Get out of the car!"

"I can't get it open!" she cried, fighting to unclip the belt.

Blake leaned inside the car to help. He gripped the buckle as tightly as he could and pried the latch. It wouldn't budge. The boy's cries got louder, but not as loud as the terrified squeal his sister gave as the building across the street began to crumble.

Dozens of people scrambled for cover as clumps of concrete and brick rained down from above. "Come on! You piece of shit!" Blake shouted, as he wrestled with the latch, using all his strength. "Come on!" Pain surged through his fingertips. "Arhhh, come on!" It was no use.

The young mother grabbed his hand tightly. "My daughter…" Blake's fingers loosened around the buckle as he stared into her teary blue eyes. "Please…" She was shaking. He held her hand for what felt like an eternity. "Please…"

With a single breath, he leapt out of the car, scooped the little girl into his arms, and ran as fast as he could towards the Golden Palm shopping centre.

"Mummy! Mummy!" The little girl reached for the station wagon, squealing in horror. The deafening impact of concrete and metal silenced her brother's cries. Blake covered the girl's mouth as they were engulfed in a cloud of grey dust.

Everything went hazy. Barely able to see or breathe, the pair moved towards the shopping centre entrance. The glass doors had already retracted, the thick air tricking the sensors as the smog blew inside. Blake glanced back; rubble and small fires now filled the intersection where the station wagon and his delivery van had once stood.

His stomach twisted. The little girl cried uncontrollably in his arms, repeatedly begging for her deceased mother. Blake didn't hear her, though; several tears trickled down his face. The girl suddenly stopped crying and began to choke on the filthy air. Blake was frozen, staring at the destroyed intersection with disbelief. Dozens of crushed cars and motionless bodies lay scattered amongst bricks and steel.

"How…?" The little girl began to cough uncontrollably on his shoulder. "We have to go… we have to go… now…" Blake snapped out of it and carried her inside under a stone archway.

The outdoor mall was long and narrow; cafes and clothing shops lined both sides of the building while tables and chairs filled the middle. Fog-like dust cascaded over the walls and poured in through the doors.

"Hey! Come on! Move it!" At the other end of the mall, a single security guard stood at an exit, yelling for the remaining people to evacuate through the doorway behind him. Blake ran between toppled chairs and tables towards him, the distraught child trembling in his arms. The security guard was bald with fair skin and appeared to be in his forties. His face was dirty, and his white button-up shirt had half untucked itself from his grey pants. "Quick! Get outside!" he urged, as they reached him.

An agonising scream echoed off the walls. Blake and the guard looked back to see a woman crawling under the stone arch he had just come through. Her face was bloodied, and her legs were broken.

Blake turned to the security guard. "I need you to watch her!"

"Okay," the shaken man agreed.

Blake lowered the little girl to the ground. She stopped crying. Her face was filthy, and her tears had left small streaks down her dusty cheeks.

"What's your name?" Blake asked.

"Amy."

"Okay, Amy, I need you to be brave. I have to help this lady, but I'm coming right back. Stay with the man, okay?" Amy started to cry again. He shouted to the guard, "Watch her!"

Blake sprinted towards the crippled woman, zigzagging back through the scattered chairs and tables, holding his breath from the smog. The ground began to tremble again. Signs and mounted fixtures fell from the walls. The tremble quickly turned into a violent tremor. Blake lost his footing and crashed into a nearby brochure stand. Another wave of dust engulfed him. Choking on the air, he lifted himself to his knees, "Miss, are... you okay?" Blake called out, sputtering and coughing. The woman didn't respond. He looked towards the entrance, but she was gone – nothing but stone and iron rods in her place. "Miss?"

Barely missing his face, a red brick smashed into a dozen pieces next to Blake's foot. He stepped back as the walls began shaking apart.

"Run, dammit, run!" the terrified security guard yelled across the mall before picking Amy up and fleeing out the doorway.

"Hey, wait!" Blake yelled back, sprinting towards the exit as one storefront after another collapsed behind him. Windows shattered, and concrete chunks slammed down like meteorites. A large metal beam smashed through a shop window. Blake reached the archway and ran out to the street, turning back just in time to see the Golden Palm shopping centre crumble into a cloudy heap.

A symphony of chaos and confusion rang out. Blake had lost all feeling in his body. Was it adrenalin or shock? He didn't know which. He searched for Amy and the security guard, but they were now lost in the scramble. News and police helicopters circled above the ruins in the smoke-filled sky, and nearby emergency sirens howled through the city streets, but neither could drown out the pandemonium as several more buildings came tumbling down close by.

"Amy!" Blake called out.

A bald man was running with a large crowd towards the next intersection. He appeared to be carrying someone. "Amy!" Blake started to run after them, weaving through the empty cars as he tried to catch up.

Suddenly, a terrifying sound shook the very foundation of the city itself. Blake stopped dead in his tracks. *What was that?* He had never heard anything like it. It wasn't a building falling or a car crashing. This was something else. The sound crackled again, bouncing off the tall skyscrapers and hotels. It was almost lion-like, only deeper and much, much louder. *Was that... a roar?*

Horrified screams from the fleeing crowd brought Blake's attention back to the intersection ahead. About fifty people were now stampeding toward him, shoving, pushing, and trampling each other.

Blake was about to run when he noticed that the bald man was indeed the security guard, still carrying Amy in his arms at the front of the pack.

"Go! Run!" the guard called out to him.

"Amy!" Blake started towards them.

The guard waved his one free arm frantically. "Stop!" he screamed in panic. Amy was squealing. Blake's heartbeat slowed to a crawl. With a thunderous crack, the same roar filled the air once again. The guard glanced behind him, and all the colour drained from his face. Suddenly, the terrified man wrapped both his arms around Amy and covered her eyes. A wave of fire, as wide as the street itself, engulfed the fleeing crowd and everything around them. Blake fell back, shielding his face from a barrage of hot embers.

Everything went silent, or maybe the shock had finally taken over. Ash floated down like a snowy winter. Cars were left burning and twisted, and streetlamps glowed white as they melted into themselves. Blake slowly lowered his arms and opened his eyes. The only remnants of the fleeing crowd were dozens of grey mounds spread across the scorched road.

"Amy... Oh no, my God, no..."

A tear ran down his left cheek, which he quickly wiped away, but another came right after it. The swirling white flakes seemed to linger in the air. Blake buried his face in his filthy hands. Each tear seemed to fall slowly, and each felt heavier than the last, dripping into his palms as if they weighed more than the rubble behind him. Gradually, the wind shrunk the mounds of ash until there was no sign of the people who had just been there.

A sudden tremor blasted through his body as something heavy slammed down on the intersection ahead. Blake looked up from his hands; he could not believe what he saw.

Dinosaur-like, with three massive claws at the end of its toes, the creature's scaly foot crushed a bus into the ground like an empty beer can. It was enormous, at least the width of two cars and over double the length. Blake's eyes followed its leg up several storeys until it swiftly moved out of sight, with only what seemed to be a massive tail trailing in its place. Covered in rough, sandy-coloured scales, the tail thinned out at the tip before forking into a pair of blade-like talons, each one curved like a sickle. The tail casually bashed into an apartment building, leaving a huge hole in the concrete as the mystery creature disappeared behind a wall of skyscrapers.

In that moment, Blake wasn't sure if any of this was all real.

The nearby crash of another toppled building was enough to get him off the ground. He stood up. Terrified screams echoed through the city. Looking around, he saw a small alley on his right. At the other end was the Gold Coast Highway, the main road in and out of town, and across the highway was the Nerang River and Chevron Island. *Water. Get to the water.* It was the only plan he could muster. Without hesitation, Blake hurried into the narrow alleyway and didn't look back.

4

PARADISE FALLS

Emma's eyes snapped open as bottles of tan tumbled from the shelves on the far side of the booth. Sandra, lowering the spray gun, asked, "Is that an earthquake?" She could hear the picture frames falling from their hooks in the hall.

"We don't get earthquakes here," Emma replied nervously. Vibrations pounded the walls relentlessly, like a tribal drum. "What is that?" She could feel the ground shifting with each resounding beat.

Before Sandra could say a word, a screech of car tyres quickly ended in a heavy collision outside. "Wait here, hun. I'll see what's going on!" She switched off the spray-tan machine and quickly left the booth.

Emma borrowed one of the silver silk robes hanging on the rack and covered her naked body. A scream came from the hall. "Sandy?" she called, as she stepped out of the booth. The lights began to flicker, then they all went black. "Sandra? Are you there?" Emma called again, cautiously making her way down the hallway. The commotion outside had been muffled following the click of the front door closing. Emma saw Sandra and two other women standing on the footpath outside the large window. Chaos seemed to be unfolding around them.

Standing behind the reception desk, Emma watched as swarms of people rushed through the street, leaving cafes, restaurants, and stores abandoned. Suddenly, Sandra threw her hands up in panic and ran into the road. A dark red sedan, flipping through the air, bounced across the asphalt like a stray beachball and slammed into her, pinning the young woman against a deserted taxi.

Emma squealed in horror before quickly covering her mouth. Sandra's body went limp. People fled in every direction, and no one seemed to care about the person trapped amid the wreckage. Sandra slowly raised her head. Only her chest and right arm were visible; the rest of her body was hidden behind bent and twisted steel. She stared at Emma through the salon window and mouthed the word, "Run."

"She's alive! She is…" Emma took a step forward then stopped. She was petrified. What was happening out there? A dozen variations of that question kept her behind the reception desk. The building shook again. A man had stopped and was trying to free Sandra from between the two vehicles. Emma didn't even remember seeing him stop.

"Go help her," she begged herself, but couldn't move. "Okay, okay," she said, and breathed in. "Deep breaths," she told herself, then exhaled. "Go!" She sprinted around the reception desk and reached for the door. Before she could turn the handle, Emma heard a deafening roar that could have split her head in two, and she skidded to a halt, covering her ears.

"Emma, run!" Emma saw Sandra mouth the words before her right cheek lit up with an orange hue. She went to scream – so did the man trying to free her – but neither could make a sound before the entire street was consumed in a blazing inferno.

Emma scrambled over the desk as fire exploded through the large window. Curling up on the ground, she tucked her face behind her knees as searing glass shards ricocheted off the walls and ceiling.

A few moments passed. Emma opened her eyes. The ceiling was scorched, and smoke filled the room. Trying not to breathe the smog, she slowly stood up from behind the desk as broken glass rolled off her silk robe.

The scene outside was nothing short of horrific. Everything was smouldering – the road, the shopfronts, even the sidewalk – all steaming with black smoke. There was not a person in sight – no bodies either – just the crackling of nearby flames as cars, signs, and trash cans burned along the street. Sandra and the man were gone; only white flakes of ash remained in their place. The taxi and dark red sedan were now twisted, half-melted heaps. Emma noticed a dozen more ash mounds spread along the road. Tears began to stream down her sticky spray-tanned face.

Suddenly, a panic-stricken crowd began to pour out of the chemist next door. Women, children, and men rushed past the salon window in a terrified frenzy. Emma wanted to call out for help but couldn't find her voice.

A young man ran by and noticed Emma standing there. He stopped, quickly turned around, and made for the salon door. It wouldn't open. He shook the door then kicked it, but it was no use; the metal handle had melted off completely. Emma, still in shock, watched as the young man climbed through the shattered window, jumped over the desk, and grabbed her by the shoulders.

"Are you okay?" he asked. Emma was silent, her eyes blank. He was right there, but she couldn't even make out his face. "Hey! Are you okay?" he asked again.

His brown eyes came into focus first; the rest of his face was caked in dust. Emma quickly realised that she had met him before – the night before, in fact, at Brooke's party – the guy with the orange vest. She couldn't, however, remember his name, but right now, none of that was important.

James quickly looked Emma up and down for injuries. She seemed okay, although still silent and clearly shaken. "Okay. We have to go right now!" He grabbed her hand and walked her to the window. "What the? Why are you so sticky?" James asked, as he quickly let go and studied the patch of fake tan on his palm.

"All those people are dead," Emma mumbled. "Sandra, she ran outside, and the car... the car hit her."

James grabbed her hand again, saying, "Hey, it's okay. Everything is going to be okay." He looked into her eyes and clenched her trembling hand tighter. "What's your name?"

"Emma," she replied, and her whole body began to shake.

"Okay, Emma, look at me for a second." James smiled as she focused in on him, "I know you're scared, but I need you to trust me. It's not safe here, and we need to go *right now*. I'm not leaving without you, so let's get out of here together." Something about his voice began to calm her.

Emma wiped away her tears and asked, "What's happening out there?"

James shook his head and replied, "I don't know. Everyone just started screaming and running." He glanced back at the street, and the low smog and crackling flames reinforced his urge to get moving. "Okay, let's climb out the window, then we head right, straight towards Surfers and get to the police station, okay? You with me?"

"Okay," Emma said, as she let go of his hand and tightened her robe sash.

Using the sole of his orange flip-flops, James kicked the remaining shards from the window frame and checked outside; seeing the scorched black street made his heart sink. He looked back at Emma, noticed her bare feet, and asked, "Do you have shoes?"

Emma remembered that Sandra had put her clothes and purse in the small steel locker by the front door. The locker was now disfigured with the small door partially melted into the frame. "Ah... no."

James cringed at all the glass on the footpath outside. "Here, take these. They should fit you," he said, kicking off his flip-flops.

"No, it's okay, I don't need—"

James interrupted her with a raised hand. "We don't have time for manners. Just put them on, and we can get out of here."

Emma slid her feet into them. "They actually fit; you must have small feet."

James didn't respond. He leaned out the window frame and checked his left, then his right. "Okay, it looks clear. We better go!" He climbed outside and offered Emma a hand.

"Turn around!" she quickly demanded.

"Why?" a confused James asked, still holding his hand out.

"I have nothing on under this robe, and I don't want to flash you."

"Seriously? You're worried about that during a time like this?" Reluctantly, he turned around.

Emma threw one leg over the window frame, grabbed James's shoulder, then lifted the other leg over. As she checked that her robe was covering the important bits, Emma noticed James's left foot was bleeding.

"Are you okay?" she asked, pointing at the small spot of blood on the simmering concrete.

"Just a small piece of glass. I'm fine," he assured her. "The floor is hot as hell, though, so let's go!"

The pair jogged down the footpath, doing their best to avoid the still sizzling sections of pavement. Most of the shops had crumbled under their own weight and covered both sides of the road in debris. James glanced at a melted wreck that sat crooked in its car park – disfigured and still glowing white. It was all that remained of his black SUV. The sight made him wonder how hot the flames must have been to do this. Yet, somehow, despite how close he and Emma were, they didn't burn, not even a little.

"My car!" Emma cried, as she pointed to the remains of her pink convertible a few spaces down. It was warped and twisted like the SUV, and tall flames were still burning where the soft-top roof had once been. A parking metre next to it looked like an ice cream that had been left in the sun too long. "What did all this?" she thought aloud. "*Who* would have done this? Do you think it was a terrorist attack?"

James pulled his phone from his pocket. "I don't know... probably," he said, as he checked for a signal.

Emma turned her gaze to the city nearby, and her jaw dropped. "Oh no! Look! Look!" she cried, as she pointed towards the Surfers Paradise skyline.

James couldn't believe it either. Dozens of skyscrapers were engulfed in flames, while several had been completely levelled. Sirens echoed from within the ruined city as black smoke filled the sky above it. He suddenly felt cold. "Blake... Blake was delivering to Surfers today! No, no, no," James mumbled, frantically scrolling through his phone's contact list. Putting the phone to his ear, he began pacing on the ruined sidewalk.

After the third ring, Blake answered. "James? Are you there? Dude, are you there?"

A sense of relief came over James as he replied, "Yeah, I'm here! Are you alright? Are you okay?"

"I'm okay. I'm okay. It's crazy here; half the city is burning! Where are you? Are you home?" Blake was breathing heavily and sounded like he was running.

"No, no, I'm on Chevron Island! Everything is messed up – so many dead people here. I don't know what's going on. We think it may be a terrorist attack."

"It's an animal, dude. It's a massive animal!" Blake yelled through the phone. "It's not terrorists. It's a lizard or something, but way, way bigger! Like the size of a building!"

"What do you mean? An animal? An animal did this?" James asked, checking he had heard correctly.

Emma tilted her head in confusion. James was confused, too. Blake wasn't making any sense.

"Yes! An animal!" Blake knew how it sounded. "A giant dinosaur or something. It breathes fire out its mouth. Like a dragon. Trust me, I'm not dicking around!"

James had never heard Blake talk like this. He knew Blake was serious, but was he right? Was all this destruction from some sort of *animal*? He couldn't even begin to process the thought and just wanted to get the hell out of there. "Where are you now?"

"Headed towards you! Meet me at the bridge!"

"Okay, we will meet you there," James agreed and hung up the phone.

Emma looked concerned. "Is your friend okay? What did he say?"

James had a blank look on his face when he said, "Um, he said a dragon did it."

"Oh…" Emma didn't know what to say, so she gave a slow nod instead.

James was putting the phone back in his pocket when the ground shook violently. "What was that?" he asked.

Emma looked over her shoulder and let out an ear-piercing scream. James spun around then pulled her towards him. A few hundred metres from where they stood, above the rubble and the scorched road, was something that neither of them could believe.

Two palm trees snapped, crushed under the enormous lizard-like foot as it stepped into the street. It was grey, with three huge claws for toes and two more claws further up, inside the ankle. The creature came into full view. It was huge – at least twelve, maybe fifteen storeys tall – as it stood upright on its back legs. Its torso was covered in large, thick, sandy-coloured scales while the underbelly had a lighter grey tone. Both its big muscular arms were also grey, covered in hundreds of large thorny scales. Its hands had three fingers and an opposable thumb with the same razor-sharp claws at the fingertips. The creature lowered itself down, violently shaking the earth as it stood on all fours. The head was terrifyingly wide and tyrannosaurus-like, with the rough skin texture of a bearded dragon lizard. The monster's eyes were mostly white but had a slight yellow tinge around the pupils. The top of its head was flat with a row of tall spines beginning at the back of its skull and continuing down the ridge of its back and onto its long, forked tail.

James and Emma took two steps back as an orange pulsing light shimmered between its scales. The mammoth creature raised its head and sniffed the air.

"It hasn't seen us yet," Emma whispered.

James couldn't stop looking at the giant lizard, particularly the long blades crowning the tip of its swaying forked tail. It took another deep sniff of the air then stopped. Letting out a deep growl, the monster lowered its head and locked its sights on James and Emma.

"Oh, shit!" James said, as he started walking backwards.

The creature's shimmering light began to pulse rapidly between its scales. The orange glow moved like a current through its entire body and seemed to accumulate at the neck. With each pulse, its throat glowed more brightly. The monster growled loudly as the whites of its eyes began to fill with a fiery hue.

"Run! Run! Run!" screamed James, as he turned around and yanked Emma's hand. The pair sprinted past melted car wrecks and weaved through the rubble. James glanced over his shoulder as the creature roared, unleashing a stream of fire that spanned the width of Thomas Drive. "Quick, down there!" James hissed, and pointed to the small alley on the right.

The pair leapt over a melted motorcycle and ran down the alley as the flames engulfed everything behind them. Crashing into several garbage bins, they tried to get through the cluttered alley as quickly as possible before crossing the next street and fleeing into a park. Emma let go of James's hand and looked behind her as they passed an empty playground. The creature was still on the main street and had not noticed their daring escape through the trees.

Two police helicopters swooped overhead and charged towards the giant lizard. Each chopper had an officer with an automatic rifle perched on the side. The two officers lined up the target and pulled their triggers. Machine-gun fire echoed over the island as Emma and James cut through several empty backyards and ran towards the bridge.

Hundreds of empty cars now littered the Gold Coast Highway as Blake approached the Chevron Island Bridge. Two abandoned taxis were now a pair of smoking wrecks in the middle of the intersection – the result of a head-on collision during the chaos. Blake ran up onto the mangled bonnet and over the roof of the closest taxi, then jumped, his feet hitting the pavement hard. A swarm of distraught people were abandoning the bridge and heading in the other direction. Blake couldn't see James amongst them. He ascended the road as automatic gunfire split the air like fireworks on New Year's Eve, then a stream of fire cut across the blue sky turning the gunfire into nothing but a brief echo.

Blake kept moving through the car-cluttered bridge as two distant voices carried from the other side. They sounded like they were screaming his name. A moment later, he could see James and a girl running towards him at the far end. They were both yelling something and frantically pointing up at the sky. "Look out!" he finally heard them shout.

Blake glanced up to see a burning police helicopter spiralling towards him. "Oh, shit!" he cried. Quickly, he lunged for the railing and vaulted off the bridge, falling into the deep river below.

James and Emma stopped in their tracks, watching helplessly as the helicopter crashed into the bridge and exploded. The impact shattered the structural supports and sent the two-lane bridge crumbling into the water, taking the helicopter wreck and a dozen abandoned cars with it.

"Blake!" James called out, fearing for his friend in the bubbling river.

Another roar cracked like thunder. Emma and James spun around just in time to see the creature open its mouth and blast the second helicopter with its fiery breath. A screaming police officer leapt from the burning chopper as it fell out of the sky and crashed into the street below. Emma closed her eyes, but the officer disintegrated to ash before he hit the ground.

"We need to jump!" James yelled, and urgently yanked on her shoulder. Emma opened her eyes and noticed his bare feet; both were covered in cuts and were bleeding quite a lot. "Hey! You need to trust me. We need to jump into the water. It's the only way."

Emma looked hesitantly at the murky river below. "You wanna jump in there?" she asked.

James nodded and replied, "Yes! Jump! It can't burn us if we're in the water."

Blake suddenly breached the surface and began to swim away from the remains of the submerged bridge. "Hey, come on!" Waving his arms, he signalled the pair to jump.

"Oh, thank God," James whispered, and sighed with relief. Before he could say another word, Emma ran and leapt off the edge, free-falling into the water below. She cleared the submerged debris by a few metres.

James took one last look behind him. The creature's massive foot crushed the burning chopper and was headed in his direction. Emma came to the surface, checked that her robe was still intact, and swam towards Blake. Taking a deep breath, James backed up a few steps then sprinted off the edge, bombing into the murky green water below. The sounds of the chaos above were quickly muffled by the water. James opened his eyes but could barely see a thing. With stiff and tired legs, he kicked towards the surface; his skinny body wasn't used to the exercise. He breached the surface and drew a long breath.

"Over here! Hurry!" Blake called to him.

A shadow fell over James's face as the creature lifted its foot over the narrow river and stepped onto the bank on the other side. Even in the water, the trio could still feel the earth move as the monster walked back into the city. James swam as fast as he could towards Emma and Blake, who were already floating away with the tide.

Emma waited for him to catch up then asked, "What now?"

Blake nodded towards a group of expensive riverside mansions a few hundred metres down the bank. "We swim over there. On the other side of those houses is Ferry Road. From there we can get to our place and call for help or something." Their three heads bobbed up and down in the current as Emma and James nodded in agreement.

The trio began to swim towards the extravagant houses. James could feel the salt water irritating the cuts on his feet, but that didn't concern him. All he wanted was to get as far away as possible. Blake paused in mid-stroke as another four police helicopters howled overhead and beelined for the smoking skyline. The now all-too-familiar roar erupted from behind a burning residential tower. The choppers banked up and circled around to get a better angle. Blake turned back and realised the other two were swimming well ahead of him. With broad strokes, he quickly swam after them.

James reached the small wooden pier first. He climbed up and rolled onto his back as he fought to recover his breath. Emma was second. The weight of the water almost caused her robe to slip off as she flopped onto the timber deck, and she pulled it back into place.

"You okay?" she asked an exhausted James, who was breathing like a Saint Bernard on a hot summer day. He simply nodded and gave a feeble thumbs up. Emma found herself staring at the massive white house as she got up. Tall glass windows reached from the floor to the ceiling, across the back wall. In fact, there was more glass than concrete across the rear of the three-storey mansion.

As Blake reached the pier, a wave of salty water rolled straight into his mouth, causing him to choke as he pulled himself up onto the deck.

"You okay, man?" James asked, sitting up.

Blake coughed and spat river water on the expensive stained timber. "I'm okay, I think," he replied, as he rolled over and immediately noticed his friend's bleeding feet. "Where are your shoes?"

Still out of breath, James pointed towards Emma. "She has them," he sputtered.

"Um, actually, I don't." The boys looked at Emma, who glanced down at her feet before smiling up at them nervously. Both her feet were bare, with James's bright orange flip-flops nowhere in sight. "They came off in the water. Sorry," she said, squeezing the river water from her long ponytail.

James and Blake slowly turned their attention to Blake's dripping sneakers. "Ah, crap," he muttered.

Emma's feet settled into the squishy soles of Blake's wet sneakers as the trio made their way around a large swimming pool. With each step, the sneakers let out a soggy *thwap*. Blake, still wearing his socks, reached the padlocked metal gate at the side of the house. Without hesitation, James pushed by and climbed over the rather high gate. Blake got down on one knee and gave Emma the signal to put her foot in his hands.

"Don't look. Close your eyes!" Emma said, with a stern finger.

"I wasn't going to look! What do you take me for?" Blake protested.

"A *guy*," Emma replied, as she smugly lifted her wet sneaker into his hand and grabbed the top of the gate. Blake pushed her up, boosting the nearly naked girl over the fence. James helped her down the other side and watched as Emma walked around the corner. Blake quickly made his way over the gate and hopped down.

Emma stood on the vacant driveway and gazed out to the suburban street. People were loading up their cars with luggage, while others were crying on the phone to loved ones. Parents ran around frantically trying to gather their children and pack their vehicles. Blake noticed one man loading two German Shepherds into the back of his ute.

"Everyone's leaving," James said.

Emma took off towards the house next door. A man with white hair in a grey business suit was loading suitcases into the back of an expensive-looking black four-wheel drive. "Excuse me, sir," she called and waved, approaching him as he rearranged the car's trunk. "Sir, can you help us? We just need a lift." Emma tightened her robe sash as she waited for him to respond. The man didn't flinch. Instead, he cursed to himself as he struggled to make the many bags of luggage fit into the rear of his car.

"Sir? Could you please give us a lift?" Emma repeated, demanding a response.

As if she had magically appeared before him, the man suddenly stopped and acknowledged her with a glassy-eyed frown. He was obviously very shaken. "Sorry, no... I have no room... My kids..." He could barely string the words together.

Continuous weapons fire broke out in the distance. Blake and James moved to a gap between the houses and looked back at Surfers Paradise. A thirty-storey skyrise – in which the pair had once spent a drunken weekend – collapsed into a fog-like cloud that gushed out of the city like a smoke machine.

Screams of horror carried across the river, almost drowning out the helicopters and their relentless attacks against the monster.

The spooked white-haired man slammed the back hatch and stood back from the four-wheel drive. "Teresa, time to go!" he yelled, then opened the front and back passenger doors. A woman carrying a baby in her left arm ran out of the house with another young boy holding her right hand. The pair secured their children in their seats and climbed into the car.

Emma moved back as the black four-wheel drive backed out of the driveway and sped off down the road.

Blake walked over and said to her, "Hey, don't worry. We will be quicker on foot anyway."

"How can he just leave us here?" Emma asked, quivering slightly.

"He's just scared and trying to protect his family." It was only then that Blake recognised Emma from the night before. Given the circumstances, he didn't bother to say anything.

James watched as many of the remaining residents got in their cars and left their homes behind. "Man, we need to move. Everyone is getting out of town."

Blake's own nerves began to take hold. His hands were trembling, too, but he hadn't noticed until now. Quickly, he stuffed them into his pockets so the other two wouldn't see. "Our house is twenty minutes from here. Unless someone else has a better plan," he suggested.

"No, it's a plan for now. Let's just go," James agreed.

Emma nodded and said, "Yeah, okay." The exhausted trio jogged down the suburban sidewalk, leaving the smoking ruins of paradise behind them.

5

A HOME ALONE

At the corner of Ferry Road, traffic was at a complete standstill – bumper to bumper – across all three seventy-kilometre-per-hour lanes. While some people honked their horns impatiently and cursed at each other through open car windows, others opted to leave their vehicles behind and try their luck on foot. Emma noticed the white-haired man hammering his horn just ahead of them; his wife, however, was seemingly in shock as her empty gaze rested on the dashboard.

Barely able to hide their exhaustion, James and Blake led Emma through a suburban maze that was rapidly becoming deserted. Other than the odd "this way" or "down here," nobody spoke at all. Instead, they each tumbled deeper into thought as a horrific highlight reel played through their minds on a loop. It wasn't until an ambulance mounted the sidewalk and forced the trio to jump aside that they realised how little they remembered of the twenty-minute trek across town. The ambulance hooked the corner, tyres screeching, before it disappeared around the bend with sirens howling into the distance.

"We're… here," James panted, as they finally approached 34 Ayles Court. All the neighbours were either packing their cars or had already left their homes behind. All the neighbours except one: 35 Ayles Court, the home of Old Lady Margret. Her rusty white sedan was in the exact same spot it had been every day since James and Blake had moved in. They had never seen her drive it or even move it, yet every Sunday morning Old Lady Margret ran the engine for thirty minutes, then dragged out the garden hose and a bucket of soapy water, and washed it with a big sponge.

Emma followed James and Blake onto their driveway and found that she was quite surprised by their house. It wasn't big, but it was modern – white rendered walls, a large timber door with a polished steel handle, a double garage and a balcony above – and not quite the dump she had expected.

"Pretty sure I lost my keys in the river," James said, as he checked his pockets. "Do you have yours?"

"Nah, mine were in the van," Blake said, nodding to the balcony above.

James sighed as he said, "Well, looks like we're doin' a Doug again."

"What's 'doin' a Doug'?" Emma asked curiously, as Blake dragged a nearby garbage bin over.

"We had this roommate, Doug," James replied, as he clambered on top of the bin, "and every time he got drunk, he would lose his keys and have to break into the house."

"Oh," said Emma, and smiled awkwardly.

Blake held the bin steady as James reached up and pulled himself onto the balcony. "Good thing we never lock this," he said, as he slid the glass door open and disappeared inside. They heard a series of muffled footsteps as James zigzagged through the house. Meanwhile, Blake pushed the bin back to the fence while Emma waited anxiously. With the click of a turning lock, the big door was flung open. "Mind the mess – Blake made it," James welcomed her.

An unamused Emma stepped inside and brushed past him. Blake clipped James across the back of the head as he came through the door. "You really think this is the time for jokes?"

"Trying to lighten the mood," James replied, but his grin disappeared. Blake followed Emma through the hall as James shut the front door behind them. "You're welcome," he muttered under his breath.

Emma looked around as she came to the end of the hall: a polished stone-top bench sat in the middle of the kitchen, and white cupboards with silver handles matched the stainless-steel dishwasher. Over a dozen empty beer cans were stacked in a pyramid next to the sink. The adjoined lounge room had a large white leather couch with a round glass coffee table in front. A fifty-five-inch TV sat on a matching glass stand, which had several game consoles and a dozen video game cases in a collapsed stack next to them. A gamepad sat on the coffee table next to half a dozen chocolate wrappers and an empty packet of corn chips.

"Sorry about the mess. I was playing *A Soldier's Duty 2* the other day… hadn't cleaned up yet," James apologised, as he quickly grabbed the empty wrappers and stuffed them into a nearby bin.

Hearing a sound, Emma turned around and asked, "What the hell was that back there?" James paused, but didn't say anything. Blake opened a glass door opposite the kitchen and wandered out onto a small timber deck.

"Maybe the news has something," James said, as he leaned over the lounge, dug his hands between two cushions, and pulled out a remote. The TV light went from red to green, but instead of finding the local news, the words "No Signal" bounced around the black screen. He changed the channel.

Same thing. He changed it again. "No signal." James rapidly flicked through the remaining channels until he finally found one that was still broadcasting. It was a live video feed from a news helicopter above the smoking ruins of Surfers Paradise.

Emma and James lowered themselves onto the couch, their eyes locked to the television as the words "PARADISE BURNS" scrolled across the imagery.

At approximately twelve pm today, Surfers Paradise was attacked by an unknown entity. Early reports suggested this was an act of terrorism. However, we are now getting reports of a much more bizarre nature. Some claims suggest this is the result of an animal attack. Yes, viewers, an animal attack! About half a dozen police helicopters are circling an area further down the city. Our chopper has been warned not to enter that airspace. The death toll is unknown at this time; it is, however, being estimated in the tens of thousands. As you can see from the images on your screen, the devastation is...

The screen suddenly switched off, as did the fridge and microwave. "There goes the power," James said, as he sighed.

"Dad!" Emma leapt up from the couch in a panic. "I have to find my dad!"

James stood up and asked, "Where is he?"

"Give me your phone, now!" Emma demanded.

James fumbled through his damp pocket and pulled out his black smartphone. "It hasn't worked since we got out of the river. I'm sorry," he said, handing it to her.

"No, no, no!" Emma slapped the phone back into his hand, turned around, and marched out onto the back deck. Blake was sitting on an old wooden bench, hunched over with his face buried in his palms. The bench looked like it belonged in a public park.

"Does your phone work?" Emma interrupted, as she kicked off his loose sneakers.

Blake looked up as the shoes bounced across the weathered timber. "Sorry, what?" A tear escaped and ran down his cheek before he wiped it away. "What's up?"

Emma tried to calm herself. She looked down at his white socks; they were now half black from the jog across town. "Thanks for letting me borrow your shoes," Emma said, pointing at the two wet sneakers lying on the deck.

Blake nodded and said, "No problem." He pointed at her arm and continued, "Your, um, thing is…"

Emma quickly noticed her robe was hanging off her shoulder. "Oh, right," she said, and pulled it up and tightened her sash. "Does your phone work? My dad is a cop. I need to make sure he is okay." Just speaking of her father brought her right back to the last conversation they had; the one she had rudely and abruptly ended.

Blake pointed to his phone, which was resting in a sunny spot on the deck, and said, "It doesn't yet, but when it dries out, hopefully, it will."

"We've got no phones, no internet and no power. What the hell do we do now?" James asked, as he joined them outside.

"We need to run," Emma said, without hesitation.

Blake stood up. "Run where? We have no car, and even if we did, we'd barely make it down the street before we'd hit a wall of traffic."

"Well, we sure as hell won't get far walking!" James quipped.

"Guess we wait it out."

"Wait?" Emma took immediate issue with the idea. "My dad is out there somewhere. I have to get home to see if he is there; to see if he is okay."

"Where is home?" Blake asked.

"Springbrook."

James scoffed, "That's almost an *hour's* drive from here!"

"I don't care! I have to find him!"

"Whoa! We get it. We totally get it," James said, lowering his tone, "but right now, we've got no choice. We're stuck here."

"He's right. We also have no idea what that thing was or if there are more of them out there. The only thing we can do is wait... and hope."

"What if he's not okay?" Emma almost choked on the words.

"Don't think like that. We got away; he probably did, too," Blake replied, glaring at James for support.

James quickly chimed in. "Yeah. You said he's a cop, right? He's probably better off than we are right now." Although James wouldn't say it aloud, after everything they had seen, he was doubtful, too.

"Let's wait it out. I'm sure, at any moment, we'll hear that the army or the police have killed that thing. Then, together, we can take you home and make sure your dad is okay." In the moment, it was the only plan Blake could think of.

Reluctantly, Emma agreed. "Okay."

"It's a plan at least," James said, conjuring a fake smile.

"What about your parents? Your family? Aren't you guys worried about them?" Emma asked.

The pair shook their heads. "Nope. All good. My whole family lives in Sydney," James explained. "But they are probably really worried about me."

Emma turned to Blake and asked, "You?"

"Mine are probably fine," Blake replied and shrugged. "Nothing to worry about." Avoiding eye contact, he walked back inside without another word.

"Did I say something wrong?" Emma whispered.

"No; it's just that Blake was a foster kid. He had a different home every two years or so," James quietly explained. "He hasn't got any real parents."

"Oh," said Emma, feeling bad for asking, "I guess you're his family then."

Blake suddenly poked his head back through the doorway and asked, "Wanna borrow some clothes?"

Emma blushed. It occurred to her that she was still naked under her filthy robe. After everything that had happened, it had completely slipped her mind. "Yes, please."

Upstairs, Blake rummaged through his walk-in closet as Emma took a nosy gander around his room, which was *much* cleaner than the rest of the house. In fact, it was immaculate. His big king-size bed was neatly made with the spotless white sheets tucked under the matching pillows. A large bookshelf stood against the left-hand wall, its shelves lined with small trophies: Grand Touring Junior Champion 2011, Rising Star 2012, Time Attack State Champion 2013, Time Attack State Champion 2014. Emma wondered why there were no trophies after the year 2014. On the shelf below were a dozen photographs of Blake standing with an older man by a race car. The grey-haired man had a beer and a cigar in almost all the photos. The shelf below that had six photos of Blake and James. The first one showed the pair standing on a small fishing boat, James holding his fishing rod between his legs to resemble a large penis and Blake casually holding a beer.

"Will sweatpants do?" Blake asked from the closet.

"Yeah, great! Anything will be better than this robe." Emma wandered over to the bedside table where a single photograph sat next to a brown lamp. Curiously, she picked it up. The photo was of a small German Shepherd puppy sitting next to a young blond-haired boy; the pair of them were filthy and covered in mud. Blake must have only been twelve, maybe thirteen years old, at the time.

"Here you go."

Emma quickly put the picture down. Blake was holding a neatly folded pair of grey sweatpants and a white T-shirt. "Thanks," she said, taking the clothes from him. She glanced back at the photograph and asked, "Your dog?"

Blake's eyes lingered on the image as he replied, "He was... I'll let you change." He left the room and quietly shut the door.

Emma dumped the clothes on the bed and stared again at the photo. She was starting to realise that her host wasn't exactly an open book. She untied the sash and removed her robe, immediately noticing a sizable gash down the back of her left calf. Emma couldn't even remember how she had got it. Compared to all the cuts James had on his feet, she realised how lucky she had been that day. They had all been lucky that day.

～～～～～～～～～

Hours passed until the sun cast a tropical glow through the smoky horizon. No message of victory had come. No policeman had knocked on the door; no solider had provided rescue. No one had come at all. The later it got, the quieter the night became. Echoes of wailing sirens had faded into silence, the honking traffic had gone mute, and the last howl of a swooping helicopter had been heard hours ago. Only the monster's horror-inducing roar could still be heard in the distance.

James lay on his back across the timber floor, positing theories about what the creature was and where it might have come from. Neither Blake nor Emma was listening. Instead, they were sitting on the bench beside one another, lost in their own thoughts.

Emma was wondering about Michelle and Brooke, trying to picture where the girls would have been during the attack. Michelle had probably been at home studying. She lived further out of town, so hopefully she was safe. Brooke could have been anywhere – at the university, at home, at a boy's house maybe. What Emma wouldn't have given for a working phone.

Normally, Blake would have told James to shut up by now. However, he could think of only one person – Amy. No matter how hard he tried, her little face kept popping up in his mind: how she and her brother were playing in the back of their mother's station wagon just hours earlier; how scared she had been when the ground shook; the scream she had let out as the clock tower fell; the guard who had carried her... the fire... the ash. Blake couldn't shake off the feeling of guilt, which filled every inch of him. "I shouldn't have left her with the security guard," he told himself over and over again.

James had never been good at processing his feelings, and this was far too much for him to even try. All he could do was keep his mind busy, which usually meant keeping his mouth busy. Eventually, Emma stood up and went inside. James was going to ask if she was okay when they heard a sudden, ear-piercing scream that resembled the word "Help!" The boys leapt to their feet and bolted through the door. A traumatised Emma was cowering on top of the kitchen bench, pointing at a large huntsman spider crawling across the floor. It was easily the size of her hand. "Kill it! Kill it!" she shrieked.

Blake sighed with relief. "Jeez, I thought..."

"Hold on. I'll get it," James said, and retrieved Blake's sneaker from the deck.

"Whoa, dude. Just hold on," Blake reproached him, snatching the shoe from his hand, "we don't have to kill it." Making his way into the kitchen, he opened the cupboard under the sink and pulled out a dustpan.

"Oh, come on! Not this again! Remember the last one? It crawled straight back into the house," James protested, cringing at the hairy arachnid.

Perched on the kitchen bench, Emma watched as Blake scooped the spider into the dustpan. "You can't be serious?" she asked incredulously.

James rolled his eyes and replied, "Oh, he is. Blondie here doesn't like to kill anything – seriously. The dude hates it when I use fly spray."

Blake ignored the pair and carried the spider out onto the deck before dropping it into the garden bed.

"That thing was disgusting," Emma said, shivering, as she climbed down from the kitchen bench.

Blake came back inside with the empty dustpan and a smile. "It was just a spider."

"He has an animal fetish. Weird, I know," James joked.

"I can't deal right now." Emma was flushed and asked, "Do you guys mind if I lie down?"

"Sure, you can take my room," Blake offered. "I'll crash on the couch."

"Thanks."

With a lit candle to navigate, the trio separated for the night. Knowing the monster could come at any moment, they each remained wide awake. However, like everything else outside, its roar had fallen silent. Blake spent the night on the lounge, staring at the ceiling as he replayed the day's events in his mind. Upstairs, Emma sat on the edge of the bed, punishing herself with a replay of Sandra's death: thoughts of how she had frozen in fear behind that reception desk; how she hadn't been there to help her friend; and how she probably would have died, too, had she been. That last thought made her feel even more guilty. James spent the night tinkering with his drone, attempting to keep his mind busy. He felt numb – cold even – but to his surprise, he didn't feel broken. Maybe he was just too scared to think, or maybe the horror of it all just hadn't sunk in yet.

〰〰〰〰〰〰〰〰

As the sun rose, James came downstairs to find Blake circling the kitchen, deep in thought. "What you doin'?"

"Trying to figure out how we get Emma back to Springbrook," Blake said, continuing to pace.

"Don't you think we should be figuring out how to get out of town?"

"And go where? We don't even know where that thing went. We promised to get her home."

"No, you promised her."

Blake finally stopped pacing. "Yeah, I did. It was the right thing to do. Don't be a dick."

"I'm kidding. Calm down. So, what did you come up with?"

"Nothing."

"How long you been doing laps around the kitchen?"

"About three hours."

"Oh, good," James said, patting his friend on the back, "nothing like a productive morning."

"Hey." Emma entered the room wearing Blake's oversized sweatpants and a fresh T-shirt. "Heard anything yet? Do the phones work? What about the power?"

"No, no, and no." Blake couldn't help but notice she was now wearing his favourite light-blue T-shirt.

"Oh, I hope you don't mind. I borrowed another shirt from your closet."

"Nah, no problem at all."

"Oh, and I used your toothbrush. Hope that's okay." Her perfectly white teeth gleamed back at him.

"Actually," Blake's face contorted as he said, "that's really gross."

"Well, too bad. You're going to have girl germs for a while," she replied, brushing off his disgust. "So, what are you guys going to do after you take me home?"

James shrugged and said, "Probably come back here, I suppose."

"You can't come back here," Emma scoffed. "You live right in the city. That thing could still be out there."

"Got any other suggestions?" Blake asked.

Emma nodded. "Stay at my house. At least for a few days until this all blows over. Springbrook is in the mountains. It should be safer than here, anyway."

"She's right. We're too close to town," James said, as he looked at Blake. "We have to go somewhere, dude."

"Yeah, okay, that would be nice. Thanks."

"No problem. It's the least I can do." Emma smiled and asked, "So what now?"

"We're about to come up with a plan," said James, reeking of fake optimism.

"We just need a car," Blake added.

"Okay, let's break down the facts." James donned his best detective impression. "Our cars are toast. Mine was barbequed back at Chevron Island. Emma's is a giant puddle of pink, and I'm assuming your old heap of junk is still parked at Bright Fart Couriers. Not to mention Houdini is at Gary's house, thanks to that crazy old bat across the street!"

"What's a Houdini?" Emma asked.

James couldn't look more pleased that she had asked. "It's Blake's stupid race car. Fun fact: it makes all his money just disappear!"

"The crazy old bat!" Blake's eyes widened as he exclaimed, "That's it! Old Lady Margret! We can borrow Margret's car!"

"Are you nuts? She hates us!"

"Got a better idea?"

Emma could barely hide her excitement. "Do you think she'll let us borrow it? How do you know she hasn't already left like everyone else?"

"Pfft!" James shook his head. "That nutter hasn't left her hut since witches were outlawed."

Blake was confident, too. "That's it! I'll sweet-talk her. We'll borrow her car and then take you straight home!"

"What if she says no?"

"Then we steal it." Blake shrugged, then headed towards the hall.

"Really?" James was stunned. "You wanna rob Old Lady Marge?"

Blake was already halfway up the stairs. James couldn't quite tell if his friend was serious or not, but soon enough, he'd find out.

6

THE ROAD TO RILEY FARM

"What? She left?" Blake was stunned. Standing on the street with heavy backpacks slung over their shoulders, the trio found themselves in front of a very abandoned 35 Ayles Court with Old Lady Margret nowhere to be seen.

James gave a certain nod and said, "Front door was wide open, too. I checked every room. The place is empty. Someone must have picked her up. Car is here, but no keys though. She must have taken them with her, too."

Blake yawned and said, "Well, at least we don't have to *ask* to borrow it."

"So, what do we do?" Emma asked.

"We borrow it."

The trio turned to the rusty white sedan. "Will that old thing even make it there?" James asked doubtfully.

"Dude, it's the only choice we've got right now," Blake replied, as he walked over to the driver's side door.

"This thing will explode before we get off the porch," James declared, as he reluctantly produced a metal coat hanger from his red floral board shorts.

Blake didn't want to touch it. "Really? You put it down your pants?"

"I had no free hands." James bent the hanger into a long hook shape and tossed it over.

"Are you *really* going to steal her car?" Emma interrupted them.

"Do you wanna get home?"

"He's right," Blake said, as he slid the metal hanger down the window seal and jiggled it around. After a minute, the lock popped up. "Besides, we're just borrowing it."

"Let's get moving." James clutched his backpack and headed for the rear door.

"Wait. We have the food. So what's in your bag?" Blake asked him.

James unslung his backpack and unzipped it. "Thought it might come in handy," he said, revealing his prized drone inside.

Disapprovingly, Blake opened the driver's door, saying, "I hate that thing."

"What is that thing?" Emma asked.

"Closest thing James has to a girlfriend."

Old Lady Margret's car reeked of musky perfume and stagnant water. Judging by the rusty holes throughout the body, the coast's tropical climate had not been kind to the forty-year-old vehicle. James sat in the back seat and dumped their hastily packed bags next to him.

"I did mention my dad is a cop, right?" Emma reiterated. "Are you hot-wiring it?"

Blake fumbled around in his pocket before producing a small screwdriver. "Not exactly," he said, as he pulled the bonnet latch and got out of the car.

Emma curiously watched from her seat as he began tinkering under the hood. "Did he used to steal cars or something?" she asked James, who was quietly gazing out at the empty street.

"Hah! Him? Steal? No; you can thank Blake's inebriated mechanic for teaching him this particular skill set. It's actually quite easy. You just use the screwdriver to connect the power to the ignition wire and—" A shower of sparks sprayed out from under the hood as the old motor sputtered to life. "That's all there is to it." James finished his sentence with a smug smile.

Blake dropped the hood and got back in the driver's seat. "Let's get out of here."

Emma slumped back in her seat, saying, "You two are so weird."

As they passed each vacant house, a sense of desolation fell over the group. While some homes had children's toys sprawled across their neatly mowed lawns, others had garage doors open and front gates swinging in the breeze. Someone had even left the sprinklers on. Each passing home told a story of a life abruptly left behind.

"Everyone's gone," James said sombrely, his face pressed to the glass.

"It's strange," Emma added. "Where did all they all go?"

"Anywhere they could. There were a lot of cars on the road yesterday. Maybe we should have gone, too."

Emma pushed the power button on the old car's radio. Nothing happened. No sound came from the speakers, nor did a single light come on.

"It's broken. I already checked it," Blake said quietly.

Emma could tell something was eating at him. Given the situation, she figured they all had concerns right now but decided to prod him anyway. "What are you thinking?"

Blake cleared his throat then said, "If everyone has evacuated, then things must be much worse than we thought."

Emma was thinking the same thing, but hearing it from him made her feel worse. Blake turned onto Southport-Nerang Road. The main road was usually busy, but now the only vehicles in sight were abandoned, crashed or damaged in some way, none of which inspired hope. Blake threaded the rattling old sedan between the scattered cars and trucks until they reached a clear section of road.

Emma was glued to the window. "I'm surprised there aren't more cars left behind. Everything was gridlocked yesterday."

"Well, at least none of them are trampled or burning," James added. "Looks like the monster didn't come this way."

Rolling over the next hill, Blake's eyes widened at the sight of the upcoming intersection. A dozen or more cars were waiting at the traffic lights. "Look!" he said, as he cautiously slowed down.

"Finally, somebody!" James said, relieved.

Blake leaned on the steering wheel as their car rolled closer; everything was very still. "Something's wrong."

Emma's attention went straight to the traffic lights. No red. No orange. No green. Just black. "The lights are out."

"So what's everyone waiting for?" James asked, suddenly feeling very cold.

Blake stopped the old sedan a few metres behind the idle vehicles and opened his door. "Wait here," he said, hopping out.

"Dude, get back in the car. Let's just go!" James barked at him.

Walking between the cars, Blake noticed that several were still running, with their headlights left on. "What the hell?"

At the front of the pack, he came to a blue sports coupe that idled with a low hum. The coupe's windshield was completely shattered, with countless shards spread over its creased bonnet. The rest of the car was fine – no damage or dents. Blake focused beyond the broken windshield to the car's interior, which made him gasp. A trail of red spots on the dash quickly led to the driver's seat, which was torn to shreds, strands of blood-soaked foam protruding from its black leather.

"Oh, shit," Blake said, as he stepped back, looking at the other cars around him. Each one had a shattered window or two, blood-soaked seats, creased bonnets or bent panels. It was like something had forced itself into them. Emma and James opened their doors and got out of the car. Emma waited by the old sedan; she was too nervous to go any further.

James walked over to the blue coupe and cringed at the sight before him. "Oh man, guess that thing did come this way," he said, covering his mouth.

"It doesn't make sense," Blake mumbled quietly. "That monster was the size of a building and burned everyone it came across." He pointed at the panels on the car. "These cars aren't burnt. They aren't crushed. The road isn't scorched, and the streetlights are still standing. That monster didn't do this."

A chill ran down James's spine as he said, "So something else killed these people."

"What are you guys doing?" Emma called out from the old sedan.

"We need to get out of here," said Blake.

James took off, saying, "No argument here!"

Emma looked at him, concerned. "What happened?" she asked.

"We'll tell you in the car. Quick, get in!"

Emma didn't need an incentive to leave and was buckled up before James shut his door. "What did you guys see?"

Blake flung himself into the driver's seat and threw the old sedan in reverse. "Nothing good." He mounted the curb and hammered the gas, leaving the horrid intersection in the rearview mirror. James began to explain their findings to Emma. She turned pale. None of it made any sense.

Blake sped down the on-ramp of the M1 motorway. The M1 was the main highway connecting the Gold Coast to the other major cities: Brisbane was an hour north and Sydney was about twelve hours south. Normally, during the early morning hours, the M1 would be bumper to bumper, with traffic backed up for miles. Instead, this morning the road was lifeless, with hundreds of abandoned vehicles spread out over the five-lane highway. Blake wove the old sedan between empty cars, buses and trucks, many of which had smashed windshields and blood-soaked interiors. Some had crashed, and some had even flipped upside down.

The sight became too much for Emma to bear. She turned her gaze to a loose strand of roof lining and watched as it danced in the wind above her open window. All she could think about was her father. Would he even be there when they arrived? What if he wasn't? What if he never made it out of the city? Would she ever see him again? As the distance to home got smaller, her fear and anxiety grew larger. Tears began to flow. Emma turned back to the window and hoped that the boys wouldn't notice. They didn't notice.

Suddenly, the familiar howl of helicopter blades vibrated the panels of the old car. Blake wound down his window to see five Black Hawk helicopters flying low over the highway toward the city ruins.

"About time! The army's here, bitches," James cried, as he leaned out and waved, hoping to get their attention. A moment later, they were out of sight.

"Well, that's a good sign, right?" Emma asked, and looked to the others.

"Hell, yeah, it is!" James couldn't hide his smile.

Blake kept his eyes on the road and didn't say a word.

After navigating the highway for some time, Emma directed them to the next off-ramp. Halfway up the incline, a school bus, with flames reaching high out of its windows, was partially embedded in the concrete wall. Blake squeezed the old sedan between the rear of the bus and the opposite wall. Emma couldn't help but notice the driver's lifeless body slumped over the steering wheel. James saw it, too. Blake quickly turned off the ramp and drove across the overpass towards the hinterland.

The country road was quiet, but it always was. Ironically, the sounds of rustling leaves and chirping birds seemed noisy after the ghostly drive through town. Two sparrows playfully flew overhead, keeping pace with the car as the early morning sunlight pierced through the trees.

After passing several farms and rural estates, Emma sprung to life when another property came into view. A white picket fence, with a matching wooden gate at the end of a long gravel driveway, ran alongside the road. "This is it," Emma announced with hopeful eyes. A small sign reading "The Riley Farm" stood next to the open gate. Blake turned onto the driveway, the car rattling as it bounced over the stony terrain. The large house loomed ahead. Emma opened her door and leapt out while the car was still moving. Blake brought the old sedan to a skidding halt. Emma raced up the steps and onto the house's front deck, calling out for her father repeatedly before disappearing through the front door.

James and Blake exchanged a doubtful glance as they got out of the car. The Riley Farm was a weathered double-storey house. The white timber walls were filthy, while the green tiled roof barely had a tinge of colour above its rusty gutters. Half a dozen shiny solar panels were mounted on it and looked particularly out of place. To the right of the front door, a three-metre-wide glass window overlooked the stained timber deck.

The deck itself stood a few feet above ground and ran the length of the house.

James immediately went inside and found himself in a wide entryway, standing before a wooden staircase to the upper floor. To his left was a narrow hall running alongside the staircase and a small arch that led to the kitchen. To his right was a large open lounge room with a brown Chesterfield couch between two black leather recliners sitting opposite a sixty-inch TV mounted on the wall. Several loud thumps in the ceiling made it clear that Emma was rummaging through a room upstairs. James figured it was best to leave her alone for the moment. Instead, he went over to the lounge room's large glass window and saw Blake walking around outside.

The gravel crunched beneath Blake's sneakers as he looked around the yard. To the right of the house stood a tall red barn that was all but consumed by cobwebs and overgrown weeds. Behind the barn was an empty field with no animals or cattle, just tall grass swaying in the wind. Around the back, a small creek ran across the length of the property and curved around the left-hand side of the house. Bordering the creek was a withering forest that stretched all the way to the mountains behind. The brown summer-scorched leaves clung to their near-dead branches as the wind played aggressively with the trees.

"My dad isn't here, and the house phone isn't working," a very distraught Emma wailed, as she burst through a door and marched out onto the rear deck. Before Blake could say a word, she turned around and stormed back into the house.

Blake quickly followed her inside and found himself in the kitchen. The room was quite large, but rather dated. The benchtops were wooden with an old navy-blue vinyl pressed over the top. The sink, however, was polished steel and was certainly a newer addition, as were the stained timber floors. Emma was pacing back and forth between a dining table and the kitchen bench.

"Hey, your dad is probably fine. Like you said, he's a cop. He's probably out there helping someone." Even Blake felt the hollowness in his words.

"I can't believe this."

"Well, the police will be busy, you know, trying to get everyone to safety and dealing with everything that's happened."

Emma stopped pacing and shouted, "I saw what that thing did to people! To Sandra and all those poor people running in the street! What chance does my dad, or anyone else, have against something like that? If he was alive, he would be here. He would be here! Waiting for me! I checked his room upstairs, and he hasn't been home since yesterday."

Blake was lost for words. "I'm sorry…"

Emma burst into tears and sank into him, saying, "I don't know what to do."

"It's okay. We can't give up yet," Blake said, rubbing her back.

"I can't lose him. I can't."

"We will find your dad," Blake reassured her, then looked over to see James standing in the kitchen doorway.

"Together," James added.

Emma let go of Blake and wiped her eyes. "So, what do we do now?"

"We wait here."

Emma nodded. "You think he will come back?"

"Well, this is the first place he'd come to look for you. So, let's wait."

"Sounds good to me," James agreed.

"Okay," Emma stammered, still choked up. "I hope you're right."

Glancing over his shoulder, James noticed the television's standby light was glowing red. "Wait! You have power here?"

"Yeah, the house runs completely on solar power. Dad hates the electric companies. He says they rip people off, so he keeps us off the grid," Emma explained.

James walked into the lounge room and found the television remote on the Chesterfield's cushion. He turned on the TV and, unsurprisingly, the words "No Signal" filled the sixty-inch screen. "Dammit," he said, as he dropped the remote and flopped into the closest black recliner. "Oh man, we need to get two of these," James exclaimed, sinking into the leather and extending the recliner's footrest.

"He'll probably be there for a while," Blake said with a sigh.

"Dude, you have to try this. It's like wrapping your arse in a cloud."

"Yeah, that's my dad's favourite chair," Emma said uncomfortably.

7

A MAN DOWN

Lorcan suddenly came to. Smoke billowed into the sky. He sat up and heaved the crumpled piece of rotor off his chest. A sharp pain shot across his torso – several broken ribs at least. With a loud groan, Lorcan stood up. His muscular arms were covered in cuts and bruises while blood trickled past his right eye from a large gash on his forehead. The lieutenant slowly looked around, caressing his ribs as his eyes struggled to focus.

The burning remains of five Black Hawk helicopters were scattered across the M1 motorway. Lorcan limped over to a motionless soldier lying next to the closest wreck. He crouched down and rolled the man over. His arm was missing; he'd already bled out. The lieutenant's vision began to clear. Two dozen lifeless soldiers were amongst the burning choppers. He unclipped his helmet and threw it to the ground, then ran his hand over his bald head. His short black beard dripped with blood.

Despite his twenty-year career, nothing could have prepared Lorcan for what he had seen that day. After recovering a rifle from the crash, the forty-five-year-old limped down the deserted highway with a sprained ankle and several broken ribs.

Leaving behind the wreckage of the five Black Hawk helicopters and the bodies of his fellow soldiers was not an easy decision, but dusk had fallen and Lorcan needed to find shelter fast. The streetlamps, billboards and road signs that normally illuminated the highway were now bleak, dull and lifeless reminders of yesterday's world. The massive cracked footprints in the road made tracking the creature's movements easy, although Lorcan wasn't sure what he would do when he caught up to it.

Early moonlight cast a Halloween-like glow on the stormy clouds above. Lorcan flicked his rifle's light on and scanned the empty cars around him; several had been completely flattened by the towering reptile. An empty bus, however, caught his attention for another reason: a huge tear in its side where the exit doors had once been. He moved closer, shining his light over every panel. It appeared as if something had forced its way into the bus.

With his rifle raised, Lorcan cautiously stepped through the opening. The missing doors were twisted and bent inwards. Almost all the seats had been ripped apart, and the floor was covered in foam, dried blood and broken glass. Shopping bags, backpacks and briefcases were also abundant, but strangely, there were no bodies or remains to accompany them. Lorcan was about to leave when, through one of the windows, a single light gleamed from a gas station at the top of the next exit ramp. Keeping low, Lorcan climbed out of the bus, switched his torch off and made his way towards the light.

The gas station was huge, with about forty pumps located out front, designed to serve the high volume of vehicles that used the busy freeway. Around two dozen empty cars were still parked at the fuel pump bays. Like the bus, they, too, all had smashed windows and windshields, except one – a shiny, red European station wagon that was parked at the pump closest to the front doors.

The gleaming light he had seen from the highway turned out to be a burning candle, flickering behind a nearby window. With his rifle butt positioned firmly against his shoulder, Lorcan cautiously approached the entrance of the gas station. A quiet whisper came from inside, and the candlelight suddenly went out. Lorcan crouched down behind the red station wagon and peeked over the bonnet; he could make out at least two moving shadows behind the glass doors.

Flicking the safety off and the light on, Lorcan emerged from behind the car and charged through the doors. "Come out!" he shouted. His mounted flashlight lit up the dark counter – nothing but a chewing gum display and a cash register. Then, hearing another whisper nearby, he shouted again, "Come out with your hands up!" Lorcan made his way between the small aisles, listening for any hint of movement. At the end of the last aisle was a small table with a box of matches; used matches were scattered around a smoking candle. Someone had put it out in a hurry. The next table over was covered in dozens of empty confectionary wrappers and crushed soda cans. "Quick, go!" a low voice murmured, as something scurried behind the front counter.

Lorcan snapped around, his finger tickling the trigger as he headed back towards the exit. "I am a lieutenant in the Australian army! Come out so I can see you!" His deep voice echoed through the empty building.

"Okay, we are coming out. Please don't shoot!" Four people stood up behind the front counter – a man, a woman and two young children, a boy and a girl.

Lorcan shone his light over them as they shielded their eyes; they all seemed unharmed. He flicked the light off and lowered the rifle. "Is anyone hurt?"

"Huh?" asked the man.

"I said, is anyone hurt?"

"Ah, no, no. Sorry! No one is hurt, thank you, sir." The man was clearly nervous, though the dark made it hard to see any of their faces.

"Are you here to rescue us?" the woman asked, grabbing her children's hands.

Lorcan spat a ball of dried blood onto the floor and replied tersely, "No."

"But you said that you're with the army?" The man came out from behind the counter.

"So?" Lorcan snorted and spat again.

The woman hung back, keeping her two children close as they huddled behind the cash register. "So what are you doing here if you're not here to rescue people?" she blurted out, clearly intimidated by the soldier's rough demeanour.

"I saw a light. Was curious who was in here."

"Will you help us get out of here?" she asked nervously.

"I'm not here to babysit."

The man choked on his words. "So you expect us to stay here with those things outside? Are you crazy?"

"Calm down. That dinosaur thing is probably miles away by now. It's a good time for you to move." Lorcan noticed the little girl hiding behind her mother's leg.

"I'm not talking about the giant lizard that just came through here. It's the snakes that we're hiding from!"

"Snakes?" Lorcan scoffed. "Trust me. You have bigger problems than *snakes* right now."

"These are not *normal* snakes."

"What the hell are you yapping about?" Lorcan couldn't tell if the man was serious or if he had lost it.

"We stopped here yesterday to get gas. When I went to pay the cashier, these huge snakes, kinda serpent-looking things, came out of nowhere and started attacking everyone. We have been hiding in here ever since."

"How huge?"

"Longer than our car! Body as wide as an oil drum! We didn't even know about that giant dinosaur until it passed by the gas station earlier." The panicked man rambled, then stepped a little too close to Lorcan. "What is that thing? I've never seen anything so big!"

Lorcan quickly shoved him back. "Listen to me," he said. "We don't know what it is either, so stop asking! Now tell me more about the snakes that attacked you here." His raised voice caused both children to cry.

"It's okay. It's okay. Come with me. Let's get you some lollies," the woman said, and shot Lorcan a look of disgust before ushering her son and daughter towards the other side of the store.

"Come," the shadowed man said, and pointed to the table with the candle on it. "Sit down. I'll tell you everything."

The candle flickered alight, finally revealing the man's face as he took a seat at the table and blew out the matchstick. He was younger than Lorcan, probably in his late thirties, had pale freckly skin, curly brown hair, and a thin moustache. Resting his rifle across the table, Lorcan sat down opposite him.

"Barry Marsh." The man introduced himself, presenting his hand for an unreciprocated handshake. "Whoa! You need to get that looked at. Are you alright?" he said, as he gestured at the large gash on the soldier's forehead.

"Tell me about the things that attacked you here."

"Right, sorry." Barry leaned in, saying, "We came down from Brisbane, booked a nice hotel in Surfers Paradise. We just wanted to take the kids to the coast for the weekend." A stern stare from Lorcan motivated Barry to quickly skip ahead.

"Anyway, we stopped here for gas. I filled up the car and went inside to pay. That's when the commotion started outside. People started screaming, started running. Samantha was in the car with the kids; she looked petrified. Then something slid out from behind the gas pump. At first, I could just see its head – bigger than a saltwater croc's – but it looked like a snake… had these long spines around its neck, too, like some kind of bony frill. Anyway, two guys ran right past it!" Barry wiped a nervous sweat off his forehead before continuing, "It made this sound, like a high-pitched cry. Chased those guys down so fast… That's when I got a good look at it. The body of a snake, but it had these long thin legs like an insect; eight legs, ten maybe. I've never seen anything like it. Those poor guys – I couldn't watch – it tore them to shreds. I can still hear them screaming. It killed them right in front of my kids while I hid behind the cash register."

"What happened next?"

"At least a dozen more came… from everywhere. Killed everyone. I ran outside and grabbed my wife and kids. We hid in the toilets and barred the door. The screams only lasted for a few minutes, but we kept our hands over the kids' ears for an hour. When I came back out, there were no giant snakes and no bodies either. We've been here ever since, waiting for help – too scared to go outside in case they're still out there." Barry took a breath, his eyes glistening with tears. "But I guess they're not. You made it here just fine."

Lorcan leaned back in his seat. He didn't know what to make of it. Giant snakes? The only creature his team had been briefed on was the fire-breathing reptile that levelled the city the day before. He wondered if his commanding officer had withheld the intel, or maybe the military didn't know about them either.

"What's your name?" Barry asked, putting his hand out to shake again.

"Lorcan," replied the soldier, still ignoring the gesture.

"So, Lieutenant Lorcan, what can *you* tell *me*?"

Lorcan spat another clump of blood on the floor, but after a moment, he figured there was no harm in answering the man. "Yesterday, at approximately twelve hundred hours, Surfers Paradise was attacked by an unidentified reptile – the one that passed through here earlier. This reptile breathes a fire so hot it incinerates anyone and anything touched by its flames. People turn to ash; steel melts into puddles. Over seventy percent of the city was destroyed. After the initial attack, the animal made its way south, burning everything in its path. The actual death toll is still unknown, but rough estimates put it at over two hundred and fifty thousand."

"A quarter of a million people? Dead? You're telling me that it killed over *a quarter of a million people* in a single day?" Barry asked, struggling to comprehend the magnitude of what he was hearing. He thought the gas station carnage had been the worst of it.

"That was this morning. Who knows what the number is now," Lorcan paused, "but, after what you just told me, maybe it didn't do all this on its own."

Barry began to feel sick. "You said it breathes fire? What is it? Where did it come from?"

"Don't know and don't care. I just want to put a nice bullet in its brain." Lorcan stood up, reached down and picked up his rifle. "I just need a bigger bullet."

Out of the shadow, Barry's wife approached the table with her son. "Lieutenant, this is my wife, Samantha." Barry stood up and forced his best smile. "And this little guy is my son, Jack."

Lorcan gave the boy a reluctant nod. Jack had messy blond hair and looked as though he'd been wearing his navy-blue pyjamas for a couple of days. Under his arm, tightly grasped, was a plush green dinosaur. Jack donned a big grin and offered the soldier his toy.

"No, thanks. Dinosaurs aren't exactly my thing today."

Jack frowned and leaned into his mother's leg. "He's tired. I'm going to take him to the bathroom then put him to bed. He just wanted to meet the army man," Samantha said, smiling at Barry but barely looking at Lorcan. "Say goodnight, Jack."

Barry leaned over and gave his son a quick hug. Samantha then took Jack's hand and led him away, the boy waving goodbye until he disappeared into the shadows. "Do you have kids, lieutenant?" Barry asked.

"Get some rest. We leave at dawn."

"Wait. You're saying you'll help us get out of here?"

Lorcan gritted his teeth. "You do as I say, when I say it! And you keep your kids in line. Understand? We don't know what's out there, and I'm not taking responsibility for you!"

Barry couldn't hide his gratitude. "Yes! Absolutely! No problem! We'll do whatever you ask. The kids will be on their best behaviour, too."

"We can't stay here; rescue won't come anytime soon," Lorcan said, and looked at the window. It was raining outside. "Sleep tonight. At dawn, we get you and your family to a refuge centre."

"Refuge centre?" Barry asked, checking that he had heard correctly.

"Yeah, the military set up a few of them. Most are outside the city, but there is one not too far from here in Robina. That's where they evacuated some of the survivors."

"I just wanna take my family home."

"Everybody does," Lorcan said, as he turned back to the table and sat down. The downpour grew heavier as a flash of lightning tore through the night sky. "Get some rest. I'll stand watch." He perched his rifle across his lap and squashed the candle's flame.

"Yeah, okay," Barry said, doubtful that the soldier would still be there in the morning. "Thanks for helping us. Goodnight."

Lorcan checked over his shoulder to see that he was alone before turning back to the window. A tear escaped down his cheek, but he brushed it away quickly.

<hr />

Lorcan's eyes opened abruptly when he heard a startling crack of thunder. It was late; he must have dozed off at the table. Peering out the window at the empty gas station, he saw that heavy rain and strong gusts continued to blanket the area. Sticks, leaves and branches tumbled between the gas pumps, while the wind violently lashed the palm trees by the road.

Lorcan was about to close his eyes again when a shadow seemed to move at the furthest gas pump. He perked up and gripped his rifle, his blurry eyes working hard to focus as they kept track of the moving silhouette. The shadow was long, exceptionally long – about twelve metres, he estimated – and over half a metre thick.

The lieutenant aimed his rifle at the snake-like shape. A chain of lightning cut across the sky, the flash revealing the mysterious animal for barely a second. Long teeth – rows of them – and dark reddish scales and yellow eyes; that was all Lorcan could make out. However, he didn't see any legs like the ones Barry had described. The huge serpent slithered just like a snake.

Only a few metres from the window, the creature stopped and directed its attention towards Barry's red station wagon. The lengthy shadow slid onto the bonnet, causing a loud clang as the hood caved under its weight. The serpent raised its head to the windshield and paused. Suddenly, it let out a shriek, that could only be described as a thousand fingernails running down chalkboards, before plunging its jaws through the glass.

Lorcan watched as it rummaged through the red station wagon before breaking out the rear window, its long body still trailing through the car. The mystery creature continued towards the road and, a moment later, it was gone.

Lorcan lowered his rifle and let out his breath; he must have been holding it the whole time. "What the hell was that?" he asked himself. He couldn't take his eyes off the station wagon; the hood was completely crushed. He didn't nod off again either.

8

CIGARS AND RED WINE

The chirps of playful birds welcomed the morning as Emma stood on the front deck, holding a warm cup of green tea. Blake was filling the radiator in Old Lady Margret's car with water, as it seemed to have developed a leak overnight. "Are you sure that thing is going to make it there?" Emma asked.

Blake replaced and tightened the cap and closed the bonnet. "Honestly," he said with a shrug, "I'm not sure."

"Aren't you worried that we'll run into the monster?"

"Yeah, I am. But I have to check on Gary; he's like family." Blake carried the empty bottle to the deck. "That's why I said that you and James should stay here."

"We're safer together," Emma replied. "I can't let you go out there alone."

"What about your father?"

Emma took a long sip of her tea. The pair had spent the night waiting for her father to come home while James slept on the recliner in the lounge room. "I wrote him a note and put it on the fridge. If he comes home, he'll wait for us to get back."

With a groaning yawn, James stepped through the front door and greeted them, wearing only his boxer shorts. "Did it rain last night?" he asked, his hair standing on end as he noticed the damp timber.

"All night. Sleep well?" Emma asked.

"That chair is something else," James replied with a smile. "Did you guys sleep?" Emma and Blake shook their heads. "So, no news about your dad?"

"No. He hasn't come home yet."

"Shit. Sorry."

"Listen, dude," Blake said, not sure how this conversation was going to go down, "I'm heading over to Gary's place to check that he's okay and bring him back here."

James's face contorted. "Really? And what about the fire-breathing monster roaming around the city?"

"I don't know, but I'm not leaving him alone."

"Well, I don't know why you're so worried. He probably got drunk and slept through the whole thing," James argued. "Besides, how do you even know he's there?"

"He has no one else. You know that. Where could he go?" Blake angrily pushed past James and headed inside. "Just stay here until I get back."

"Fine with me," James said stubbornly. "Let him go visit his dumb mechanic without us."

Emma was surprised at James's sudden disregard for his friend; it wasn't in his nature. "You really don't like this Gary guy, do you?" He didn't answer her. "Even after what has happened, you don't want to check if he's hurt? Do you hate him that much?"

James avoided eye contact and walked over to the railing. "I don't hate him; he's just not good for Blake. He's a drunk, and he's dangerous. Blake shouldn't risk getting himself killed for someone like that."

Emma joined him by the railing and said, "Listen. We agreed to stick together, and he is going to check on him, with or without us. I don't know what Gary is like, and I don't care, but something tells me that you are not really going to let him go alone."

James knew she was right; it wasn't the time for pettiness. "I know. But if Blake asks – I fought you really hard on this. Oh, and if we get roasted, I'm gonna hate you both." Without another word, he marched back inside the house.

Emma raised her tea to her mouth and blew on it. "Boys," she said with a sigh.

〰〰〰〰〰〰

"Is it just me, or are cars not supposed to sound like that?" James mocked, enjoying his "I told you so" moment.

Blake kept his eye firmly on the temperature gauge. Despite topping up the radiator earlier, the needle was clearly rising, and the subtle rattle of Margret's rusty sedan was now a ballad of clangs and backfires. Taking every back road and short cut he knew, Blake cut through several abandoned suburbs before arriving in Ashmore, the suburb where Gary lived.

Lounging in the back seat, James reached out and tapped Emma on the shoulder. "So, if this thing breaks down, how long will it take us to walk back to your house?"

"Not as long as it takes for you to realise your fly is open."

James checked his jeans. His fly was open. "Right," he said, and awkwardly zipped it up and sat back in his seat.

"We're here," Blake announced as he pulled into the driveway of an old red brick home. Gary's truck was parked under the carport with a pile of spare parts and rusty tools alongside it. Houdini was still on the trailer, which was parked on the curb out front. The lawn featured three rusty old cars that were up on bricks and missing wheels, hood and doors; in fact, most of their removable panels were gone.

James's disgusted expression spoke volumes. "This doesn't surprise me."

"It's like a junkyard," Emma said, as they got out of the old sedan.

"No," James objected, "junkyards are organised."

"Give it a rest, man," Blake replied, as he made his way to the front door and gave it a hard knock. "Gary! You in there?" Emma and James swapped nervous glances as they stood behind him. Blake knocked louder. "Hey, Gary, you there or what? It's me." There was no response, just the rustle of the trees swaying by the roadside.

"Maybe he's not home," Emma said.

"His truck is still in the driveway; he must be here. He has no family. Where else could he be?" Blake knocked again. "Gary?"

"Maybe we should check the pub?" James remarked, only to be jabbed by Emma's bony elbow. "What?" She nodded to Blake who was clearly worried. "I mean… is it locked?" James reluctantly added. Blake grabbed the handle and turned it. The door creaked open.

"Gary, you home? It's me." Walking through the front door, the trio were immediately overwhelmed by the smell of something rotten.

Emma clamped her nose. "Yuk! What is that?"

"This is probably a bad sign," James said, lifting his shirt over his nose.

Blake led them into a narrow hallway. The old raggedy carpet was riddled with stains while stacks of car magazines and rows of empty beer bottles lined both walls. The smell only intensified as they entered the kitchen and living room.

"Dude, seriously, it smells like something died in here," James said.

"Let's just find him." Blake took a long look around the room. More empty bottles covered the kitchen bench, dirty dishes were stacked in the sink, and three full bags of garbage sat next to an overflowing bin.

"Who lives like this?" Emma asked, as a plague of blowflies swirled around her.

After noticing an old television with a cracked screen in the adjoining living room, Blake went to take a closer look. James followed him but was the first to see it: Gary's lifeless body lying on the floor. He was covered in cuts and surrounded by a sea of shattered glass. A deep red stain around his head had soaked into the carpet. His greasy fingers were still clutching the stem of a broken wine glass.

"Blood," James gasped. "He's dead. He's dead." He felt sick.

Blake was silent, his eyes firmly locked on the old mechanic.

"Oh no," Emma said, stopping behind them, "is he?" She covered her mouth in shock.

"What do you think happened?" James asked.

"I know exactly what happened," Blake said, and quietly left the room.

"Was he attacked?" Emma asked, keeping her distance from the body.

A moment later, Blake re-entered the room carrying a mop bucket full of water. "Yeah, by a bottle of Shiraz." He tipped the bucket over Gary's head. The man suddenly sprung to life, causing Emma to let out an ear-piercing squeal.

"What the heck! Who wants a knuckle sandwich?" Gary barked as he sat up, his moustache dripping and his eyes struggling to open.

Dropping the bucket on the floor, Blake turned to a speechless James and pointed at the red stain and broken wine glass. "It's not blood; it's red wine. He wasn't dead. Just passed out."

Gary squinted up at his visitors and asked, "Kid? Is that you? What time is it?"

"So what the hell is with all the broken glass then?" James asked, ignoring the disorientated man at their feet.

Gary looked over at the broken TV and chuckled. "Had that bloody thing for twenty years, and suddenly it decides it doesn't want to get a signal anymore! I think I lost my temper with it. Can't really remember." He brushed the glass off his clothes and shakily stood up. "Hello, darlin'," he greeted Emma, water still rolling down his face. She was completely speechless, her hand still over her mouth.

Blake walked back into the kitchen and smelt the garbage. "Well, that explains the smell," he said, kicking the bin. "Shit, old man, I know the last couple of days have been rough, but seriously, this place looks like a dump."

An embarrassed Gary rubbed the back of his head as he realised he had a severe hangover. "Yeah, today is my cleaning day."

"Is cleaning day an *annual* thing?" James muttered, as he followed Emma and Gary into the kitchen.

"Wait. What are y'all doing here?" Gary began searching his fridge for something to drink. "I normally meet you at your place."

Blake thought the answer was obvious. "We came to check on you. You know, to see that you were okay."

Gary pulled his head out of the fridge and smirked at him. "That's sweet, kid, but why wouldn't I be?" He then grabbed a half-smoked cigar off the kitchen bench and lit it with a match.

James snapped. "He doesn't even know. Damn it! I told you he would be fine. All he does is get pissed until he passes the hell out."

Gary immediately saw red. "Hey! You think you can speak to me like that? Under my own roof? Boy, you got another thing coming. Now, get out!"

"Enough!" Blake said, as he tried to calm them, but had no luck.

"Fine!" James finally cracked. "Thousands of people are dead. But you wouldn't know. You were too busy picking a drunken fight with your *prehistoric* television," he shouted, then stormed into the hallway. "Oh, and your TV was fine, dickhead. No one has a signal anymore." The front door slammed as he left the house.

Gary looked to Blake with a stunned blank face.

"I'm going to check on him," Emma said quietly, and left a mountain of tension in the room behind her.

"Kid, what the hell is he talking about? Thousands of people dead?"

Blake hadn't thought about how he'd explain the situation. He was too tired to sugar-coat it, so he told him straight. "There was an attack in Surfers Paradise on Saturday. Some sort of dragon thing tore down half the city. I was there. So were James and Emma, the girl with us. We can't contact anyone. There's no phone, no power, no internet. We don't really know what is going on; we've barely seen anyone since it happened. We came here to check if you were okay."

Gary expelled a puff of smoke from his nostrils and paused, seemingly processing the information. He began to squint quite hard at Blake's face and eventually asked the only question he believed mattered. "Are you *high*, boy?"

"No, I'm not fucking high!" Blake threw his hands up in the air. "You think I don't know how crazy I sound? Just pack some shit, grab your truck, and come with us. You can see for yourself."

It did sound crazy, but Gary could see that Blake was shaken. "Okay, kid, it's gonna be alright. I'll pack some stuff and come with ya." He put his cigar out on the kitchen benchtop and slipped it into his shirt pocket.

"Pack your tools," Blake instructed, "as many as you can, and bring food."

"How long are you expecting this to last?"

"Just in case," Blake replied, and quietly left the room.

Gary turned to his cigar box on the counter; he was down to his last five cigars. He picked up the box and tucked it under his arm, saying, "Can't leave my babies."

Outside, Blake found James and Emma studying the front grille of Old Lady Margret's sedan. "So, I don't think we're gonna get Marge's car back to the farm," James said, pointing to a large amount of oil dripping from under the engine.

"Just great," Blake sighed.

"We can fit in Gary's truck, right?" Emma asked.

"Actually," Blake said with a smirk, "I've got a better idea." He pointed to Houdini; the car was still parked on the trailer by the curb.

〜〜〜〜〜〜〜〜

Eventually, Gary emerged from his home wearing a cowboy hat and carrying several garbage bags full of clothes. He loaded them into his truck's rear tray and lit a fresh cigar. "Okie dokie, y'all good to go?" Blake, Emma and James stood by Houdini, looking rather unimpressed. They had been waiting for over an hour. Gary pointed to the race car, which was now parked at the foot of his driveway. "Houdini has one seat. You're taking it?"

"Well, I'm not leaving it here. Only a matter of time before someone steals it," Blake said, as he leaned through the window and started the engine.

"Right. You mean the same way you stole this heap of junk from that old woman across the street?" He nodded at Margret's broken-down sedan, which was still dripping oil all over the pavement.

"Shut up. I didn't steal it. I'm gonna give it back," Blake said, as he opened his car and got in.

"Okay then." Gary pulled the handle on his truck's passenger door and opened it for Emma, saying, "The lady rides up front. Jimbo, you're in the tray."

James huffed and replied, "Thanks, but no thanks. I'm driving. Sober people in the front, drunk geriatrics in the back."

Gary was too busy helping Emma into the seat of his truck to reply. "Name's Gary. A pleasure to meet you."

"Nice to meet you. I'm Emma." She wasn't sure what to make of him just yet.

Gary gently closed the door and threw James the keys. "Fine, you drive. Wake me up when we get there." He climbed into the tray and made himself comfortable between the bags, covering his eyes with his hat but leaving enough room for his cigar.

James got in the truck and slammed the door shut, clearly irate.

"He seems… nice," Emma said, hoping to soften the tension.

A loud belch came from the back of the truck. "Whoops, tastes like sangria!"

James stared at her blankly. "He's a peach," he said, as he started the engine and began backing out of the driveway.

〰〰〰〰〰〰

9

DISOBEYING ORDERS

Over the many years he had served, Lorcan had never had a civilian escort quite like this one. The Marsh family had been following him down the desolate highway for over two hours and, so far, had kept relatively quiet. But as the sun rose higher, the M1 motorway grew hotter, and patience began to evaporate, along with the puddles left by the storm.

Simmering and profusely sweating, Lorcan removed his shirt and wrapped it around his bald head like a bandana. Unbeknownst to her husband, Samantha caught herself admiring the soldier's muscular physique. Unbeknownst to Samantha, however, Barry was looking, too. A tattoo on Lorcan's upper back, reading "R.I.P. David," had captured his curiosity though he found the soldier far too intimidating to dare ask about it.

Mindy Marsh, their happy-go-lucky daughter, skipped alongside her father to a tune only she could hear, while just a few metres behind them, Samantha was witnessing the unravelling of their overtired and overheated son, Jack. The young boy had begun kicking and scuffing his feet while groans of boredom and discomfort grew louder and more frequent. After a several minutes of unattended attention seeking, Jack decided to take a new approach and began to hum loudly, which immediately irritated Lorcan.

"Cut it out," the lieutenant snapped.

Jack immediately ceased humming. Samantha ran her fingers through the boy's blond hair, saying, "We need to stay quiet, honey. Okay?"

"Daddy, I'm tired. Carry me?" Mindy asked, pulling on Barry's hand. Her dad scooped her up, and she climbed onto his back.

Jack immediately began to yank on Samantha's hand. "Mummy, Mummy, Mummy, carry me," he insisted, holding his arms up in the air.

"You're too heavy for me, sweetie," she declined, giving him a pat on the head instead. Jack groaned and immediately ran ahead of Lorcan with his arms up.

"No." Lorcan's glare was enough to scare most grown men.

Undeterred, Jack lowered his arms and began to walk in pace with the army man. Before long, he began to hum again.

Lorcan gritted his teeth and ordered, "Stop it."

"Jack! Cut it out," Samantha growled at her son.

Jack groaned, ran in front of Lorcan again and threw his arms into the air.

Lorcan stopped and stated roughly, "I said no!"

Jack returned to humming, only this time it was much worse.

"Cut it out! We need to stay quiet," Lorcan ordered.

Jack's hum turned into a high-pitched whistle.

"Stop that! Right now!"

Samantha walked over, snatched her son by the hand and dragged him away. Jack kicked and thrashed until his tantrum went into overdrive.

Lorcan stopped the group in its tracks. "Do I need to explain to you people that we need to stay as quiet as possible? We don't know where those things are or how many are out there. It's at least another hour's walk to the refuge centre!"

Jack's screaming turned to crying.

Samantha, struggling to get her son under control, had also had enough. "Well, clearly, you don't have kids, lieutenant. We are trying to be quiet. Maybe you could show a moment of patience."

"Lady, I'm trying to keep you alive. I don't have the luxury of patience. Do you want to end up like the rest of the people in this city? Do you want to—" Lorcan stopped in mid-sentence as Jack let out an ear-piercing squeal.

Samantha let go of him and threw her hands into the air with frustration. "Are you going to do anything, Barry? He's your son, too."

Barry's face dropped. "What do you want me to do? You know how he gets."

"And who does he get that from?"

"Your mother," Barry answered, a little too quickly.

"My mother? Oh, really?"

Jack left his parents arguing and ran back to Lorcan. The soldier gave the kid his most intimidating stare, but Jack didn't care. He just let out the highest squeal his little voice could produce and lifted his arms high. Lorcan kept glaring at the child until, eventually, the young boy cheekily smiled. The soldier didn't smile back.

〜〜〜〜〜〜〜〜

Jack wrapped his small arms tightly around Lorcan's neck and poked his tongue out at his sister.

"Extortionist," Lorcan muttered, as the boy on his shoulders made himself comfortable. Barry and Samantha couldn't help but share a quiet chuckle with each other as the hardened soldier continued ahead. The group wandered for almost an hour, passing hundreds of empty vehicles and abandoned buildings.

"How do we know we're not heading towards that big monster?" Samantha asked.

Lorcan removed Jack's hand from his beard for the fifth time. "You see all these cars? All the bridges we passed under?"

"Yeah."

"The cars are not crushed. We haven't seen any footprints in the road for a while, and the overpasses have all been intact. That thing leaves destruction wherever it goes. It must have left the highway shortly after it passed the gas station."

"That's good then," Samantha said, feeling a little relieved.

The distant rumble of a car's engine stopped the group in their tracks. Lorcan turned around to see a white delivery truck zigzagging through the scattered vehicles, speeding towards them. Jack ducked his head and strengthened his grip around the soldier's neck. Barry, Mindy and Samantha quickly moved as the truck continued to speed up.

"Jack, cover your ears," Lorcan ordered as he crouched down, allowing the boy to climb off his back.

Samantha pulled her son close and covered his ears while Barry did the same for Mindy. Lorcan stepped into the path of the oncoming truck, raised his rifle and fired three rounds into the sky. The driver slammed the brakes, bringing the small truck to a screeching stop in a swirl of white tyre smoke. The driver was a young man, who immediately removed his hands from the wheel and surrendered.

"Get out of the truck! Now!" Lorcan yelled, firing another deafening round into the air.

The young man got out of the truck and rested his hands on his head. His white baseball cap, black shirt and jeans were covered in dried mud. "Please! Don't shoot!"

"What are you doing?" Lorcan asked, keeping the rifle on him.

"Please, I have survivors in the back. We are heading for the refuge centre."

Samantha put her hand on the rifle. "He is terrified," she mouthed to Lorcan, who begrudgingly lowered his weapon. "Do you have room for us?" she then asked the driver.

The young man slowly lowered his hands. "Ah, yeah, I do. It will be tight, but the refuge centre isn't far from here."

The young man led the group to the back of the truck and opened the rear doors. A dozen people were huddled inside. Most of their faces were dirtied or bloodied, but all were clearly exhausted.

"Okay, kids, get in," Barry instructed. Mindy and Jack climbed into the truck while the young driver helped Samantha up. Squeezing between the others, they found space on the floor.

"You coming with us?" Barry asked.

Lorcan shook his head. "I've got to report in. My base isn't far."

"Thank you for your help," Barry held his hand out.

"Be safe." This time, Lorcan shook his hand.

Jack immediately began to cry and leapt out of the truck, wrapping his arms around the soldier's leg. "Please come, please. Come, army man," he pleaded.

Lorcan was caught completely off guard and didn't know what to say, so he just patted the boy's head as if he were a

Golden Retriever. Barry picked up his son and lifted him back into the truck. Samantha hugged her teary child and handed him his plush dinosaur. "Thank you," she mouthed to Lorcan. Barry climbed into the truck, and the Marsh family waved goodbye as the driver shut the doors.

"Okay, best of luck, man," the young driver said, as he locked the handle into place.

Suddenly, Lorcan snatched the boy by the collar and slammed him into the back of the truck, knocking his cap off. "Anything happens to them, I'll hunt you down and shoot your nuts off!" He raised his rifle to the driver's crotch area. "No stopping for anyone else. Don't make noise. Don't speed or draw attention to yourself – straight to the refuge centre! Got it?" The young man nodded. "Got it?" Lorcan shook him again.

"Yes, I promise. I've got it! I've got it! No stopping, no attention," he agreed in a nervous sweat. Lorcan let go of his collar and stepped back. The young man snatched up his cap and couldn't get to the driver's door fast enough.

A cloud of black smoke coughed from the exhaust as the delivery truck drove away. The noisy engine echoed off the highway's concrete walls. Once the truck was out of sight, Lorcan slung his rifle over his shoulder and began the long walk back to base camp.

〰〰〰〰〰〰〰〰

Night had settled over the Riley Farm as Blake, James, Emma and Gary gathered around the dining table to discuss their next move. "It would take days, though. I mean, we're not exactly in the suburbs out here. It's going to take time for the government, the police, the army or whatever to come tell us that the coast is clear, right?" James argued.

"Yeah, it would. But we need to be proactive just in case it's not over yet. We can't just assume that they killed the bloody thing," Gary debated. "Food is going to go first. We got a week's worth here if we start rationing right away."

"Rationing?" James's frustration was getting the better of him. "Seriously? Do you really think this is going to last for weeks? It was an animal attack. Yes, a very big scary animal, but still *just* an animal. Hardly end-of-the-world stuff. Just a horrible event."

"An animal the size of a building that can breathe fire," Blake corrected him.

"Exactly!" Gary slammed his hand on the table. "A goddamned dragon destroyed half the city, and you figure everything is just going back to normal? Where the heck has that thing been all this time? Why is it here now? Huh? I'm seeing a lot of big questions, and no damn answers, boys. So, I suggest we play it safe until we know what the hell is going on."

"It's *not* a dragon," James muttered under his breath.

"What?" Gary turned his good ear in James's direction.

"I said it's not a dragon. Dragons have wings. It didn't have wings, so, you know, it's not a dragon."

Gary just stared at him blankly. "Well, thank you, James. I'm just going to put that right at the top of my useless fuckin' information pile."

Everyone was quiet for a moment.

"Can I say something?" Emma interjected. "Gary might be right. We haven't seen any sign of people returning or even driving on the road. Maybe it's over. Maybe it's not, but we are going to need supplies. My guess is, if there is a search-and-rescue team, they'll be set up around the large structures – like a mall maybe. And if they're not, we grab what food and supplies we can before looters take everything. Then we can come up with a new plan."

Gary and James stared at each other before nodding in agreement.

"Pacific Town Mall is the easiest to get to," Blake suggested.

James almost choked. "Pacific Town? Are you nuts? That's a little too close to the city, don't you think?"

"Yeah, but it's a straight trip across the highway from here."

"Not to mention, it's huge," Gary added, pulling a cigar from his pocket. "It's a one-stop shop. We'll find everything we need."

"And what about that fire-breathing monster we were just talking about?" James asked.

"It could be anywhere by now." Blake faced his friend directly. "Listen, man, I don't think we have much choice. Every move we make is a gamble right now."

"I guess you're right," James conceded. "Please, let there be a rescue party…"

"Hopefully, looters haven't cleaned out the mall already," Emma added.

"Wait a sec," James said, grinning conspicuously. "If we take stuff from the shops, doesn't that make us the looters?"

Gary and Emma thought it over. "Yeah, pretty much," they both agreed.

Blake shrugged. "Well, we've already stolen a car this week. May as well rob a store or two."

"I did mention my dad is a cop, right?"

10

THE RING BEARER

Caught in an updraft, a flock of seagulls watched over the famous Surfers Paradise Beach, waiting for their next meal to be discarded by one of the thousands of beachgoers below. With a rainbow assortment of blankets and towels littering the sand, families and friends frolicked in the crystal blue water, built sandcastles, played games of volleyball or soaked up the beaming Saturday morning sun.

A little further out from shore was the usual congregation of surfers paddling out to catch the next big wave. One of the surfers, however, was less interested in the rolling sea and far more interested in the small glistening object resting in the palm of his hand.

With his scruffy brown hair tied in a man bun, Will's board bobbed up and down as the ocean rolled under him. He hadn't looked up in over ten minutes and wasn't even aware that the current was gently pulling him back to shore. But today was the day – the one he'd been planning for months. Never had something so small weighed so much. The gold diamond ring gleamed in the sun as he recited the proposal in his head. It was a simple question; nothing fancy. She didn't like fancy things anyway. All she had to say was *yes* or *no*.

Will and Lila had been together for just over four years. They rented a small house further down the coast in Burleigh Heads and had a white cat called Milky. Both had part-time jobs. Will waited tables for a popular Italian restaurant in Broadbeach, while Lila worked at the chemist in the Pacific Town Mall. Today was Will's day off, and he had spent it the only way he knew how – surfing.

Will had never been one to get nervous before, but ever since he had bought the ring two weeks earlier, he hadn't let it out of his sight. He'd kept it in his pocket at work, hidden it among his clothes as he showered, and even wrapped it in an airtight bag and brought it surfing over a dozen times – despite almost losing it twice to the depths of the sea.

Will unzipped his board shorts pocket and pulled out the sealed plastic bag containing the blue ring box. Carefully, he placed the ring back inside, sealed the bag around the box and returned it to his pocket. "A few hours to go," he said, checking his watch.

Craving a final decent wave, he began to paddle back out to the barrelling water. A group of surfers ahead were sitting on their boards, talking amongst themselves with their backs to the waves. "Come on, guys, talk somewhere else," Will grumbled to himself, waiting for them to realise their ignorance. The three men, however, didn't move; instead, they just floated on their boards and stared at the shore. Will was about to go around them when he noticed that, one by one, everyone in the water had stopped paddling and had turned their gaze back to the city.

"What is everyone looking at?" he wondered, turning his board around.

Screams of panic and terror erupted from the beach. Parents gathered their children, sunbakers abandoned their towels, and volleyballs were left rolling across the sand. Will and dozens of other surfers watched as the crowd of thousands scattered like a nest of aggravated ants.

"What's happening?" one man asked.

"I don't know," another answered.

Will couldn't see anything either. Everyone seemed to be running from nothing.

Suddenly, an explosion rocked the city itself. Black smoke began rising from the skyline.

"Look!" a shocked surfer cried and pointed to the clock tower, the source of the smoke trail. A moment later, the tower began to sway, and before another word could be uttered, it collapsed behind the massive skyscrapers in clouds of grey.

"No way," gasped one man.

"Did that just happen?" another asked in disbelief.

"What is that?" a woman shrieked.

Will saw it, too, although he didn't know what *it* was. A massive spiny creature walked through the city, smashing building after building. Dinosaur-like, and as large as a small hotel, its roar echoed off the city walls. Two police choppers circled the ocean, swooping over the surfers' heads before flying above the skyline and opening fire behind a large tower.

"No!" Will started to paddle towards shore, leaving the stunned surfers behind him. Two streams of fire cut through the air, sending both police choppers spiralling down somewhere beyond the city.

Will had only one thing on his mind: Lila. He had to get to her fast. Lila was at work, about six kilometres south of the beach. He had surfed his way up the coast that morning, leaving his car parked in Broadbeach, about halfway between him and the shopping centre he needed to get to.

Will hit the shore running, leaving his board in the water behind him. People were running in every direction, scared and confused, and no one knew which way to flee. He sprinted across the sand and up the concrete stairs to Cavill Avenue. Standing under the famous "Surfers Paradise" sign, he looked around for some way out of the city.

At the far end of Cavill, the tram sped through its station, leaving a group of frightened tourists stranded on the platform. A man trying to navigate the chaos on his bicycle quickly abandoned it at the side of the road and took off on foot. Will didn't hesitate; he ran over to the bike and jumped on. Pedalling like an Olympic athlete, he swerved and shunted through the frantic crowd, barely able to keep upright as he collided with one person after another. A stampede of horrified shoppers burst out of Cavill's popular shopping mall and joined the fray. Will kept moving, inching forward against the current of fleeing bodies.

Fire suddenly engulfed the tram station at the far end, turning the stranded tourists into a shifting cloud of white flakes. "Oh, shit!" Will yanked the brakes and banked left into the mall. Racing past one boutique shop after another, he hopped, ducked and weaved through the shopping complex towards the exit.

He shot out the doors like a bullet, clearing the steps and nearly knocking over two women in the process. Riding off the curb, he threaded the bike between two taxis and jumped on the next curb. The street was rapidly filling with traffic as more and more people began abandoning their vehicles to escape on foot. Will overtook a father leading his distressed wife and three children down the sidewalk when he noticed the tram ahead. Its rear carriage was now a rolling inferno as it sped through another station.

Will launched the bike onto the road and followed the tracks, his bare feet tearing on the plastic pedals as he quickly closed in on the runaway tram. Stray flames from the rear carriage swirled and crackled. Will shielded his face and raced past the moving fireball until he caught up to the second carriage. Holding the bike steady, he inched closer to the moving tram and reached out for the door's hand supports. After a few attempts, he finally grabbed hold and lifted his feet off the pedals, the bike's rubber tyres letting out an unsettling whine as the tram rapidly gathered momentum.

Holding on with an iron grip, he rocketed out of Surfers Paradise and over to the Gold Coast Highway. The tram line ran right through the middle of the northbound and southbound lanes. Hundreds of vehicles, none of which were moving, filled the road south. Several motorists decided to leave the gridlock and crossed the tramline to try their luck in the northbound lanes. The panicked drivers sped directly into oncoming traffic. Will cringed as one of the cars collided with a small truck. Feeling helpless, he could do nothing but look away as the tram zoomed by.

A wide sweeping shadow briefly darkened the road. Car doors were flung open, and dozens of motorists began abandoning their vehicles. Will looked at the sky but couldn't see anything. The shadow passed over once more, this time with a thunderous roar. Cries of panic broke out. A street-spanning wave of fire was unleashed upon the road, incinerating everything behind the moving tram. Will looked back over his shoulder. All six lanes of the Gold Coast Highway were smouldering. Hundreds of cars were melted to the pavement while their owners' ashes drifted across the area like flakes in a snowstorm. Frantically, he searched the skies once more but found nothing but blue.

The bike continued to shake along the tracks, but the tram seemed to be slowing down. Will realised that the fire had melted the power lines, and the three carriages were now free-rolling into the Broadbeach area. To make matters worse, an empty bus was blocking the intersection that the tram was rapidly approaching.

"You've got to be kidding me," Will said, and quickly let go of the hand support and pulled the brakes. The bike skidded to an eventual halt as the tram ploughed into the bus, derailing in the process. The tremendous crash sent the second and third carriages jack-knifing across the northbound lanes, wiping several cars clean off the road and into nearby apartment blocks.

"Lila. Get to Lila. Just get to Lila." Will quickly found his bearings. He was in Broadbeach, the suburb where he had parked his four-wheel drive earlier that morning. "Come on. Move it, Will!" He gripped the handlebars and began to pedal. His car was parked at the beach only a few blocks away.

A conga line of police pursuit vehicles raced down the next street in a flash of red and blue. Will hopped the curb and cut through a local park, passing swaying swing sets and half-eaten picnics. He could see the oceanfront on the other side. He ducked his head under a tree branch and exited onto the esplanade's two-lane road, which was also completely backed up with traffic. His yellow, open top, four-wheel drive was still parked in its space; the oversized tyres and off-road suspension made it an easy car to spot.

Will discarded the bike and cut across the road, squeezing between the honking vehicles and cursing motorists. Removing his keys from his zip-up pocket, he felt the jewellery box still inside. He needed to hurry. Will climbed over the door and fired up the V8 engine. Shifting into reverse, he realised the obvious: he was blocked in. "Damn it." He looked ahead; wave after wave rolled upon the sandy beach. "Screw it." Will shifted into first and hit the gas. The big four-wheel drive mounted the curb and crashed through the wooden fence, descending on the sandy beach with a howl. He flattened the accelerator and headed south along the shore.

Another spine-chilling roar echoed close by. To his horror, Will saw a monster moving through Broadbeach along the esplanade. Fortunately for him, the creature hadn't noticed his four-wheel drive bouncing along the sand, or if it had, it didn't seem to care. The sheer size of the animal was jaw-dropping, but the swift reptile moved like a panther on all fours. It pounced at the side of a tall hotel, its long spines slicing through the building with a spectacular explosion of concrete and steel. Will kept his foot planted on the accelerator and checked his rearview mirror as several more buildings collapsed in the reflection.

The top of the Pacific Town Mall peered over the bank. He hooked right and charged up the sandy slope, propelling the vehicle into the air and back onto the road with a loud clang.

Will held down the horn as he drove up the sidewalk and barged through the perfectly trimmed hedge of an office building. Pedestrians dived out of harm's way as the four-wheel drive ploughed through garden beds, park benches and several more hedges. Bursting through the next gate, Will crossed back over the Gold Coast Highway, mounting the trunk of a limousine to make it through the narrow gap in the intersection.

The Pacific Town Mall came into full view. Once again, Will stuck to the sidewalk and, with the horn depressed, drove straight through the brilliantly sculpted garden to get to the carpark. People were leaving the mall in masses. Will crossed the carpark, attempting to part the sea of scared shoppers with repeated honks of his horn. It was no use. People shoved and shouted as they all tried to squeeze through the open glass doors. He stopped the car and leapt out, then pushed his way inside the building.

A massive skylight ran through the middle of the building, providing the only light in the darkened mall. Will passed a large supermarket and countless clothing shops as he fought to get through the crowd. A man carrying his two children off the escalators warned him to get out while he could. Will took little notice and kept pushing through until the chemist sprung into view. "Please still be there," he said to himself.

Before he could reach the doors, an inhuman shriek came from within a nearby store. It was like nothing he had ever heard.

"Will! Oh my God, Will," a familiar voice called out.

Will spun around and, to his great relief, saw Lila running towards him. They must have almost run past each other. Still wearing her white lab coat over her jeans, Lila threw herself at Will, almost bowling him over. The pair hugged each other tightly. Lila's coconut-scented blonde hair brought Will right back home.

"Are you okay?" Will asked, as he checked her over. "Are you okay? I was so worried… that thing outside. So many people… just gone. I thought you… might have…"

Lila quickly broke free of his embrace, saying, "We have to go right now!"

"No way, honey! Trust me. We're safer in here! There is this monster burning—"

"No! We can't stay here!" Lila cut him off. "There are these things in here; they are eating people. We have to go!"

"What?" Will stammered, then put his confusion aside. "Okay, okay! Let's get out of here. We need to get as far away as we can."

Lila's face suddenly turned completely white.

Will felt a warm breath tickle his back before an ear-piercing shriek sent him to his knees. Lila squealed. Will gazed up at a pair of yellow snake eyes staring down at him. Letting out another shriek, it opened its gaping jaws and lunged. Will's body spasmed as rows of serrated teeth sank into his chest. Lila screamed out his name, but her voice quickly faded. Everything went black.

∽∽∽∽∽∽∽∽∽∽

Will sat up in a cold sweat, his heart beating like a drum.

"It's okay; it's okay. You're okay. I'm here."

Everything slowly came into focus. Lila was sitting next to him, smiling as she gently stroked his head. "You're all sweaty," she added, wiping her hands on her dress. "Same dream, babe?"

Will drew a deep breath, then rubbed his eyes. "Yeah, same one."

Lila switched on a flashlight and stood up. "We got away. Those things didn't get us."

"Yeah, well, they did in my dream. Right after I found you." He looked around the dark storage room. "I'll be fine once I find a way to get us outta here."

"Honey, we'll figure something out."

Will stretched out over the makeshift bed they had been sleeping on - a pile of brand-new clothes spread across the tiled floor. Lila picked up a pink toothbrush from a small wooden table and began brushing her teeth in the torchlight. While she was facing the other way, Will discreetly checked his shorts pocket and, to his relief, the ring box was still there.

"I think we need to tip this out," Lila said, as she picked up a mop bucket and spat her toothpaste inside. "Yeah, we definitely do." She cringed.

"Did you sleep at all?"

Lila didn't answer; she was too disgusted by the bucket of spit. Will removed a white singlet from their new bed, pulled the tag off and slipped it on, but even in the confines of a dark storage room, he couldn't take his eyes off Lila. Wearing a new dress that she, too, had plucked from the bed, her shoulder-length blonde hair brushed over her freckly pale skin, she was as beautiful as ever. He was simply happy he got to her in time.

"That looks good on you," Lila said, placing the bucket on the floor.

"Huh?"

"The singlet; it shows off your arms. I like it!"

"Thanks. It's from our new bed." Will walked over and picked up the bucket. "I'll empty this. I have to go to the bathroom anyway."

Lila quickly put herself between him and the door. "What if those things are out there? Maybe we do the bucket tomorrow?"

"I have to go to the bathroom anyway. Don't worry. It's the very next room."

"I know, but they're still out there. You heard them call out to each other last night, right? No wonder you keep dreaming about Saturday." Lila slid down the door and sat on the ground.

"Listen, I'm going to get us out of here. I promise." Will crouched down and kissed her forehead. "My car is outside the main entrance. I just need to create a distraction so we can make a run for it."

"Maybe we should just stay in here until help arrives. You know… like we said we would."

"We have waited. This is day three. For three days, we have hidden in the back of this supermarket. We haven't seen anyone come through here – not to help us, not to kill those things. I'm starting to think that help just isn't coming."

"It can't just be us out here, can it?" Lila asked.

"I don't know. That big one did a lot of damage. Even if help is coming, we don't know how long it's going to take for them to get to us."

"That's *if* they get to us before those things do," said Lila despondently.

"All I'm saying is we can rely only on ourselves right now. Okay?" Will wiped a tear from Lila's cheek. "All we need is a good distraction."

11

LOOTERS

"Tell me when!" Blake shouted, as he backed Gary's old truck though the mall's entrance towards the supermarket.

James signalled him to stop. "That's far enough."

Having recently been renovated, the new Pacific Town Mall was the crown jewel of shopping malls on the coast. With over two hundred designer stores, three supermarkets, a cinema, an exotic car dealership, and almost every other kind of shopping experience you could ask for, it was something of a "must do" for locals and tourists alike. Or, at least, it had been.

"Jeez," James said, as he took a good look around. The foyer's marble floors were now buried under a layer of shattered glass and plasterboard, the sculpted indoor gardens were mostly uprooted, and every store was severely damaged. Oddly, however, most still had stock on the shelves – if they hadn't been ripped from the walls.

Blake climbed out of the truck and went to the rear tray.

"Don't you think it's weird?" James asked. "We drove all the way here and didn't see a single person. It's like the whole coast has become a ghost town."

Blake unclipped the tailgate and noticed Emma emerging from the supermarket with a trolley full of groceries. "Yeah, dude, it's weird. What's your point?"

James gestured toward the vacant shops. "Even this place! It just doesn't make sense. All the shops are totally trashed, but no one stole anything. Why smash the joint up if you're not even gonna take stuff?"

"You guys are not going to believe this! The shop is full," a beaming Emma interrupted, as she pushed the trolley to the rear of the truck. "Like, I think we're the first ones to come back here. I've got everything: lots of pasta, bread, cans of soup, more beans. This will last us a while. Even got something for myself," she said, and winked, holding up a tube of lipstick.

"Oh, and you didn't get any for Blake?"

"Very funny," Blake replied, as he began to unload the groceries into the tray.

James quickly snatched a bag of liquorice from the trolley. "My favourite! Yes!"

"Thought you'd like that," Emma said, and smiled.

Blake lifted the last bag and noticed eight boxes of herbal tea protruding from the top. "Not sure if you got enough green tea. What will we drink *next* year?"

"Shut up. It's good for you."

"How come Gary got to stay at the farm anyway? He could be here, helping us," James complained, stuffing a piece of liquorice in his mouth.

Blake sighed and said, "He is helping. He let us use his truck. Can you imagine using Houdini for a run like this?"

"I'll meet you guys inside," Emma said, as she reclaimed the trolley and headed back towards the supermarket.

James waited until they were out of earshot before continuing his rant. "I'm not talking about the truck. I'm talking about the whole *he's planning to grow vegetables in Emma's backyard* thing. It's dumb. Like seriously, look at all this food. We're all set!"

"So what if he's digging a few holes and planting a few seeds? Emma said she's fine with it, and it probably makes him feel better, you know? He's just trying to help out."

James's face fell flat. "The man hasn't had a drink in two days. He's probably planting a vineyard."

"You're an arse," Blake said, snatching the liquorice bag from his hand. "Besides, it's good to have someone there just in case her dad comes home."

"You know he's probably dead, right?" James whispered. "Come on. It's been days. I don't want her to get hurt, but I think she needs to deal with the facts right now."

"Really, dude? You're gonna go there?"

"If he was alive, then don't you think the first thing he would have done is look for his daughter?"

"We don't know what happened to him."

"Okay, fine. But what's the deal with her mother? It's like she doesn't care what happened to her at all."

Blake looked toward the supermarket and saw Emma perusing the shelves along an aisle. "Listen to me," he said, as he stood in front of James and kept his voice low. "Right now, all she has is hope. Maybe he's dead. Maybe he's not, but after everything we just went through, I'm sure as hell not gonna take that away from her. Are you?" he asked, as he shoved the bag of liquorice in James's hand and headed toward the spare trolleys.

As he neared the supermarket, something James had said earlier returned to centre stage in Blake's mind. *Why is everything in the mall trashed?* But more curiously, *Why, after three days, hasn't anyone ransacked it?*

As if on cue, an ear-piercing shriek cut through the air. James and Blake stopped in their tracks and turned toward a nearby clothing store. Inside, through the darkness, a pair of large yellow eyes was glaring at them.

"Hey, what the hell is that?" James asked nervously.

Blake took a step back. "I... don't... know."

A metal rack of garments crashed to the ground as shadows began to shift within the store. Slowly, the yellow eyes emerged from the dark, revealing an enormous snake-like creature. Covered in glossy red scales, its head was wide and flat, with a frill of white ivory horns around the top of its neck and continuing down the entire length of its ten-metre spine. The red serpent was at least half a metre thick and had five unusual horns evenly spaced down each side of its body, the last near the tip of its tail.

"Holy... shit," James stammered.

The creature opened its huge jaws, and thick strands of saliva dribbled from rows of serrated teeth as it let out another gut-wrenching shriek.

"That's why looters haven't come here," Blake whispered, continuing to move back.

After a reciprocal shriek from the clothing store, another large serpent emerged from within. The yellow-eyed monsters acknowledged each other with a low screech before focusing on the two pale-faced young men.

"What do we do?" James whispered, as the creatures began to inch closer.

"Don't trip up," Blake whispered. From the corner of his eye, he could see Emma still browsing in the supermarket aisles. The monsters hadn't spotted her, nor had she spotted them. "On my count, ready? One... two..."

"Screw it!" James jumped the gun and tossed his liquorice bag into the mouth of one of the serpents, causing it to choke, with a loud squeal. "Run, dude!"

"Emma, get out of here," Blake cried out, as he and James ran into the mall.

Emma glanced down the aisle and saw the two serpents out front giving chase. "Oh, my God," she gasped, dropping a bag on the ground. Suddenly, the large head of a third serpent slithered around the end of the aisle with drool pouring from its open jaws. Emma went cold. She turned to run but was met immediately by the penetrating eyes of a fourth red-scaled monster at the opposing end.

"Stay back!" she shouted.

With a loud shriek, the serpents called out to each other as they closed in from both sides.

"I said stay back!" Emma kicked the trolley as hard as she could, sending it hurtling down the aisle before crashing into the thick skull of the closest reptile. She quickly grabbed the shelves and began climbing. The two serpents met below with a deep hiss.

Clambering onto the top shelf, Emma carefully checked her balance as she looked around. There was only one way to go. Taking a leap of faith, Emma jumped across the aisle to the next stack of shelves. She landed with a loud clatter as several glass bottles fell to the floor. Turning back, Emma watched as both serpents slithered up and over the shelving in pursuit of their prey. She leapt across to the next row. With another shriek, they kept coming, but the enormous weight of the animals sent the stack of shelves beneath them tipping into the next one, like a giant game of dominoes.

Emma jumped from aisle to aisle, barely outrunning the wave of collapsing supermarket fixtures before the next shelf buckled under her weight and gave way. Emma went down with the Pet Food section. She opened her eyes and groaned loudly as she lay amongst cans of Finest Feline. A lurching wall of red scales quickly blocked out the ceiling, and a pair of yellow eyes lingered over her. Emma frantically crawled backward as the serpent opened its gaping jaws.

She tried to scream.

Suddenly, the roar of a V8 motor filled the supermarket, and the monster was ripped from her sight with a splash of glowing orange blood. Emma sat up to see a yellow four-wheel drive only metres away and the serpent crushed between its front grille and the back wall. Two strangers, a guy and a girl, were calling for her to get to the car.

"Will, go help her," the girl cried, as a shriek from the second serpent escaped from beneath the collapsed shelving.

"Okay, hold on." Will jumped out of his vehicle and lifted Emma to her feet.

"Thank you," Emma said, catching her breath.

"Quick! Get in!" Lila extended a hand and helped the girl into the rear seat of the open-top off-roader. Will reversed out of the supermarket with haste, leaving the bloodied remains of the huge serpent behind.

〰〰〰〰〰〰

James and Blake continued through the mall at full speed, shoving trolleys, jumping tables and leaping counters in a vain effort to elude the two pursuing predators. A frustrated shriek came from the serpent hot on James's heels, who glanced back to see rows of razor-like teeth getting a little too close.

"We have to split up!" Blake panted alongside him.

"And go where?"

"Just keep running!" Blake took a sudden right turn towards the food court, taking a serpent with him.

"Shit," James muttered, and continued straight ahead, passing countless grocery-filled trolleys and scattered shopping bags. The snake ploughed through everything in its path, sending carts spinning into shopfronts or flipping into the air. Ahead, an escalator descended to the floor below and was James's only obvious way out.

"Head downstairs, get outside," he reasoned.

Only one obstacle stood in the way of his planned escape route: a single trolley nestled between the hand railings, blocking the staircase.

"Up and over. Up and over," he whispered. Just as James attempted to leap over the stranded cart, the striking jaws of the serpent flicked him upward. Painfully, he slammed into the very trolley basket he'd tried to hurdle over and began bouncing down the escalator. With each step, he banged his head on the cage a little harder. The tenacious serpent forced itself between the hand railings, snapping its jaws just inches from the runaway trolley. James hit the ground level and, to his amazement, the cart didn't tip over. Instead, he found himself spinning across the floor as he attempted to free himself from the rolling prison.

It didn't take long for the salivating monster to catch up to its prey. A wide shadow fell over the basket, followed by the fiercest shriek yet. James opted for the fetal position, and the serpent lunged. The trolley suddenly came to an abrupt halt. With his eyes shut tight, James awaited the inevitable agony, but instead of pain, something warm dripped onto his arm.

"Oh no," James whispered. He was now staring deep into the creature's throat, with thick strands of saliva pouring over his face. Two retractable fangs pierced the metal cage on either side of his head, and the serpent was attempting to swallow the trolley whole.

Frustrated, the serpent lifted the cart into the air and began to thrash it around. James felt like the last mint in a packet as he crashed from one side to the next. Refusing to join the stench of rotting meat, he began to kick the roof of the reptile's mouth. "Let... me... go... you... sack... of... shit!" he cried, stomping his heel.

Several strong kicks were enough to shake the trolley free of the monster's grip and send it crashing through the window of a nearby store. James rolled out onto the floor, his head ringing and the room spinning. At the rear of the shop, he spotted an emergency exit leading outside, which brought him to his feet. He sprinted towards the exit as the confused serpent searched the foyer for its lost meal.

Bursting through the door, James crossed a large green lawn, checking over his shoulder for any signs of his attacker. The main road was straight ahead. He had no idea where Emma and Blake were, but right now wasn't the time to stop.

A nearby pair of glass doors exploded into thousands of pieces as a yellow four-wheel drive crashed through them and onto the lawn. "Get in!" a voice called out.

James turned to see Emma hanging out of the rear of the vehicle with her hand out. He gripped her wrist tightly and pulled himself up. "Are you okay?" she asked, as he flopped exhaustedly onto the backseat.

"No," he replied.

"Are you hurt?"

"Wait," James said, as he locked eyes with Lila, then Will, both of whom were staring at him from the front seats. "Where is Blake? And who are these people?"

〜〜〜〜〜〜〜〜〜

Blake raced through the food court as if it were an obstacle course, narrowly outpacing the relentless serpent as it crushed every chair and table he leapt over. A fire escape at the far end was his only glimmer of hope. Blake charged through the door and slammed it shut behind him before sprinting up the concrete staircase. Before he reached the next floor, the monster's head burst through the door. The creature ploughed through the confetti of splintered timber as it continued its hunt upward.

Around and around, floor after floor, an exhausted Blake ascended the claustrophobic fire escape until he eventually reached the mall's rooftop. Small vents and air-conditioning units were all that kept it from being a barren wasteland. With nowhere to go or hide, Blake could hear the monster nearing the top of the stairs. A recently installed Pacific Town Mall sign stood at the edge of the building, its big white letters still surrounded by tall scaffolding. He ran to it and quickly began climbing. Reaching the top, Blake glanced down to see the serpent crash through the fire escape door with a loud hiss. It didn't take the reptile long to spot its prey standing at the top of the structure.

"Ha! What's wrong?" a relieved Blake mocked. The yellow-eyed snake slithered back and forth at the base of the scaffolding like a prowling cat. "Can't get me, dickhead?"

With a deafening screech, the horns along both sides of the serpent's body began to extend, revealing dark slimy bone beneath the ivory. Blake turned pale. Each horn grew longer and longer until they were at least three metres in length. After a series of gut-wrenching snaps, the bony limbs began to reconfigure themselves. Blake couldn't believe it. They were not horns at all; they were legs.

The now ant-like serpent raised its body off the ground. While eight of its newly formed legs carried its weight, the two front limbs seemed to serve a far more sinister purpose. Flat, long and sharp, the blade-like arms resembled those of a praying mantis.

The serpent latched on to the side of the scaffolding and began to ascend. Blake had nowhere to go. He was far too high to jump down, and even if he could, that meant being on equal footing with the eight-legged nightmare. Standing at the edge, he peeked over the side of the building. A series of white sails, supported by high tensile cables, had been erected two storeys below over a large body of water.

The serpent's bladed arms pierced the wooden floorboard as it reared its head over the top of the scaffold. Blake took one last look at the white sails. "Screw it," he said, and jumped.

Free-falling towards the vinyl, air whipped past Blake as if he'd been dropped from a plane. With a loud crack, he hit a sail and immediately began to slide down the slippery surface.

Blake frantically scrambled for something to grab onto but found nothing. He slid right off, and only at the end did his hands finally grasp one of the high tensile cables. With a painful jerk, he suddenly stopped and found himself dangling several storeys above the mall's moat. Blood trickled down his wrists as the cable had buried itself in his palms.

A series of unmistakable shrieks cried out from the rooftop as the aggravated serpent perched at the top of the scaffolding.

With its yellow eyes fixed on Blake, it rose up on its hind legs and stretched the other six into the air.

"What now?" Blake wondered, as he tightened his grip on the cable.

One at a time, the monster's legs began to split apart until the two sides fanned out and revealed a thin colourful webbing in between. Each was a cocktail of blue, orange and green, displayed in beautiful patterns like those of a butterfly. The serpent began to flap these wings rapidly and, like a bee, began to hover above the scaffold.

Slithering through the wind like a Chinese New Year dragon, the monster's wings painted the air with a moving rainbow. Blake couldn't help but be in awe of the stunning creature; however, that admiration quickly dissipated. The flying reptile changed course and headed straight for the young man hanging from the white sail.

Panic took over, but it was useless. The only way out was three storeys down. Blake hoped the moat was deeper than the paddle boats it had been built for. He took a deep breath and let go of the cable. Seconds seemed like minutes. Clamping his nose, he tucked his knees into his chest and plummeted into the murky moat like a bomb going off at sea.

The serpent, undeterred, nosedived like an eagle, its wings retracting into its body before it crashed into the water after its prey.

Winded and desperate for breath, Blake breached the surface and swam towards a small dock. Ignoring the deep gashes in his hands, he pulled himself out of the water and tried to find his bearings. The broken doors of the mall's entrance were at the far end of the nearby carpark.

With wet clothes and soggy shoes, Blake began running as the giant snake emerged from the murky water with a ferocious howl. He crossed the carpark at full speed, hoping only that the monster hadn't seen him. As he neared the mall's entrance, a pair of familiar voices desperately called out to him.

"Blake!"

"Blake! Stop!"

James and Emma were in the back of a yellow four-wheel drive, gesturing for him to get in.

"Go! Get out of here!" Blake ignored their pleas and sprinted into the mall.

"What the hell is he doing?" James asked.

"He's going for the food," Emma answered fearfully.

Blake pulled the keys from his pocket and flung open the door to Gary's truck. He jumped in, started the motor and began to back up when a serpent's massive head slammed into the side of the tray. Blake flattened the gas pedal. He reversed the truck out of the mall and back into the carpark, dragging the latched-on snake with it.

"Oh, shit!" James flinched when he saw the huge reptile hanging off the side. "We better move, dude," he added, frantically tapping Will on the shoulder.

"Is your friend crazy?" Will asked, as he hit the gas.

Blake tried to keep up with the modern four-wheel drive, but the weight of the massive serpent was too much for Gary's old truck. Then a series of concrete columns gave him an idea. He swerved towards the next column and scraped it along the side. With a big shunt, the serpent's head was severed cleanly and its limp body was left gushing orange blood onto the pavement.

The two vehicles sped out of the carpark and left Pacific Town Mall in the rearview mirror.

"Let's never do that again," Emma said.

"I second that," Will added.

"Me too," Lila concluded.

Emma and James slumped back in their seats, giving Blake an exhausted wave as Gary's old truck caught up to them.

∿∿∿∿∿∿∿∿∿

Gary tossed another shovel load of dirt onto the mound beside him and wiped the sweat from his brow. Having spent most of the morning digging holes and planting tomato seeds, he now resembled someone who had been swimming with his clothes on. The sound of approaching cars provided the perfect incentive to take a break and wander around to the front of the house.

Sure enough, Blake pulled into the driveway in Gary's old truck followed by a second vehicle – a yellow four-wheel drive. "Made some new friends, did we?" Gary asked, as he put a fresh cigar in his mouth and lit it with a match.

"You could say that," Blake answered, as he hopped out of the car and stressfully ran his fingers through his hair. It didn't take long for Will, Lila and Emma to join Blake and Gary at the front of the house. The group took a moment to introduce themselves formally.

"Nice place you have here. Thanks for taking us in," Will said.

Gary pulled the cigar from his mouth and said, "Actually, this is Emma's place. We're all guests here."

"Well, thank you, Emma," Lila added.

"So, what did I miss?" Gary was pointing to the obvious section of red paint missing from the scraped side of his truck.

"This shit," James replied, as he came over and dropped the serpent's severed head by his feet.

Gary was startled at first. "Well, I'll be damned, kid! What the hell is that?" He crouched down to get a better look.

135

Blake shrugged and said, "Hell if I know, but they're not friendly."

"In all my years…" Gary mumbled to himself, running his fingers over the rough scales of the serpent's snout.

"Makes me wonder what else is out there," James said, knowing that everyone was thinking the same thing.

"I'm sure we'll find out."

12

SQUAD SEVEN

Lorcan sat silently on a small wooden chair in front of a cold metal table. The old chair was intentionally uncomfortable – too small for a grown man to relax on but big enough to hold him up. This was an interrogation chair, the kind Lorcan had used many times while on tour in the Middle East. An iron door, grey brick walls and the dim light of a single swaying bulb were the only features of the repurposed maintenance room.

Five hours had passed since he had been summoned to this room to be debriefed by Colonel Henrickson. This wasn't normal protocol, but Lorcan knew this wasn't a normal day. The iron door's loud screech brought his posture to attention. A pair of uniformed soldiers entered the room along with Colonel Henrickson, who was carrying a thick white folder under his arm.

Lorcan immediately saluted his superior.

At forty years of age, Samuel Henrickson was a decorated soldier and a well-respected colonel in the Australian army. Not a single strand of his perfectly combed black hair was out of place nor was there any sign of stubble on his immaculately shaven jawline. In comparison to Lorcan's bald head and scraggly beard, the two men could not have appeared more opposite. A third soldier brought in a comfortable leather chair before leaving the room with a clang of the iron door.

"Lieutenant Lorcan Edwards, it's been a while. At ease." Henrickson dropped the folder on the table and gestured to the small wooden chair. Lorcan sat back down. "You've had quite the start to your week, lieutenant." The colonel opened the folder and slid an image across the table. "I want to know exactly how this happened." The aerial shot of five burning Black Hawk helicopters was all too familiar to Lorcan.

Lorcan didn't bother to pick the photograph up. Instead, he leaned back in his chair and began to divulge the requested information. "We received numerous reports indicating the creature had been located on the M1 motorway. As you know, the animal disappeared after the attack on Saturday; these were the first sightings since then. With very little time to be briefed, we were immediately dispatched under the command of Captain Richards."

〰〰〰〰〰〰

Under the rumble of their spinning rotors, five Black Hawk helicopters glided through the summer sky in perfect formation over the M1 motorway. Lorcan leaned out the side of his chopper, nodding to the soldiers in the adjacent aircraft. "I can't see it, cap."

"Intel says it was spotted right around here," Captain Richards said, leaning out the opposite the side.

"Maybe it's just bad intel from a spooked truck driver."

"Nah, it wasn't just the truck driver's report. One of our recon drones spotted it, too, before its GPS went offline. That bastard is here somewhere." Richards leaned back inside the chopper and turned to the pilot. "Just keep following the motorway!"

"Ah, sir," the pilot called out, "you better come see this."

Richards and Lorcan stepped into the cockpit and looked out the windshield. The monstrous reptile was moving down the highway in their direction, breaking through multilane overpasses and bridges like they were made of paper.

"Okay, people, this is a shoot-to-kill order! Understood?" Captain Richards directed the choppers over his radio. "Take us down," he told the pilot.

Lorcan braced himself as the Black Hawks descended until they were hovering only two dozen metres above the highway.

"On my mark!" Richards yelled.

Lorcan leaned out of the chopper and took aim.

The towering reptile halted as it reached the next overpass. The howl from the five helicopters had drawn its attention.

"It spotted us! Light it up!" the captain screamed into his radio.

A barrage of gunfire and heat-seeking missiles were unleashed over the highway. Smoke trails and glowing bullet streaks cut through the air until all that could be seen was a rising ball of fire in the creature's place.

"Hold your fire!" ordered the captain.

The thick white cloud spread over the highway like fog. Lorcan could hardly see the road below them, let alone the target ahead.

"We can't see, captain! The smoke's too thick," a voice yelled over the radio.

"Did we get it?" another asked.

Lorcan, still fingering the trigger, didn't take his eyes off the overpass.

"Wait, I see something!" a third voice yelled.

Deep within the smog, rays of orange light began flickering, and with each surge, the foggy silhouette of their target became clearer. "No goddamn way," Richards stammered, as the smoke began to part. The enormous creature stood before them completely unharmed, flames swirling around its eyes.

"Fuck! Pull up! I repeat, *pull up!*" the captain barked across the channel.

The Black Hawks jerked violently upward, the force causing Lorcan's strong legs to buckle under the pressure. A stream of fire blasted through the air, narrowly missing the rising aircraft. Richards stared through the cockpit windshield at the monster below. It roared in furious fashion at the now out-of-reach Black Hawks.

"Phew, that was a close one, cap!" the pilot said, as he clenched his chest in relief, but after another roar of frustration, the animal's thick skin suddenly split open along the ridge of its spine.

The captain didn't even blink. "What the hell is it doing?"

The reptile's skin lifted from both sides of its wide back, revealing more armoured scales underneath, then unfolded into a pair of wings that spanned the entire width of the highway.

Richards's jaw dropped as he stared at the gigantic wingspan. "Fall back!" he ordered.

Before his order could be acknowledged, the animal launched itself into the air, swinging its massive arms into two of the choppers and sending them hurtling to the ground below. Circling around like a fighter jet, it then engulfed a third Black Hawk with its fiery breath. Lorcan unloaded a full clip into the monster as it banked right and flew straight for the last two helicopters.

"Hold on to something!" Captain Richards yelled, as he reached for the pilot's chair.

Lorcan grabbed the nearest support handle as rows of long teeth clamped down on the rear of their chopper and tore it off. Alarms bells rang out from the cockpit while Lorcan and Captain Richards clung to their half of the spiralling helicopter. The creature spat the crushed fuselage from its mouth and impaled the last Black Hawk with its forked tail before flinging it to the road below.

∿∿∿∿∿∿∿∿∿

"When I came to, it was all over; everyone was dead. Richards lost an arm and bled out, and the monster just walked off into the sunset. We didn't even scratch it." Lorcan leaned on the table and looked Henrickson in the eye as he said, "We're nothing but ants to that thing."

The colonel sat back in his leather chair, seemingly in deep thought. "I've heard enough. I'll read about the rest of your movements in your report. Have it on my desk in one hour." He slid a form across the table and tossed Lorcan a pen before standing up from his chair. One of the uniformed soldiers opened the iron door.

"Sir!" Lorcan interrupted the colonel's exit.

"Yes, lieutenant?"

"There is something else. That thing isn't the only one out there. I saw something else – some kind of snake."

Henrickson nodded and said, "We are aware, lieutenant, and big snakes aren't the only strange things we're seeing. But that's not your concern. I have something more important for you – search and rescue. Oh, and congratulations, lieutenant. You're a captain now. Report to me at oh four hundred."

The uniformed soldiers followed the colonel out of the room, leaving Lorcan alone with his report. Begrudgingly, he picked up the pen and began filling out the necessary paperwork.

~~~~~~~~~~~~~

The following morning, Lorcan stood by Henrickson's door for over thirty minutes. Keeping people waiting was one of the colonel's more infamous traits. Soldiers carrying boxes of equipment passed back and forth like worker ants.

"With me, Edwards!"

Lorcan turned to see the colonel standing at the far end of the hall, carrying the same white folder he had the previous day. As requested, he followed Henrickson out of the building and into a large open parking lot.

"Castra Dam," the colonel announced. "You ever been here before, Edwards?"

"No, sir. Have you?"

"Yes, my youngest daughter loves the place. Little bookworm, she is."

The morning sun had only just touched the surrounding mountains, leaving the dam itself draped in a nightly shadow. Military vehicles and olive-green tents filled the once public carpark, while trucks and supply choppers delivered a steady flow of weaponry and office supplies.

"Why here, colonel? Why set up base at the dam?" Lorcan asked.

"Captain, this dam holds over three hundred thousand megalitres of water and supplies more than ninety percent of the region. Spanning over eighteen hundred and fifty metres in length and over one hundred metres high, it was built in 1976 and named after the Castra family who once lived right here, in this valley. Tactically speaking, its secluded location and close proximity to the city make it ideal for deployment."

The colonel led Lorcan up to the dam wall to take in the view.

The sight was captivating: green valleys rolled on for miles before blending into the sprawling suburbia that culminated at the desecrated skyline of Surfers Paradise, and the endless ocean backdrop reflected the rising sun with a pink hue.

"If we lose this place, we lose the whole coast."

Lorcan stared at the distant ruins. "From where I'm standing, sir, we've already lost the coast."

Henrickson stepped back from the railing and straightened his posture. "There are still survivors out there. People held up in their homes, people trapped under all that rubble. People waiting, hoping, for someone to help them. That's where your team comes in, captain."

"My *team*, sir?"

Perfectly on cue, two uniformed soldiers walked over and saluted them. "At ease," the colonel said. "Captain, these gentlemen will be under your command."

The soldier on the left was in his late twenties, maybe, with dark brown hair and olive skin, and was rather short. "This is Mitchel Kay, an expert marksman and sniper. He has been in the army since he was eighteen and has a decade of service under his belt. You won't find a better shot on the east coast," Henrickson stated, and gave Mitchel a respectful nod before turning to the other soldier.

"This is Damien Saunders. Forty-two years of age, he has served his country for the last twenty years. A qualified mechanic turned explosives and demolitions expert, this man can fix almost anything – or blow it up." Taller and more muscular than Mitchel, Damien had buzz-cut ginger hair and deep forehead lines, as well as a long scar above his left eye. Judging by his facial expression, he didn't want to be here anymore than Lorcan did.

"Two men, colonel? Not much of a squad," Lorcan grunted, sizing the pair up.

Henrickson was about to respond when a loud and clearly out-of-breath voice interrupted him. "Sorry! So sorry! I'm not used to twenty-four-hour time."

The four men turned to see a woman jogging towards them, pushing past a dozen busy soldiers and apologising to each one as she went. Fumbling and frantic, she tucked her white blouse into her business skirt and rushed over to Colonel Henrickson, saluting him with the wrong hand. "Sorry I'm late, colonel," she apologised, pushing her thick-framed glasses up the bridge of her nose and checking that her black curly hair was still tied in a bun.

"That's fine," Henrickson assured her. "This, gentlemen, is Amanda Stone. She is a renowned expert in herpetology and will be joining you as a civilian consultant."

"What is her-pet-ology, exactly?" Mitch asked, unsure if he had just insulted the woman.

"I study reptiles," Amanda answered, in a soft English accent.

Damien folded his arms with clear disapproval and asked, "Where are you from, lady?"

"I grew up in London, graduated at the top of my class from a school you probably can't pronounce, and moved here when I was twenty to study your big lizards and snakes."

Lorcan smirked. She was clearly not intimidated easily.

Damien scoffed, "Well, you hit the jackpot, lady! Got a building-sized gecko running around those smoking buildings over there. Go nuts, but you don't belong with us; you'll just get in the way or get yourself killed."

"That is not your decision, Saunders," Henrickson growled. "I suggest you remember your rank before you make suggestions about the structure of this squad."

Damien immediately retracted his statement. "Yes, sir. Understood, sir."

As much as Lorcan didn't want to admit it, he agreed with the arrogant soldier. "With all due respect, sir, given the circumstances, I don't believe we are in a position to babysit a civilian in the field. We already have a large number of unknown variables to contend with, sir."

"Point noted, captain. But let me be clear: this is not a negotiation. If I wanted your input, I would have asked you for it. Yes, Ms Stone is a civilian, but I believe getting her up close to these monsters will provide us with some insight as to what they are and how to deal with them. This is your team, Captain Edwards. Call sign Seven – Squad Seven."

"Very well, then, that is sorted. What now, chaps?" Amanda asked, seemingly excited.

"There is one more thing," Henrickson added, as he pointed to a truck being unloaded in the carpark. "Come with me."

The newly formed Squad Seven waited at the rear of the white semi-trailer as two soldiers locked wheel ramps into place. Several blinding white lights lit up the interior of the trailer as an engine fired up with a low rumble. A vehicle emerged from the trailer. Its matte black paint and six wheels (four at the back, two at the front, all fitted with large off-road tyres) caught the soldiers completely off guard.

It was unlike anything the team had ever seen – not ugly and brash like most military vehicles, but sleek and almost exotic. The large front headlamps featured horizontal daytime running lights, and the grille in between was chrome and reflected the faces of the team members like a mirror.

The armoured front bumper was low slung and fitted with two LED fog lamps. The driver and passenger side doors had black tinted glass, while the rear of the vehicle had no windows at all, just flat armoured walls with a retractable hydraulic door built into each side. Mounted on the roof was a fifty-calibre chain gun that seemed to be remotely operated.

"Squad Seven, this is the all-terrain vehicle experiment – the ATV-X," Henrickson announced. "Or, as some of us call it, the Wombat."

"The Wombat?" Mitch mouthed silently to Damien, who simply shrugged back.

"The first of its kind, this prototype was co-developed with the Americans. She is the future of all-terrain vehicles. Built to withstand all conditions, she can take a direct hit from a missile or a fifty-calibre bullet. The tyres are heat resistant, and the turret is operated remotely from inside." Henrickson pushed an electronic pad next to the side door, and the door swiftly retracted into the vehicle's armoured wall.

The squad leaned inside and looked around. The rear cabin, containing an intercom and three large monitors, was separated by a thick wall from the driver's cabin. Each screen displayed an exterior camera feed while the monitor in the centre appeared to be for the turret's controls. The rest of the cabin was mostly open. A dozen air vents seemed to be circulating fresh air, and seating along the walls provided enough room for twelve people. A gun cabinet against the rear wall was the final touch.

Mitch gawked. "I'm in love."

"The Wombat features submerged traversal capabilities and its own air circulation system to protect the occupants from chemical attacks," the colonel explained.

"You mean it can be driven underwater?" Mitch couldn't hide his grin.

"Precisely."

"That's so awesome."

"Oh, and one more thing. The Wombat features a lockdown mode. Should you find yourself immobilised, hit the red switch next to the monitor and the vehicle will seal the doors and disable all excess electronics, including the engine. All power will be diverted to the air filtration system, with the camera feed and the turret controls remaining functional. The Wombat's systems will automatically send a distress beacon, and we will deploy a recovery team immediately to assist you. Any questions?"

Mitch raised his hand. "Can I drive?"

"I assume you have an assignment for us, sir?" Lorcan got straight to the point.

Henrickson opened the folder he had been carrying and handed each member of Squad Seven a mission briefing. Amanda looked confused as she read it over, mouthing the words to herself as she went down the page. "Your objective is to locate a group of government officials who went MIA during the initial attack. Their last known position was the White Sun Hotel in Broadbeach. Our intel suggests that it is one of the few buildings that remain standing in that area. Our targets are likely held up inside, awaiting rescue."

"What makes these government pencil pushers so important? We haven't even located the mayor yet," Damien asked.

"That information is above your pay grade," the colonel countered. "You are to radio in once you reach the hotel, and we will provide you with more intel from there. Let me be clear. We have lost too many birds to these monsters, and until we receive additional support, our resources are running very low. There will be no air extraction or backup on this mission, so watch yourselves out there! Do whatever it takes and extract them at any cost. They are invaluable assets. Gear up! You deploy in thirty minutes."

Lorcan saluted then turned to his squad. "Alright, you heard the man. Mitch, get the civilian a vest. Damien – weapons check."

Damien leaned over to Amanda and put a hand on her shoulder. "Welcome to the army, Civi," he snickered, before walking off towards the munitions tent.

Amanda straightened her glasses, turned to Lorcan and asked, "What do I do?"

Lorcan ignored her and headed off in his own direction, leaving the young woman standing by the Wombat. "Not getting much of that team-spirit feeling. Rude buggers," she said quietly.

13

INTO THE ASHES

One wrecked car after another crumpled against the Wombat's armoured grille as Mitch ploughed through the congested Gold Coast Highway. While Lorcan rested his eyes from the comfort of his seat in the rear cabin, Amanda flinched with each impact the vehicle endured. Manning the turret controls, Damien surveyed their surroundings via the screen in front of him. Thick rain clouds painted the sky a bleak grey while black smoke still rose from several smouldering buildings within the Broadbeach area.

"We're one click from the target area, captain," Mitch announced over the intercom, taking a hard right over the tram line. Lorcan opened his eyes and noted the nerves Amanda was failing to hide.

"Damn, look at this shit," Damien sombrely referred to the devastation displayed on-screen.

"Road's blocked, captain. Want me to go up and over?" Mitch asked.

Lorcan got up from his seat and joined Damien at the turret's camera feed. Surf Parade, the once renowned restaurant strip, was completely levelled. Dozens of hotels and eateries – once recognisable establishments – were reduced to fragmented piles of rubble. Mitch swallowed a massive lump in his throat and brought the ATV-X to a complete stop. His favourite coffee shop used to be right across the street.

"Hold here," Lorcan ordered. "We go in on foot. We can't risk crushing anyone who may be trapped in the debris."

"Probably do them a favour," Damien remarked, "and put them out of their misery."

"That's disgusting," Amanda retorted. "How can you say that? What if it was you trapped under there?"

"Trust me, Civi. I'd rather be dead."

"Enough," Lorcan interrupted. The pair went quiet. "On foot. Now!"

"Yes, sir," Damien said resentfully, as he grabbed his rifle and hit the touchpad. A gust of wind blew through the side door as it retracted.

"Move out, Seven!" The squad disembarked from the vehicle. "Eyes open! Ms Stone, you're on my six," Lorcan ordered, much to the civilian's confusion.

"That means stay close behind him," Mitch helpfully whispered to her.

With their rifles at the ready, the three soldiers moved in formation, checking their surroundings for any sign of hostile activity. While dozens of small fires still burned amid the mountains of broken concrete and bent steel, white flakes of ash swirled through the air like an arctic winter.

"All this ash; it's everywhere. Must have been quite a fire," Amanda remarked, as she opened her palm and let a single white flake fall into her hand.

"It's all that's left of the people here," Mitch said, gazing up at the thousands of flakes floating through the air.

"What?" Amanda quickly brushed it off her palm. "That's awful!"

"Try not to breathe it in," Damien chuckled.

The ominous clouds finally gave way, and a slow drizzle began to fall. The squad moved across a tilted slab of concrete which contained the remaining half of a swimming pool and several broken tanning lounges, probably from one of the fallen hotel's rooftops. Lorcan noticed a lifeless arm crushed between a steel beam and fractured brick wall. Amanda, however, hadn't noticed it, so Lorcan kept quiet.

"No offense, Civi, but I don't understand why the colonel sent you with us. This isn't the place for a tea-sipping bookworm," Damien said, clambering over a small ledge.

"She's here, dumb-ass," Mitch interjected, "to collect samples from any creatures we may encounter and bring them back for further study and, hopefully, provide intel on what they are, right?"

"Yes, I suppose that is correct," Amanda concurred.

The squad reached a clearing in the rubble that revealed the road beneath. The remainder of the street was scorched black, with half a dozen vehicles melted to the pavement. Amanda's attention lingered on a once beautifully landscaped park which was now a charred field, containing only a deformed set of monkey bars and a warped frame that loosely resembled a swing set.

The light drizzle steadily turned to heavy rain.

"That's our target, captain," Mitch said, and pointed to two forty-storey hotels standing tall at the far end of the road.

"How can you tell that from here?" Damien asked.

"The White Sun Hotel, right? My wife and I spent our anniversary there. Best steak I ever had."

"Okay, stay sharp," Lorcan instructed.

Squad Seven remained in formation as they closed in on their target destination. As the intel had stated, several hotels remained intact and undamaged. One such location was a bar called The Big Cow.

"I got kicked out of there once," Damien recounted. "Too much tequila and the manager's wife were not a good combination."

"Why does a story like that hardly surprise me?" Amanda jibed snarkily, in her British accent. "You seem like such an honourable man."

"Actually, Civi, I'm lovely – once you get to know me."

"Quiet!" Lorcan snapped, as a dark object scurried off behind The Big Cow's glass doors.

"We've got movement inside, captain," Mitch confirmed, raising his weapon.

Shadows continued to shift from one side of the bar to the other. Lorcan aimed down his rifle's sights, ignoring the rain as it trickled down his face. Amanda kept her distance as the three soldiers closed in on The Big Cow. "Hold your fire," Lorcan ordered, as a silhouette approached the glass door and opened it.

A middle-aged woman carrying a young child stepped out of the bar. "Please don't shoot," she begged them.

"Stand down!" The squad lowered their rifles. The woman's face was severely bruised. Her blood-soaked scrubs indicated that she was a nurse, but she seemed frail, barely able to hold the child in her arms.

"Are you okay?" Lorcan asked.

"I'm fine, but I have five others inside. We've been held up here for days. Can you please help us?" The nurse was clearly desperate. Amanda went to the woman's side and greeted the little boy.

"Don't worry, ma'am. We'll get you out of here," Mitch reassured her, then disappeared into the bar to see who she had with her.

"Ms, we are looking for three government pencil pushers in the area. Are they in there with you?" Damien asked.

"Government? No one like that here, but I've seen a man down the street; he's in one of the hotels. Sometimes he comes outside and searches through the rubble. I have never spoken to him. To be honest, we're too scared to leave the bar."

Entering the bar's kitchen, Mitch found two teenage boys and two women huddling around an elderly man who was clearly struggling to breathe.

"Are you here to rescue us?" one of the teenage boys asked.

Mitch radioed Lorcan outside. "Captain, we have five more survivors – two men, two women, and one elderly male in need of urgent medical attention, sir."

"Understood," Lorcan replied. He moved back from the nurse and radioed Command. "This is Captain Edwards. We have located seven survivors – one child, three adult females, three adult males, and one man in need of urgent medical attention. Permission to extract."

"Understood, captain. Have you located your objective?" a woman responded in Lorcan's earpiece.

"Negative, Command. Civilians must take priority. Permission to extract?"

"Permission to extract denied, captain. Remain on target to your objective."

"This is bullshit!" Mitch emerged from the bar, shaking his head.

"They can't do that," Amanda protested. "We can't just leave them here!"

Lorcan tried again. "Command, I repeat. We have a child here. I request that you reconsider."

"What is the sex of the child, captain?"

"What kind of question is that?" Lorcan replied. "The child is male, Command! What the fuck does that matter?"

"Understood, captain. The request is denied. The objective must remain top priority. Henrickson's orders, Edwards! You are to move on your target. Radio in once you reach the destination for further instructions. Over and out." The voice went quiet in Lorcan's ear.

"What difference does the kid's sex make?" Mitch couldn't make sense of it.

"Alright, Seven. Move out!"

Amanda stood by the nurse's side and glared at Lorcan with contempt. "You can't be serious! You're not actually going to leave them here?"

"Please help us," the woman pleaded, as she put the child down and dropped to her knees before the squad. "Please don't leave us here. My father needs help!"

Lorcan couldn't even look at her when he said, "I'm sorry. We have our orders. I suggest you remain inside. You'll be safer there."

"Please! There must be another way. Let us come with you," she pleaded, tugging on Lorcan's hand, which he quickly pulled away.

"Lady, there is nothing I can do. It's not up to us. I'm sorry."

The three soldiers regrouped on the street and waited for Amanda to join them.

"Civi, let's go," Damien insisted.

Amanda stubbornly folded her arms and said, "No, I'm not going anywhere without them."

The young boy ran back into the nurse's arms.

"You are soldiers, for God's sake!"

"I told you we shouldn't have brought her," Damien muttered.

Frustrated and short on patience, Lorcan marched over to the defiant consultant and pointed to the street. "Let's go. Now!"

"No."

"That's an order!"

"Well, captain, I'm not military – as you three have made *abundantly* clear. I'm just a tea-sipping Brit, so you can shove your order up your bravado-filled arseholes! I'm staying here, and I'm going to do what I can to help them, seeing as you cowards won't do a damn thing!"

"I have orders to bring you back."

"I don't give a rat's arse, captain."

It was then that Lorcan noticed the young boy's beaten face. He grunted, then said, "Fine. Have it your way. We will extract them. But only after we have located our targets. Until then, they are to remain inside this bar until we come back for them. Deal?"

Amanda donned a suspicious frown. "How do I know you'll actually come back for them?"

"I'm a man of my word. We'll take them with us. Deal?" Lorcan asked again.

"You have a deal, captain." Amanda shook his big hand before turning back to the nurse. "We will be back for you, I promise. Stay indoors till we return. We won't be long."

"Thank you! Thank you!" The woman praised Lorcan with a teary gaze. "I knew you were a good man."

"Okay, okay, that's enough. Have everyone ready to leave before we get back."

The woman ushered the boy inside the bar and shut the doors behind her.

Amanda winked at the three saturated soldiers standing in the rain. "Cheer up, boys. I'll make heroes out of you yet."

She strutted past them, leaving dumbstruck expressions across their faces.

"Civi's got balls," Damien said, and grinned.

"Big hairy ones," Mitch agreed.

Lorcan glanced back at the bar where seven hopeful faces watched from behind the doors as raindrops rolled down the glass. He lifted his rifle, turned around and led his squad down the quiet damp road.

The entrance of the White Sun Hotel was something to behold – tall stone columns, sculpted statues and a staircase of polished marble. It was an impressive greeting for its exclusive guests and elite clientele. For Squad Seven, however, it was just another harrowing reminder of what had been lost. Inside, spilled luggage bags, suitcases and garments littered the lobby while a polished stone reception desk stood resolutely before a mural of the Gold Coast that spanned the entire wall.

"How the hell did you afford to stay in a place like this?" Damien asked Mitch.

"My uncle used to work here; he hooked me up with a discount. Still, it took me a whole month to save up the money. My wife didn't even like it that much. She complained that the service was terrible."

"Where is your wife now?" Amanda asked.

"She's in New York, visiting family with my twin baby girls. My wife's American."

"Oh, so she wasn't here when everything happened?"

"No. We were the lucky ones. The girls left the week before the attack. They were supposed to come back on Sunday, but... Hopefully, I can see them soon."

"Married a Yank, huh? Always knew Americans had poor taste," Damien teased.

Mitch's middle finger couldn't spring up fast enough. "So, what about you, Ginger? You married?"

Damien shook his head. "Nah, I was. A long time ago. She was a hard woman – hard to live with. I'd rather be in a room with those fire-breathing bastards than spend another minute with that witch."

"I like her already," Amanda quipped.

"So, no family?" Mitch asked, taking a closer glimpse at the four inactive elevators.

"Cancer got Mum a few years back, and Dad, well, he left with a waitress when I was five and never came back." Damien laughed as he said, "She must have given great service."

"So, just you, then," Amanda said, feeling slightly sympathetic. "You must get lonely."

"Lonely? Nah, I'm a free man. Just how I like it. Don't worry, though, you're welcome to visit my tent anytime, Civi."

"Oh, very smooth," Mitch said sarcastically.

"Well, thank you for that kind offer, but I'll have to decline. You seem to be quite content with a one-man show anyway."

Damien shrugged and said, "Nothing wrong with handling things yourself."

Behind the desk, Lorcan found an emergency map of the building fixed beside a computer monitor. "Command, we are in position. The building appears to be structurally intact. Awaiting further instructions."

Children's clothing had spilled from an open luggage case onto the floor. Amanda crouched down and picked up a small brown teddy that had fallen out. "Everyone left in a hurry," she said, examining the stuffed animal.

"Yeah, well, if you had seen that thing, you would have got your arse out of here, too," Damien replied.

"So you didn't see the attack?" Mitch asked Amanda.

"No, I was on a study trip in Tamborine Mountain when it happened. We could hear it, though, even all the way up there. The buildings coming down, all the sirens, the roar that thing made – can't describe what it sounded like."

"Well, guess we're the lucky ones. Living on a military base finally paid off, right, captain?" Mitch asked, but Lorcan was too busy studying the layout of the building on the map to take notice.

"After all the commotion, we packed our things and left the nature reserve," Amanda continued. "Military jeeps began driving through the village streets, telling us to leave the area and make our way to the nearest evacuation zone. When we asked one of the soldiers what had happened, he said the city was under some sort of animal attack. I thought he was crazy, but I told him what I did for a living and he brought me to see the colonel. The rest is history."

"Captain Edwards, proceed to the twenty-second floor, room twenty-two-zero-two. That is the targets' last known location. You are to retrieve the three female individuals inside."

"Affirmative, Command. Moving out." Lorcan's finger located the twenty-second floor on the map.

"Twenty-two floors with no working lift," Damien said, as he opened the fire escape door. "That's a lot of stairs, captain. These politicians better be worth it."

"Mitch, you take point," Lorcan ordered. "It's going to be dark in there. Lights on."

Three simultaneous clicks echoed in the lobby as the tactical lights mounted on the soldiers' rifles were turned on. Lorcan gave the signal to move out. Mitch entered the fire escape, checking the stairs to his left while Damien entered behind him and checked the staircase on the right. The fire escape was indeed dark, and very narrow. With only their lights to guide them, Squad Seven made their way up to the twenty-second floor – much to Damien's annoyance.

"This is it, captain." Mitch stopped at a door with a large number twenty-two etched into it.

The squad exited the fire escape and entered a long hall. A room service cart lay tipped on its side, littering the carpet with several broken dishes and half-rotten food scraps.

"Hungry?" Damien joked, shining his light over a maggot-covered chicken wing.

"Charming," Amanda replied, and turned away.

After navigating the hall's bends and turns, Mitch finally came to a halt at the next suite. "Twenty-two-zero-two. Got it. Right here."

Damien attempted to turn the handle, but the door was locked. "It's no good, captain. The room is electronically locked, and seeing as there's no power and this is a fire safety door, it's gonna take a bit of force to breach it."

Without hesitation, Lorcan lifted his leg and kicked the door straight off its hinges, taking part of the doorframe with it.

"Or, we could just do that, sir."

The suite was quite large, with two double beds, separated by a timber bedside cabinet, and a black leather lounge that faced a curved high-definition television. The bathroom featured a spa bath and modest shower.

"Nice digs," Damien noted.

"Very nice. This is a lot fancier than the room I got for my wife," Mitch agreed.

Resting on the furthest bed, an open suitcase remained half-packed with a child-sized bikini folded next to a tiny summer dress. "Looks like they were about to go for a swim when they had to evacuate," Mitch said, picking up an adult-sized bikini from the other bed.

Lorcan noticed a holiday brochure next to a pink Gold Coast tourism cap on a nearby table.

"So, I'm going to say they were planning for a day at the beach," Amanda said, as she emerged from the bathroom, holding a set of beach towels and a bottle of coconut-scented lotion.

"The high-flying life of government douchebags," Damien said in a snarky tone. "Probably paid for this with taxpayers' money, too."

Lorcan studied the vacant room closely. Something was off, although he hadn't a clue what it was. "Command, this is Seven. We have reached the location; the room is a bust. There is no one here. I repeat, the room is unoccupied."

"Understood, Captain Edwards. It is imperative that you locate the targets. Search the remaining rooms. You are to report in if you locate any individuals within the tower."

"Search every room? That's a lot of rooms, Command."

"Search every room, captain. Those are your orders."

Damien couldn't believe what he was hearing. "Man, this is bullshit," he said.

"I don't get it," Mitch huffed. "What is so important about these politicians anyway?"

Lorcan searched for any sign of their targets' identities. Sure enough, a woman's purse was wedged between the mattress and bedside cabinet. He picked it up and opened the clasp. A car rental agreement was folded around a driver's licence.

"Does it have a name?" Amanda asked.

It did. Lorcan had to read the name twice before the horrific realisation set in. "Split up! Damien, you sweep the lower floors. Mitch, you sweep above. Meet in the foyer in thirty minutes. Now move it!" he barked, stuffing the licence and rental agreement into his pocket.

"Yes, sir," the two soldiers responded, then departed quickly.

"What are we doing?" Amanda asked, clearly confused by the captain's sudden urgency.

"We're checking the basement carpark."

Lorcan and Amanda made their way back to the fire escape and descended twenty-four flights of stairs until they reached the basement. The hotel's derelict parking lot was in complete disarray. The tangle of criss-crossing cars would have prevented anyone from being able to leave. Lorcan scanned the rental agreement and noted the registration number on the paperwork: 578-34T.

"So what are we doing down here?" Amanda asked.

"Locating a vehicle that our targets had leased," Lorcan answered, reading each number plate as he went.

"Why does their car matter? Do you think they will be hiding in it?"

"If the vehicle is still here, then we know they fled the building on foot. If it's not here, then we know we're looking for a red convertible out on the street."

"A red convertible? Doesn't sound like government issue to me."

"It isn't."

"I'm not sure that I follow you, captain."

"Just help me find this thing."

The pair searched the remainder of the basement but had no luck locating a red convertible. Damien and Mitch were already waiting when they regrouped in the hotel lobby.

"All rooms above the twenty-second floor are clear, captain," Mitch reported.

"Lower levels, too," added Damien, who was sweating horribly. "That was a lot of doors to kick in. Just saying."

"Good work."

"You guys have any luck?" asked Mitch.

Lorcan held up the discovered paperwork. "I found this in their hotel room. It describes a red convertible with plate number five seven eight, thirty-four tango. We're gonna check the surrounding area and see if any of the wrecks match this description. Watch yourselves. Don't forget what's out there."

Following Lorcan's orders, the squad departed the White Sun Hotel and began routine checks of all vehicles – or what was left of them – in the immediate area. The fact that most were now hardly recognisable as cars, let alone a specific type, didn't help the situation.

Amanda found herself fixated on the drooping chassis of an SUV. "How many died?" she eventually asked Mitch, as they moved to another vehicle.

"Come on. Don't ask me that," he brushed her off.

"You know, don't you? How many?"

Mitch reluctantly answered, "Henrickson told me they were estimating the death toll at over two hundred and fifty thousand, within the first twenty-four hours."

"What? That many in one day?" Amanda wished she hadn't asked. "And what's the estimate now?"

Mitch eyed Lorcan and Damien, both of whom decided to keep walking. "Around four hundred thousand."

"Four… hundred…" Amanda was stunned. "I had no idea it was so many."

"The big one hit us the hardest. But, pretty soon after, we started getting reports of other weird things popping up all over the coast."

"Enough chatter. Focus on the mission," Lorcan interjected, partly to save Mitch from his uncomfortable conversation.

"Can you hear that?" Damien asked, directing Lorcan to a faint whistle lost in the patter of heavy rain.

"Yep, I hear it alright."

Outside a nearby office building, a man vying for the squad's attention was whistling, albeit poorly, and waving for the soldiers to join him. "Over here, boys!"

"Must be that guy the nurse told us about earlier," Mitch said.

"Eyes open. We don't know who this guy is," Lorcan ordered, as he cautiously began to move in. Suddenly, the man ran off and ducked into another hotel. "Don't lose him! Move it, Seven!"

The squad sprinted down the street and entered the hotel's lobby with rifles raised and itchy trigger fingers. The man was waiting for them under a glistening chandelier that hung from a magnificently sculpted ceiling. He, too, had a rifle in his hands, but it was pointed at the floor.

"Hold it!" Mitch ordered him. "Put down the gun and get on your knees!"

"Whoa! Easy mate! I'm not one of those things," the man said, but kneeled down and complied with the soldier's demands.

Lorcan picked the rifle up and handed it to Damien. "Where did you get this?"

"Found it at one of those crashed police helicopters a few blocks from here," the man said, his hands raised in surrender. "The bloke holding it didn't seem to need it anymore – being dead and all."

"What are you doing here?"

"Been here since that dinosaur tore down the city. Got myself set up in one of the rooms upstairs. Can see the whole city from up there. Well, what's left of it, anyway."

"Why did you call out to us?" Damien asked, slinging the stolen rifle over his shoulder.

"I got something to show you upstairs – one of those monster things."

"You have one upstairs?" Mitch questioned him doubtfully.

"Sure, I'll show you."

"Finally," Amanda said, "something I can take a look at."

Damien frisked the man and removed a wallet from his pocket. "Your licence here says your name is Gareth. And your business card says you're a dentist."

The man nodded and said, "Yep, name's Gareth, and I'm a dentist. Good work, detective."

"Hey, smart-arse, keep this up and I'll give you some dental work to fix."

"That's enough!" Lorcan lifted Gareth to his feet. "You got one of those things upstairs? I want to see it. Lead the way."

Mitch and Damien escorted the strange man towards a fire escape.

"Captain, I don't think you can trust this bloke; something feels off," Amanda said quietly.

Lorcan couldn't help but agree. "We'll see what he has, then we'll cuff him and bring him back with the others."

"Great, more fuckin' stairs!" Damien's voice echoed in the stairwell.

Gareth led Squad Seven up to the twenty-eighth floor and into the hotel room he had been squatting in. The suite was a complete mess. Crumpled food packets, empty bottles and half-eaten scraps were scattered throughout the room. All the furniture had been stacked against the left-hand wall, except for a mattress that remained on the floor. Mitch noticed that the sliding door to the balcony had been left open, despite the rain blowing inside.

Damien tapped Gareth on the shoulder and asked, "You waiting for housekeeping to show up?"

"So, where is it?" Lorcan asked.

Gareth wandered onto the balcony and gazed out at the ruined city. "I can see the whole area from up here. Let's me keep track of things; saw you lot the moment you left the fancy hotel down the street."

Lorcan wasn't feeling particularly patient; he still had three people to find. "Alright, Gareth, you have ten seconds to show me this monster you have, or I'm dragging your creepy arse out of here."

"It's right there," Gareth said, and pointed to a school's soccer field a few blocks away.

"Great. All those steps for nothing," Damien complained, also out of patience.

Lorcan examined the field, at least two-thirds of which had been converted to mud by the downpour, but no creature of any kind was to be seen. "Alright, doc. You're coming with us."

"You're not seeing it," Gareth protested. "Pay attention!"

Hesitantly, Lorcan took a second glance, and to his bewilderment, Gareth was right. The muddy soccer field was not a field at all. It was a muddy gaping hole. No, not a hole – a burrow.

"The big one, the monster that did all this, it's in there," Gareth stated.

"How do you know?" Mitch asked.

"A few days ago, it burst out of the ground there. I didn't get a good look at it then. Was too busy watching my wife and sister burn in its breath. But that's okay, because us boys, pardon me, *and girl*, are going to kill it today!"

"I'm... sorry," Mitch stammered. "We're going to do *what* now?"

"Every day, at around this time, it leaves that hole and flies off to God-knows-where," Gareth explained. "Not today, though. The second it leaves that hole, we can shoot that bitch right outta the sky!"

Lorcan snatched Gareth by the shirt and dragged him back into the messy hotel room. "Listen here, you crazy son of a bitch! Bullets don't do shit against that thing. The only thing you're going to do is get yourself killed, along with anyone who tries to help you."

"I say we let the crazy bastard go," Damien suggested. "No need to rescue a man with a death wish."

"You three are unbelievable!" Amanda waltzed over to Lorcan and removed his hand from Gareth's collar. "Sir... Gareth, I mean. I'm so sorry about your family. I can't imagine what you are going through, but I can imagine that your wife and sister wouldn't want you to throw your life away like this."

"My family was my life," Gareth wearily replied. "Don't you see? I have to kill it. For my wife, for my sister... for everyone."

Before Amanda could respond, a howling roar erupted from the depths of the soccer field.

"Hold him," Lorcan instructed Mitch, before returning to the balcony. Gareth was right again. A monstrous creature was climbing out of the ground. He was wrong about one thing though. "That's not the one that attacked the city."

"It's just as big though," Damien said, and shuddered as the animal dwarfed nearby apartment blocks. "That's gotta be over fifteen storeys high, maybe higher."

Whereas the grey monster Lorcan had encountered was muscular and bulky, this creature was bony and thin. Black scales covered its long skinny limbs. The creature looked malnourished, as you could see its massive ribcage through the white scales that covered its chest. Long and limber, its arms nearly reached the ground as it walked, and four razor-sharp claws protruded from the end of its lengthy fingers. Its long snout and wide skull reminded Damien of an alligator, but that's where the likeness stopped. No alligator had countless rows of serrated teeth and glowing blue eyes. A series of protruding horns crowned the ridge of its spine and continued down to a pair of long black tails. Behind its shoulders were not one, but two sets of bat-like wings.

"I'm going to have nightmares about this thing," Damien whispered, as the black monstrosity let out another ferocious roar.

Mitch gulped, eyes glued outside. "That's if you can get to sleep."

"We need to stay quiet," Lorcan whispered. Suddenly, Gareth broke free of Mitch's grip and snatched the handgun from the distracted soldier's holster.

"Gun!" Mitch yelled.

Gareth raced out to the balcony and fired four rounds. Lorcan reacted a moment too late, tackling Gareth to the ground before prying the weapon from him. With a flap of its wings, the monster kicked off the ground and made a beeline for their hotel.

"Captain, we've got incoming!"

The monster was already there, hovering outside the building like a Harrier Jump Jet. The force of its four wings sent a salvo of heavy rain and wet ash hurtling through the balcony doorway.

Lorcan stepped away from Gareth and took aim. "Light it up!"

Gareth and Amanda covered their ears as the squad opened fire. Round after round, each bullet ricocheted off the creature's thick scales until all three clips were reduced to a collection of casings littering the carpet. The flying black reptile let out a low growl as blue light began to surge through its body in an all-too-familiar fashion.

"Everybody out!" Lorcan seized Amanda by the hand and whisked her into the hallway, with Mitch and Damien hard on their heels. Gareth had no intention of following them. Instead, he proceeded to the balcony and glared into the monster's flaming blue eyes. "See you in hell, bitch."

A stream of blue fire cut through the building like a laser. Amanda glanced over her shoulder. An inferno now raged where Gareth's suite used to be.

"Captain, look! It's leaving," Mitch cried, as he gestured to a nearby window. The monster had taken to the sky and was heading the opposite way.

"Well, that was easy," Damien said. "Oh, hold on." His face dropped. The black monster banked left and circled around before it came hurtling back towards them with immense speed.

"Shit! Hold on to something," Lorcan shouted.

The flying lizard propelled itself through the lower levels of the hotel like a hot knife through butter. Squad Seven tumbled to the ground as the floors between the third and seventh storeys were completely obliterated. As the severed building crashed to the ground, it tipped into the neighbouring hotel, sending the squad sliding down the hall towards a large window.

A passing doorframe was Lorcan's only chance. He slammed his hand on the timber and latched on, stopping his descent, but the weight of Amanda in his other hand painfully jarred his shoulder. Mitch and Damien hastily found the next two doorframes and grabbed hold.

"Great! What now?" Damien asked, feet dangling against the inclined carpet.

Lorcan spotted their rifles, now resting on the windowpane at the end of the hall. A drop of several storeys filled the gap between the glass and the balcony on the next building over. "Damien, shoot the window!"

"What? Are you nuts?"

"Shoot the glass! We can jump to the next balcony." Lorcan's one-handed grip on the doorframe was beginning to slip.

"You mean the balcony on the *other* building?"

"Do you really wanna stay in this one, Saunders?" Mitch interjected. "Just shoot the damn window!"

"Fine." Damien pulled the pistol from his holster and fired two bullets into the glass. The window shattered, sending the four rifles and countless shards of glass into the street below.

"Go, go, go!" Lorcan urged, as cracks began to spread across the walls.

Damien let go of the doorframe and slid down the hallway. Up on his feet, he raced towards the broken window and readied his jump. A glimpse of the huge drop was enough to make his stomach turn. Pushing his feet off the ground, he launched himself out of the window. He crossed the gap and collided with an assortment of outdoor furniture on the opposite balcony. Damien brushed himself off, then yelled, "Better hurry the hell up in there!"

A moment later, Mitch came flying out of the window with considerable speed, easily clearing the gap before collecting Damien and taking him right back to the balcony floor.

"I can't do this! I can't do this!" Amanda panicked, still dangling from Lorcan's hand in the crumbling building.

"Yes, you can," he assured her. "Push your feet off the ground as you reach the window. You'll make it!"

"No, no, no! I can't do it!"

"Look at me! You have to do this, or we are going to die." Lorcan loosened his grip on her hand. "Trust me. You can do it."

"Okay, okay," Amanda said, as she skittishly peered at the dreaded hall.

"Ready? One… two…" Lorcan abruptly let go, causing the terrified woman to scream the whole way down the slope. Nearing the window, she pressed her feet against the floor and pushed off as hard as she could. With every limb flailing, Amanda soared over the multistorey drop, but it wasn't enough. She hit the railing hard. Scrambling for something to grab onto, she slipped off the balcony with a horrific squeal.

Within mere moments, her forearms were under incredible pressure. She couldn't tell if they hurt or not; she wasn't even sure what was happening. Amanda opened her eyes to find Mitch and Damien stretched over the railing, each gripping one of her arms tightly in their hands. The two soldiers heaved her over the railing and onto the balcony floor. The traumatised woman wept in Damien's arms as Mitch stood up and called for Lorcan to hurry.

Lorcan let go of the doorframe and sped towards the window, but before he could make the leap, the hall twisted and broke away, sending the big man slamming into the wall before tumbling out of the window.

Mitch snatched Damien's pistol from the ground and quickly fired the rest of the clip into the glass door behind them. The three hurried into the room just as a mass of falling concrete tore the balcony off.

"Captain! Can you hear me? Captain Edwards!" Mitch shouted over the radio.

"I'm here. I landed in a room a few floors below you," Lorcan's voice came through the earpiece. Mitch breathed a sigh of relief.

"Meet me in the fire escape."

"Roger that," Mitch acknowledged.

Lorcan was in another hotel suite. Having danced with lady luck, his tumble out of the window and into the adjacent building was nothing short of a miracle, but a nearby roar was the perfect reminder that he wasn't out of the woods yet. Bursting out of the room, the soldier headed for the green exit sign. Mitch, Damien and Amanda were descending the fire escape when Lorcan entered one floor below them. The reunited Squad Seven raced to the ground floor and into the lobby. The fallen hotel had crushed several small apartment blocks and spilled over the road.

"Oh no! What are they doing?" Amanda raced to the nearby window, her face pressed to the glass. The survivors hiding in The Big Cow were now fleeing into the street. The teenage boys were assisting the elderly man, while the nurse and the two women escorted the young child. "No! Get back inside!" Amanda shouted.

A swooping shadow passed overhead, and a barrage of blue fire was unleashed upon the group. All that was left was a cloud of ash dispersing amid the rain drops.

"No…" Amanda slid down the window, completely inconsolable. Damien had no words for her; all he could do was kneel by her side.

Gritting his teeth, Lorcan punched the glass, creating a web of cracks, and exited the hotel. The winged nightmare flew high into the sky, giving one final roar before disappearing behind the storm.

"We should have extracted them when we had the chance," Mitch said, as he joined Lorcan outside.

"Retrieve the Wombat," Lorcan ordered. "This mission is over."

"Yes, sir," Mitch said, and sombrely wandered off.

A small access road quickly drew Lorcan's attention. He hadn't noticed it before as the squad had been too busy pursuing Gareth into the hotel. About halfway down the alley, a scorched wreck was wrapped around a melted lamppost. Curiously, he made his way into the alley and approached the twisted vehicle. The wreck didn't appear to have a roof and, judging by the lack of heat, it seemed to have been there for several days. Lorcan stopped at the rear of the vehicle as half the number plate was still intact: -34T. He quickly double-checked the registration number on the rental agreement: 578-34T. This was it – the reason they were here. Lorcan slammed his fist on the warped metal. Like the survivors they had failed to rescue, the people they had been searching for were nothing but ash – likely killed whilst trying to flee the first attack.

"Command, this is Captain Edwards. We have located the targets. Confirmed DOA. I repeat the targets are deceased."

"Understood. Roger that, captain. Targets are confirmed DOA. I'll inform the colonel."

"Is that the government folks we were looking for?" Damien asked, as he escorted an emotional Amanda out into the street.

"Worse." Lorcan removed the woman's driver's licence from his pocket and quietly read the name back to himself: Lisa-Anne Henrickson. The colonel's wife.

14

FAMILY

"**O**uch! That really stings!"

"Don't be a baby! That cable cut your hands deep," Emma said, pouring disinfectant over the gashes across Blake's palms.

"Yeah, but they hurt less before you started to fix them."

"Well, just be grateful my dad always keeps a first aid kit in his drawer."

Sitting at the foot of the impeccably made bed, Blake found himself in Emma's father's immaculate room, which was also rather plain. Other than several photos of Emma on top of a wooden dresser, there was really no sign that anybody had ever occupied the space. There were no books, no TV, and no cologne or personal effects, other than the evenly spaced garments hanging in the walk-in closet. The master bedroom could have been mistaken for a freshly readied hotel suite.

"You know, you could have slept in here last night. My dad wouldn't mind," Emma said, as she finished wrapping the bandage around his left hand.

"Thanks, but the couch is fine. Besides, I wouldn't want to mess his room up; everything is so clean in here."

"Yeah, I know. Dad's a neat freak. He can't even walk in my room because it stresses him out so much."

Blake replied with a smirk, "Guess we'll never invite him to one of Gary's barbeques."

"No," Emma agreed, "although I would love to see Dad's face." She finished the bandage on his right hand. "All done!"

"Thanks. How's your leg?"

Emma glanced at the cut down the back of her left calf; it was red with irritation. "It's a little sore, but just a small cut. Nothing to worry about."

"Aren't you forgetting something?" Blake asked, as he nodded at the bottle of the disinfectant by her foot.

"Oh, that's not necessary."

"Really? Who's being a baby now?" Blake asked. "Suck it up. Switch places." Reluctantly, Emma plonked herself on the end of the bed while Blake kneeled on the floor. "Okay, let's see here." He lifted her leg and surveyed the wound. "This is more than a little cut!"

"You're being dramatic. It's not that bad."

"Good. This shouldn't hurt too much, then." Blake dabbed the disinfectant on her leg and was met with a flurry of curse words. "And I'm the baby?"

Emma winced. "You're enjoying this, aren't you?"

"A little." He removed the cotton and began applying a bandage. "So, can I ask a personal question?"

"I'd say no, but you're clearly skilled in torture. So ask away."

"I noticed there's no photos of your mother anywhere, and you've never really mentioned her."

Emma was silent for several seconds. "My mother passed away."

"Oh, I'm so sorry. I shouldn't have asked."

"No, it's okay. I don't exactly talk about it. There used to be dozens of photos of us, but I made Dad take them all down."

"Why?"

"A few years ago, I was at the beach with Brooke when I got a call. It was a police officer; my mother had been in a car accident. The driver of the car she was in lost control and collided with a truck. My dad used to be in the military; he was on an overseas tour when it happened. The army sent him home immediately. The investigating officer found some text messages in my mother's phone. Turns out the man driving was some famous writer; he wrote kids' books or something. She had been having an affair with him for almost a year."

Blake really felt awful now. "That must have been hard," he murmured.

"I still don't know how she could have done that to us – to our family – or how she could have done that to my dad, while he was risking his life overseas. The worst part was that Dad acted like none of it mattered. He just forgave her and never spoke about it. He quit the military to be with me and became a cop. I blamed him for not getting mad. I used to tell him that he had a right to hate her, but he never did. I did. Guess I still hate her for it. It's like we didn't know her at all."

Blake felt for her. He wanted to say something profound, but instead he said, "I'm sorry. I had no idea."

"Now Dad is gone, too, and I'll never get to tell him that I'm sorry." Emma turned away and smeared several tears across her cheek. "I treated him so badly. He came home for me – quit his career for me – and I kept punishing him for something that *she* did. I never really appreciated him until all this happened. How messed up is that?"

"You're being too hard on yourself."

"Am I? Maybe it's about time that I was."

Blake became quiet. He pinned the bandage around her calf, smiled, and said, "All done."

"Thank you," Emma said, "for my leg and for listening to my pity party."

"Anytime." Blake's eyes lingered on her brown ones for a while. "For what it's worth, I don't know what James and I would have done had you not taken us in. I think your dad will be proud of you."

"*Will* be? You think he's still out there?"

Blake stood up. "I don't know, but we're not going to give up until we find out."

Even Emma's tears couldn't hide her smile. "Thank you." She got up from the bed and pecked him on the cheek. "I'm glad you're here."

"Are you out of your mind, old man?" An outburst from James in the next room immediately spoiled the moment.

Blake sighed and said, "Sounds like James and Gary are up."

Emma nodded, "Yep."

"Shall we?"

The pair quickly joined a curious Lila and Will on the deck to find James and Gary arguing on the driveway. "What's this about?" Blake asked.

"We were wondering the same thing," Will said, amused.

James was pacing back and forth. "What's the point? You're going to do all this for nothing. We just got food yesterday."

Gary, who stood with his arms folded, was far calmer than the young man before him. "That food won't last all of us more than two weeks. That's *if* we start rationing it right now. I'm tellin' ya, it's gonna run out real fast!"

"Come on! Everything will be back to normal in a day or two. Once the army kills these things, it's all over. They're just animals. You're being dramatic."

"What are you guys fighting about now?" Emma finally interrupted.

James quit pacing and addressed the spectators. "The *old woman* here wants to spend the day planting crops in the yard because he thinks the world has ended. Someone please tell this guy that he's going senile!"

All eyes fell on Blake who, after some thought, said, "What if Gary's right? Look, man, we have no idea what's going on out there, but I do know that we were almost killed getting that food yesterday. Maybe being prepared is the smart thing to do right now."

"Figures you'd take his side," James said, and kicked a rock before pointing a stern finger at Gary. "You're going to bust a hip."

Gary gave him a heavy-handed pat on the back. "Nah, I'll be fine. You're gonna do all the digging."

James shrugged him off, saying, "Your grave, maybe."

Lila, who was thoroughly enjoying the show, let out a small snicker. James shot her an unimpressed glare. "I'm sorry. But you two are like an old married couple," she said, laughing.

"Hey! Only one of us is old!" James kicked another rock and stormed off towards the barn in a huff. "Whatever! You guys are paranoid! They're just big reptiles, you lunatics."

"Is he okay?" Emma asked Blake.

"Just let him be. He'll be alright. We're all dealing with this in our own way."

"So, are you guys sure you wanna come with us?" Lila asked. "It could be dangerous. Milky is our family, but we can't expect you to put yourselves at risk for us."

"Milky? Cute," Emma smiled. "After what you did for us yesterday, we can't let you go alone."

"Safety in numbers," Blake added.

Will and Lila nodded with appreciation. "Thanks."

"Well, you four be careful out there." Gary swung a shovel under his arm and picked up a bag of fertilizer. "Just get what ya need and get back here. You know that city ain't safe."

Blake nodded and said, "We will. Keep an eye on James for me, will you?"

Gary replied with a devious grin, "Oh, don't worry. I'll watch the little whiner."

∿∿∿∿∿∿∿∿∿

Flattened homes, burning shopfronts and collapsed buildings had become an uncomfortable, but familiar sight for Blake and Emma. This was the furthest south they had ventured since the attack, but the devastation was the same. For Will and Lila, the sight of the levelled city brought a new sense of the severity of recent events. Nobby Beach, one of the most active local hotspots on the coast, was now a concoction of charred ruins and melted cars.

Lila grabbed Will's hand and held on tight. She was shaking, but Will wasn't even sure if she realised it.

A quick glance down the next street revealed the glistening ocean, which ran parallel to the Gold Coast Highway. Lila mumbled something to herself about not looking and shut her eyes. Will couldn't make out what she had said, but he didn't need to. She was obviously frightened. He abruptly turned left down the next street and headed straight for the oceanfront homes. At the end of the narrow road, between two beachfront mansions, a large set of wooden stairs descended from the street to the sandy shore. "Babe, what are you doing?" Lila asked, opening her eyes.

"Changing the scenery," Will replied, as the four-wheel drive mounted the curb and bounced down the steps. Blake and Emma clutched their seatbelts. Sand sprayed from the tyres as they bounded onto the beach and headed south along the shoreline.

"Great idea," Lila said, and kissed his cheek.

"Anyone like a shower?" Will asked as he veered off, sending the left wheels cutting through the shallow water and flinging sea spray into the air. Emma and Lila squealed as cold water rained down, drenching almost everyone in the car.

"Will, you jerk!" Lila laughed, as water dripped from her face.

Emma wiped her eyes and flicked her fingers. "Yeah, thanks for that."

Blake, who was mostly dry, smirked to himself and relaxed in his seat.

"Well, at least you're smiling now," Will said to Lila, feeling rather pleased with himself. That smile, however, didn't last. A wild howl in the distance turned their moment of joy to overwhelming dread.

Several kilometres back, a massive reptile soared through the air above the ruins of Broadbeach like a stalking eagle. Emma gasped, "Blake, is that—?" The horrid creature was covered in black scales, and had four wings and two long tails trailing behind it.

"That's something else," Blake said, as his eyes widened. "That's not the same one we saw on Saturday."

Lila was quivering. "So there are two giant dragon things?"

Will swallowed a golf ball-sized lump in this throat. "Looks like it."

"Please just get us home," Lila whispered, her eyes glued to the monster in the clouds. Will sped off, continuing south towards their home, but more importantly, away from the flying nightmare in the sky.

Burleigh Heads was known as a local getaway – the perfect spot for those eager to enjoy beautiful scenery and entertainment without any of the craziness that tourist centres like Surfers Paradise and Broadbeach were known for. Widely regarded as a local treasure, thousands of people flocked from all over to enjoy its picturesque setting. Palm trees and curved pathways meandered along a grassy hill that overlooked the blue sea and white beach, making for a perfect picnic site. Even the sharp rocks and boulders along the shoreline failed to deter countless locals from surfing the waves or taking long swims.

It was also Will and Lila's favourite spot on the coast, which is why they lived so close by. Will turned onto a narrow suburban street which, to the group's amazement, appeared completely unscathed. There were no scorched roads or burnt cars; just one vacant house after another.

Lila watched each home pass by. "So weird – Alison's place, Jess and Greg's place – they're just empty. I hope everyone's okay."

"Try not to think about it," Will said. He eased on the brakes, pulled into a weed-riddled driveway and announced, "Home sweet home." To the couple's relief, their house was exactly as they had left it that fateful Saturday morning. A lime-green front door and a pair of square windows were lost behind the overgrown bushes and tall grass. A lofty gum tree, reaching over the tiled roof, had coated it in a layer of dead leaves and old branches, while vines stretching along the timber walls had grown into the overflowing gutters.

"Milky!" Lila opened the car door, leapt out of the vehicle and ran around the side of the house.

Will unclipped his seatbelt and turned the engine off. "You guys coming? We're just grabbing a few things; we won't be long." Blake nodded. Emma, however, remained rather quiet in the seat next to him. Will got out of the car and approached the front door, walking along the one thin stretch of pavement that hadn't been completely consumed by the garden.

Blake climbed out of the car and offered Emma a hand. "You coming?"

"Yeah," Emma answered quietly, taking his hand as she lowered herself out of the high vehicle.

"I've always wanted to visit the jungle," Blake said, eyeing the tangled branches and knee-high grass.

"That's very funny," Will said, as he unlocked the front door and pushed it open. "Lila is kinda obsessed with anything that's living. She won't let me trim the trees back or even mow the lawn because I'm 'hurting' them."

Watching her step, Emma followed the paved path through the grass to the front door. "Doesn't the council send you fines or something if you let the garden get like this?" she asked.

"Yeah, it does. Lila uses them as wrapping paper at Christmas time," Will said, as he held the door and gestured for Blake and Emma to enter.

Inside, the lounge room closely resembled the outside. Dozens of potted plants sat on the floor and hung from the walls. The room also contained a couple of folded-out trestles (also covered in plants) and a tall bookshelf displaying dusty photos of the happy couple. The six-foot-four-inch Blake carefully threaded himself between several dreamcatchers hanging from the ceiling as he followed Emma and Will into the kitchen.

Cluttered with cutting boards, pans and a few dirty dishes, the kitchen bench was also home to a line of potted sunflowers and a small Venus flytrap. Blake locked his sights on the carnivorous plant and reached out to touch one of its open-mouthed leaves.

"Don't touch that! It's delicate," Lila unexpectedly snapped behind him.

A startled Blake yanked his hand away from the small plant.

"Sorry, I didn't mean to make you jump."

Blake turned to see Lila standing in the doorway, holding a purring, fluffy white cat.

"It's cool. I've never seen one of these up close before," he said, glancing back at the flytrap.

"They're beautiful, aren't they? I'm a little overprotective."

"A little?" Will mocked, emerging from the pantry with a bowl of fresh cat food. "The cat once knocked my surfboard on top of her favourite fern. She made me sleep outside that night."

"Okay, maybe I went too far that time," said Lila, and blushed with a half-embarrassed smile.

"Oh, so cute! She's so white!" Emma gawked with excitement at the yawning white cat in Lila's arms and rushed over for a closer look.

"Everyone, this is Milky!" Lila held the cat out, its back legs dangling in the air. "Milky, this is Blake and Emma. You will meet the other two later."

"So, you're quite the gardener," Blake said, as he looked around at the various plants scattered around their kitchen.

"Yeah, I'm obsessed. The sunflowers are my favourites! But I love them all. My mother had a real green thumb. She taught me everything I know."

"Where is your mother now?"

"She passed away when I was ten."

"Oh, I had no idea. I'm sorry," Blake apologised, hoping that he hadn't hit a nerve.

"Oh, no, it's fine. It was a long time ago. My father passed from cancer a few years back, and Will hasn't talked to his parents in years; they weren't exactly nice people. So, yeah, it's just us two. Living in our own little paradise."

"Her fur is so soft," Emma said, patting Milky who was now purring with closed eyes.

Will placed the bowl of cat biscuits on the floor. "We had a carpet python under the sofa three weeks ago, and a kookaburra perched on the shower head the week before that. I'm one loincloth away from swinging to work on a vine."

"Oh shoosh. I never complain about the sand you drag in every morning, do I?" Lila pecked him on the cheek before placing Milky on the ground. "Look what Daddy has for you!" The hungry cat dove straight in, devouring the food within a matter of minutes. "She must have been so hungry."

"Speaking of hungry..." Will opened the cupboard under the sink and pulled out a yellow watering can, saying, "I'm sure your other children are thirsty."

Lila smiled and said, "This is why I love you." She took the watering can and disappeared into the lounge room.

"I'm going to pack some things. Want me to pack your stuff, too?" Will called out to her, as he ventured into the hallway.

"Sure, honey, just pack whatever clothes you want, and don't forget my toothbrush."

Emma couldn't help but admire the couple; they seemed perfect for each other. Taking care of the cat food, filling the watering can, and packing Lila's clothes for her – Will had scored solid boyfriend points in her eyes. Emma, however, would never have let someone choose her clothes, let alone a *boy*. No; she would have sorted outfits with matching shoes and co-ordinated her handbags – probably three times over.

Lila didn't seem to care for any of that. All she wanted to do was make sure her plants were cared for and her cat was fed. Emma found something humbling about it all, though she kept it to herself.

Lila made her way around the lounge room, humming a soft melody as she catered to her leafy children. The sound of the front door swinging shut made Emma realise that Blake had left the house. Feeling out of place, she decided it was best to join him.

Emma found Blake leaning against the ticking bonnet of Will's four-wheel drive as she quietly closed the door behind her. "What are you doing? Too many flowers for ya?"

"Just needed some air."

"It's that girl, isn't it?" Emma asked, joining him at the hot car. "Amy? James told me what happened."

Blake couldn't look at her. Instead, he focused on the crack in the pavement and ignored the tears welling in his eyes. "I keep seeing her face."

"I know what you mean."

"Her mother trusted me to take her. I can't stop thinking about it."

Emma cleared her throat then said, "Right before James pulled me out of the salon, I watched my friend die. She was hit by a car. I was so scared. I couldn't move. By the time I went to help her, that monster had killed everyone in the street." Emma turned to Blake, placing a comforting hand over his. "I still see her face, too."

"So what do we do?"

"I don't know."

Will barged out the front door carrying two bags and a small potted sunflower. "Well, I'm ready to go, but Mother Nature is still inside."

"I heard that, William," Lila yelled from somewhere in the house.

Blake walked over, grabbed a bag and helped Will load their stuff into the car. Emma stayed quiet, still thinking about her conversation with Blake. Eventually, Lila exited the house carrying Milky in her arms. "Sorry, everyone, so sorry. Everything is watered, so we are ready to hit the road!" She held Milky's paw up and waved it at the others.

"Okay then." Will opened the car door as everyone climbed in and retook their seats. "Let's get back to the others."

"Hopefully, James and Gary haven't killed each other yet," Blake said, buckling his seatbelt.

"I'm sure they're fine," Lila said, as she longingly stared at the overgrown garden she had become so fond of. She wondered how long it would be before they saw their home again – *if* they saw their home again.

"Everyone buckled up?" Will asked, backing out of the driveway. Emma and Blake glanced at each other once, though not at the same time. Their fingers became intertwined, but neither spoke a word of it.

15

BEHIND THE CREEK

From the comfort of a shaky fold-out chair, James sat by the creek, muttering profanities as he attempted to fix his waterlogged phone. The wires inside were in far worse condition than he had thought, and he was beginning to doubt whether it could be fixed at all. "Come on, you piece of crap," he mumbled. Twisting a small screwdriver, he removed a tiny circuit board from the plastic casing and surveyed the damage, which was quite extensive. "Great. Just great," he said, as he tossed the phone into the creek and flopped back into his chair.

"You know, you could give me a hand instead of dicking around with that thing." A sweaty Gary was standing behind him, holding a bucket of water and a shovel.

James didn't bother to turn around. "Why?" he muttered, watching the creek water break along the rocks.

"I don't know what your problem is, but boy, you had better check yourself." Shaking his head, Gary headed towards the barn.

"Are you kidding me?" James leapt up from his chair, sending it toppling over, then marched over, red-faced and steaming from the ears. "Wanna know what my problem is?"

"Here we go," said Gary, and stopped and turned back around.

"Let's see... maybe it's the constant drinking? Maybe it's the smoking, the swearing, or the never-ending belching? Wait, no, I can handle all that. No – maybe it's the fact that Blake looks up to you like a father! Maybe it's the fact that when he needed you most, you were passed out on your lounge room floor!" James was now only inches from Gary's face. "You weren't there! Where were you? Huh? Were you trying to help him? Did you even call him? No, you didn't because you were too busy at home, having a good time, smoking your cigars, drinking your booze, and thinking about the only person who matters – you."

"Blake is like a son to me," Gary shot back, and dropped the bucket, spilling water on the dirt.

"Bullshit! A son to you? This isn't the first time you have let Blake down, is it? Nobody needs a father like you – the man who was too drunk to turn up to his own adoption hearing! The only chance for Blake to have a real home, and you were passed out in some bar, right? Just like you were too drunk to help him when the city fell. Let's face it. You're just a drunk old man – at best."

Gary tossed the shovel aside, too. "For once, boy, we agree on something," he said, then quietly walked off.

Having barely taken a breath during his rant, a panting James watched as Gary crossed the creek and disappeared into the foliage of the old forest.

Dead leaves littered the ground as Gary strolled through the woods deep in thought. Reaching in his shirt pocket, he pulled out a half-smoked cigar and flicked his lighter open, but before the flame could singe the tobacco, he froze. Something big and round was hanging from the tree before him. Something he had never seen before. Taking a step back, he found a dozen more clinging from branches all around him.

James was reaching for the back door when Gary's cry for help echoed out of the forest. "Old man?" He spun around and bolted towards the tree line.

James charged into the forest and found Gary standing before a strange object. "You better look at this," he said.

"Whoa! What the hell is that?" James yelped, skidding to a halt.

Gary was studying the object closely. "I have no idea."

Shaped like a teardrop, the two-metre-long pod was covered in thick reptilian scales and hung from a slimy purple tongue that seemed to have suctioned itself to the branch above. The green scales were shiny and reflective, with small patches of moss growing between the plates. The tongue seemed to be breathing, letting out a gooey squishy sound with each convulsion.

"This is nine kinds of crazy," Gary muttered.

"Look," James said, as he pointed to the branch where the tongue had attached itself. It was drained of all colour, as if the tree had been dead for years, with not a single leaf on any of the nearby branches. The other side of the tree, however, was still brown in colour and covered in the usual summer-scorched leaves.

The pair backed up a little. There were dozens of pods around the area. Each one clung to the branch of half-white trees. "Oh boy," Gary exhaled nervously. "They're killing the trees. It's like they're feeding off them."

James turned to leave. "I think I saw a machete leaning against the barn. We need to cut them down."

"No, don't," Gary said, as he grabbed James's arm. "We don't know what they are or what put them here. If we cut them down, we don't know what will happen – or what we might piss off."

"So, what – we're just gonna leave them here?"

"No," Gary said, "I'm saying we figure out what these things are before we go poking them with sharp objects."

"Fine," James conceded, "but let's get out of here. These things are freaking me out."

"No argument here."

For the next forty minutes, Gary and James manned a pair of fold-out chairs from the back deck and watched the forest slowly decay. Piles of dead leaves were now covering the ground in an orange and brown blanket, and the longer they studied the trees, the more pods they noticed among them.

"Well, this isn't good," James said, reaching into his half-eaten packet of chips.

"That's one way of putting it," Gary agreed, puffing on his cigar.

"Where do you think they came from? I mean, how did all of these creatures just suddenly show up?"

"Aliens? Maybe they're dinosaurs? Or some lab experiment gone wrong."

James nodded, stuffing another chip into his mouth. "Maybe they're mutants."

"I read a story about this old lady who would feed a crocodile every morning from her local pier. Eventually the croc grew as big as a bus and started eating people. They brought in a special team to hunt the darn thing down."

"You didn't read that. That's the movie Blake made us watch for his birthday last year."

"Right," Gary said, as he expelled a cloud of smoke from his nostrils, "I remember now. Damn kid, he loved that movie."

"He sure did. I hated it."

"Me, too."

James paused for a moment then said, "Listen, about what I said before…"

"It's okay." Gary stopped him, lowering his cigar. "You were right. I haven't been there – not the way I should have been."

"Still, I shouldn't have said—"

"My ex-wife and I tried to have kids for years," Gary said quietly. "We didn't have much luck. Eventually, we realised the doctors were right. I couldn't give her the family she wanted, no matter how much I wanted to. After she left, that's when the drinking started. Helped me block out the noise, you see. Problem was, the noise never went away, so I drank more and more. Cost me my career, my family and, yeah, it cost me the one last chance I had to have a son."

"Man, I'm sorry." James turned to him and said, "Blake never told me you were married."

"He doesn't know. It was a long time ago." Gary took another puff of his cigar. "When they told me I could adopt Blake, I was thrilled. Really, I was. But I wasn't that man anymore. Shit, I could barely take care of myself, and I knew it. So, the day I was supposed to sign the papers, I buried myself under the hood of some car and told the kid I was at a bar, too drunk to get to the meeting."

"You were hiding."

"Yeah, I was hiding alright, and I let him down. That's why I'm out here planting damn seeds in a stranger's field. Truth is, I don't know what the hell I'm doin'. I'm just trying not to let him down again."

"Well," James said, as he slumped back in his seat, "I don't care that you're planting seeds. That's not the reason I didn't want to help you. I guess I was afraid that if I helped you, then I was somehow admitting that my old life is over. Despite how much I complain, I actually love my life. I love my home, my university, my friends. You know, I'm a straight A student. I worked hard to get to where I am. Just feels like, if the world doesn't go back to normal soon, then all my hard work – everything I have ever done – will have all been for nothing."

Gary tipped his hat back and tapped the ash off his cigar. "The way I see it, maybe life will go back to normal, maybe not. Either way, all your knowledge, all that fancy stuff you can do… the world needs people like you. You're the future, kid."

"Thanks." James was humbled. He didn't know what to say. "That means a lot."

"Anytime."

"Chip?" asked James, as he reached out, holding the open packet.

"Sure." Gary grabbed a handful and shoved them in his mouth, only to cough, wheeze and spit them back out again. "Fuck me! They're disgusting!"

James shrugged. "I know. They're Emma's vegetable chips," he said, eating another one.

"Women," Gary said, shaking his head, "make even less sense than these damned dragons."

"They're not dragons," James said, with a smirk.

"Agree to disagree."

"Deal. Chip?"

"Get those things away from me."

"Okay."

"Can you hear that?" asked Gary. The rumble of a V8 engine coming down the driveway propelled the pair out of their chairs. "Sounds like they're back."

"It's about time!" James darted inside and headed for the front of the house. Will and Blake were already walking across the deck with bags slung over their shoulders when he came bursting out the door to greet them. "You won't believe what we found!"

"Was it a giant black dragon with four wings and two tails?" Will asked, tossing one of the bags to him.

James caught the bag and turned pale. "Wait – what? Another dragon thing?"

"Ha, thought they *weren't* dragons," Gary mocked, as he came outside and relieved Blake of one of the heavy bags.

"Yeah, another one. We saw it flying over the city. It was huge."

"Definitely not the one we saw last Saturday," Blake added.

"Hey, guys, this is Milky," Lila announced, as she squeezed between Will and Blake, holding the placid cat out for all to see.

"Ah, who's cat is that?" James screwed up his face. "This is the family member you went to get?"

"Yes," Lila replied, "isn't she cute?"

"You took all that risk for a cat?"

"Is this a problem?" Will asked.

Blake snickered. "He's allergic. That's why we didn't tell him."

James let out a violent sneeze, dropping the bag on the ground.

"Well, tough. Milky is family, and we don't leave family behind, do we Puss-Puss?" Lila nuzzled into the hesitant cat's face.

James tried to respond but was too busy sneezing to get a word out. Blake, Will and Lila made their way inside, leaving him on the deck to combat his allergic fit.

Emma walked onto the deck carrying a small potted sunflower. "Hey, you two, how was your day?"

"Just wonderful," Gary replied, giving James a heavy-hand-ed pat on the back, which only made his sneezing fit worse. "Except Jimbo, here, is allergic to cats."

"Oh, that's a shame. Milky is so cute, though!"

"Nice flower."

"It's Lila's," Emma said with a smile. "I'm gonna put it on the back deck where it can get some sun."

"Good idea," Gary agreed. James, still sneezing profusely, tapped Gary on the shoulder as Emma entered the house. "What?"

"The… the…" James sneezed again. "The trees!"

"Oh, shit!" For a moment, Gary had completely forgotten about the weird pods in the forest.

"Hey, guys?" Emma's concerned voice carried through the house. "What happened to the forest?"

James and Gary rushed inside and headed for the back deck. The rest of the group were already outside. "We were about to tell you…" James stepped through the back door to find every word fade from his vocabulary. "About the trees… What the hell?"

"Well, I'll be damned." Gary scratched his head in bewilderment. "That doesn't make sense." He pushed through the group to get a better look.

All the mysterious pods were now gone. In their place, fresh green leaves enveloped every tree in sight, with each trunk now a healthy dark brown. The sea of dead leaves covering the ground had vanished under a blanket of thick tall grass and an assortment of colourful flowers.

James didn't blink once; his mind was racing to make sense of it all. "The trees… They were almost dead a few minutes ago." A strong gust of wind left the picturesque forest swaying back and forth, as if it were waving to the stunned group of people staring at it.

"You boys care to explain this?" Blake asked, stunned.

"I wish we could, kid," Gary replied.

16

BROKEN

Upon returning to Castra Dam, Squad Seven disembarked from the Wombat to find themselves greeted by several military personnel. A pair of nurses tended to a visibly traumatised Amanda, who hadn't spoken since their ordeal in Broadbeach. They escorted her to a nearby medical tent. While Damien and Mitch sombrely went their own ways without obstruction, Lorcan found himself intercepted by three uniformed soldiers. "The colonel will not be debriefing you today, Captain Edwards."

"What do you mean, *not today?*"

"The colonel has taken a day's leave. No interruptions. His orders, sir."

"Like hell." Lorcan shoved his way past the soldiers and headed straight for Henrickson's office. When he arrived, he found two more soldiers standing guard by the door.

"The colonel won't be seeing anyone today, captain," the young woman informed him.

Lorcan held up the recovered licence. "You see this face? The lady in this picture is the colonel's wife. Either you step aside or I will move you. Either way, Sam and I are having a conversation."

Neither soldier budged, but before Lorcan could move them, the colonel called out from behind the door, "Let him in." As ordered, the two soldiers parted, allowing Lorcan to enter the office.

It wasn't the aroma of cigars or the bar-like stench that caught him by surprise. It was the colonel, Samuel Henrickson, himself. Clutching an expensive glass of whisky in one hand and a cigar in urgent need of an ashtray in the other, the colonel was hunched over his desk, with his tie loosened and his sleeves rolled up to his elbows. "You know I could have you arrested for insubordination."

Lorcan walked over and dropped Lisa's driver's licence on his desk. Henrickson lifted his head. His eyes were red, and his cheeks were flushed. He put down his glass and picked up the licence. "I was supposed to be there, you know. With them. I was on leave this week. Lisa thought I should spend some quality time with the girls before they got older. She didn't want me to miss out on them growing up."

"Why didn't you tell me who we were really looking for?" Lorcan asked.

"When I was on tour, Gracie was only three or four. She would stand by the window every afternoon and ask Lisa if I was coming home that day. Now, she barely says a word when I see her – too busy texting boys or watching whatever it is that kids watch now. Even Bia; she grew up so fast. Every time I came home, she was taller, smarter, funnier."

"Eight people died today," Lorcan bluntly interrupted, "seven of which my team could have extracted."

Henrickson leaned back in his chair and placed his wife's licence on the table. "What would you have done, Captain Edwards? If it was your family out there? If they were your little girls? I had to know if they were alive."

"My team risked our lives for you today. You should have come clean with us before we went in."

"You and I both know that military personnel are not to be deployed for personal operations. I would have been stripped of my command."

"You should be," Lorcan said through gritted teeth. "My men were nearly killed. That monster dropped a building with us inside it! Amanda – that civilian you forced into our squad – she almost fell out of a twenty-eight-storey window. She's a mess! You made the wrong call. We found survivors, colonel. Survivors that we could have saved. Should have saved!"

Henrickson opened his drawer and removed a Polaroid photo, then handed it to Lorcan. The picture was of two young girls and the colonel's wife, Lisa. "Bia was only seven years old, and Gracie was thirteen. Now, you take a good look at those faces, Edwards. Because I'd make that call all over again."

Lorcan dropped the photograph next to Lisa's licence. "I guess we're all haunted by faces now, colonel."

Henrickson picked up his glass and sipped his whisky. "Just go. Get out of here."

Lorcan obliged and headed for the door. "I'm sorry for your loss, Sam," he said sincerely, before leaving the room. The colonel poured himself another whisky to the click of the closed door. He picked up the Polaroid and stared at the three loving faces in the picture. "They were so happy that day," he thought, before knocking back the whole glass in one swig.

17

BLACK AND WHITE

A three-quarter moon shone over the Riley Farm like a white spotlight. James, Blake and Gary had planted themselves on the deck that afternoon and had barely moved from their chairs since they were too afraid to take their eyes off the lush trees across the creek.

"So, you're saying they were two metres tall?" Blake asked again, much to James's annoyance.

"For the twelfth time – yes!" James groaned. "They were hanging on the branches with these long slimy purple things. Actually, they kinda sounded like Gary's stomach after he eats stir fry."

"I'm just trying to get my head around this," Blake said, leaning back in his chair. "But if they were so big then wouldn't they be really heavy? How did the branches hold them up?"

Gary and James shot Blake a daft look. "That's what you're confused about?" James asked, shaking his head. "They turned the dying forest into the damn botanical gardens in a few minutes!"

"Shut up. I'm working that out, too."

"Hate to say it, boys," Gary said, mid-yawn, careful not to spill the cup of warm tea in his hand, "but I don't think we're gonna find the answers sitting on this deck."

"You're right," Blake agreed. "As soon as the sun comes up tomorrow, I'm gonna go in there and take a look."

"That's not what I meant."

"I'm coming too," James added, ignoring Gary's objection.

"Suit yourselves, ladies," Gary said with a shrug, then stood up from his chair. "I'm going to call it a night. A man needs his beauty sleep." Blake and James nodded then returned to their conversation.

Gary opened the back door and found Emma sitting by herself at the dining table, seemingly deep in thought. "Thanks for the tea, darlin'," he said, placing his cup in the sink.

Emma lifted her head and tried her best to smile, "You're welcome." It was clear by the streaks under her eyes that she had been crying.

Gary walked over and pulled out the chair opposite her. "You okay?" he asked, taking a seat.

"Yeah." A stray tear escaped down Emma's cheek, which she quickly wiped away. "I was just thinking about my friends. Wondering if they're okay."

Gary reached across the table and clasped her hands in his. "There is always hope."

Emma couldn't look at him or she risked totally falling apart, so she focused her eyes on the steam rising from her untouched cup of tea. "Two of my friends – Brooke and Michelle – they've been like sisters to me. I want to find them, but I have no idea where to start, and then there is Dad. He's still missing, and the trees in the backyard are now going crazy and—"

"It's overwhelming," Gary softly interjected.

Emma nodded and wiped away another tear. "I just don't know what I'm supposed to do now."

"Well," Gary gripped her hands tighter, "none of us knows what to do next. But whatever it is, we'll do it together. I can promise you that."

"Thank you," Emma said quietly, appreciating the warmth of his sentiment. "I'm so glad I found all you guys. I don't think I could do this alone."

Gary chuckled and said, "None of us could. But I think it's us that should be glad that we found you. Who knows where we would have ended up if we hadn't? You took us in. You saved us."

"We saved each other."

"That we did, darlin'," Gary smiled in agreement, "that we did." Letting go of her hands, he slid his chair back and stood up from the table. "I'll leave you to your thoughts."

"Thanks," Emma smiled back at him, "for what you said. It means a lot."

"Anytime." Gary winked before exiting the kitchen and making a beeline for the recliner in the lounge room. "Hah! You snooze, you lose, Jimbo," he praised himself, then settled into the soft cloud that was the armchair's black leather. Emma couldn't help but smile as she listened to him relish the childish victory.

⬦⬦⬦⬦⬦⬦⬦⬦⬦⬦

Standing side by side with the creek to their backs, Blake and James found themselves staring into the dense greenery of the forest. The early morning sunlight cascaded between the treetops in a heavenly fashion, providing the only patches of light under the dark canopy.

"You're sure these things aren't dangerous?" Blake asked.

"Nope," James answered with a shrug, "but all they did was hang from branches. They didn't really move."

"If they didn't move, then where the hell did they go?"

"Good point," James agreed, shuddering nervously at the thought.

"Hey! Wait for me!" Blake and James turned to see Emma hopping across the creek, waving at them. "You're not going without me!"

Blake wasn't as eager. "Not sure that's a good idea. We don't know what these pods are. They could be dangerous."

"Dangerous? Seriously?" Emma rolled her eyes at him. "A giant lizard is walking around that could show up at any moment and burn this place to the ground, unless, of course, one of its giant flying-snake cousins decides to devour us first. I'm thinking some big green egg things sound pretty good right now, don't you?"

Blake wanted to argue, but he knew it was pointless. "Fine. Suit yourself," he replied, turning back to the forest. "Okay then," he said, as he took a deep breath, "shall we?"

Emma pushed through the two boys and walked on ahead. Blake quickly followed her, leaving a hesitant James taking one last look at the farm behind them. "Guess that's a yes," he muttered rhetorically before jogging into the trees, eager not to let the others get too far ahead.

As the trio ventured deeper into the woods, the air grew thicker, damper and more humid, with a subtle fog-like haze sifting through the trees. Blake wasn't sure if it was condensation running down their faces, or sweat. Either way, it was uncomfortable and left him yearning for a cool breeze. Emma walked ahead, examining the assortment of colourful flowers as she went. In all her years at the farm, she had never before seen this kind of plant life. She wondered if they had grown there at one time, before countless hot summers had taken their toll on the aging forest. James trailed behind, studying each tree branch for any sign of the green pods from the previous day, but as he expected, there were none – just the deep brown branches and vibrant leaves they had left behind.

"How could they all just disappear?" Emma asked, as she stepped over a fallen branch. "Are you sure we haven't missed any?"

"Trust me, you can't exactly miss these things. They're pretty big," James assured her.

"The real question is, how did all of this grow so fast? You said they were killing the trees when you and Gary found them," Blake wondered aloud, investigating a thick green moss growing up one side of a tree trunk.

"Beats me! They sucked on the branches, the wood went grey, and all the leaves fell off," James recounted, ducking under a low branch. "Then you guys came home, and when we came back, everything looked like this."

"My neighbour's house isn't too far from here. Maybe they know something," Emma suggested. "They might have even seen where the pods went."

"Maybe," James said doubtfully.

Emma crouched beside some flowers that surrounded an old stump and ran her fingers along the red petals. "All these plants and flowers – I've never seen them grow here before. Do you think they're native?"

"How the hell would I know?" James asked. "I'm not a florist."

"You mean botanist, dumb-arse," Blake replied. He parted the trees and spotted a large clearing ahead. "I think we found your neighbour's house."

Emma took one last look at the unusual flowers before moving on. "Wait up for me," she called, jogging after the boys.

Blake and James emerged from the tree line to find themselves standing on freshly mowed grass. A ride-on lawnmower was parked alongside a brown timber barn. To the left of the barn was a faded blue house with white handrails, window frames and doors.

"Think anyone's home?" James asked.

Several muffled voices came from within the barn, which had both its tall wooden doors wide open. Emma followed the boys as they crossed the lawn and cautiously approached. Blake noticed an aluminium shed on the opposite side of the barn. Its dark grey paint was immaculate, and it was clear that the shed had been a recent addition to the property.

The trio stepped in front of the barn's open doors and looked inside. Two men and three women sat on green plastic chairs around a small white plastic table. They were chatting to one another, smiling and laughing, as they played a game of poker. It was only when one of the women spotted Emma, James, and Blake standing by the doors that the chatter became a murmur.

"Well, hi there," one woman said, as the other four lowered their cards with nervous looks on their faces. The trio just stared back at her; only James bothered to lift his hand for a wave. "Don't be shy," the woman said, standing up from the table to greet them. Her black curly hair stopped just above her shoulders and bounced as she walked. Her long summer dress was a similar blue to the faded walls of the house, even down to the white buttons and stitching. A pair of narrow reading glasses, which were attached to a beaded chain around her neck, sat perfectly straight on her nose. "Hi, my name is Patrice. Welcome to our home." She introduced herself with a big smile. "You three here for some medical treatment?"

"Huh? Medical treatment?" Blake asked, surprised by her question.

Patrice pointed at the dirty bandages wrapped around Blake's hands. "Yeah, sweetie, you're not here for the hospital? Didn't you see the sign out the front? *We can heal any wound!*" She reached down and grabbed his palm. Blake watched curiously as the odd woman began to unwrap the bandage around his left hand.

"Actually," Emma intervened, "I live next door. My name is Emma. This is Blake, and this is James. We just came to see if there was anyone still here."

"Oh, you're Thomas's girl!" Patrice's face lit up with delight. "Your dad has popped over to borrow a thing or two from time to time. He's a lovely man," she said, pulling the bandage off as she studied the deep gash along Blake's palm. "Oh, honey, that's an angry wound. Let's take a look at the other one," Patrice said, as she grabbed his right hand and unwrapped the other bandage.

"Are you a nurse?" James asked.

The happy lady let out a laugh before she looked at James. "Oh, dear heavens, no. I'm just a housewife with some *very* good medicine," she chuckled. The trio cracked half-smiles as Patrice's upbeat attitude made them unsure of how to take her. "Come with me. My husband is around somewhere. I'll make some tea, and we can get those wounds taken care of."

"Oh, that won't be necessary. I'll be fine," Blake politely declined. "We really didn't come here to bother anyone. We actually wanted to ask about—"

"Oh please, don't be silly. Trust me, young man. You want our help. Those cuts are not happy chappies – and you're not bothering anyone." Patrice pointed to the people at the table. "See these happy faces? My husband brought all these people here for medical treatment. Many of them were badly hurt by those monsters. Now look at them! All better!" One of the men raised his hand and gave a thumbs up of approval, but it didn't diminish Blake's reluctance.

"That would be great! Thank you, Patrice," Emma blurted out, before he could decline again.

"Great, it's settled. Follow me, please." Patrice led them out of the barn like a shepherd guiding her flock. Emma followed her closely, ignoring Blake's disapproving gaze as he and James trailed behind her.

As they crossed the yard, Blake noticed a teenage boy wrapping a heavy chain around the doors of the dark grey aluminium shed. After he clamped a padlock shut, the boy turned around to see Blake staring at him, which seemed to make him nervous, as he lowered his head and quickly walked away from the shed.

"I like to take my guests through the front door. It's more formal." Patrice led them around the side of the house, past a rotating washing line that was slowly turning in the wind, and towards the front yard. "Please excuse the mess, though. My husband and son have been very busy keeping our hospital stocked up and ready for lovely people like yourselves."

As they rounded the corner, a ute with its bonnet propped open was one of four cars parked under the large rusted carport. Scattered tools and fuel cans left lying on the floor seemed to indicate that someone was currently working there. A red brick driveway curved from the carport through an expertly maintained garden before joining up to the same quiet road that Emma's house was located on.

"Here we are!" Patrice walked them up to the big white door. "Please make yourselves at home," she said, opening the door with a polite smile.

Emma was the first to go in, followed closely by James and a hesitant Blake.

The sweet smell of baked goods made James smile from ear to ear, and he was instantly carried back to a time when his late grandmother would pack his lunchbox with an assortment of freshly made goodies. Emma looked around the living room: an old television with a DVD player on top sat across from a worn-out yellow couch and a coffee table. Blake took note of a fancy timber cabinet but was far more distracted by the large head of a crocodile mounted on the wall above it. "Is that real?" he asked, pointing to the reptile's head.

"Sure is," Patrice said proudly, as she stood behind him and gazed up at it. "My husband Rodney caught it on a fishing trip up north. Took him two hours to trap the darn thing."

"Blake hates hunting," James blurted out with a snicker.

"Oh, really?" Patrice turned to Blake and asked, "Have you ever hunted before?"

"No," Blake said bluntly.

"Well, you can't say you hate something if you have never tried it," Patrice said, with a pointed finger.

"Have you ever murdered somebody?" Blake asked her.

"Blake!" Emma snapped, hitting him on the arm.

"No, I have not," Patrice's smile faded, though she tried to maintain her polite manner.

"Well, me either, but let's agree that some things shouldn't be done." Blake was clearly not fussed by how rude he was being.

Keeping up appearances, Patrice's smile quickly returned before she turned her attention to James and Emma. "Please, have a seat, and I'll get my husband to fetch the magic cream. Oh, and I have blueberry muffins in the oven, too. Just relax. I won't be too long." She clapped her hands in joy before leaving the room.

As soon as the coast was clear, Emma scowled at Blake and gave him one more punch on the arm. "That was so rude!"

"Tell that to the crocodile," Blake whispered, trying not to laugh.

"So excited for these blueberry muffins," James cheered, rubbing his hands together.

"Really? With everything that's going on, you're excited for blueberry muffins?" Emma asked. "What about the pods we're supposed to be looking for?"

"Are you kidding? They can wait." James flopped back onto the yellow couch and said, "I don't know how many muffins I'll ever get to eat again."

"Unbelievable." Emma rolled her eyes and plonked down next to him.

Another ten minutes passed as the trio sat silently on the couch, waiting for Patrice to return. Eventually, the door to the next room swung open, but instead of Patrice, the teenage boy whom Blake had seen locking the shed stepped into the room carrying a jar of what looked like neon-green engine coolant.

The young man had freckled pale skin with ash blond hair. His faded yellow shirt coincidently matched the couch they were sitting on, but it was his brown leather sandals that caught the eye, mostly due to the fact that his jeans were rolled up to three-quarter length – which seemed to be a conscious fashion choice rather than a practical necessity. The boy looked at them awkwardly as he placed the jar of green liquid on the small table next to the kitchen doorway.

"Hey," Emma greeted him.

"H… Hey," the boy replied, too nervous to make eye contact with the pretty girl.

"What's your name?"

"Bernard."

"Nice to meet you. I'm Emma. This is James, and this is Blake," she said, as the two boys waved half-heartedly.

The rustle and clang of plates and cutlery came from the kitchen, along with the muffled sound of Patrice singing. Without uttering another word, Bernard scurried through the doorway to help his mother, leaving Emma feeling slightly bewildered.

"Hey, Em," James snickered, "do you think Bernard is a saint? Get it? Saint Bernard? It's a dog joke."

"If you were a dog, I'd have you neutered," Emma said, jabbing him with her elbow.

A moment later, Patrice entered the room carrying a tray with three blueberry muffins on a plate, followed closely by Bernard, whose tray held three steaming hot cups of cocoa. "Now, you have one muffin each. They are fresh out of the oven so be careful not to burn your mouth," Patrice said, placing the tray down on the timber coffee table.

"Thank you," Emma said politely.

"Yeah, thanks!" James reached out and snatched a muffin before Patrice's hands had even let go of the tray. Bernard sat his tray next to the muffins and quickly walked back to the doorway. Blake couldn't help but wonder why the strange boy was so nervous.

"Stand up, dear," Patrice said. "Let's get those hands sorted. It'll give your muffin a chance to cool down." Patrice picked up the jar of green liquid before strolling over to him. "And don't think I didn't notice that wound on your leg, young lady. We'll get to that next," she added, smiling at Emma.

Emma glanced down at the bandage covering her calf. The wound was a little sore, but she hadn't really given it a second thought.

Blake stood with both his palms open as Patrice opened the jar of thick green liquid. Bernard was perched like a lemur, watching intensely from the doorway. "What is this stuff?" Blake asked, as Patrice scooped the goo onto his left palm and rubbed it into the large gash.

"It's our own secret recipe," Patrice winked, as she massaged the green substance into his wound.

Before long, Blake's hand began to tingle, then turned completely numb. "I can't feel my hand," he told her. Emma looked at James to see his reaction but found that he wasn't paying any attention. Instead, he choked, coughed and then spat a piece of hot muffin into his hands, huffing and wheezing as he battled the intense heat burning the roof of his mouth.

"Your hands will feel strange, but trust me, sweetie, it will be worth it," Patrice assured Blake, as she rubbed the last of the green goo into his wound then reached for the bandages in her dress pocket. Sure enough, Blake quickly lost feeling in his right hand, too.

Patrice hummed a soft melody while she wrapped his hands in fresh bandages. "All done," she said with a wink of reassurance, before turning to Emma. "Okay, your turn, young lady. Stay seated, and lift your leg up on the table." She slid the tray of muffins to the side to make room.

Suddenly, the front door swung open with a loud thud, followed by the clonk of heavy footsteps. The trio peered over the back of the couch to see a large man standing in the doorway with a rifle in his hand. He had messy short black hair, a beard, blue jeans and a dirty red flannel shirt. "Is that blueberry muffins I smell?" the man asked excitedly, before noticing the strangers staring at him.

"Your muffin is in the kitchen, darling. There is warm tea in there for you, too," Patrice said, as she focused on rubbing the green gunk into Emma's calf.

"This is why I married you," said the man, and he chuckled as he leaned the rifle against the wall and kicked off his boots. "So, who are our new patients?" he asked with a friendly nod.

"Rodney, dear, this is Emma – you know, Thomas's girl from next door – and these are her friends, James and Blake."

"Oh, great! How's the old man doing?" Rodney asked, as he came over.

"We don't know," Emma said, causing the man's smile to fade. "He's been missing since the attack."

"Well, darlin', don't you give up. He's a tough son of a bitch, your old man is," Rodney said, then went to stand by Bernard, who now seemed even more uncomfortable. "Well, you probably made Bernie's day. He's a big fan of yours."

"Dad, shut up," Bernard snapped at his father with embarrassment.

"Bernie follows you on that Insta, Face, thing. Whatever you kids call that social media stuff. Heck, he's had a crush on you for years," Rodney said, letting out a loud chuckle at the expense of the humiliated young man next to him.

"You're such a jerk!" Bernard shouted, throwing a minor tantrum before storming out of the room and leaving his father with a rather amused smile on his face. Blake and James looked at Emma with mischievous grins as the sound of the back door slamming made it clear that Bernard had left the house.

"Rodney, did you really have to embarrass the poor boy?" Patrice asked, as she began to wrap a bandage around Emma's calf.

"Oh, come on. I was just playing." Rodney dismissed her with another chuckle. "The boy needs to toughen up a bit. He's too old to still be spitting the dummy like that."

"Oh, wow! I can't feel my leg either," Emma announced nervously, as all senses below her knee faded away.

Patrice finished wrapping the bandage and stood up. "There now, leave those bandages on for about ten minutes, and you should be good to go."

Patrice joined her husband by the kitchen doorway and gave him a peck on the cheek. Blake was beginning to wonder if their hosts were *all there* upstairs. "Ten minutes? So I'll be able to feel my hands again in ten minutes?" he asked, wondering why they had even let this stranger apply green slime to their wounds in the first place.

"Oh, yes, you will feel much better, dear," Patrice reassured him, but her eyes were busy watching James who was reaching out for another muffin from the tray. "Young man, there was one for each of you," she barked, startling him just as he was about to take a bite.

"She won't eat it anyway," James squabbled, pointing at Emma.

Emma shot him a sarcastic smile. "It's fine. He can eat it. I'm not hungry anyway."

James smiled back with pieces of muffin wedged in his teeth. "See?"

Patrice straightened her glasses and glared at James for a moment. "Right, then. Well, I'm going to take some cocoa to our other guests outside. Please relax. I'll be back in time to help take those bandages off." The three nodded, then she and Rodney left the room.

Emma shook her head at James, who had stuffed the second muffin into his gob and was now struggling to chew all the food in his mouth. She turned away and looked at her numb leg resting on the table. She couldn't even wiggle her toes. Next to her, Blake was staring at his hands when he, too, realised that he couldn't move his fingers.

"I can't feel anything. What do you think that stuff was?" he asked Emma.

"I have no idea, but I'm starting to freak out."

Blake then noticed James staring at him from the other end of the couch, holding the third and last muffin in his hands, waiting like a puppy for permission to eat it. "Just have it," he sighed.

"Thanks!" James didn't hesitate. He bit into the muffin, and a blueberry euphoria exploded in his mouth.

It was almost another fifteen minutes before Emma and Blake began to regain feeling in their bandaged limbs. Strangely, as relieved as she was to move her toes again, Emma found herself wondering about Bernard. He was odd for someone his age, almost childlike in some ways. Maybe he had been a sheltered child, or maybe his father had bullied him. Patrice seemed nice, but she, too, seemed rather out of touch. Not only that, but the family was just a bit too upbeat, given all that had happened recently.

The slam of a door closing turned the trio's attention to the kitchen doorway as Rodney and Patrice stepped into the room. "Okay, Blake, let's look at those cuts." Patrice clapped her hands in excitement.

"Ah, okay," Blake uttered, unsure of what the crazy lady expected to find after fifteen minutes. Reluctantly, he stood up and held his hands out, wriggling his fingers as Patrice walked over and began to unwrap the bandage on his right hand. Rodney watched with a grin of anticipation that left Emma feeling uneasy.

"What the hell?" Blake almost choked as he stared at his hand in disbelief.

"Good as new," Patrice said, as she turned his palm so that the other two could see. James and Emma turned pale. Blake's hand was perfectly healed. No gash, no scar – no sign that he had ever had a wound in the first place.

"How did you do that? What is that stuff?" Blake asked, as he frantically began unwrapping the bandage on his other hand.

"Magic," Patrice replied, as she winked at him.

Blake's left hand was the same. The large gash was completely gone, with no sign that it had ever been there. He looked down at Emma who had already begun to unravel the bandage around her calf. After removing it, she ran her hands over her skin. She, too, was healed. There was, however, one thing that was strange – a patch of long hairs had grown where the cut had been.

"How? What was that stuff?" Emma asked, looking up at Blake who was clearly just as confused as she was.

Rodney let out a deep laugh at the three lost faces staring at him. "Come on. I'll show you."

"Are you sure that's a good idea?" Patrice asked hesitantly.

"It's fine. They're our neighbours. They might even be able to help us. Two strong boys would be handy to have around if we're going to keep treating people," he assured her, though his wife seemed reluctant to agree.

"Okay, if you think it's best."

Emma, Blake and James couldn't hide their bewilderment, and Rodney seemed to be lapping it up. "Okay then, follow me. You're all looking like your heads are gonna explode."

Rodney escorted the trio through the kitchen and out a back door to the yard where they had first arrived. Passing the barn, which still contained a very active poker game, they arrived at the same dark grey shed that Bernard had been chaining up earlier.

The shed was quite narrow, with double doors that were almost the width of its frame. Rodney pulled a keyring from his pocket and unlocked the padlock, holding the thick chain around the handles. "My old man used to take me hunting when I was a boy. Nothing quite like the thrill of a good hunt, ya know. I tried to take Bernie out a few times, but the boy is more interested in his video games than doing real sports. Anyhow, I spent my whole life hunting until bloody cataracts took my eyes. I couldn't read, let alone shoot. Don't get me wrong. I wasn't blind. I could still see, but everything was real blurry." Rodney unwrapped the chain and pushed the shed doors open. "Come on in."

James, Emma and Blake glanced at each other as they curiously followed Rodney inside.

The shed was indeed narrow, but also longer than expected, with the far end shrouded in shadow. Along the left-hand wall was a mounted board with dozens of hand tools neatly hanging in their respective places. Below it, a large machete and several empty jars rested atop a timber sheet supported on an old rusty frame. Standing along the right-hand wall, an out-of-place bookshelf contained dozens of the same jars – only, these jars were filled with the same mysterious green substance that Patrice had administered to their wounds.

Rodney continued past the shelving and headed for the rear of the shed. "So, a couple of days ago, Bernie comes running inside yelling nonsense about something he found in the woods. The boy was really shaken. So, I grabbed my gun and that machete there, and went into the woods to find it. I walked for ten minutes straight and saw nothing. I almost came home, too. Thought the boy had lost the rest of his marbles until I saw something latched onto a big gum tree. This green egg thing had skin like a croc and was hanging off a branch with a slimy tentacle sorta thing. Thought I was seeing things. Anyway, I realised there were hundreds of the bastards, all around me! All the trees were nearly dead. Those things had sucked the life out of 'em."

"Yeah, we've seen them, too," James said. "That's actually what led us here."

Rodney flicked a switch on the wall. A yellow spotlight above them illuminated the shed, revealing a black plastic tarp hanging like a curtain by a thin wire at the far end.

"Anyhow, I took my blade to the closest one and cut straight through the purple cord it hung from. This green shit sprayed out of it, got right in my eyes, and stung like shit, too. By the time I got inside to wash it out, I couldn't feel my face. The wife panicked; she didn't know what to do. When I could finally open my eyes again… well, I couldn't believe it. I could see, dammit! I don't mean a little better either. I mean my cataracts were gone! Perfect bloody vision!" Rodney turned around and continued towards the rear of the shed. "So, I went back out to the woods, grabbed that thing by its purple tentacle and dragged its arse back here. For something so big, I couldn't believe how light the bloody thing was! It couldn't have weighed more than fifteen kilos."

"So, what happened to it?" Blake asked.

"Well, I dumped it in this shed here and went to find Patrice. When I came back, it was still sitting *where* I left it, but not *how* I left it."

"What do you mean?" Emma asked.

Rodney grinned and explained, "It wasn't no egg anymore. It was standing up. These things aren't eggs or pods, you see. They're animals. Big animals, with eight legs – like a fucking spider! It just stared at me with all those eyes. Good thing I had my gun. I blew off a few of its legs before it could make a move."

"So, what did you do with it?" James asked, not sure if he really wanted to know the answer.

"I kept it," Rodney said smugly, then reached out and pulled the black tarp to one side.

Emma, Blake and James gasped simultaneously. A green spider-like creature was chained by its limbs to the wall behind it, groaning, as the light shone over its countless eyes. Emma covered her mouth in shock as six of its eight legs had been dismembered.

Blake leaned closer. He wasn't sure *what* exactly he was looking at. Unlike a normal spider, this creature's head and body were one and the same – one perfect dome covered in big square scales that retracted to reveal dozens of eyes beneath.

Rodney reached a hand towards a group of the creature's eyes before it quickly closed its scales over them. "You see, each one of those scales has a cluster of eyes hidden behind it. The damn thing can open and close them as it wants. Full three-hundred-and-sixty-degree vision! Those scales are thick, too – real thick, like bulletproof thick!"

A purple tongue-like appendage hung from underneath the animal's domed body, leaving trails of saliva as it felt along the wall, seemingly looking for something to grab onto.

Eight dark green legs extended from under the domed body, each one covered in long coarse hairs up to its knee. After the knee, on the two legs that hadn't been shot off, was a green boot-like armoured shin made of the same thick green scales that covered its body.

James then pieced the puzzle together. When the creature's legs retracted into the dome-shaped body, its armoured shins formed the top of the pod's teardrop appearance, leaving only enough room for its tongue to emerge between them. This also explained how the pods came and went so quickly. The creatures had to scale a tree, attach themselves to a branch and hang upside down before folding into their pod-like state.

"Turns out that the green gunk running through their veins can heal almost any wound. Like I said, the green shell parts are as hard as a diamond, so you gotta cut through the soft part of the leg. The best part is, the limbs grow back pretty quickly, so it's a renewable resource. Can't tell you how happy we were. You know, with everything that's happened, we've finally found a way to help people. Patrice and I set the barn up with beds and put that hospital sign out front for any injured that passed by. Only a few people have come through. I've had to find most of our patients myself, but once we can get the word out, we'll help a lot of folks out there." Rodney moved back, allowing James and Emma to get a closer look at the creature.

"Is it in pain?" Emma asked.

"Well, it squeals like a bitch when I take its legs, so probably," Rodney cackled. "It's a monster though – 'bout time we got some revenge on these bastards."

Blake felt a large pit form in his stomach. "So, you just cut this thing up and bottle its blood?"

"You betcha! It's a lot of work, but it's worth it. We're doing a lot of good here."

"Right, you're just going to torture it," Blake sneered, "cut it up, then have a cup of tea while you wait for its limbs to grow back?"

Rodney glared at him. "I'm starting to sense a lack of appreciation from you, son."

James stepped in front of Blake with a surprised expression on his face. "Dude, are you serious? We don't even know what this thing is. Look at your hands. Look at her leg. This could help a lot of people."

Blake pointed to the creature in chains and asked, "And what does that make us? What kind of people are we? The ends don't justify the means."

"I'm sorry, man. You know I've always had your back. But you're wrong this time," James said, and looked painfully at his friend. "We don't even know what it is."

"What difference does that make?"

"Oh, come on," Rodney argued. "Son, you can still smell the smoke from the city blowing through the trees up here, and you're gonna defend this thing? Why do you care? These fucking things lost their rights when they burned our homes to the ground! When they killed innocent children!"

Blake confronted the big man and stared him down. "This thing didn't burn down the city. I know. I was there! This thing is innocent, but you're too fucking backward to see it."

"What did you just say to me?" Rodney grabbed Blake by his collar and raised his fist.

"Whoa! Everyone calm down," James urged, as he pulled the two apart and put himself in between them.

Rodney unclenched his fist and lowered his arm. "Emma, darlin', you need to take your ungrateful friend here and leave," he said, his eyes glaring into Blake's.

"Yes, of course, I'm so sorry," Emma apologised. "We're leaving right now." Grabbing Blake's arm, she dragged him behind her and made for the doorway.

"This idiot can't be serious?" Rodney said to James.

James stared at the creature hanging in chains. It was staring right back at him. "Please thank your wife for the muffins," he said, unable to take his gaze off the helpless animal.

"Just get out of my shed," said Rodney, and pointed to the door.

"Sure thing," James replied. He left the shed and jogged across the yard, eager to catch up to the other two and get back to Emma's farm.

Ahead, Blake entered the overgrown forest, rambling and cursing under his breath.

"Hey! Wait up," Emma called out, as she tried to keep up with him. Blake ignored her and continued on. "Hey, I said stop!"

Blake spun around and looked her in the eye. "Why didn't you say anything?"

Emma's face twisted. "What did you want me to say?"

"Oh, I don't know. Maybe that you think what he's doing is messed up? Or maybe that it's wrong to torture innocent animals?"

"I'm not so sure that what he is doing is wrong," Emma said quietly, as James finally caught up to them. "I mean, come on. This isn't black and white. It's pretty remarkable what that stuff can do."

"I agree with her," James said, out of breath from his short sprint.

Blake glared at him. "Yeah, you made your point perfectly clear," he said, then turned around and walked away.

"You know what?" James shouted. "You're a real arsehole when you don't get your way!" Blake didn't respond and kept walking. "He hates being wrong," James muttered angrily.

"Is he wrong?" Emma asked quietly, before walking off, leaving James standing by himself.

"Great. Just great." James threw his hands in the air, then jogged after her.

18

THE DRAGON AND THE ARCHANGEL

Lorcan heaved himself up to the top of the chin-up bar as the door at the far side of the room opened. Lowering himself down, he exhaled, not bothering to check who had entered before pulling himself up again.

"So, they turned the day-care room into a gym, huh," Mitch said, stepping over a pair of heavy dumbbells as he gazed around the room. A variety of children's toys, painted artwork and colourful plastic furniture had been stacked along the walls to make room for the half a dozen workout machines that now filled the day-care's floor space.

As the shirtless Lorcan continued his workout, Mitch noticed the many purple bruises covering most of his muscular torso and an 'R.I.P. David' tattoo below his right shoulder. "You should probably get a medic to check those broken ribs out," he said, fully aware of the response he would receive.

"You want something, Kay?" Lorcan grunted, finishing a final rep before dropping from the bar.

"We've got orders," Mitch replied. He grabbed a red towel from the shelf and tossed it to him.

Lorcan caught it and noticed a manila folder tucked under Mitch's arm. "What kind of orders?" he asked, before dabbing the sweat off his forehead.

Mitch pulled out the folder and handed it over. Lorcan flung the towel over his shoulder and flicked through the pages. Among them were four photographs – each a portrait shot of a different soldier.

"Missing squad?" Lorcan asked.

Mitch nodded.

Reading through the names, the last one caused him to pause. "Private Daniel Kay. Your brother?"

Mitch nodded again. "Yes, sir. My brother Danny and his squad were returning from a supply run when we lost contact with them on the M1."

"Colonel Henrickson approve of this yet?" Lorcan asked, closing the folder.

"No, sir, but I was going to request that he deploy our squad. Just wanted to run it by you first."

Lorcan handed the folder back to Mitch. "Get Damien and gear up. Meet at the Wombat in fifteen," he instructed.

"What about Henrickson?" Mitch questioned.

"A mission to find your missing brother. I have a feeling he won't have much to say about it."

Mitch nodded and said, "Thanks, captain."

"You have fourteen and a half minutes left. Move it."

"Yes, sir!" Mitch snapped to attention, tucked the folder under his arm and quickly made for the door.

Lorcan pulled the towel off his shoulder and wiped his face. "Don't thank me yet," he thought, as the young soldier exited.

〰〰〰〰〰〰〰

With Mitch at the wheel, the ATV-X sped down the M1 motorway, bulldozing through any vehicle that got in the way.

In the rear cabin, Damien watched as Amanda clenched her eyes shut and gripped her seat tighter with each shunt and bump.

"So, Civi, you got a death wish or something? I was expecting you to be hiding under a desk or something after yesterday," Damien said, handing her a Kevlar vest.

Amanda slid the vest over her head and didn't bother to look at him. "I am assigned to this squad," she said quietly, still clearly shaken from the ordeal. "I just want to help stop all of this."

Damien loaded a clip into his rifle and sat opposite her. "So, you think what we do out here... you think it actually makes a difference? That's cute," he said with a chuckle. "Soldiers don't make a difference, Civi. We don't even make our own decisions."

Lorcan stood at the rear of the cabin, holding onto the support brace above him. He knew Damien's words were born of frustration, and he was usually cynical. But after losing eight people the previous day – seven of whom they could have saved – he found himself agreeing with the disgruntled soldier.

"So, why join the army then?" Amanda asked.

Damien grinned. "I like to shoot stuff," he said, knowing it wasn't the profound answer she was prodding him for.

Amanda sighed and slumped back against the armoured wall. "Very heroic."

"No such things as heroes or villains, Civi." Damien stood up. "Just circumstances and choices," he added, then moved over to the Wombat's turret controls.

Amanda glanced down at her hands; they were shaking. She quickly tucked them under her arms so no one would notice, but Lorcan was already staring at her. Amanda waited for him to say something, but he didn't. He just looked away and ignored it.

The Wombat rammed through another wrecked car as Mitch announced their arrival over the intercom. "Captain, we have a military vehicle up ahead. It's on fire, sir."

Lorcan moved to the middle of the cabin as they came to a halt. "Okay, Seven, this is our stop. Watch your arses! We have no idea what we're walking into here."

"Roger that." Damien hit the touchpad and the armoured door retracted. A waft of burning flesh blew through the cabin, forcing Amanda to cover her nose. Damien and Lorcan disembarked and checked their immediate surroundings. The sight of a burning military truck was one that no soldier ever wanted to see.

"We have bodies, sir," Damien reported, gesturing to three motionless soldiers next to the burning wreck.

"No, no, no! Daniel?" Mitch climbed out of the Wombat and raced to the bodies. "It can't be him! It can't be him! It can't be—"

Damien was about to pull Mitch away when Lorcan placed a hand on his chest. "Let him be," he said, gently pushing him back.

Mitch rolled the first soldier over. It wasn't his brother. Surveying the body, he immediately noticed a bloodied hole in the man's chest – a bullet hole.

"These damn monsters have to go," Damien muttered, grinding his teeth.

"Monsters didn't do this," Lorcan said, staring into the flaming wreck.

"What do you mean?"

"The bodies…" Amanda interrupted, as she finally stepped out of the ATV-X. "They don't leave bodies."

"That thing turned people to ash," Lorcan agreed. "The truck is on fire, but it's not melted. Not to mention, there is a single bullet hole in the left passenger door, but I bet if you walk around to the right-hand side, you'll find that it's riddled with them."

Damien's eyes widened. Lorcan was right. The longer he stared at the wreck, the more the signs of a human ambush revealed themselves.

"Captain! This man was shot," Mitch cried out, further confirming Lorcan's observations. Mitch turned the next body over. The young man's face felt cold. It wasn't Daniel, either.

"Spread out," Lorcan ordered. "We need to know what happened here."

Damien and Amanda split up and began to check the surrounding area.

Mitch tended to the third body, dropping to his knees at the sight of the woman's familiar face. It was Sarah. Having gone through basic training together, Sarah had been friends with the Kay brothers for years. "No, Sarah, not you, too."

Damien circled the truck and rejoined Lorcan. "All their weapons are gone, captain. Looks like whoever did this took them," he reported.

"Why would they take their guns?" Amanda asked, immediately feeling naive as the answer then dawned on her.

Mitch stumbled back from Sarah's body. "Where is my brother?" he asked himself, but there was only one body left. Among the flames of the burning truck, a lone soldier was slumped over the steering wheel. "Daniel?" Mitch dropped his rifle and ran for the wreck, only to be quickly restrained by Lorcan and Damien. "I have to get him out! I can't leave him! Let go!" he cried, and thrashed about in their arms as tears cascaded down his face.

"There is nothing you can do, mate," Damien said gently. "He's already gone."

"I can't leave him there," Mitch said, as his strength seemed to leave him. Lorcan and Damien loosened their grip, watching as their distraught squad mate fell to the ground. Amanda rushed to his side.

"Stay with him," Lorcan whispered to Damien, before turning his attention to the two-lane overpass ahead.

"The bridge made for a perfect ambush spot," he thought. Sure enough, the underside of the bridge was riddled with holes, likely from what little fire the soldiers managed to return. Lorcan took the ramp up and made his way across the overpass, stopping at the railing to run the attack through his mind. Judging by the series of bullet holes down the right-hand side of the truck, the ambushers would have opened fire from where he was standing. Lorcan glanced down at his boots: a trail of bullet casings confirmed his suspicions. He followed the shiny breadcrumbs which ultimately led to a pair of muddy tyre tracks at the far end of the overpass. The tracks indicated that a vehicle had stopped, turned around and left the bridge the same way it had come. Lorcan's eyes followed the tracks to a service road that ran alongside the highway. A mound of dirt that had spilled onto the road seemed to be the cause of the muddy tracks, which continued onward to a nearby industrial estate.

~~~~~~~~~~~~~

Moving in tight formation, Squad Seven followed the service road to a slew of factories and warehouses. Lorcan took point while Mitch and Damien hung back to guard the rear, leaving Amanda tucked in the middle.

"You sure you're up for this?" Lorcan quietly asked Mitch, who had barely spoken a word since he'd been shown the tyre tracks on the overpass.

Mitch's eyes were still watery and bloodshot. "I'm fine. Just wanna find these bastards," he said, moving up on Lorcan's left side.

The industrial area was eerie, to say the least. Trucks waiting to be received at open gates, vans full of undelivered goods, and company cars abandoned on curbs, driveways or in the street were all caked in a layer of ash that the wind had carried over. A dump truck full of gravel, with its rear box inclined, had spilled its cargo into an overflowing container in a nearby yard. Another site had a crane with a long steel beam still suspended in the air, slowly turning in the wind. It was as if someone had hit the world's pause button.

A white delivery truck abandoned at the side of the road brought Lorcan to a stop; it looked familiar. He signalled Mitch and Damien to flank the vehicle while he cautiously approached the open rear doors. Several bullet holes in the right-hand side of the truck cast beams of dusty light through the rear storage compartment. Lorcan switched his rifle's spotlight on and immediately noticed a green plush toy sitting in the corner. It was a dinosaur – Jack's dinosaur. This was the same truck he had left the Marsh family in, a couple of days earlier. Lorcan rushed to the front cabin and yanked the driver's door open. A dirty white baseball cap toppled out and landed by his boot.

"Poor bastard," Damien muttered, glancing over Lorcan's shoulder at the body inside.

"Yeah…" Lorcan stared at the young man bent over the steering wheel. The blood-stained seats were peppered with bullet holes and shards of glass from the shattered windshield. "I told him to go straight to the refuge centre," Lorcan said, as he crouched down and picked up the boy's baseball cap. He placed it on the dash and shut the driver's door.

"Nothing here, sir, just some kid's toy," Mitch reported as he walked over, holding Jack's green dinosaur.

Lorcan took the toy and noticed a bloody smudge down the side of its face.

"You okay, captain?" Amanda asked, trying to read his face.

"We need to find who did this," Lorcan said, stuffing the dinosaur into his thigh pocket. "Move it!"

"Yes, sir," Damien acknowledged before taking point.

As the squad regained formation, Amanda kept low and tucked herself in behind Lorcan. Something was off with the captain. The van had spooked him, but she didn't know why.

Squad Seven passed several blocks before Damien raised his hand and signalled them to stop. "Captain, we've got movement ahead," he whispered, leading the squad behind the cover of an old sedan.

Standing in the carpark of the next warehouse, a group of men were smoking cigarettes as they laughed and joked among themselves. A woman's horrifying scream echoed from the warehouse's open roller door, interrupting their banter, but only briefly. The three men quickly went back to their conversation and continued their mockery of one another.

Lorcan peered over the sedan's bonnet and pointed to a hedge that ran the length of the warehouse yard. "Keep low. We use the bushes for cover," he whispered. Damien and Mitch nodded in agreement. Lorcan turned to Amanda and said, "You stay here. Don't move!"

"Okay," she complied.

The three soldiers crept around the back of the sedan and made their way towards the warehouse, taking advantage of any available cover until they reached the hedge.

Amanda watched through the sedan's dusty windows as Damien, Lorcan and Mitch positioned themselves directly in front of the three smoking men on the other side of the hedge. Another agonising scream came from inside, but the banter didn't stop this time.

Using the scream as cover, the three soldiers leapt over the hedge and tackled the three men to the ground. Lorcan pinned the man in the middle to the pavement before knocking him out with a hefty punch. Damien choked the man on the left while Mitch clocked the man on the right with the butt of his rifle. Seconds later, all three men were unconscious, lying next to their half-smoked cigarettes.

Amanda exhaled in relief as the soldiers came back into view over the hedge.

With their rifles at the ready, Lorcan, Mitch and Damien cautiously made their way inside, ducking under a partially open roller door.

Sunlight filtering through several skylights provided the only light in the building, but it was enough to see that the place was a complete mess. Empty bottles of alcohol were scattered amongst hundreds of cigarette butts littering the floor. Dozens of empty beer bottles and confectionary wrappers covered an old wooden table in the middle of the room. A corroded old ute was parked near the left-hand wall. Full of rust and cobwebs, it had clearly been there for quite some time. Other than some flimsy shelving along the right-hand wall, the rest of the warehouse was mostly empty.

The squad stopped several feet from the table and looked at a pair of red doors along the rear wall. The door on the left had a green 'Exit' sign mounted on the wall above, while the door on the right had 'Maintenance' etched into it.

"Sir!" Mitch pointed to four military issue rifles leaning against the wall near the exit. "Squad Twelve's missing weapons."

"Gonna kill these arseholes," Damien said, fingering his trigger.

With a loud creak, the maintenance door opened and another scream escaped from the room. A tall muscular silhouette closed the door and began heading towards them. The squad raised their weapons and kept their sights firmly locked onto the shadowy figure.

"Can I help you, gentlemen?' the man asked aloud, laughing at the sight of his intruders.

"Get on your knees! Hands on your head!" Mitch barked.

The silhouette emerged from the shadows and approached the wooden table. The skylight above revealed the man's long silver ponytail and muscular physique. "Now, tell me, do I look like the kind of man who gets on his knees?"

Seemingly in his fifties, the man's long grey hair and unkempt goatee matched the rest of his haggard appearance. With scuffed black boots, filthy denim jeans and a singlet stained with so much blood that it was more red than white, the man was utterly unnerving.

"So, what can I do for you boys?" he asked, casually pulling a cigarette from his pocket with his bloodied fingertips.

"You have five seconds to get on the ground," Lorcan warned him.

The man put the cigarette in his mouth and flicked his lighter open. "Five... four..." he mocked. The tobacco sizzled alight, revealing a tattoo that covered the left side of his face – a long serpent-like dragon, with its jaws draped around the man's eye, while its long body coiled over his cheek before the tip of its tail touched his chin. "Three... two... one... nothing?" he said with a grin. "Thought so."

"We're not asking again, arsehole," Damien shouted.

"Hold that thought. Hey, boys," the man shouted, "bring out my little buddy! We've got guests."

"No! Not my son – please!" a woman screamed, as the maintenance door opened once more. Four silhouettes exited the room. Lorcan made out three adults, while the fourth appeared to be a child. Sure enough, three men, dressed in flannelette attire and armed with handguns, emerged from the shadows and joined them at the table. One of the men was holding a squirming young boy by the wrist. It was Jack.

Mitch and Damien aimed their rifles at two of the armed men while Lorcan kept his sights on the one holding Jack at gunpoint. "Let him go. I swear to God, I'll blow your head off!"

"Hah!" Everyone relax," said the man with the dragon tattoo. "Listen, fellas, we're just a couple of blokes letting off a little steam."

"Is that what you call ambushing a military vehicle," Damien growled, "and killing four innocent men?"

"Hey, now, one was a woman," the man said with a wink.

"Give me the kid," Lorcan said bluntly.

The man walked over to Jack and kneeled before him. "What's your name, son?" he asked.

The boy was trembling as he replied, "J… Jack."

"Nice to meet you, Jack." The man clasped the boy's hand and shook it. "My name is Gabriel."

"I wanna see my mum." Jack began to cry.

"Oh shoosh," Gabriel said, as he wrapped his bloodied fingers around the boy's cheeks and squeezed them together. "Real men don't go running to their mothers. Are you a real man, Jack?"

Lorcan's finger skimmed the trigger as he kept his sights locked on the man with the gun to Jack's head. He just needed an opening.

"Do you like stories, Jack?" Gabriel asked, still clenching the boy's face. "Of course, you do! Let me tell you a story. So, I'm in this bar, keeping to myself, just having a drink. And this hot little bitch comes up next to me and asks the bartender for a couple of vodka somethings. Hmmm, she smelt like strawberries. You like strawberries, don't you, Jack? Anyway, I reached over and whispered something in her ear. I can't tell you what, Jack – it was a little naughty." Gabriel paused to take a long drag of his cigarette. "Guess what this bitch did? She slapped me and left the bar! Crazy! Right?"

"I like this girl already," Damien said, still aiming at one of the armed men.

Gabriel flinched at the remark. It seemed to irritate him, but he didn't take his eyes off the young boy. "So, Jack," he continued, "when a woman treats you like that, you don't just let her walk away. You're a fucking man, Jack! So, I followed her little arse outside to give her a chance to make up for the way she acted. I'm a reasonable guy, you know. But that little bitch wouldn't even stop. She tried to run! I caught her, though. Oh, yes, I did. Got a little carried away, I did. She wasn't that pretty when I was done, Jack."

"Let the kid go," Mitch said calmly.

Gabriel twisted Jack's face until he was looking at the three soldiers. "You see, Jack, men like this hide behind rules and ridiculous laws. Men like this, Jack, wanted to put me away for killing that bitch – even though she deserved it. They don't get it, Jack. Not like we do. But they will. You'll see. When the police were taking me away in that van, I prayed. That's right; I prayed for my freedom. For all freedom." Gabriel turned Jack's face towards him and pressed the boy's forehead against his own. "And do you know what happened, Jack?"

"No…" Jack started crying.

"My prayers were answered. By him," said Gabriel, and pointed to the dragon tattooed on his face. "He came and freed me, Jack. He melted those doors off that van, and when I stepped out into the world, all those rule-following, law-pushing, self-righteous pricks were turned to ash. He's here because of me, Jack. Because of my prayers."

"This guy is batshit crazy," Damien whispered.

Gabriel finally let go of Jack's face, leaving a bloody streak across the boy's cheek. "Oh, shit. Sorry about that, Jack. I left a bit of your daddy on you." He sucked his bloody thumb clean and wiped the smear off Jack's face.

"Where are the others?" Lorcan asked.

Gabriel stood up and faced him with an unnerving grin. "Can you be more specific?"

"Where are the other survivors from the truck?" Lorcan demanded. "What did you do with them?"

"You still don't get it, do you? There are no rules anymore. No police. No government. None of that equal rights bullshit all the sheilas used to rant about. The only rule that matters now is the oldest one of all – survival of the fittest. Take what you want, from who you want."

"Does that mean I can shoot him now, cap?" Mitch asked, frustrated by the current standoff.

Gabriel smiled. "Clearly, the big man is upset about the boy. You want the boy? You can have him," he said, then nodded at the man holding Jack hostage. The man lowered his gun and shoved the kid forward.

Crying hysterically, Jack ran straight to Lorcan and hid behind the soldier's leg.

Lorcan checked that Jack was behind him and then turned back to Gabriel, saying, "The others – let them go."

"The two girls?" Gabriel exhaled smoke from his nostrils and shook his head. "Nah, the girls are ours. I haven't even had any fun with them yet. Like I said, fellas, no rules." He flicked his cigarette on the ground and put it out with his boot. "Now, you can leave with the kid or we kill you three and shoot the kid for fun. Up to you, fellas. What will it be?"

Amanda, who had grown tired of waiting by the sedan, leaned around the open roller door and saw Jack crouched behind Lorcan's leg. Amanda waved, quietly mouthing for the boy to come to her. Jack nodded, then ran as quickly as his little feet could take him. Lorcan glanced back just in time to see Amanda lean in, scoop the boy up and take him outside.

Gabriel licked his lips. "Oh, I see you got a lady of your own there. Tell you what, let me have some of that, and you can take the bitch I've got in the back room. She's a bit busted up, but all the important stuff works."

"Actually, I got something else for ya," Damien said, as he whipped a grenade from his belt, flicked the pin and pegged it between Lorcan's legs. The grenade bounced along the ground and rolled right up to Gabriel's boot.

"Bastard!" Gabriel snatched the man who had held Jack hostage and tripped him to the ground, over the explosive. Lorcan, Mitch and Damien darted left and dived over the rusty ute as the grenade detonated. Shrapnel and body parts exploded over the warehouse like bloody confetti. Gabriel made a break for the exit, leaving the other two men firing their weapons blindly as they, too, tried to flee.

Lorcan popped up and fired several rounds, dropping the pair instantly. Awakened by the gunfire, the three men who had been left unconscious in the parking lot charged into the warehouse with firearms drawn. Mitch and Damien came out from behind the old ute and took them down before they even noticed the soldiers were there.

"He escaped out the back! You two get after him!" Lorcan clambered over the bonnet and headed for the maintenance door at the back of the warehouse. Mitch and Damien acknowledged his order and sprinted towards the red door with the 'Exit' sign. As the pair barged outside in pursuit of Gabriel, Lorcan kicked the maintenance door open and entered the room.

The stench hit him right away – the stench of a dozen decaying bodies. Each one was slumped forward, but held up by chains that bound their hands to the grey brick wall behind them. Each of their faces had been beaten beyond recognition.

"Help us," a woman's frail voice said softly.

Lorcan turned to see Samantha and her young daughter, Mindy, chained to the right-hand wall. He raced over and quickly tended to them. Samantha had been badly beaten. Her face was purple, and her left eye was almost consumed by swelling. Her legs, arms, and shoulders were covered in scratches, while her clothes were bloodied and torn. Her daughter, Mindy, was shaking but seemingly unharmed.

"I need both of you to close your eyes," Lorcan said, as he aimed his rifle at the bolt holding Mindy's chains to the wall. "This is going to hurt your ears. Sorry, kid."

He fired a single round, and the chains dropped to the ground.

"Daddy!" The little girl frantically began crawling across the floor towards the back wall. Lorcan fired another round into the bolt holding Samantha's chain in place.

"Barry!" Samantha cried out, before feebly crawling across the floor towards her daughter. Lorcan attempted to help her up, but she pushed him away. "Barry…" Samantha grabbed

Mindy and hugged her tight, diverting her attention from one of the lifeless bodies chained to the wall. That was when Lorcan recognised the dead man's clothing. It was Barry Marsh.

"Captain! We lost Gabriel," Mitch reported, as he entered the room. "Oh, my God," he stammered, gasping at the horrendous sight.

"Civi and Jack are secure," Damien announced, then covered his mouth from the stench as he stopped in the doorway. "Jesus, what did those bastards do?"

"Call it in," Lorcan ordered. "Medical evac. They're coming with us. We're not leaving them here. Any of them."

"Yes, sir," Damien sombrely acknowledged.

19

THE MONSTER IN SHACKLES

"Where would we go?" Lila asked, tucking the warm blanket around her neck.

Will, seated on the edge of the bed, looked at her glumly. He didn't have an answer.

Since returning from their trip home the previous day, the couple had spent most of their time tucked away in Emma's spare bedroom. The rather narrow room felt claustrophobic, with countless boxes of old belongings stacked along every wall surrounding the double bed. Most of them were marked 'Emma'. The sight of another flying monster and the discovery of the Riley Farm's new Amazon forest had locked the couple in a debate of what to do next.

"I don't know," Will eventually said. "Maybe south? We need to get away from all this. We could head for Sydney."

"How do we know that it's not just as bad down south?" Lila countered. "What if it's worse?"

"Honey, look at the trees across the creek," Will said, as he stressfully ran his fingers through his long brown hair. "All that from some big scaly egg things. I can't keep you safe here. Everything is getting weirder and weirder."

Lila sat up and leaned against the wall, dragging the bedspread with her. "I know, but at least we have each other."

"Each other?" Will scoffed. "What can the two of us do here?"

"I meant all of us."

Will shook his head in frustration and said, "All of us? Honey, we don't even know these people. They just spent the day out in the woods and have barely said a word since they got back."

"Well, maybe they didn't find anything out there," Lila said. "I'm sure they would tell us if we asked them."

"I don't know." Will sighed, then said, "I don't trust that Blake guy. Just something about him."

"He's just a quiet guy," Lila said, snickering at Will's sour expression. "Don't be so judgemental."

"Fine," Will replied, wanting to stay on topic. "So, where should we go?"

Lila reached over and held his hand. "I think we should give this place a shot. I know you're trying to keep me safe, but I feel safer here, right now. There has been no sign of rescue, no sign of any police, no medical aid. If things were better south, then why hasn't someone come to help?"

Will hated to admit it, but she had a point. "Okay," he said, "we'll stay – for now. But you have to promise me that if things start to get too dangerous here, then we leave. Deal?"

Lila's smile widened. "Deal," she said, pulling him closer before kissing him. The couple's loving moment was quickly interrupted as Milky leapt onto the bed and nestled between them. "See, Milky likes it here, too."

Will looked at the purring white cat scornfully. "Taking her side, huh?"

"Oh, honey," Lila laughed, "there is only my side."

Near midnight, Blake stood at the kitchen table checking over his equipment: a flashlight and one set of bolt cutters – hardly the gadgetry of a secret agent about to perform an impossible mission. Dressed like a cat burglar, in black sneakers, shorts and T-shirt, his messy blond hair and pasty legs seemed even paler than usual.

"Are you sure about this, kid?" Gary asked, as he watched the determined young man stuff his equipment into a navy-blue backpack.

Blake zipped up the backpack and slung it over his shoulder, saying, "I know what you're thinking, but I can't let them torture that thing – even if I don't know what that thing actually is. I just can't stand by and let that happen."

"Fair enough. But are you sure you don't want to let the others in on your little plan?"

"I'm not bringing Emma and James into this. They don't agree with me anyway."

Gary nodded, but obviously didn't agree. "And what about Will and Lila? They don't even know about the monster in the shed. Don't you think you should at least tell them about the green gunk in those jars and what it can do?"

"I'll tell them tomorrow. Let them sleep tonight."

"You had all day to tell them about it, kid, and you haven't. Why keep them out of it?"

"Because I don't have time to run this by a committee," Blake muttered, eager to end Gary's inquisition. "That thing needs help."

"This ain't a committee. They have a right to know."

"I don't have time for this right now," Blake snapped. "Can we drop it?"

"Sure thing," Gary conceded, taking a step back from the table.

"So, how do I look?" James asked, as he entered the kitchen wearing a black tracksuit and a pair of black sneakers, but it was the black stocking pulled over his face that made Blake and Gary look sideways at him.

"Like an idiot," the pair answered in unison.

"What are you doing here? And why do you have that over your head?" Blake asked.

"Oh, this?" James said, as he pointed to the stretched pantyhose over his face.

"Hey! Is that my stocking?" Emma asked, as she stepped into the kitchen and whipped the hosiery off James's head. "Do you know how expensive these are?" She, too, was wearing only black attire – a pair of yoga pants, sneakers and a T-shirt.

"Wait!" Blake objected. "What are you two doing? Why aren't you asleep?"

"Well, I knew that you'd be too stubborn to let this go, so I decided to come with you," James said, before nodding towards Emma. "No idea what she's doing here, though."

Emma ignored him. "Well, I also knew that you'd be too stubborn to let this go. And, I also knew that *he* would be too stupid to let you go alone. So, I'm coming too! Someone has to keep an eye out and make sure that you two don't get yourselves shot."

"Keep an eye out…" James grinned from ear to ear. "Emma, you're a genius! I'll be right back," he blurted out, before dashing out of the room.

"I don't get it," Blake said with a confused shrug. "You both think that Rodney is doing the right thing, so why are you helping me?"

"I don't know what I think yet," Emma said, "but we need to stick together. You're not going in there alone."

"She's right," Gary agreed. "I'll feel better knowing you're looking out for each other, too."

"I knew this would come in handy!" James raced back into the kitchen and plonked his drone on the dining table.

Blake sighed. "And what are we gonna do with that?" he asked.

"It's gonna be our eyes in the sky," James replied with a grin.

"How are you going to fly that *and* sneak into the shed with us?"

"I'm not. Emma can go with you, and I'll stay here and guide you guys in."

"That's a great idea," Emma piped up. "Dad keeps some old two-way radios in his room for emergencies. We could use those to talk to you."

"Sweet!" James enthusiastically agreed.

"Great," Blake muttered. "Knew I should have snuck out earlier."

"Well, this ought to be interesting," Gary said restlessly, unsure if he should be supporting their behaviour or trying to talk them out of it, but knew that the latter idea would be pointless.

∞∞∞∞∞∞∞∞∞∞∞

A short while later, James dragged one of the old chairs across the back deck and settled into it. "Night vision on, spotlight off," he mumbled, tapping several buttons on the tablet's screen.

The back door opened and Gary stepped out, holding a bottle of whisky and two glasses. "Care for a co-pilot?"

"Where did you find that?" James asked.

Gary pulled a chair over and sat next to him. "Will brought it here from his place. Left it on a table in the living room. Figured he wouldn't mind."

The answer was good enough for James. "Well, then, you're on radio duty. Buckle up, co-pilot. This bird is ready for take-off." The drone lifted off the deck and rose into the air with a low hum. "You better pour me one of those, too."

Blake and Emma were already standing at the edge of the moonlit forest, waiting for James to radio the go-ahead.

"You sure you wanna do this?" Blake asked her. "Rodney has a gun, you know."

"Can't be worse than what we've been through, right?" Emma said, checking her ponytail. "Besides, I thought about what you said to Rodney – about what kind of people we become. To be honest, I don't know who I am anymore. But I do know that I want to do the right thing, and I think setting that thing free is right."

"Okay then," Blake said, slightly surprised. "I guess we better go save a monster, then."

"This is Eagle One to Eagle Two. We are good to go. I repeat, the mission is a go!" James's voice crackled over the radio.

Blake raised the radio to his mouth and replied, "Roger that, Idiot One."

"Huh? That's Eagle One, I said."

"We're not calling you that. Over and out," Blake responded.

"You suck. Over and out."

Blake and Emma turned their gaze upward as a silhouette resembling James's drone flew overhead and disappeared above the treetops. The pair quickly jogged into the trees and flicked their torches on. As they made their way through the forest, Emma couldn't help but feel dazzled by the sheer variety of plant life shimmering under her light. It was as if the forest was constantly flourishing, with countless new flowers and bushes now growing along the same path they had taken that morning.

Blake, however, was less enthralled by the rainbow of flora and more interested in looking out for any reptilian creatures that might be sneaking up on them. He waved his torch back and forth, constantly checking their surroundings as he led them deeper into the woods.

"Still haven't seen any pods around here," Emma noted, shining her light over several tree branches.

Blake cautiously stepped over a log, also pointing it out to Emma. "Watch your step. I don't think we'll see pods here. Seems like after they've done their thing to the trees, they leave the area, probably to find the next spot."

"Still can't believe what they can do," Emma added. "Just look at this place. Look at your hands. It's pretty amazing."

"Yeah, that's some blood they're carrying around."

"But why do the pods nearly kill the trees before healing them? Remember, Rodney and James both said that all the trees had turned grey – that they looked almost dead when the spider things disappeared."

"Probably the same reason that you lost all feeling in your leg before your cut healed. I mean, I couldn't feel my hands for ten minutes either. It must be something in the way their abilities work. Doubt we'll ever know for sure, though." Blake then noticed a distant light shining through a gap in the foliage ahead. "Looks like we're here," he said.

"Oh no, they must still be awake," Emma whispered.

The pair switched their torches off and carefully approached the edge of the forest. About half a dozen spotlights illuminated the exterior of the house, most of them shining upon the path between the barn and the shed holding the spider monster captive.

"James, we've reached the house," Blake radioed in.

"Right above you."

Emma and Blake glanced up to see the drone hovering high above the house.

James zoomed his camera out and studied the image on screen. He had a full bird's-eye view of Rodney and Patrice's farm. Gary was leaning over his shoulder, trying to decipher what little of the imagery his aging eyes could make out.

"I can see movement at the shed," James warned them.

Blake and Emma could see it, too. The shed's doors were opening as Rodney and Bernard stepped out, carrying two crates of jars containing green blood.

"Um, Blake, Farmer John and Freak Boy just stepped out of the shed. Looks like they're carrying a fresh batch of magic blood."

"Yeah, we see them, too," Blake responded. He and Emma peered around the trunk of a large tree, watching until Rodney and Bernard were inside the house.

Careful to keep the drone out of sight, James flew over the left side of the rooftop and waited. In the corner of the screen, the clothesline came into view. Patrice was there with a basket of washed towels, hanging them on the line. "And here, we have the Nobel housewife hanging her freshly cleaned and monster-blood-free towels near the front door. God, I'd kill for one of her muffins right now."

Blake and Emma turned their attention to the large barn in front of them, which appeared to be empty. There were no lights on inside, and it seemed rather quiet. Blake was about to step out from behind the tree when Emma grabbed his wrist and yanked him back. "Stop! See that?" she whispered, pointing to a moving shadow near the barn's open doors. Blake squinted. He wondered if his eyes were playing tricks on him or if the pair of moving silhouettes were real.

"Hey, dude, I know it's probably not the best time to bring this up, but Rodney is a hunter. What if he shoots us, after this? I mean, he isn't stupid. He's gonna know it was us, right?"

Blake quickly wound the radio's volume down and raised it to talk. "Dude, he's not going to shoot us. Now, shut up and tell me what else you see."

"Hold on," James said, and guided the drone back towards the barn.

Suddenly, several bright spotlights flashed along the barn's wall, causing Emma and Blake to quickly take cover behind the wide gum tree again. Two men – the same ones they had seen playing cards earlier that day – exited the barn and placed a pair of plastic chairs on the grass to sit on.

"Blake, there are a couple of guys sitting down right where you two are about to come out."

"We see them," Blake whispered into the radio. "We just need to get to that shed."

"We could go around the back of the barn," Emma suggested.

"We can't. They can see the shed doors from there. As soon as we reach it, they'll spot us…" Blake trailed off as a very questionable idea came to him. With a cheeky smirk, he lifted the radio and hit the talk button. "Hey, I've got an idea! I need you to create a distraction. Let them see you."

James exchanged a confused glance with Gary, then responded, "Um, Blake, I think you're missing the point of a top-secret mission. If they see the drone, they will definitely know it was us! We won't be able to make it look like an accidental escape!"

Blake stared up at the drone hovering above the house. "Dude, it's just like you said; they will know it's us anyway! Don't worry – they're farmers, not killers. They probably won't shoot us. Probably."

"Probably won't?" James's voice crackled through the speaker. "Fine. Hold on."

Blake and Emma watched as the two men clinked their beers together and chatted from the comfort of their plastic seats. The whizz of the drone's rotors was enough to grab their attention as it suddenly hovered over them. The two were clearly startled. One toppled over in his seat and dropped his beer on the grass while the other scrambled backwards, trying to catch his frightened breath.

"Bit jumpy, are we?" said James, and quickly pulled the drone back and flew it around the side of the house. "Here, boys! Come on!" Sure enough, the two men followed. Pointing and shouting, they curiously pursued the drone until they disappeared from Blake and Emma's sight.

"Okay, I've got their attention!" James guided the drone over to the clothesline, giving Patrice a big fright, too. The startled housewife fumbled with the towel in her hand and almost lost her balance completely. The two men from the barn ran to her side and began conversing with her in a rather alarmed manner. James couldn't help but giggle as he watched the three confused people panic on-screen. Before long, two more women emerged from the front door and joined them in pointing and shouting at his drone. "Uh, Blake, the villagers are gathering. You better go now – like right now!"

Blake and Emma ducked out from behind the tree and sprinted across the lawn. Passing the barn, they could hear the fuss and commotion James was causing on the other side of the house. When they reached the shed, Blake unzipped his backpack and removed the bolt cutters. He quickly cut through the padlock and unwrapped the heavy chains from the handles before tossing them into a nearby bush. Emma quietly opened the door, leaving just enough room for them to squeeze though before closing it behind them.

The air inside was thick and humid, making it feel more like a greenhouse than a shed. Two subtle clicks echoed in the dark as Blake and Emma switched on their torches. Dust particles danced through the white beams of light as they shone over the nearby benchtop. The dozen empty jars they had seen earlier that morning were now filled with green blood and neatly lined up beside the recently used machete. Blake and Emma glanced nervously at one another before turning towards the rear of the shed where the hanging black tarp glistened under their torchlight.

"Okay, we can do this," Emma told herself quietly.

"Yeah, we've got this," Blake joined in. He was just as nervous as she was.

Reaching the rear of the shed, an agonising groan came from behind the tarp.

"You ready?" Emma asked, taking a deep breath as she reached up and clenched the curtain. Blake gave her a nod. She whisked back the tarp and took several steps back.

Seemingly half-conscious, the shackled monster cried out as if it were terrified by the sight of the two people before it. Blake scanned his torch over the creature's domed body, causing each of its retractable scales to close as the light passed over its countless eyes.

"Oh, God, that poor thing!" Emma saw that another one of its legs had recently been dismembered, neon-green blood still dripping from the stump. Five of the seven severed limbs seemed to be growing back, as they were significantly longer than they had been that morning.

"I hate people sometimes," Blake admitted, as he shone the light away, allowing the creature's eyes to open. "It clearly can't walk out of here. Rodney said it wasn't heavy, though, so I might be able to carry it."

Emma shone her light over the thin wire holding up the crumpled black tarp beside her. "Wait!" An idea dawned on her. She spun around and pointed to the rusty machete resting on the bench next to the jars of blood. "Quick! Pass me that knife."

Blake retrieved the blade and handed it to her, causing the creature to thrash around in its chains. Emma grasped the machete tightly and began cutting through the thin wire.

"We need to hurry," Blake urged quietly, as the spider continued to squirm, causing its chains to clash together which, in turn, caused the shed walls to vibrate. "Someone will eventually hear this."

"Almost there. Got it!" The wire snapped and the plastic tarp fell to the floor. Emma handed Blake the machete, which he tossed into a dark corner near the front of the shed, far away from the creature's sight.

Emma dragged the tarp over and laid it flat over the concrete floor.

"Care to fill me in on this plan?' Blake asked, watching curiously.

Emma slid the tarp underneath the suspended animal. "My dad and I used to drag piles of bark chips like this when I was a kid. We'd load the tarp up with a big stack of bark, grab a corner each and just pull it along."

"So, we're just gonna drag it out of here?"

"Got a better idea?"

"No," Blake said, quite impressed. "In fact, it works for me."

"Good." Emma stood back and glanced at the eight chains holding the monster in place. Each chain was bolted high on the wall at one end, while a shackle was clamped around the spider's legs at the other. Rodney clearly knew what he was doing. Even after a leg was severed, the creature's weight provided too much tension on the chain for the shackles to slide off its severed limb.

"So, it looks like if we cut the chain holding its one good leg, then all we need to do is lift it a little and the other chains should slide off!" Blake explained, pulling the bolt cutters from under his armpit as he found a milk crate to stand on.

"So, what do I do?" Emma asked.

Blake stood on the crate and found himself face to face with the creature's many watchful eyes. "Well," he gulped, "when I cut through this chain, I'm gonna need you to lift it so I can quickly slide the other shackles off."

"You want me to hold it?" Emma asked, squirming at the thought. "Why can't I cut the chains?"

"Because I'm taller than you. You couldn't reach them, even if you stood on this crate."

Emma looked over at him squeamishly. "Do I *have* to hold it?"

"Yep," Blake said, and carefully reached over the creature's body and readied his bolt cutters around the chain holding its one intact leg. "Any time now, if you don't mind."

"Fine. I normally hate spiders. Count yourself lucky, buddy," Emma huffed. Squeezing herself between Blake and the creature's scaly body, she was hit by a truly foul odour. "Yuck, this thing stinks."

"Stop your whinging," Blake remarked with a slight grin.

Closing her eyes, Emma reached under the creature's wide domed body. While the top was covered in hard mossy scales, the underside was soft, slimy and dripping with the creature's saliva. Emma cringed. "Hurry. It's so gross!" Suddenly, Emma felt something wet on her stomach. She glanced down to find the creature's purple tongue feeling its way under her T-shirt. "Blake!" she squealed.

"Hey! Keep it together," Blake shushed her, as he struggled to cut through the thick chain.

"I'm sorry," Emma growled at him, "but your friend here is taking advantage of the situation."

Blake glanced down and snickered once he realised what was taking place. "Look, you two could at least wait for me to leave."

"Ha ha, very funny. Now hurry up."

With all his strength, Blake pushed on the bolt cutters' handles and sheared through the chain. "Hope you don't mind bracelets, dude," he muttered, realising that the monster's armoured shin prevented the shackle from sliding off.

"Did you get it?" Emma asked, trying not to squirm.

"Yeah, I got it. Now, I need you to lift it a little while I slide these off. Can you do that?"

"Yeah, I can. It really isn't that heavy after all," Emma said, lifting the creature upward. "Okay, go!"

Blake quickly made his way around to each of the severed limbs and carefully slipped the shackles off. "Okay, let me help you," he said, stepping down from the crate.

Together, Blake and Emma lowered the big reptilian spider onto the tarp. The creature let out another loud groan as its slimy purple tongue retracted out of Emma's shirt and back into the underside of its body. Cringing from the warmth she felt on her stomach, Emma lifted her shirt above her belly button. Thick strands of saliva dangled between the black cloth and her toned abs. "Oh, my God, that's so gross." She shivered, lowering her shirt.

Blake pulled out the radio. "James, are we good to go out there?" he asked, enjoying Emma's moment of disgust.

"Well, I'm still entertaining the locals, if that's what you're asking."

Back at the Riley Farm, James and Gary were watching the commotion unfold on the tablet's screen. Patrice, now joined by her husband, Rodney, and their son, Bernard, had gathered with several of their guests by the clothesline while James flew the drone in a circular pattern above their heads.

Excited by the flying contraption, Bernard crouched down and picked up a rock.

"Don't you dare do it, Bernie!" James yelled at his tablet.

Bernard pegged the stone, which bounced off the drone's mounted camera, much to James's outrage. Following the teenager's example, the man next to him bent down and picked up a rock of his own. "That little shit! Okay, Bernie, you and your friends wanna start throwing rocks? You can't throw them if you can't see." James tapped the screen and switched on the drone's powerful spotlight. Gary and James cheered, then clinked their glasses of whisky as the people on the screen protected their faces from the bright light. "How do you like that, suckers?" James cackled.

"Damn it, James! Are you there? Are we good to go or not?" Blake yelled through the radio speaker.

James realised he'd been celebrating too loudly to hear Blake. He quickly snapped the radio up. "Ah, yeah, you guys are good to go. All clear! Over!"

"Okay, we're clear." Blake turned to Emma. "Open the doors," he said, crouching down as he clutched both corners of the tarp.

Emma walked over to the shed doors and pulled the latch. With a loud creak they popped wide open. Blake began dragging the tarp and the crippled animal along the floor. The creature squirmed on the slippery plastic and let out another uncomfortable whimper. Once the monster was outside, Emma quickly closed the shed doors and grabbed one corner of the tarp from Blake.

"Head for the trees!"

"Good idea," Emma agreed.

The pair dragged the spider across the lawn and past the barn. Soon they reached the forest's edge. For some unknown reason, the reptilian spider began to let out a pleasant hum as if it knew it had been rescued and wanted to celebrate.

"Hold up!" Blake dropped the tarp and grabbed Emma's arm, stopping her in her tracks.

"What are you doing?" she whispered.

"Just listen," Blake said, directing her attention to the trees in front of them.

Playing like a soft melody, a second hum was emanating from within the shadowy forest. Growing louder with each passing second, its tune seemed to match that of the spider on the tarp.

"There's something there! In the shadows!" Emma said, cautiously moving back from the trees, pulling Blake back with her.

The rustling of leaves and the creaking of several branches made it clear that something big was about to join their company. With their soft hums turning to welcoming howls, a pair of green scaly spiders emerged from the darkness of the forest and strode into the moonlight. Standing at over two metres each, Emma and Blake hadn't realised just how big the mystery spiders were at full size.

"Oh, crap. Hey there, fellas," Blake said, carefully moving away from the tarp.

But the impressive animals showed no interest in Blake or Emma. Instead, they turned to their injured sibling lying on the ground. The crippled spider let out a loud hum, seemingly happy to see its own kind as it reached for them with its one remaining leg. The two large spiders moved to either side of it and extended their purple tongues from their bodies, feeling the creature's severed limbs.

"What are they doing?" Emma whispered.

"I have no idea," Blake whispered back.

One of the spiders withdrew its tongue and stepped aside, leaving the other to climb over its injured friend and suction its tongue to the top of is domed shell. Using its front and back legs to lower itself, it then positioned its four middle legs underneath the crippled spider's body and lifted the helpless animal up. The three spiders let out a unified cheerful whine, then together they disappeared into the shadowy forest.

"They came for him," Emma said to Blake with a wide smile.

"They sure did." Blake nodded happily.

"Ah, guys? You there?" James's muffled voice came from Blake's pocket.

"Oh, crap, James!" Blake whipped the radio out and pushed the talk button. "We did it, man! We got it out! You won't believe what happened."

"That's great, but I think it's time to go. The village people are getting a little nasty over here."

Back at the Riley Farm, James was clenching his radio as the image on the tablet's screen showed rock after rock bouncing off the hovering drone, and the entertained mob cheering and laughing after every direct hit. "These people are savages!"

"Where is that guy going?" Gary asked, as Rodney disappeared through the front door of the house.

"He better not come back with more things to throw," James said, as he attempted to manoeuvre the drone away from the barrage of flying rocks. A moment later, Rodney retuned to the group on-screen, armed with his rifle. "No, Rodney, no! Don't you do it, you hillbilly!" James shouted at his tablet.

Rodney cocked his rifle and took aim. The gunshot echoed through the air. James slumped back in his chair as the tablet displayed nothing but white fuzz.

"Gotta admit," Gary said, sipping his whisky, "that man sure can shoot."

"Shut up," said James, sulking and tossing the tablet across the deck.

Suddenly, Will burst through the back door and rushed out onto the deck. "Was that a gunshot?" he asked, wearing only sweatpants and fresh bed hair.

"Sure was," Gary chuckled in reply. "The neighbours shot James's flying car thing."

Will breathed a sigh of relief, then quickly asked, "Wait. What neighbours? And why would they shoot your toy? Where are Blake and Emma?"

"There they are," Gary answered, pointing over the deck railing at Emma and Blake as they came running out of the trees and across the creek.

Frustrated, Will waited on the deck for someone to answer him. "Anyone gonna fill me in on what's going on here?" Blake and Emma walked up the steps, panting and out of breath. "Again, does someone wanna fill me in? What the hell is going on?" Will yelled. Gary, James and Emma looked at each other nervously.

"Everybody, give us a minute," Blake said, still trying to catch his breath. "This was my idea. I'll fill you in."

"Come on," Emma urged James and Gary, who quietly followed her into the house.

Blake turned and faced Will, saying, "Okay, I'll tell you everything."

"You'd better," Will warned him.

20

THE CHOICES WE MAKE

"So, what you're telling me is you and Emma snuck into the neighbour's property – the same neighbours who miraculously healed the huge gashes on your hands – then broke into their shed and unchained a monster that might have killed you both. A monster that produces miracle blood? Miracle blood that can heal anything. Are you out of your fucking minds?" Will was furious.

Blake stood on the deck, waiting for a break in Will's rant so he could get a word in, which he eventually did. "It was the right thing to do."

Will looked at him scornfully. "Says who? You?"

"You didn't see it, man. It was inhumane!"

"Inhumane? Blake, it isn't human. We don't know what the hell it is."

"I don't care. It wasn't right!"

Inside, Emma, James and Gary sat around the kitchen table in silence, trading awkward glances as they listened to the argument outside. Lila entered the kitchen with a long yawn and was greeted by three uneasy smiles.

"What's going on?" she asked, yawning again as she stopped at the foot of the table. "I heard yelling."

"Maybe you should sit," Emma said, pushing a chair out from the table with her foot. "I need to tell you something, and you're probably going to be mad."

"First thing you should know," James started, "is that this was all Blake's idea."

"James!" Emma quickly hushed him.

Outside, Blake found another break in Will's fury. "Listen, man, you didn't see what they did to that thing! I wasn't gonna sit here, drink tea and just let them cut the legs off an innocent animal."

"Innocent animal?" Will screwed his face up in disgust. "Look at our city! Look what these monsters have done! They've murdered thousands!"

"Bullshit!" Blake shouted. "A building-sized dragon did that. So, this spider thing should suffer for what something else did?"

"Pfft! Don't be naive. They're all the same. Or did you forget about the giant flying snakes that tried to kill us, too?"

"Whatever, man. I'm glad I saved it."

"Fine," Will snapped. "Have you even thought about what you saved us from? I mean, come on, did you even think of the cost? The ability to heal wounds in minutes! How many lives could those people have saved?"

"You're gonna talk to me about saving lives?" Blake scoffed at him. "When everything went down, I tried to help everyone I could. Shit, I almost died trying to help them! More than once! What did you do, Will? You ignored everyone and went straight for Lila. So don't lecture me about the people we could have saved."

Will glared at him. "Let me make one thing clear. That girl is the only reason I'm still here. She's the only reason we stayed to help you three in the mall and the only reason I'm not knocking your teeth in right now. The only thing that matters to me is her. So, if you, or anyone else, have now put her in danger, then God help me, fire-breathing monsters will be the last thing you have to worry about."

"You don't scare me," Blake said, staring back at him.

"Not yet," Will grunted, then shoulder-barged Blake out of the way before storming inside.

The sudden slam of the back door sent the group around the dining table into immediate silence as Will entered the kitchen. "We're leaving," he snapped at Lila, clearly annoyed to find her sitting at the dining table with the others. "And, you three should know better," he added, glaring at Emma, James and Gary, who just stared back with blank expressions. Will then left the room in a frustrated huff.

Lila sighed and slowly rose from the table. "I'm sorry. I'll go talk to him," she said, smiling awkwardly at the group before leaving the room.

"You should know better!" James mocked, snickering to himself until Gary and Emma's disapproving gaze caused him to zip it.

◇◇◇◇◇◇◇◇◇◇◇◇

By the time Lila entered their room, Will was already packing their clothes into a suitcase on the bed. "What are you doing?" she asked, knowing full well what his answer would be.

"We're leaving," Will grunted, stuffing one of his shirts into the case.

Lila quietly closed the door behind her. "That was a little harsh, don't you think?" she said, leaning her back against the wall and folding her arms. Will didn't even look at her, but she could still read his face.

"Harsh?" Will shook his head. "Are you serious? I should have punched Blake in the face."

Lila shrugged. "And he would have punched you back. Then what?"

"I take it Emma told you what they did?"

"She did," Lila replied, "and I get why they did it."

Will tossed another bundle of clothes in the case, then he turned to her with a look of disbelief. "How could you agree with them? We should be helping those people at the other farm. Think of how many lives they could save with medicine like that."

"It wasn't medicine, Will," Lila said bluntly. "They were cutting its legs off."

Will shrugged and said, "It was a monster."

"Says who? We don't even know what it is!"

"Exactly!" Will frustratedly ran his fingers through his hair. "That thing could have killed them!"

Lila stared into his eyes. "It made some trees grow, Will. It didn't hurt anyone."

"Great," Will huffed. "You sound just like Blake."

Lila turned to the boxes next to the wall and picked Milky up from the cat's now regular napping spot. "So, could you cut her legs off? Could you do it to Milky? If it was her blood that saved lives? Could you do it, Will?" she asked, holding the white cat out in front of him.

"You know that's not fair," Will snapped, pointing his finger at her.

"Yes, it is. It's a simple question," Lila countered. "Would you cut her limbs off and bottle her blood to save lives?" Milky jumped from her arms and returned to the stack of boxes.

"You know I could never hurt her," Will said, as he turned back to the suitcase. "But it's not that simple."

"Exactly!" Lila reached out and grabbed his hands, forcing Will to face her again. "It isn't that simple. Blake thought he was doing what was right. Should he have talked to us first? Yes, he should have told us, and I don't blame you for being mad about that. But don't confuse the two. You can't be mad at him for setting it free when you're not even sure how you would have handled it yourself. We can only do what we believe is right. You know that. You used to tell me that."

Will took a deep, slightly defeated breath. "Ever the voice of reason," he said, reluctantly smirking at her.

Lila smiled. She always knew how to calm him down. Wrapping her arms around him, she buried her head into his chest and said, "I love you, William."

Will conceded and hugged her tightly. "You know I hate it when you call me that."

"That's why I say it," Lila answered, smiling to herself. "Honey, I really like these people. I don't want to leave them."

"I know." Will sighed, then looked over at the case on the bed. "Guess I can give them one more chance."

"Thank you."

It was in that moment, during Lila's warm embrace, that Will felt the weight of the ring box in his pocket. It was heavier than before, not physically but emotionally. So much had changed since that fateful Saturday at the beach. Suddenly the prospect of marriage seemed so irrelevant. Would she care anymore? Did it even matter anymore? "I love you, too," Will whispered, kissing Lila on her head while he contemplated his looming questions.

The following morning, Emma made her way to the rear deck to enjoy the country air, wearing her sky-blue pyjama shorts, a white shirt and her favourite pair of pink slippers. However, it was the aroma of her freshly made green tea that really tantalised her nose. Holding the mug with both hands, she let out a long yawn, acknowledging another sleepless night.

The lush greenery of the forest was touched with an orange hue from the early morning sun, and Emma couldn't help but replay the previous night's events in her mind as she stared at the woods. In fact, all she had thought about since freeing the monster in shackles was how much pain the poor creature had seemed to be in – the sight of its severed limbs flashing like a disturbing slide show.

A sudden growl from a loud engine kicking over made Emma quickly realise that she wasn't the first one up for the day. Following the rumble, she stepped down from the deck and made her way around the side of the house where she saw Blake backing Houdini up next to the barn. She hadn't spoken to Blake since his fight with Will, but judging by the constant opening and closing of cupboard doors and footsteps throughout the night, she gathered he hadn't slept much either.

"Good morning!"

Startled by the unexpected greeting, Emma turned to see Gary coming towards her, clutching a cup of coffee. "Morning," she said, calming her nerves and taking a sip from her mug.

"I see you slept as well as he did," Gary said, and nodded towards Blake, who was now hunched under Houdini's open bonnet by the barn.

"What is he doing?" Emma asked.

"Thinking," Gary said, slurping his coffee. "When Blake gets stressed out, he closes off, buries himself under the hood of that car, and barely speaks to anyone."

Emma frowned, saying, "Well, that's stupid. He can't just do that. We're all in this together."

"Hah!" Gary let out a chuckle. "Together. Group therapy ain't gonna cut it here, darlin'."

"Well, you may be willing to let him wallow in self-pity, but I'm going to talk to him." Emma, however, barely managed a single step before Gary reached out and put a hand on her shoulder.

"Hold up, darlin'," he said, turning her back toward him. "If it's all the same to you, let me take this one. I've known the kid most of his life. Navigating his stubborn side is kinda my specialty at this point."

Reluctantly, Emma agreed. "Okay. Sure."

"Thanks." Gary gave an appreciative nod, then headed towards the barn, leaving Emma, after a long pause, to head back inside.

〰〰〰〰〰〰〰

Blake gave the screwdriver a final twist, loosening the clamp holding the intercooler piping in place. Wearing a pair of shorts and a maroon singlet, his pale shoulders gleamed under the brightness of the rising sun. He removed the section of rubber pipe and looked it over for any signs of splits or cracks.

"You know, we replaced those rubber sleeves only a few weeks ago," Gary interrupted, as he strolled through the grass towards the barn.

"Can never be too careful." Blake dismissed him, still looking over the pipe.

Sipping his coffee, Gary glanced over the engine bay as he came to a stop at the front of the car. "Here's the thing, kid. Every time you get angry, you fiddle with Houdini, pull things apart, and then afterwards, I have to fix what you've done."

"I'm not angry," Blake said quietly, before turning back to the engine to continue his tinkering. "I gotta keep these clamps tight. Can't afford to have the piping blow off like it did at Mount Cotton."

Gary sighed and said, "That was an old clamp, and we replaced it. But you already know that."

Blake pulled himself out from under the bonnet and asked, "Is there something you came over here for?"

Gary reached past him, unhooked the support strut, then dropped the bonnet shut. "Yeah, actually there is," he said, taking a seat on the nose of the car. "We need to talk about last night."

Blake begrudgingly sat alongside him. "I don't regret letting it go," he said quickly, opting to stare at the barn wall instead of facing Gary directly.

"I'm not asking you to," Gary replied. "Listen, I don't know whether letting that thing go was the right thing to do or not. All I do know is the world is never black and white – good or bad. It's all a matter of perspective, and there is a lot of grey in between. Those people next door, they probably believed that they were doing the right thing, too."

"I couldn't leave it there – not like that," Blake said softly.

"I'm not saying you should have, kid. I'm not saying that at all." Gary exhaled a loud sigh through his nostrils, and the pair went silent for a moment. "As a man, all you can do is try to make decisions that you believe are right. Make the decisions that help people, choices that keep your loved ones safe – and pray for forgiveness when you get it wrong. And believe me, kid, you will get it wrong. This won't be the last hard decision you'll have to make, and not everyone will agree with your choices. Just be the best man you can be and trust yourself, 'cause at some point in your life, you're gonna look back at the kinda man that you were, and when you do, you wanna hope that you like what you see."

Blake looked at him then asked, "Did your father give you that advice?"

"No, he didn't," Gary replied, shaking his head then tipping the remainder of his coffee into the grass, "but I wish he had." Standing up, he brushed off his pants and pointed at Blake with a stern finger. "Now put this car back together. And if I see you touching that clamp one more time, then so help me God!"

Blake remained seated on Houdini's bonnet and watched Gary walk off towards the house. "Hey, old man," he called out. Gary paused and glanced back at him. "Thanks."

Gary simply nodded back, then continued towards the house. After a few steps, Gary yelled once more, "Don't touch that frickin' clamp!"

Blake let out a small laugh and stood up, removing the screwdriver from his pocket. "Yes, *Dad*," he said, shaking his head, as he lifted Houdini's hood and put the support strut in place.

21

THE MOURNING AFTER

Whistling a soft melody, the nurse entered the room carrying a tray of fresh fruit and placed it on a table by the open window. Rays of sunlight rolled across the walls like waves on a beach as the breeze wafted through a gap in the curtains.

Various documents and files regarding the dam and its maintenance schedules had been put into boxes and stacked in the corner alongside a cruddy rosewood desk, reminding anyone who came to the makeshift hospital wing that it was really just a strip of old office spaces. Well, that was what Lorcan was thinking anyway. As he stopped in the doorway, he noticed a long rectangular photograph of the dam's construction hanging on the wall, its worn timber frame matching the rosewood desk perfectly. However, old photographs and crappy furniture were of no interest to the soldier, so he turned back to the nurse – or more importantly – the patient she was tending to.

Samantha Marsh was strapped to a heart rate monitor and morphine drip as she drifted in and out of consciousness from her hospital-grade bed. Most of her face was covered with purple bruising, and her left eye was lost somewhere within its swollen socket.

"How are you feeling, Sam?" the nurse asked, as she picked up a chart and read it over. Samantha mumbled something in response, but it was barely audible. "Well, you have a visitor." The nurse gestured to Lorcan standing in the doorway.

Samantha slowly turned her head on the pillow and produced what little of a smile she could muster, "H-hi."

"I'll give you a moment. Ring the bell if you need me, okay?" the nurse said, before heading to the doorway. "She's very weak. Please, don't take too long," she whispered in Lorcan's ear, then left the room.

"I thought... you were a hallucination," Samantha said weakly, "but you were real... you found us."

"Not soon enough," Lorcan apologised, as he walked over and stood at her bedside. "I should never have left you in that truck."

"You could never have known..." Samantha took a long painful breath, then tears began to trickle down her face. "They made the kids watch, you know... The one with the tattoo on his face... he made them watch as they beat Barry senseless." Samantha feebly reached over the rail and clutched Lorcan's hand. "One after another, they took turns... They hit him so hard... but, Barry... he just looked at us, and kept saying, 'It's gonna be okay'. He told the kids to close their eyes, but those men wouldn't let them... Then, he stopped moving... stopped speaking..." Samantha burst into a hysterical cry and let go of his hand.

Lorcan could do nothing but watch. There were no words of comfort that could help her.

"Have you ever lost someone you loved?" Samantha asked, still sobbing.

"Yes," Lorcan answered simply.

"Does the pain ever go away?"

"It hasn't yet."

"Then... I'm sorry for your... loss." Samantha began drifting out of consciousness.

"I'll let you rest," Lorcan said quietly, then headed for the door.

"What will you do now?" Samantha asked, still awake but coughing on her own words.

Lorcan clenched the door handle with his calloused fingers as he said, "I'm gonna hunt down the man that killed your husband."

Samantha relaxed her head back into the pillow. "Make him pay," she said softly, then turned to stare out the window.

"Yes, ma'am." He nodded, then closed the door behind him.

Lorcan made his way down the hall and checked each office window, hoping to find the room that Mindy and Jack had been admitted to. Reaching the third door, he peered through the window and found Mindy sitting on Amanda's lap inside. The young girl was crying profusely and burying her teary red face into the woman's shoulder. Amanda rocked the child back and forth, hoping to calm her down. Neither of them noticed Lorcan on the other side of the glass, so he figured it was best not to interrupt. Truthfully, he didn't know if he could handle seeing the young girl falling apart.

He moved on to the next room. There he found Jack sitting in the middle of the floor with the same nurse who had just tended to Samantha. She handed Jack an action figure, but the boy didn't even look at her. Instead, he just stared at the carpet and picked at the threads with his fingers.

With one hand on the door handle, Lorcan contemplated whether to go inside or keep walking. He reached down and felt the soft squish of Jack's plush toy in his pocket. The nurse looked up as the door swung open, and Lorcan stepped into the room holding the green dinosaur.

"Can I help you?" the nurse asked.

"This is his favourite," Lorcan said, holding the toy out for her to take.

The sound of Lorcan's voice caused Jack to perk up, and at the sight of the solider, he leapt to his feet and raced over to wrap his little arms around Lorcan's calf.

The nurse was shocked. "That's the most he's moved since they brought him here. Does he know you?"

"Ah, yeah, guess you could say that," Lorcan said, as he glanced down at the child clinging to his shin.

"Well, he seems to like you."

Unsure of how to handle the affectionate child, Lorcan reached down and patted the kid on the head. Jack quickly snatched the toy from his hand with a happy grin. Brushing dirt off the dinosaur's face, he returned to his spot in the middle of the room and sat down to play.

The nurse donned an uneasy frown as she watched the boy amuse himself. "He hasn't spoken a single word since he got here. The doctors say he's still in shock."

"How is he? Physically?" Lorcan asked.

"He's fine. A few bruises and a couple of small cuts on his right hand, probably from falling over. No visible signs of abuse. Well, not physically anyway. It's unimaginable… what those people did."

"Take care of him," Lorcan said to the nurse. "I'll be back to check on him later."

"Wait!" she said, clearly surprised. "You're just gonna leave? He could use a friendly face."

Lorcan was about answer her when Jack's quiet voice interrupted them. "Are you going to kill the monster now?" he asked, turning the nurse's frown to an expression of astonishment.

"Yes," Lorcan answered, "I'm going to kill the monster now."

"Good," Jack said, without taking his focus off the green dinosaur, and then he began to hum to himself.

Stunned and confused, the nurse leaned over and whispered into Lorcan's ear, "I don't understand. Does he really think that the dragon did this to his family?"

"No, he knows what happened," Lorcan said, reaching for the door. "He just learnt an important lesson."

"What lesson?"

"Not all monsters breathe fire."

Lorcan left the nurse standing in silence as he left the room. After a moment, she turned to the quiet boy sitting in the middle of the floor and watched him with unwavering concern. Jack didn't even seem to notice her. He just growled playfully and made his dinosaur walk across the carpet.

Leaving the medical wing behind, Lorcan had only one more stop to make. When he reached the colonel's door, he was surprised to see the two uniformed guards were no longer posted outside. With a sturdy hand, he knocked three times and awaited a response.

"Who is it?" Henrickson asked, as if he were already expecting someone.

"Captain Edwards."

"Come in, captain."

Lorcan opened the door and was immediately hit with the same aroma of whisky and cigar smoke he had encountered during his last visit. This time, however, the colonel seemed a little more put together. His uniform was *almost* straight, and his demeanour was calm, albeit a little drunk.

"Have a seat, Edwards. I was expecting you." Henrickson gestured to the vacant chair before taking his own seat behind his desk.

"You were expecting me, sir?" Lorcan was surprised.

"Well, I assume you're here to debrief me on that *un-au-thorised* mission you deployed Squad Seven on?" Henrickson snarled, lifting half a glass of whisky to his mouth.

Lorcan leaned back in his chair. He was ready for a fight. "Actually, yes, that is why I am here."

"Well, you can save yourself the trouble." The colonel knocked back his whisky and immediately poured himself another. "I read through your squad's reports, and it seems you made the right call."

Lorcan didn't know if it was the whisky talking or if the colonel was trying to justify their previous mission in Broadbeach, but either way, he liked what he was hearing and preferred to have Henrickson on his side. "Thank you, sir."

"You brought back two children and their mother, captain. I call that a win."

Lorcan agreed. "So do I."

"Which brings me to your next assignment," Henrickson said, sipping his whisky. "There is a scientist, Doctor Diane Tate, who has crucial information about the creatures we've encountered. She will be arriving at the refuge centre tomorrow. I need your squad to rendezvous with her and bring her here."

"The refuge centre is in Robina. Why not send a chopper?" Lorcan asked, not overly keen to play babysitter.

Henrickson shook his head. "We can't afford to lose another bird, captain. Besides, there is another reason I am asking you to do it."

"Another reason?"

The colonel removed a folded map from his top drawer and laid it out across his desk. "You see this area?" he asked, pointing to the suburb of Robina. "For almost a week now, our squads have been clearing out these surrounding areas of all supplies. Everything they find either gets shipped back to us here or is taken to the refuge centre." Henrickson then pointed to an industrial region that connected to the M1 highway, which was far closer to the refuge centre than Lorcan had realised. "This, captain, is where your squad encountered Gabriel and rescued the Marsh family."

Lorcan looked up from the map and said, "You think that Gabriel is heading to the refuge centre?"

Henrickson nodded. "From what your report said, he fled with nothing. He's gonna need supplies – every man needs to eat – and we have it all, for at least several miles anyway."

"It's our best lead," Lorcan said, standing up from his chair.

"I must stress that your priority is still Doctor Tate, captain. But find this bastard, and he'll pay for what he's done. I promise you that."

"Thank you, colonel." Lorcan saluted him.

Henrickson stood up from his chair and swirled his glass. "Happy hunting, captain."

22

CONSEQUENCES

As per Gary's rather insistent request, Blake tightened the clamp around the intercooler piping and dropped Houdini's bonnet shut, wiping the sweat from his forehead afterward. Before he could think of resting for a moment, what could only be described as a cry of pure terror bellowed from the house, causing him to stand upright and drop the screwdriver somewhere in the grass.

"Emma?" Blake had heard that scream before.

Tall grass whipped at his shins as he sprinted through the field towards the front of the house. Crossing the gravel driveway, Blake hopped over the steps and onto the deck, then barged through the front door, shaking the very walls it was hinged to as he skidded into the lounge room. Another horrified squeal turned Blake right around, where he found Emma standing on the dining table in the kitchen, trembling and pointing to something on the floor.

"It was on my neck!" she yelped, shaking her hands off in disgust.

Blake scanned the timber floorboards until he spotted it – the monster that struck fear into the hearts of many. Near the foot of the bench, a huntsman spider was crawling up the cupboard door.

Gary and James sat at the other end of the dining table, eating their breakfast with amused smirks on their faces. Emma continued to squirm in her pyjamas, shaking the table under their cereal bowls.

"Blake, get it! It was on my neck, and these two didn't even help me," Emma cried, quivering. "They just sat there eating and laughing as I tried to flick it off!"

James spoke up with a mouthful of corn flakes. "We told you. We can't hurt the spider, or we will have to deal with him," he said, pointing to Blake.

"That's right! The kid hates killing the darned things," Gary joined in, as he shovelled another spoonful of cereal into his mouth and wiped the milk off his moustache.

Blake proceeded to give them both the finger and then turned his attention back to the arachnid making its way up the cupboard.

Emma growled in frustration, "You idiots do realise that milk is probably off by now, right?"

James and Gary glanced down at their cereal bowls, then looked at each other. "Yeah," they responded in unison before putting another large spoonful into their mouths.

A clatter of footsteps on the stairs preceded Lila and Will, both wearing bathrobes, as they rushed into the room and quickly came to a confused halt. "We were in the shower. We heard a scream. What happened?" Will asked.

"Emma found a spider," Blake answered, pointing to the culprit, which had now reached the kitchen benchtop.

"Oh, cool!" Lila beamed, hunching over to get a better look.

"You're all chickens. I'll get it," said Will, as he reached down and grabbed one of Emma's pink fluffy slippers by the door.

"Hey! Put that down," Emma barked at him, protecting her favourite morning footwear.

"Everybody relax. It's harmless. I'll just put it outside," Blake said, as he walked over to the benchtop and picked up a cutting board.

"Mate, just squash it," Will scoffed, tossing the pink slipper onto the floor.

Emma nodded, "I agree. Like, seriously, just knowing it could crawl back in here, I won't be able to sleep at night if you put it outside!" The four boys paused and then looked at her with dumbfounded expressions on their faces. "What?" Emma shrugged.

"Really?" James asked, wiping the milk from his chin. "That's why you won't be able to sleep at night?"

"Hey, I'll take a fire-breathing lizard over disgusting spiders any day," Emma defended herself, ignoring the plethora of judgemental eyes.

"I think they're kinda cute," Lila added. "They are an important part of the ecosystem, you know."

Blake swiped a dirty bowl from the sink and quickly cupped it over the spider. Then, in one swift move, he slid the cutting board under the bowl.

"You can throw that bowl out, by the way, and the cutting board, too," Emma said, squeamishly watching Blake as he headed for the doorway with the trapped spider.

Will followed him outside, keeping a few steps behind as they stepped onto the front deck. Blake deemed a large bush next to the driveway the perfect spot to set the monster free.

"Mate, what's the deal here? Are you trying to be some kind of hero? Is that what this is? Trying to impress the girls?" Will asked provokingly. "Why couldn't you just step on it, man?"

Blake stopped at the bush, put the cutting board down and lifted the bowl. The large spider ran into the thick shrub and quickly disappeared into the green. "Why kill it?" he said, turning to Will, who was standing up on the deck looking rather annoyed. "Because we can? Because we are bigger? Should I end its life just because it might crawl on me later? Is that what it deserves?"

Will shrugged and replied, "It's just a spider, mate."

"A life is a life," Blake said, then pushed past Will and headed for the door. "You wanna kill it, you know where it is."

Will looked at the bush as the front door slammed shut behind him. The spider was crawling up a thin leafy branch that swayed under its tiny weight. Walking over to it, he quickly found a heavy rock in the garden bed and picked it up. The hairy huntsman clung to the leaf as it struggled to reach the next branch over. Will raised the rock over the spider. He wanted to get back at Blake; he knew he did. He was furious with him. How could he not be?

He watched the spider for several minutes, then slowly lowered the rock to his side, eventually dropping it beside his foot. Will sighed and said, "Have a good life." Then he turned around and headed back inside the house.

~~~~~~~~~~

Protected from the sizzling afternoon sun by the cover of a cloudy sky, James picked another orange from the tree and placed it in his basket. After breakfast, Gary had asked James to assist him in picking some of the ripe fruit from the now flourishing trees by the creek. Normally, picking fruit would have been the last thing he wanted to do, but with all the tension in the house, keeping busy to avoid uncomfortable conversations sounded pretty good to him.

"The hell with ya! Damn it!" Gary, who had volunteered to pick fruit from the trees that weren't supercharged by giant super-bugs, cursed and flailed his arms about as he attempted to combat a pesky blowfly by swiping at it with his hat.

Hearing the curses of a frustrated Gary, James looked to the more barren fruit trees near the front of the house. He couldn't help but snicker. "You got everything under control over there, grandma?" he yelled, but Gary was too busy trying to karate the annoying insect to respond.

Something else, however, did respond. A high-pitched cry from the forest sent a flock of cockatoos fleeing from the treetops with panicked squawks. James dropped his basket and turned to face the forest. He had heard that sound before. He suddenly felt very heavy. *Shrieker.* James gulped as he stared into the darkness under the thick canopy. The shadows of the forest seemed to be moving.

James spun around to see Gary in the distance, and with two fingers he whistled as loud as he could to get the old man's attention. Gary didn't even look his way. "Stupid deaf ear," James moaned, as another shriek from within the woods sent a shiver down his spine. He took off running, straight to the oblivious fifty-two-year-old mechanic near the front of the property. "Gary! You deaf bastard, look at me!"

Much to James's relief, Gary soon noticed him and said, "Hah! What's wrong, boy? Can't lift your own basket?" He chuckled.

James came in fast, sliding across the dirt before coming to a complete stop at Gary's feet. "We have... to get inside... those serpent things... are in the trees," he sputtered, hunched over, trying to catch his breath.

"What?" Gary dropped his basket in alarm. "Why the hell didn't you just call out to me?"

"I did!" James snapped, between gasps. "But my Aunt Hilda… has better hearing than you. And she's dead!"

Gary straightened his hat, saying, "We better get inside!"

Leaving the fruit behind, the pair ran towards the house as fast as their legs would take them.

With Milky purring on her lap, Lila snuggled into Will as they chatted on the couch in the lounge room. Suddenly, James and Gary burst through the front door in a panic, startling the couple and causing Milky to skittishly leap from Lila's lap. "You guys, okay?" Will asked.

"Lock all the doors!" James instructed, as he ran over to the windows and began frantically closing all the curtains in the lounge room.

"What happened?" Will stood up from the couch. "What did you do now?"

"Why are we locking the doors?" Lila asked nervously.

"Everything okay?" Emma stepped out of the kitchen and looked at the others.

"There's no time! Those things are in the woods! Cover everything!" James rushed past her and entered the kitchen.

Emma gave Will and Lila a confused shrug before turning back to James. "The spider things?" she asked him.

"The shriekers," Gary answered her.

"I heard them in the forest!" James closed the curtains above the kitchen bench and began dragging the dining table to the back door.

"Oh, God." Lila shuddered at the thought.

"We'll lock all the windows upstairs," Will yelled, then raced up the staircase with Lila right behind him.

Gary entered the kitchen and looked around the room. "Wait," he said, as James pressed the dining table against the door. "Where's Blake?"

James looked at Emma, whose face turned a pale white.

"Oh no! He's out there," she cried out, pulling the table back towards her.

"What do you mean? Where is he?" James asked, concern spreading over his face.

Emma struggled to put words in coherent sentences. "Um, he said he was going to talk to the neighbours and smooth things over. You know, so everyone would stop freaking out about letting the monster go!" She pushed past James and reached for the back door.

James grabbed Emma's shoulder and stopped her. "How long ago?" he asked, spinning her towards him.

A tear ran down her cheek as she said, "Not long... ten, fifteen minutes maybe."

James nodded. "He's gonna be okay," he assured her, then turned to Gary. "You stay here. Lock everything behind me. I'm going to get him."

"I'm going too," Gary said, approaching the back door.

James halted Gary with a firm hand on his chest. "I'll be faster on my own – no offence."

"Boy, you barely made it across the yard without collapsing! You're about as fit as my hernia."

"True... and gross," James said, tilting his head. "But I'm still going – alone."

Gary sighed. They didn't have time to argue, so he let the young man have his way. "Bring him back."

James nodded and said, "I will."

"Be careful." Emma looked at him nervously.

"Don't worry! I'll be back with that lanky mofo in no time." James opened the back door and bolted outside. Emma locked the door behind him. Feeling a lump in her throat, she glanced back at Gary.

"Those boys are tougher than they look. They'll be fine," Gary reassured her with one of his signature winks. "Don't worry. He'll bring him back."

Emma didn't feel any better.

〰〰〰〰〰〰〰

Emerging from the trees, Blake entered Rodney and Patrice's yard. "Hello?" he called out, but a quick howl from the wind and the creak of swaying barn doors were all that greeted him in return. Next to the barn, a pair of fold-out chairs remained on the lawn where the two men had been drinking the night before. One chair was still tipped on its side from James's improvised distraction. At the far end of the yard, the now infamous dark grey shed rattled as both its doors clanged in the breeze. "They must have gone to check on the monster, or maybe Emma didn't shut the doors properly. Either way, they know it has escaped by now," Blake thought to himself. He had been secretly hoping that Rodney had not noticed the monster was gone yet.

Blake headed down the left side of the house, the same way that Patrice had taken them during their first visit. The rotating washing line slowly spun in the wind. Several hanging towels were still pegged on the line. Blake noticed a basket full of clothes sitting in the grass, and next to it was a long black object. He crouched down by the basket and ran his fingers over a towel; it was bone dry. His attention then turned to the black object – Rodney's hunting rifle.

"Weird," he thought, as he grabbed the weapon and stood up to examine it. "Why is all this stuff still here?"

Blake had never held a gun before. It was heavier than he'd imagined. He couldn't even tell if it was loaded but decided it was best to take it anyway. He slung the gun's strap over his shoulder, then noticed several scattered pieces of plastic in the grass not too far from the washing line: all that remained of James's drone.

Moving around to the front of the house, Blake found that the carport hadn't changed either. The large red ute was still there, its bonnet still open, and tools were still lying around on the ground. The other three cars remained parked in the exact same spots, too. The white front door, however, was different. It was covered with deep scratches, and a long gouge that spanned the width of the door and would have folded it in two if it hadn't been for the hinges holding it to the frame.

"What happened here?" Blake wondered, but pushed the crippling answers from his mind and cautiously entered the house. "Hello? Is anyone home? Rodney? Patrice?" He aimed the rifle ahead, unsure if he was even holding it correctly.

The scene in the lounge room could have been ripped straight from a horror movie. Blood spatter covered the floor and the walls. The yellow couch was torn to shreds with blood-soaked foam spewing from each gash in the fabric. The coffee table that Emma had rested her leg on was nothing more than a splintered heap on the floor. A wide hole in the back wall, spanning around two metres across, suggested that something had broken through the plasterboard from the hall on the other side. Blake noticed that the mounted crocodile head he detested so much was now buried under the debris.

The sight was all too familiar. The intersection they had driven through the morning after the attack came flooding back to him: the blue coupe, its shattered windshield, its blood-soaked seats. It was the same grizzly sight.

Blake made his way to the kitchen, noticing several broken jars and a large, green, monster-blood stain in the carpet, as he went. Shattered plates and teacups covered the kitchen's tiled floor, crunching under his shoes as he walked over them. The oven door was hanging by a single hinge, whilst the cupboards alongside had been crushed inwards. Blake felt his foot kick something. He crouched down and picked up a pair of narrow reading glasses; they were bloodied, bent and twisted. The beaded chain had been snapped, and several beads fell off as he examined it. Patrice had been wearing the glasses and the beaded chain the last time he saw her.

Blake had seen enough. As he placed the glasses on the bench, he heard the sound of crunching glass coming from the next room. The hairs on his arms stood on end, and a cold shiver rushed over him. He spun around, raised the rifle and took aim.

"Whoa! Don't shoot! It's me!" James stood in the kitchen doorway with his hands held up.

Letting out a deep sigh of relief, Blake lowered the gun. "Dude, you scared the shit out of me!"

"Sorry," James said. "Is that Rodney's gun?"

Blake nodded. "Yeah. I found it outside near the washing line."

"Do you know how to use it?"

"No, do you?"

"Nope." James shook his head, then looked at the state of the kitchen. "Man, we need to get out of here."

Blake agreed. "I think the snake things did this."

"That's why I'm here." James urged him towards the door. "We heard them in the forest. Everyone else is locked up in the house. I came to get you, so we better go." Blake stared at the twisted and bloodied glasses next to him. James knew what his friend was thinking. "Hey, man, there is nothing we could have done here. But we really need to go, like right now!"

"Is this my fault?" Blake asked, looking down at Rodney's gun. "Everything here is exactly the way we left it. This happened right after we left last night."

"Don't do that to yourself. None of this in on you," James said, making a point of looking his friend in the eye. "We can talk about this once we get back. I need you to focus, man."

"Yeah," Blake eventually agreed, "let's go."

The pair left the house with haste. James glanced at his broken drone as they passed the washing line and headed for the overgrown forest.

23

WHY

Emma stood anxiously at the kitchen window, her eyes glued to the trees across the creek. "Here, I made you one." She turned around to see Lila holding two mugs of tea.

"Thanks," Emma said, taking one.

"They'll be back soon," Lila said with a reassuring smile.

Emma turned back to the window. "They never left me," she said softly.

"Huh?" Lila moved a little closer. "Sorry, Em, I missed that."

Emma continued to stare outside. "They never left me. The world fell apart around them; they didn't even know me. They stayed here." Emma turned to Lila with glassy eyes. "They didn't have to stay here. They only stayed so I wouldn't be alone while I waited for Dad."

Lila smiled and said, "My mother used to say that a crisis separates the men from the boys." She reached out and grabbed Emma's free hand. "And the women from the girls. You have been there for them, too."

Emma put her tea down on the table and wiped her eyes. "What if I've put us all in danger? Staying here, I mean, hoping Dad will show up. I wouldn't leave, and now those things are out there."

"Em, those monsters are everywhere. And everyone made their own choice to be here. Besides, who is to say it's safer anywhere else? You gave us all a home when we had nowhere else to go. You say the boys didn't leave you, but you never left them either. Whatever happens, you've done the best you could."

"Thanks," said Emma, and smiled.

"Family sticks together, Em," Lila added. "Wait, can I call you Em?"

Emma let out a small laugh. "Of course, you can. All my best friends call me Em."

Lila beamed. She didn't really have a best friend – other than Will, of course. Emma held out her arms and embraced Lila with a warm hug. After a moment, the pair turned back to the window to see James and Blake sprinting out of the woods like a pair of marathon runners.

"They're back," Lila cheered.

Emma frantically unlocked the door, and the two boys came bursting through.

"You two okay?" Lila asked.

The pair were hunched over and fighting to catch their breath, but James managed to give a thumbs up. Emma lunged forward and wrapped an arm around each of their necks. "I'm really glad you're okay," she said, squeezing them tight.

"We were gone for like… half an hour?" James puffed.

"Shut up. I was really worried," Emma said, before giving the pair some breathing room.

"What's that?" Lila asked, pointing to the black object tucked under Blake's arm.

"It's Rodney's gun," James answered.

Blake pulled the rifle out from under his armpit and rested it on the kitchen table.

Emma's warm affection turned to immediate disapproval. "You stole his gun. Blake, he's gonna be so pissed!" James and Blake glanced at each other nervously. "What is it?" Emma asked, hands on her hips.

Feeling responsible, Blake swallowed the lump in his throat. "Something happened at your neighbour's farm. The house… it's a mess. There was a lot of blood. No bodies, though."

Emma covered her mouth in shock.

James took over. "We think it happened last night, after you guys left. When I was flying the drone, Patrice was hanging washing outside. The basket is still there with clothes and towels in it. It's also where Rodney shot the drone out of the sky and where Blake found the gun," he explained.

"Something chased them inside the house," Blake continued. "I found Patrice's glasses with blood on them in the kitchen. There was a massive hole, like something broke through the wall in the lounge room, too. Everything was… yeah, a mess."

"Are we sure that the spider thing didn't come back for revenge?" Lila asked.

"No way." Blake shook his head. "It was the snakes – same things from the mall, same things James heard outside."

Goosebumps ran down Lila's arm. "I hate those things."

"Sounds to me like the gunshot attracted 'em," Will shot Blake an accusing glare as he and Gary entered the kitchen.

"We don't know that, Will!" Lila snapped.

"Come on," Will scoffed. "We're all thinking it. If you hadn't broken into that house – if you had just minded your own business – then that man wouldn't have shot the drone, and that gunshot wouldn't have brought those things here. Well done, boys! You just got more people killed."

James and Blake had nothing to say.

"That's enough," Lila shouted at her boyfriend. "No one could have known! What has gotten into you?"

"No," Blake stopped her, "it's okay. He's right. This was my idea. I did this. It's on me."

Will pointed an accusing finger at him. "You're damn fucking right it is!"

Lila walked out of the kitchen, eager to distance herself from the tension but mostly to distance herself from Will.

The room went silent for a moment. Before long, Will left the room to find Lila.

Gary looked at a very silent James, Emma and Blake, who, judging by their sombre expressions, were deep in regretful thought. "Right, we don't have time for this. What has happened, has happened, and there ain't much you three can do about it. Now, those things are out there, so we need to focus and come up with a plan."

"We need to leave," James suggested. "We need to leave while we can."

"And go where?" Emma asked.

Blake finally looked up. "There is nowhere to go. The gunshot attracted those things, and our cars aren't exactly quiet – not to mention the bigger fire-breathing monsters that are still out there somewhere."

"Okay, so what do we do?" James asked.

"We stay here," Gary suggested.

"Oh, great plan!" James said, as he rolled his eyes.

Gary glared at him, then added, "I say we stay low. We've got enough food and water for a few days. We kill the lights and wait it out. Let those things pass by and leave the area."

"How will we know when they leave?" Emma asked.

"We won't be certain, but from what Lila told me, those things shriek the most at night," Gary explained. "When we get through a couple of nights without a sound coming from those woods, we should be in the clear. Maybe."

"It's the best shitty option we've got," Blake agreed. "We stay low-key. No lights on, no loud noises, and we keep out of sight."

"I've got some lanterns. They're not too bright, but are bright enough to help us see in the dark," Emma said, before heading to the lounge room.

"That should help," Gary said, then turned back to James and Blake and grabbed each by the shoulder. "Now, you two listen to me. I don't care what Man Bun says. What happened next door wasn't your fault. You boys did what you believed was right. These things could have shown up anyhow. You hear me?"

"I appreciate the gesture, but no." Blake removed Gary's hand from his shoulder. "Those people paid for what I did." He then walked out of the room, leaving Gary with James.

James offered half a smile. "Thanks for trying, old man. I get you. I really do. Just let him process it for a minute." He gave Gary a pat on the shoulder, then followed his friend out of the kitchen.

◇◇◇◇◇◇◇◇◇◇◇◇

Will stormed into his bedroom like a charging bull, cursing under his breath as he slammed the door shut behind him. Lila was sitting on the edge of the bed, crying into her palms.

"I seriously can't believe them," he vented, picking up their luggage case and tossing it on the bed next to Lila. "We've got to get away from these people."

Lila didn't look at him; she just continued to sob. "I'm not leaving," she said, her words muffled by her own tear-filled hands.

"What?" Will paused before he said, "You can't be serious! Honey, those people are dead because of what they did. We have to get away from them."

Lila finally lifted her head. Her rosy cheeks were shimmering with wet streaks. "The only person I want to get away from right now is you," she said softly.

Will squinted angrily and said, "Me? You agreed that if it got too dangerous, we would leave. Well, guess what, honey? Those serpents just killed half a dozen people, less than a half a kilometre from here. So, yeah, I'm thinking it's too dangerous." Will yelled loudly enough that the rest of the house could hear. He immediately regretted it.

"Are you hearing yourself? I've never seen this side of you before. It's like I don't even know you," Lila said, still crying. "You're being so mean. So cruel. It's like you're looking to blame someone for everything that has happened, and I get it. You're angry, but I'm angry too."

"Of course, I'm angry," Will protested. "Blake should never have—"

"But this isn't Blake's fault," Lila cut him off, "or James's fault or Emma's. It just happened. They didn't cause this. Monsters are hunting and killing people all over the place, Will. You know that; you've seen it, too."

Will's angry demeanour faded. He moved away from the bed and crouched down beside her, taking a moment to think before he said, "When your father died, I promised him that I would keep you safe. I have no idea how I'm supposed to do that anymore."

"You could start by being the man that my father spoke to. 'Cause this isn't him." Lila stood up from the bed and walked over to the doorway. "I'm gonna help the others. If you want to leave, I won't blame you. But I'm not coming with you."

She opened the door and left the room. Milky jumped down from its box and quickly followed her out before the door closed.

Will slid down to the ground and removed the velvet ring box from his pocket. Flicking it open, he stared at the diamond engagement ring. How could something so valuable now feel so meaningless? He snapped the lid shut and put the box back in his pocket. He had a lot to think about.

~~~~~~~~~~~~

Lila entered the lounge room to find Blake and James fortifying the room. The pair had just dragged the bookshelf across the floor to the large window beside the front door. Gary was following them around, holding up a pink lantern with a candle flickering inside. The lantern didn't provide much light, but it was enough to see around the rapidly darkening room. Emma came out of the kitchen holding two more pink lanterns.

"Aw, they are so cute," Lila said, as she looked at the small candles burning inside.

Emma glanced at the lanterns and said, "My dad made them for me when I was a kid. I've always been obsessed with pink, so he painted them for me. My friend Brooke and I used to take them into the forest when we were little." She held one of the lanterns out.

"Thanks," Lila said, taking the lantern. "He sounds like a cool dad."

Emma smiled and said, "He was."

"He *is*," Lila corrected her. "He's still out there."

"I know," Emma said, watching as the boys dragged the Chesterfield lounge across the room. "So, are you okay?" she asked and turned back to Lila. "I don't mean to pry. I overheard the yelling."

"Yeah, I'm okay. Thanks," Lila replied and smiled, but was eager to change the subject.

"So, did your dad happen to make any manly lanterns back in the day? I don't exactly do pink," James interrupted, as he and Blake pushed the lounge up against the bookshelf. "Got any red ones?"

Emma shot a raised eyebrow his way. "It's either pink lanterns or you can walk your thick head into the walls. Which will it be?" she asked, holding up the other lantern for one of them to take.

James and Blake looked at each other for a moment. "We'll take it," they both answered.

Lila let out a small giggle.

Emma shoved the pink lantern into Blake's hands. "Hold on, I've got one for you, too," she said to James before ducking back into the kitchen.

"I'm just kidding, Emma. I love your girlie lanterns," James mocked, "especially for Gary. They really bring out the blue in his eyes."

Gary placed his lantern down by his feet, then slumped back into the leather armchair. "It ain't a crime to be beautiful, boy. These are my mother's eyes."

"Is that your mother's moustache, too?" James asked.

Emma returned with two more pink lanterns. "Here, this one is yours," she said, handing one to James, "and I'll give this one to Will later."

"What about you?" James asked. "Don't you need one?"

Emma brushed a strand of hair from her face. "I don't have any more. It's fine. I'll share with Blake or something." She looked at Blake for his reaction but was met with a blank expression. He was clearly lost in his own thoughts.

"Oh, right," James said, and gave Emma an obvious wink. "I'll leave you crazy kids to it. Nature calls." He went into the hall and headed for the bathroom, mumbling, "Ah, young love!"

"It's not like that," Emma protested, but he was already long gone. Feeling slightly embarrassed, she folded her arms and went into the kitchen. Blake snapped out of his reverie and watched her go to the sink and begin washing a teacup. Letting out a yawn, he looked back at Lila and Gary who were both staring at him with disappointed faces. "What?" Blake asked.

"Boys are so dumb," Lila huffed, then walked off into the kitchen.

"Did I miss something?" Blake asked Gary, who said nothing and reclined in his chair.

"Wake me up if the monsters come to kill us," he mumbled, shutting his eyes.

<><><><><><><><><>

Several hours passed before Will emerged from the spare room. After thinking hard on Lila's last words to him, he pulled himself together and thought it was best to finish their conversation – starting with an apology from him. Emma explained that she had let Lila borrow her room for some much-needed alone time. Now, Will found himself standing outside Emma's door, holding up a pink lantern and reciting an apology, which sounded like rubbish however he said it.

"Come in," Lila eventually called out from the other side of the door, having grown tired of listening to him pace the hall.

Will opened the door and entered Emma's bedroom. Lila was sitting on a wooden chair beside the bed, staring silently out the window with her lantern resting at her feet. Will gently closed the door and made his way across the room, his lantern causing shadows to crawl over the walls.

Surprisingly, everything in Emma's room was clean and in its rightful place. Even in the dark, he could see that pink and white was the obvious colour scheme throughout. A tall wall-mounted mirror reflected the flickering candlelight.

Lila blew her nose and then tossed the used tissue into a dustbin beside her chair. The bin was overflowing with scrunched up tissues, and several had fallen onto the floor. "Not sure I feel like talking," she said quietly.

Will placed his lantern on the floor and lowered himself onto the end of the bed. "That's okay. I think I should do the talking."

"I think you've said enough already."

"You're right," said Will, and nodded. "I deserve that."

"I really don't want to talk to you right now."

"I know. I just wanted to say that I'm sorry. I know I've not been the easiest person to deal with."

Lila got up from her seat and turned to face him. "Please go."

"You got it." Will grabbed his lantern and stood up from the bed, but as he went to leave, he noticed the reflection of Lila's blonde hair in the window behind her. Something wasn't right about it. He focused on the glass and saw that there were two yellow lights twinkling across her back.

"Please just go," Lila insisted, but then realised he wasn't staring at her. "What is it?" She turned to see what he was looking at.

"I don't know," Will said, watching as the two yellow lights moved across the glass towards his own reflection. He raised his lantern and looked down at his chest, but nothing was there. He looked back up; the two yellow lights twinkled back at him. "Can you see those… No! wait!"

Lila was already holding her lantern up to the window. Glossy red scales and two yellow eyes stared back her. She dropped the lantern and froze.

"Shrieker!" Will yanked Lila away from the window as the flying serpent plunged its head through the glass with a high-pitched roar. Lila squealed as the monster's jaws slammed shut mere inches from her face. Will threw his lantern at the serpent's head, which harmlessly smashed into several pieces against its ivory frill. Taking Lila by her arm, he flung the bedroom door open before fleeing with her into the hallway. Each of the serpent's colourful wings snapped closed and retracted into its thick body as it slithered in through the window. Letting out a frustrated growl, it slid through the room, squashing the two burning candles as it pursued its prey into the hall.

Standing in the dark, Emma was scrubbing her hands at the kitchen sink when Lila's scream reverberated through the house. "Lila?" She quickly turned the tap off and heard a low hiss coming from the other side of the curtain above the sink. Emma whipped the curtain back and found two yellow eyes on the other side of the glass. "Blake!" she cried out, taking two steps back.

The serpent's jaws opened, dripping saliva strands between rows of serrated teeth and two long fangs. The monster seemed fascinated by its own reflection. Emma slowly moved towards the lounge room, but its yellow eyes were already tracking her. With a spine-tingling shriek, the monster burst through the glass. Emma ran for the lounge room. Two bladed legs pierced the kitchen benchtop as the creature forced itself through the narrow window frame, which fractured, then crumbled, under its heavy weight.

Blake charged to the doorway, catching Emma as she ran into him. The enormous snake filled the entire kitchen, its body crushing the dining table against the far wall as it coiled around. Its ant-like legs knocked Rodney's rifle off the benchtop, twisting the barrel in the process and rendering it completely useless.

Blake rapidly searched for a weapon but found only Emma's favourite morning footwear by the doorway. He snapped them up and pegged the pink slippers at its large skull. This only made matters worse. With an angry growl, the serpent raised its head off the floor. Its two machete-like front arms stabbed the timber floor, allowing it to boost itself high over their heads. Blake was looking around for something else to throw when James and Gary emerged from the hall, armed with a cricket bat and a fire poker.

"Here, kid," Gary said, as he tossed Blake the fire poker.

"Eat this!" cried James, hurling the wooden cricket bat like a javelin, but the serpent snapped its jaws and shattered the bat between its teeth, mid-air.

"We've got to get outside!" Emma panicked as the sound of more commotion came from upstairs. Gary was already unlocking the front door.

"Everybody out!" Will shouted, as he and Lila came racing down the staircase.

"This way!" Gary reefed the front door open.

"Go now!" Blake yelled, standing his ground in the kitchen doorway so that the others could make a run for it.

Will snatched the fire poker from Blake's hand and threw it at the serpent. The monster didn't even flinch. "No time for heroics, mate," Will said, as the other serpent reared its head at the top of the staircase.

James's jaw dropped when he saw the second serpent. "Oh, shit…"

Multiple high-pitched shrieks erupted from other areas of the house, followed by several shattering windows upstairs. "Time to go!" Blake yelled.

Gary, Emma and James were the first ones out the front door, followed closely by Blake, Lila and Will.

"You got keys? Blake asked, as the group ran towards Will's four-wheel drive.

"No, they're inside!" Will glanced at him. "You?"

"Mine are inside, too!" Blake cursed himself.

With a loud snap, one of the pursuing serpents ploughed through the front door, shattering the frame and ripping the door from its hinges. The lounge room window shattered next, sending splintered pieces of the bookshelf spilling onto the deck. Then the second shrieker emerged from the house, followed by a third.

"I haven't got my keys either," Gary panted. "Just keep going!"

The group veered left, passing Gary's truck and Will's four-wheel drive and running towards the orange trees where Gary had been picking fruit earlier that day. Emma glanced back over her shoulder; two more serpents rose above the roof of the house, flapping their colourful wings under the moonlight. Together the five monsters let out a unified shriek, then charged towards their prey. The timber railing snapped like a twig as the three serpents that had stormed through the house slithered off the deck.

"Run faster!" James yelled, struggling to see in the dark field.

"There is nowhere to go!" Emma shouted, as they passed the barn and the orange trees.

Loud shrieks echoed through the air like warning sirens.

"Just keep going!" Will shouted.

Lila squinted to see ahead, but even the moonlight didn't help much. "I can't see a thing!" she shouted, just before her foot collided with a rock that felt more like a mountainous boulder and sent her crashing headfirst into the grass.

It took Will a moment to realise what had happened. "Lila?" he called out, but struggled to see her.

"Hey, wait!" Emma yelled, as she noticed Will was quite a way back. Everybody stopped running and turned around.

Lila felt every grain of dirt drop from her face as she lifted her head up from the ground. "I'm here." She coughed, feeling winded and sore.

Will quickly spotted her, but as soon as he did, his heart felt like it had stopped beating. Three serpents slithered up behind the fallen girl with a delighted hiss.

"Honey, move!" Will screamed, as he ran towards the only person he had ever loved.

"We have to help them!" Blake started running. James was quick to follow him.

"Kid! Don't!" Gary shouted, but it was too late.

Lila glanced up to see three salivating shriekers above her.

"Run!" Emma cried out.

The closest serpent extended its two bladed arms from its body. Lila glanced at Will one last time. He was sprinting towards her as fast as he could. She reached out for his hand. He reached out for hers. Lila mouthed the words "I love you," then closed her eyes and accepted her fate.

Bright orange light suddenly cut through the night sky, distracting the monsters for the briefest of moments. Without warning, a stream of fire exploded over Lila's head and obliterated the three serpents where they stood, leaving only three wriggling tails beside a crater of tall flames.

Lila scrambled to her feet as Will grabbed her hand and pulled her close. "What... what happened?" he asked, turning to James and Blake who had skidded to halt a few metres from them.

"Watch out!" Emma yelled, pointing to the sky.

Shrieking loudly, the two flying serpents swooped. Their massive jaws were open as they hurled themselves at Blake and James.

Another stream of fire blasted through the sky and consumed the shriekers, leaving another burning crater in the ground nearby. The flames decorated the area with an orange tinge while the scorched half of an orange tree began to flake off in the wind.

"There's more coming!" Lila shouted, squeezing Will's hand.

Huddling together, the group watched as dozens of shrieking serpents began closing in from every direction.

"Oh, God!" Emma panicked. "They're everywhere!"

Blake slowly looked up as fire rained across the starry night like a meteor shower, systematically incinerating each serpent as it approached.

"Finally," Lila cheered, "the army shows up!"

"Well, it's about bloody time!" Gary celebrated with her.

Blake traded a nervous glance with James as fireballs destroyed the remaining serpents swarming around the group. "I don't think that's the army..." A bone-chilling realisation came over him. "Everybody run! Get back to the house! *Go!*"

"The house? Are you crazy?" Will protested.

"Trust me! Run!" Blake wasn't about to argue.

"But why would we—" Emma stopped in mid-sentence, and the penny quickly dropped. "Oh, God... Everybody run!"

But before they could take a single step, an enormous scaly tail slammed down in front of the group, blocking the path to the house. "Quick! The other way!" Emma screamed, but the ground immediately trembled from a second impact behind them. The group froze, and with pure dread smeared across their faces, they slowly turned around. Their eyes followed the giant spiny tail until it became clear which terror was towering over them. It was none other than the same monster that had started this nightmare – the so-called dragon that had levelled a city in a single day. Now, it's swirling fiery eyes were bearing down on them.

"Sweet... mother... of..." Gary could hardly string his words together. He had never seen it before.

For the first time in a long time, James was speechless.

Emma had almost forgotten how big the creature was.

"Will," was the only word Lila could muster as her whole body started shaking.

"I know..." Will wrapped his arms around Lila and kissed the top of her head, feeling the weight of the ring in his pocket more than ever.

Moonlight flickered between the bony spines of the dragon's back as it lowered itself on all fours, its huge three-fingered hands crushing several trees and bushes as its claws dug deep into the earth. A fiery orange light surged between its scales, illuminating the area with each pulse.

Blake pushed past the others and stood at the front of the group, pointlessly placing himself between them and the gargantuan creature. The dragon lowered its tyrannosaurus-like head; swirling fire burned within its eyes.

"This is it," James said softly.

Gary relaxed his body and braced himself with a silent prayer. Will clutched Lila's hand and held her close. Emma stood completely still. All she hoped was that her father would know that she loved him. And that she was sorry.

Blake didn't even blink. A single memory played like a slideshow in his mind: the silver station wagon, the young mother, the little boy, the clock tower, Amy. This monster had done it all.

The dragon blasted the group with a deafening roar. They covered their faces, feeling the sweltering heat from its charred breath. What was only mere seconds felt like excruciating hours. Nevertheless, nothing happened – no fire, no pain. One by one, the group opened their eyes and gazed up at the dragon.

"What is it doing?" Lila asked, as she squeezed Will's hand.

"I don't know…" Will glanced at James and Emma, but they looked just as confused as everyone else.

The dragon belted out another fierce roar, then another. The group plugged their ears and did their best to withstand each deafening cry. Much to his surprise, Blake quickly began to recognise something. Each roar sounded slightly different from the last; each was becoming more defined.

Blake lowered his hands and began to listen carefully. The dragon roared again. Blake inched a little closer. Keeping their ears covered, the group watched him with utter bewilderment.

"What are you doing?" Emma snapped.

"Listen," Blake said. One by one, the rest of the group removed their hands from their ears. Seemingly frustrated, the monster raised its head and let out a thunder-cracking roar.

"Do you hear it?" Blake turned back to the others, but they all stared at him with a mix of terror and confusion.

Gary was sweating profusely. "Kid, I don't hear—"

"WHY?" The word suddenly roared from the dragon's mouth.

Blake felt every muscle in his body tense up. *Why?* Did he hear that correctly?

Emma cupped her mouth.

"It spoke. It actually spoke," James said, choking on his words.

"Will," was again the only word Lila could utter.

"What the hell?" Will couldn't believe it.

"WHY?" The dragon blasted them again.

Blake took several steps back from its gaping jaws and asked, "What? *Why what?*"

Lifting its massive tail off the ground, the monster violently dug its claws deeper into the ground and roared once more. Blake protected his face from the heat while James glanced back at the now clear path and wondered if they should make a run for the house. The monster swung its tail through the air, obliterating countless trees and bushes before slamming it down behind it. "WHY DIDN'T... YOU..." It failed to get the words out coherently.

"I don't understand! Why didn't I *what?*" Blake found himself in a race to understand the creature, fearing that if he didn't, it might lose its temper.

With fire swirling around its pupils, the dragon finally asked, "WHY DIDN'T YOU KILL IT?"

24

THE GUARDIAN

The colossal dragon stood over the grassy field on all fours. Its razor-sharp claws etched deeper into the earth as both its muscular arms, which were covered in hundreds of thorny scales right up to its shoulders, pressed hard into the ground. Lowering its head, moonlight shimmered over its sandy scales as it let out a throaty growl. A row of tall spines ran from the rear of its skull, along the ridge of its back and onto its long tail, which was swaying back and forth like a curious feline's.

The dragon belted out another fierce roar. "WHY DIDN'T YOU KILL IT?" Its voice was exceedingly deep, and its mouth moved only slightly as it spoke.

"Everyone get back!" Blake shielded his face from its hot breath. Flaming craters where the shriekers had been incinerated began to slowly spread along the tall grass.

"Dude, it's speaking," James said in amazement, stumbling back and colliding with Will and Lila. They barely noticed him.

"Quick!" Emma said. "Say something!"

"Yeah, I don't think this thing wants to be ignored, kid," Gary agreed, his face drenched in a nervous sweat.

"I'm trying," Blake replied, as he stared up at the vocalising creature. "I don't know what you mean. Kill it?"

"WHY DIDN'T YOU KILL IT?" the dragon repeated.

"I don't understand! Why didn't I kill *what*?"

"Oh!" James began to anxiously hop on the spot. "It means the pod thing. Try that!"

"Of course!" Blake's face lit up. "The big shell-like spider thing! You mean that?"

"NO!" The monster's growling voice sent birds scampering from nearby trees.

"No?" Blake turned to the group for assistance. "Got any other ideas?" All James gave him was a helpless shrug. Lila was too petrified to watch, so she buried her face in Will's chest, who was also struggling to comprehend the predicament they were in.

"WHY DIDN'T YOU KILL IT?"

Blake shuddered. "I'm sorry! I'm trying! I don't know what you mean!"

The dragon reared up on its hind legs and let out another cracking roar, only this time a stream of fire erupted from its jaws and incinerated an approaching shrieker from the night sky. Emma squirmed as the creature's ash showered over them.

Slamming both of its claws back into the ground, the dragon lowered its wide flat head, growling angrily and revealing rows of enormous teeth.

"Hey, just relax…" Blake raised his hands, hoping to calm the creature which, admittedly, didn't seem too effective. "I'm trying to answer you! But you're not giving me much to go on here. I don't understand what you mean."

Something suddenly dawned on Emma, but it was far too silly to be the answer they needed – or was it? "It couldn't be *that*?" She dismissed the thought with a whisper. "Surely not."

"What did you say?" Blake asked her, eager to keep the giant monster talking before it decided to pre-emptively end the conversation. "Hey, if anyone has a suggestion, *now* is the time!"

"Blake, the spider," Emma murmured, but then blurted out her answer like she had the final number in a game of bingo. "The spider! The one you put in the garden! It wants to know why you didn't *kill* the spider!"

James sneered at her. "Really, Em? *That's* what you come up with? We're so dead."

"The spider!" Blake didn't hesitate to spit it out. "Is that right? You want to know why I didn't kill the spider this morning?"

"YES," the dragon answered. "WHY DIDN'T YOU KILL IT?"

"Um... I didn't... I didn't kill it because..." Blake's nerves had well and truly taken over. How was he supposed to think with those teeth hanging over him? It was a spider. Why did it matter to a giant reptile anyway? Frazzled and lost, he was now scrambling to string a competent sentence together. "I didn't... I don't..."

"TELL ME!" the dragon snapped, its eyes flaring brightly. "WHY DIDN'T YOU KILL IT?"

"I'll tell you!" Blake suddenly shouted. "The spider *didn't know* it was in our home. It wasn't *trying* to get in our way. It *didn't know* it wasn't supposed to be there. It has a life. Who am I to end it? All I had to do was take it outside. It didn't deserve to die." He finished his short rant, gasping for breath – and nervously awaited the monster's response.

"You." The dragon's eardrum-shattering voice lowered to a softer – yet still terrifying – tone. "You are a protector," it growled, as the fire swirling around its pupils dissipated, and the orange glow between its scales faded to black.

Blake drew a deep relieved breath, and then the creature's words clicked. "A protector?" What did it even mean by that? "Me? A protector – of spiders?"

"A protector of life," it corrected him.

Blake was sweating all over; he had no idea what was going on. The murderous monster that had levelled their city had just saved their lives. It was now talking to them and becoming more fluent with every sentence its gravelly voice belted out. "What are you?" he asked, not even sure he wanted to know the answer. But the question had already slipped out.

"Blake, be careful," Emma whispered nervously.

"Yeah! What are you?" James brazenly called out. Gary quickly clipped him across the ear and covered his mouth, but the dragon didn't seem to care or even notice. It only seemed interested in Blake for the moment.

"Where did you come from?" Blake asked again. "Does your species have a name?"

The monster's gaze shifted to the cloudy night sky. "We have existed for a great length of time. We are not foreign; we are not alien. We were born here – have always been here. Your kind once walked among us. Some fought wars over us. Some feared us, some hunted us, and some prayed to us. For a time, you celebrated us – carved our likeness in stone, created images in our honour, told stories about us to your young. You put a great many names to our species – monsters, demons, griffins, titans, dragons, gods. We come in many forms, but we are of *one* race. We are Dreyan. We have awoken."

"Dreyan?" The monsters now had a name, but Blake still had a laundry list of questions. "What do you mean, *awoken*? Like, you were sleeping?"

"Yes," the dragon growled. "Much like your own species, we require regular rest. Deep underground, where land is warmest."

"You came from underground…" Blake remembered hearing reports of unusual earthquakes over the radio in Gary's truck. "Why are you here? Why tell me any of this?"

"Because we have much to discuss," the dragon replied. "My kind has awoken from our slumber to find our home in a state of devastation. Humankind has consumed much of this earth, leaving our coming reign in jeopardy."

"Your reign?" Blake didn't like the sound of that.

"The Dreyan have reigned over this earth for many past cycles. Once awoken, our reign spans over a thousand cycles, so we must take greater periods of time to rejuvenate in between."

"A thousand cycles?" Blake asked. "Do you mean years? You're awake for a thousand years?"

The monster didn't respond right away; it seemed to be studying Blake's reaction. Eventually, it did answer him. "Yes. There is an order of leadership within the Dreyan. A name you cannot pronounce, but in your language, it means *Guardian*. The Guardians are the pinnacle of our species; only the most powerful and devoted are bestowed this title. It is the duty of the Guardians to ensure that all life continues to flourish for many cycles to come. Some Guardians protect the skies, while others watch over the seas. Alarak, the Guardian of Balance, ensures that all species remain in a natural, equal order, so that none consume beyond their needs. The most powerful Dreyan, Grannus, is the first Guardian. He is the respected voice of our species and the overseer of all existence."

"And where do you fit in all this?" Blake asked.

"I am Drakken, the Guardian of all Living," the dragon said, "the protector of all living beings. I am charged with the preservation of all species."

Rapid memories flashed through Blake's mind: the silver station wagon, the clock tower, Amy's dusty face, the security guard, the fire that engulfed them both, the ash. A tear escaped down his cheek. "You're a guardian for everything that lives, huh? The protector of all?" Blake was shivering as the words rolled off his lips. "Is that what you were doing when you dropped a building on a woman and her child? Were you protecting them? When you burned all those terrified people in the street? Was that you, Drakken, the Guardian of all living things? You murdered thousands," he screamed in an outburst of tears and anger.

Everybody remained dead silent.

The dragon stared at him. Blake didn't care if it killed him right there. But it didn't. Instead, the dragon's deep growling voice uttered a single word, "Yes."

"Yes?" Blake wiped his eyes. "Some Guardian you are."

The dragon lowered its head, then growled at him. "You speak of murder, of my actions, with anger, yet you have taken no reflection of your own. Tell me: how many creatures of this land perished when your kind removed their homes to build your cities? How much life has your kind eradicated so that you may wear their skins? How many lives has your kind carelessly ended because they were simply not of your own species? Your kind murders and consumes without hesitation or remorse, without consequences or punishment. Your kind has committed earth-wide genocide. Even the humans behind you wanted to kill an innocent being out of pure inconvenience."

"The spider…" Blake's heart raced. "You watched me put it in the garden. But how? How could you have seen that?"

"I have tracked many scents over great distances to ensure your kind's eradication. Your scent brought me to this area, and from the skies I observed you."

"Eradication?" Blake asked. "You mean, you're going to kill everyone?"

"That is our intent. Humans have spread far, and your numbers are too great. Your consumption of this earth's resources has left it crippled. Several Guardians have already risen and commenced a purge across this land. Other Guardians will soon awaken around the earth, and together we will ensure that harmonious life continues."

"But... You can't..." Blake couldn't even finish the sentence. "If you're here to kill us, then why tell me this?"

The dragon paused for a moment, seemingly to decide if it was going to answer him. After what felt like a tediously long wait (it was merely seconds), the Guardian of all Living spoke again. "Your choice to protect a life has brought me to question my own actions. If a single human can be re-educated, taught to preserve instead of consume, then perhaps your species need not perish. As the Guardian of all living beings, I cannot ignore this alternative to your species' extinction as I have witnessed your capacity to influence another with these traits." The dragon's gaze then shifted to Will. "This human also chose to spare the creature's life."

Everyone slowly turned to Will.

"Honey?" Lila peeled herself from her boyfriend and stumbled back. "What happened?"

Blake didn't get it either. "What is it talking about?"

"The spider..." Will was struggling to find a way to explain himself. "I had a rock... I was going to kill it... but, I left it in the bush... It didn't feel right... so, I just left it there."

Reaching out, Lila grabbed his hand and clutched it tightly as the significance of Will's choice was realised by all around him.

"I always liked spiders," James sheepishly muttered, hoping the dragon wasn't about to turn on those who weren't named Blake or William.

Blake turned back to the dragon. "So, what happens now? What does all this mean?"

"You are an example of what your species is capable of. An example I require the other Guardians to witness if I am to convince them to spare your kind."

"No problem!" Blake agreed without hesitation. "What do I have to do?"

"I am no longer familiar with your kind. Humans are young to this earth but have evolved quickly," the dragon replied. "You will teach me about your species. When we are ready, we will meet with Grannus and I will educate him in my learnings."

"Just hold on a damn minute!" Gary emerged from the group and stood alongside Emma. "I'm not gonna let this monster parade you around for all his overgrown buddies to see, like some puppy at show and tell!"

"Gary!" Blake quickly hushed him. "Not now."

Reluctantly, Gary calmed down, but his wrinkled blue eyes did all the talking. Trembling and fearful, he could only watch as the closest thing he had to a son surrendered himself to the most frightening creature he had ever seen.

Emma reached out and clutched Gary's hand.

"So, can you ask the other Dreyan or Guardians to stop, too?" Blake asked, desperate for some good news.

Drakken's nostrils flared. "Alarak believes humanity will never stop consuming and is certain that your extinction is vital. He will not be swayed as easily."

"But you can convince him to help us, right?" Blake asked.

"Alarak is the Guardian of Balance and a stubborn Dreyan. But he is loyal. He will follow Grannus's command."

Blake nervously ran his fingers through his sweaty hair. "So, we need to convince this Grannus guy…"

"Grannus must witness that your kind has the capacity and devotion required to preserve this world. My duty as Guardian is to make him aware of my observations so he may decide the rightful course for our home."

"And how do you suggest we do that?" Blake's head was spinning. It wasn't exactly a conversation he was prepared to partake in.

"You will be a beacon for your species, an example for them to follow," Drakken growled.

"Me? I'm a nobody! No, no, no! I know you don't understand how humans work, but trust me, I have no say in what we do. You need to speak to someone important, like the prime minister. Maybe go to America and knock on the door of the White House." Blake was flustered and could feel the weight of everyone's eyes on him.

"Human social structure is of no interest to us," the dragon gruffly disagreed. "The Guardians will only care about your intent. Your value is decided by your actions, not by your species' social ideals. If your kind is to survive, then *you* must show them how."

"No pressure, though," Blake replied, unsure if he was on the verge of a panic attack. "So, what are you suggesting?" he asked, trying to keep the conversation moving.

"I request we form a union. I will follow you, learn from you – for a time. If I am to convince Grannus of your species' potential, then I must be educated in current human behaviour."

"Okay," Blake agreed nervously, "I guess we can do that."

"Then it is done," Drakken agreed.

Blake nodded. His palms were sweating. "So, what do we actually do now?"

"That is for you to decide. You possess an understanding of human culture that I do not. It would be unwise for me to ignore this. Your judgement is what brought me before you; I will trust it and do as you require."

"I don't know about this, kid," Gary murmured. "This thing was happy to kill us all yesterday."

Blake was too scared to do anything but agree with the monster. "Can't we go see this Grannus now?"

"No," Drakken replied. "Grannus is yet to awaken. We must use this time to prepare for his arrival."

"How much time do we have?"

"One cycle."

"A year," Blake sputtered. "The other Guardians will have wiped us out by then!"

"It is possible." The dragon didn't seem to care for this argument.

"Um, okay," said Blake, and pulled himself together and tried to focus on what to do next. "Well, you may not care for our social structure, but humans do. So, let's start with the army. If we can locate them, they should be able to reach the prime minister or someone high up. We need to explain all this to them, if we are really gonna do this."

"One problem," James interrupted, "we don't know where anyone is."

"We don't, but he might." Blake looked at Drakken. "You said you tracked our scents to find us. Could you find others?"

"Yes," Drakken acknowledged. "There is a large gathering of humans not too far from this land. Their numbers grow each day. I can lead you to them."

"If you know about them, then why are they still alive?"

"Humans seek one another during times of desperation. It is efficient to allow them to gather and terminate them when their numbers are greater."

"Oh." Blake regretted asking the question. "That's horrifying. So, wait – one more thing. If we do this, it's gonna take some time. You have to agree not to kill anyone else, okay?"

"Yes," the dragon said, "a Guardian does not seek to harm what is not necessary."

James inched a little closer, then whispered in Blake's ear, "Dude, this is crazy! I don't think you can trust this thing."

"Please, shut up right now," said Blake, and glared at James. "I don't want to piss it off!"

"Human insults inspire no such intention within me," Drakken's gravelly voice quickly silenced them both. "I do not experience such emotion the way you do."

"Good to know," Blake said, and gulped. "So, I guess we better get started then, right?"

25

A PLACE OF REFUGE

After dousing the fires spreading through the field with its massive hands, Drakken, the Guardian of all Living, circled the skies over the Riley Farm like a watchful hawk and remained there for several hours. Sunlight was now kissing the tips of distant mountains, and with each pass overhead, the dragon's shadow routinely cast the house into darkness.

"I can't do this," James complained. "Every time that thing comes back around, everything goes black, and I shit myself!"

"Yeah, well at least you can still tell you've shit yourself," Gary said, as he and James tossed the broken couch onto a pile of rubble beside the barn. "I have to double-check sometimes," he added, brushing the dust off his hands.

"So, what now?" James continued. "Blake's just gonna go off with this thing to find the army? Am I the only one who feels like we're screwed, no matter what?"

"I hear ya," Gary agreed, "but I don't think Blake had much choice. Not to mention, if he thinks he can stop all this, then… well, you know him."

"Yeah, I do. But what if this Drakken thing changes its mind? Just decides humans are too far gone, then barbeques all of us?"

Gary gave James a not-so-reassuring pat on the back. "After hearing what that thing said last night, sounds like we're all living on borrowed time anyway."

"Very encouraging," James said, shaking his head as Gary walked off in the direction of the house.

Will, who hadn't said much since Drakken had appeared, continued to sweep the shattered glass off the front deck into a green garbage bin, doing his best to ignore the monster's looming shadow when it passed overhead. Working alongside him was an uncomfortably quiet Blake, who was busy filling a wheelbarrow with pieces of timber and plasterboard from the obliterated front door and lounge room window.

"That thing hasn't stopped circling this place for hours," Will quietly said, breaking what seemed like an eternity of awkward silence. "It's obviously watching us."

Nodding in agreement, Blake dropped another piece of the splintered window frame into the wheelbarrow. "Well, it – or he – said we shouldn't leave here until the sun comes up. I wasn't about to argue with it."

"He? It's a he now?" Will scoffed. "Well, I don't trust your new friend."

Blake gave him a what-do-you-want-from-me look. "Friend? *It* said it was a *he* before he flew up there. It – crap, *he* – can probably hear you, too. You know that, right?"

Will shook his head. "If you wanna clean this place up and pretend that what just happened didn't just happen, then fine – but don't expect me to play along."

Blake lowered his voice to a whisper. "We'll be leaving soon anyway, so just chill till then, okay? Things are crazy enough. I don't need your mood swings, too."

"Whatever, man," Will said dismissively.

"You're unbelievable," Blake replied. "You do realise that this could be a chance to save everybody? We could stop this from happening anywhere else. You get that, right?"

"Right," Will muttered. "Is that why you're doing this? Or are you just trying to save your own arse?"

"Figures you'd think that way. Tell me, what would you have me do? Just ignore his proposal? Not even try to stop this?" Blake asked, angrily throwing his hands up. But Will ignored him and continued to sweep the deck in silence.

∞∞∞∞∞∞∞∞∞

Inside the house, Lila quietly leaned against the doorway of Thomas Riley's bedroom and watched as Emma frantically tossed all her father's clothes from the wardrobe onto the bed. "Em, are you sure you need to take any of this?" Lila gestured to an open backpack on the mattress that Emma had already filled to the zipper with clothes.

"Um, no," Emma said, then stopped and looked over at the mess she had just made. "I don't know. It was Blake's idea. This gathering of people... he said maybe Dad would be there. I'm probably fooling myself."

"Hey, Blake's right, but I don't think he meant for you to pack a suitcase," Lila said. "Are you sure you're okay?"

Emma flopped onto the end of the bed. "I can't think straight." She sighed, then began to re-tie her ponytail for the third time in ten minutes. "How about you?" She looked at Lila. "Those things last night; that was a close call. Are you okay?"

"I don't know," Lila said, as she joined Emma at the end of the bed. "It was a close call – for all of us."

"Can you believe it?" Emma asked. "That Drakken creature, I mean. Do you believe what it said? About all of this?"

"I do," Lila said. "When those things caught up to me, I thought it was all over. Will's face – I could see the helplessness he felt. Then that Drakken saved my life, saved all our lives. Why do that if it's not trying to help us? We're like ants to that thing; it has no reason to lie to us. For the first time since this started, I feel like I finally know why this happened. And, as messed up as this is, I kinda understand it. Do you think that makes me a bad person?" she asked, turning to Emma.

Emma threw an arm around Lila and rested her head against her shoulder. "No, I don't think you're a bad person."

"Thanks." Lila smiled as the pair aimlessly stared at the opposite wall. "You're handling everything pretty well, all things considered."

"You mean considering the world might end because some really old dinosaurs are going to wake up and hate what we've done to the place? Considering we almost got eaten last night? Or considering the same giant monster we've been hiding from saved our lives, can talk for some reason, and has been flying over my house like the world's scariest vulture for the last few hours?" Emma sighed again. "I think I'm just numb, at this point."

"Me too," Lila added quietly. "I feel anxious."

"So do I." Emma lifted her head off Lila's shoulder but continued to stare at the wall. "I'm really scared, you know."

Lila nodded. "Me too."

〰〰〰〰〰〰

A short time later, the group gathered on the driveway to discuss their next move. While Blake, Emma and a very disgruntled James agreed to follow Drakken to find this "human gathering,"

Lila, Gary and Will chose to stay behind and attempt to make the Riley Farm liveable again.

"So, it's settled then," Gary concluded, then turned to Blake. "You can take my truck."

"Actually, you should take mine." Will dug into his pocket and pulled his keys out. "It's still got half a tank of gas and plenty of power – if you need to run from something."

"Why does it feel like everyone is expecting us to die?" James remarked.

"Thanks," Blake said, catching the keys as Will tossed them over.

With a backpack full of her father's clothes slung over her shoulder, Emma was clearly nervous about the journey ahead. "Ready to go?" she asked, somewhat hesitantly.

Blake and James both nodded, but neither could shake their nerves.

Lila, who was holding a very skittish Milky in her arms, was feeling worse about their plan with every passing minute. "You three be careful."

"We will," Emma assured her before turning to Blake. "So, what do we do now?"

Blake looked dumbfounded, then turned his gaze to the sky and the gigantic wingspan that occupied it. "I guess I just call out to it? To him, I mean."

"You mean, like a dog?" James asked apprehensively.

Blake shrugged. "I guess so."

James drew back with raised hands. "Your funeral, dude."

"Hey, there. Ah, Drakken? We're ready to go." Blake raised his voice barely a single octave and immediately found himself a sweaty mess. "Do you think he heard?"

Without hesitation, the dragon executed a swan dive like an enormous falcon, folding its wings onto its back a mere second before slamming into the ground with the force of a nine on the Richter scale. A shockwave of dirt and dry leaves sent the group into a coughing fit as they struggled to keep their balance.

"Guess…" Blake gasped, "that means… we're good to go."

"Great," James coughed beside him.

Drakken lifted his head to the sky and stood on his back legs, eclipsing the area in his shadow.

"You three be careful," Gary said, still trying to wrap his head around it all. "We don't know where this place is – or what it is."

"He's right," Will said, earning a raised eyebrow from Gary. "You don't know what you'll find there. Watch yourselves."

"Alright then, let's not waste any more time," Blake said, then gave Drakken a nervous nod. "Lead the way."

Drakken's concealed wings unfolded from his back and spread out like an eagle's. With a single broad stroke, the dragon launched off the ground with an earth-shaking leap and began to hover several metres above the driveway.

Blake, Emma and James headed over to Will's four-wheel drive and buckled themselves in. Lila went to the passenger's side door and gave Emma a heartfelt goodbye, while Gary came over to the driver's side to add a few cautious words of his own. "Now, you all listen here. You three take care of each other. Watch out for each other, you hear? If something don't seem right, then you turn right 'round and come straight back!"

Blake nodded. "We will. You be careful, too."

"I never thought I'd say this, but I'd rather be staying here with you," James uttered, "and I wouldn't say that lightly."

Gary leaned into Blake a little closer and said, "If you don't come back with him, everyone will understand."

After all the goodbyes were said, Lila and Gary rejoined Will and Milky on the deck and watched as the yellow four-wheel drive left the gravelly driveway in a cloud of dust.

The car quickly disappeared behind the roadside trees, but Will waited until Drakken was further away in the distance before speaking up. "Now's our chance."

Lila and Gary looked at Will with confused faces. "What do you mean?" Lila asked, taking the restless cat from Will's hands.

"They're leading that thing away from here. I say we make a run for it." Will opened his hand, revealing the keys to Gary's truck in his palm.

Lila and Gary looked at each other. They both knew exactly what the other was thinking.

∿∿∿∿∿∿∿∿

At first glance, it appeared to be just another beautiful day on the Gold Coast – a crystal blue sky with barely a cloud in it. Unlike any other day, though, there was something else in the sky – the Guardian of all Living. Drakken's incredible wingspan extended over the width of the highway that Blake was currently weaving the four-wheel drive through. Admittedly, Emma found that there was something almost majestic about the way the monster effortlessly glided through the air – from the way the sunlight gleamed over its sandy-coloured scales to the way its long tail rolled over the updrafts.

Aware of Drakken's heightened hearing, no one had spoken a word since leaving the Riley Farm. James kept remarkably quiet in the back seat. He had no joke, no funny tension-breaking line to whip out. The magnitude of what he had become involved in was quickly overwhelming him. His mind flicked through questions and scenarios like a bored child searching for the right TV station. What if Blake had rejected Drakken's proposal? Would it have killed them? Could they really stop this from happening everywhere else? Did the government know of the Dreyans' existence? Would the world ever go back to normal? He couldn't stop himself, and the longer he thought about it all, the worse he felt.

In the front passenger seat, Emma unzipped the backpack on her lap and pulled out a crumpled photograph of her father. He still had black hair at the time and was smiling on the front deck in his military uniform, with an eight-year-old Emma on his shoulders. *Thomas Riley, Emma Riley, 40 Walker Road, December 23rd 2008,* was scribbled on the back in pencil. Her mother had taken the photo moments after her father had surprised Emma by coming home to spend Christmas with them. It was her favourite Christmas memory. After staring at the photo for some time, she folded it over and put it back inside the bag.

Drakken banked left, causing Blake to take the next exit into the suburb of Robina. The throaty V8 howled as they rounded the next bend to find something quite unexpected. Blake slowed the car to a crawl as Emma and James leaned out of their seats to get a better look.

Home after home had been consumed by overgrown vegetation. Trees twisted and curved through windows and doorways, vines clung to lampposts and gutters, concrete footpaths were reduced to grey patches between lush grass, and the road itself was riddled with tree roots growing out of the pavement. It was as if the area had been deserted for decades.

"Man, those spider things really went to town here," James said. "It's like nature has retaken this place."

"I guess that's what they are supposed to do, right?" Emma agreed. "The big monsters cleanse the land, and those weird spiders repopulate it. It's actually starting to make sense. They're repairing the damage we've done."

"Do you think your farm will end up looking like this?" James asked.

"I don't know," Emma replied.

"Well, it can't be that bad," Blake chimed in. "Lila and Will have been living like this for years."

James studied a tall tree that curved over the road. Several vines draped from its branches and were swinging in the breeze. A rustle in some nearby bushes revealed a group of kangaroos feeding on the vegetation. A female perked up her ears and stopped eating, then cautiously watched the passing vehicle as a joey poked its head out from her pouch – much to Emma's excitement. "Oh, look! It's a baby one! So cute!" she gushed.

"Did we really ruin the world without realising it?" James asked sombrely. Blake and Emma looked at one another, but neither said a word.

"We should get moving," Blake insisted. "Don't wanna lose sight of him." He then checked the sky to find that Drakken was nowhere to be seen. "What? Where did he go?"

"How could we lose it?" Emma asked, twisting in her seat, but she couldn't spot the dragon either.

"Maybe we're close," James said. "We're looking for a big gathering of people, right? The Robina shopping centre is just down the road from here. It's big enough."

"Worth a shot," Blake agreed, shifting into gear.

Several grassy streets and two overly green roundabouts later, the massive Robina Mall came into view at the far end of a long narrow road. Crossing through the final jungle-like junction, Blake noticed that the large mall wasn't consumed by overgrown trees, wild grass or creeping vines. It appeared that someone had maintained it well.

"This is it! It has to be!" Emma eagerly pressed her nose up to the windshield as they approached the mall's carpark.

Three military trucks were parked at each side of the multistorey carpark's entrance, leaving just enough space to drive a single vehicle through the middle. "Hold it!" an unknown voice barked at them. Blake slammed the brakes. Four armed soldiers darted out from behind the vehicles and surrounded the yellow four-wheel drive.

"Hands up! Right now!" the first soldier yelled, his rifle aimed directly at Blake's head. James raised his hands first, and Emma and Blake quickly followed. "Are you armed?" the soldier asked.

"What?" Blake hadn't heard properly.

"Are you armed?" the soldier yelled this time.

"No, no. We're not armed," Blake quickly assured him.

"Looks clean, sir," another solider said, looking over the car with the flashlight mounted on his weapon.

"Alright." The soldier nodded to his squad mate at the passenger's side door and lowered his rifle. "Man, I can't believe there are still people out there," he added, looking pleasantly surprised. "You guys looking for a safe place to stay?"

Emma quickly pulled the photo from her backpack, leaned over Blake and handed it to the soldier. "We are looking for someone. Have you seen him?"

The soldier squinted at the picture, then shook his head. "Look, I don't know. There are a few thousand people crammed in here. You're welcome to head inside and look for yourselves."

"Thousands?" Blake was stunned. "What is this place?" he asked

"You guys don't know?" The soldier was even more surprised. He removed his helmet and scratched his buzz-cut head. "The mall has been turned into a shelter. An emergency call was put out on the radio when the city was attacked. Not many people got the message, though, as we lost some of the radio towers that afternoon. If you guys didn't get the message, then how did you find this place anyway?"

Blake subtly checked the sky for their winged guide, but Drakken was still nowhere to be seen. This time he was glad, since the last thing he wanted was to start a panic. "We were just passing though, saw the army trucks and thought we'd check it out," he lied convincingly.

"Listen, everyone here is homeless, sick, injured or all of the above." The soldier put his helmet back on. "It's crowded in there, but it's safe for now. If you guys need somewhere to stay, this here is your refuge. All are welcome here."

"Thanks, but we have people to go back to," Blake declined.

The soldier nodded respectfully and handed the photo back to Emma. "Your choice, although I'd recommend staying here. Some of the things we've seen out there…"

Blake glanced up at the sky one more time. It was still clear. "Hey, while I have you, who is your commanding officer here? We might have some information that could help him."

The soldier raised a suspicious eyebrow and asked, "Information? What kind of information?"

Blake had to think quickly. "Oh, it's no big deal. Um, yeah, just a few places that may still have food inside, medical supplies even. Could help the people here," he lied again. Sweating in their seats, Emma and James smiled at the surrounding soldiers.

"Great!" the soldier said appreciatively. "Any supplies we can get will help. Thanks! Colonel Henrickson oversees all military operations across the region, but he isn't stationed here. One of his squads arrived a short while ago, though. I think they're here to retrieve a civilian. Captain Lorcan Edwards is the man you're looking for. Let him know; they might pick up the supplies on their return trip to base. We're shorthanded right now, but it's best to get to that stuff before some scumbag looters do, right?"

"Right," Blake replied, and gave the soldier a grateful nod. "Thanks for your help."

"What does the captain look like?" James asked.

The soldier chuckled, stepped back from the car and signalled the rest of his squad to stand down. "Oh, don't worry. You'll know him when you see him. They don't breed them that big anymore."

"Oh, great, that's really helpful," James said sarcastically. Emma reached back and pinched his leg for being rude. "Ouch! What the hell!" He slapped her hand away.

"Thanks again," Blake said to the soldier.

The soldier returned the gesture. "Good luck in there. I hope you find who you're looking for. Park anywhere you find a space. Oh, and I'd hold on to those keys tight. People don't care much for the law right now, and a lot of folk would love a big car like that in a time like this."

"Got it." Blake allowed the squad to move back before he shifted into gear. Emma glanced down at her father's photo. She prayed that he was inside. With only several inches of room on either side, Blake squeezed the big yellow four-wheel drive between the military vehicles and entered the Robina Mall carpark.

"Well, no one's driving out of here in a hurry," James said, looking around.

He was right. The enormous undercover carpark was packed. Vehicles of all types and sizes were parked in total disarray. In what appeared to be an attempt by the military to preserve space, thousands of cars had been crammed together, many of which were now scraped, crashed or backed into. Emma watched as a military operated forklift carried a car from one space and then carelessly dropped it in another. Blake followed the only open lane through to the other side, emerging from the carpark into the beautiful landscaped gardens of Robina Mall's entrance.

"It's crazy," Emma mumbled.

"What is?" James asked.

"Michelle and I were shopping here the other day. Now look at it."

The centrepiece of the Robina Mall's entrance was a large pond with three water fountains in the middle. The once grand entrance to the popular shopping centre was now a flat, murky green body of water. The surrounding lawns and flower beds had been trampled under a gathering of military trucks, ambulances and police cars.

Blake quickly spotted a patch of grass between the road and the murky pond, then mounted the curb and parked on it. Swinging the backpack over her shoulder, Emma clenched her father's photo and was out of the vehicle before Blake had even switched the engine off.

Unlike the touristy Pacific Town Mall in Broadbeach, the Robina Mall had been a popular social hub for local Gold Coast residents. Hedges, pretty flower beds and illuminated trees decorated the exterior of half a dozen restaurants and bars that bordered the mall's main entrance. On any given day, crowds flocked to the mall for its variety of stores, award-winning food outlets and first-class cinemas. While Emma always preferred to shop at the Pacific Town Mall, the Robina Mall had been her friends' – Brooke and Michelle's – favourite shopping destination.

Now, the mall was a breeding ground for desperation. To the right of the main entrance, a large congregation of people slowly shuffled into a defunct steakhouse. Hungry men, women and children queued between armed soldiers as an elderly woman handed out warm bowls of soup and plastic cups of water. On the left, a pair of female doctors carried an emotional young man between them. He couldn't have been much older than James. The young man's face was battered, but it was his amputated leg that caused Blake to feel a deep pang of guilt. The kind ladies did their best to calm the distraught man, whispering sweet words and assuring him that he would be okay, before they escorted him into a cafe-turned-recovery ward.

Realising Emma was already quite a way ahead of them, Blake and James hurried across the gardens to catch up. As they neared the mall's entrance, much to their surprise, a group of laughing children came barrelling towards them in pursuit of a runaway soccer ball, which rolled straight to James's foot. A young soldier came out from behind a parked sedan with another mob of happy children latched onto her legs. James smiled and kicked the ball back to her.

"Thanks," said the soldier, waving, but several children playfully tackled her to the ground. A little girl with blonde hair picked the ball up and ran off with it. "Hey, Lenny! No hands!" The private laughed, as she pried giggling children from her fatigues.

Blake checked the sky for Drakken's silhouette once more. Still no sign of him. He just prayed that he wasn't making a mistake. The last thing these people needed was more horror brought upon them.

Emma entered the mall through its tall glass doors. The immediate area had been cordoned off with wooden barriers, blocking the path ahead. Three plastic tables were set up along the right-hand wall with a spotlight shining over them.

"Well, this is welcoming," James grunted, as he followed Blake through the doorway.

"Sorry, were you expecting a red carpet?" a uniformed soldier snarled, squeezing through the barriers before coming over to greet them. "Maybe some champagne, too?"

James was embarrassed. "Ah…no…I didn't mean it like that."

The soldier was around forty years old; her uniform was pressed and tidy, and her red hair was neatly tucked under her camouflage-patterned hat. There was a certain strength about her that Emma instantly admired. Striding with her shoulders back and holding a clipboard with her right hand, she carefully looked each of them up and down. "Have you registered?" she asked firmly. Emma, James and Blake responded with blank faces. "I said, have you registered?"

"No, no, we haven't," Emma quickly answered her. "Registered for what?"

"Fill these out – name, address, date of birth, family members," the woman said, as she handed each of them a paper form from her clipboard. "We use these to keep a record of the people who come through here."

"What for?" James asked.

The soldier stepped to the side and pointed to a wall beyond the barriers. "The names go up on the wall. If a name is up there, then that person is here or was here."

The white marble wall was covered in hundreds of forms like the ones they had been handed. A crowd of people were huddled around it, bumping and shoving into each other as they tried to search through the names on the wall for missing loved ones. An elderly lady stood out among them. Her green cardigan was frayed, and her curly grey hair was clumped and knotted, while fresh scabs and dark bruises covered her arms and face. Clutching a scrunched-up tissue in her right hand, she slowly made her way around the noisy crowd, standing on the tips of her toes to read each name back to herself, while respectfully trying not to impose on those around her.

The soldier's gaze lingered on her for some time. "That lady has read every name on the wall a dozen times. She is looking for her husband. They got separated when they evacuated the casino. The whole place is rubble now. Poor thing, she won't give up, though – not till she finds him. Reads that wall every morning, hoping to see his name up there."

Emma, James and Blake silently watched the wall for several minutes. It was hard to watch. Every piece of paper taped to the marble offered a small glimmer of hope, but most left with heart-crushing disappointment. Looking for the name of a loved one was like a prize pool. The people lucky enough to find someone cried as if they had won a grand lottery – as if all their dreams had come true and their life had changed forever. The not-so-lucky people also cried – most falling on their knees and burying their teary faces in their hands. Then they got up and did it all over again the next day, praying that the next lot of names that went up would be their winning ticket.

Blake looked down at the form in his hands. "You said some people on the wall *were* here. Did they go somewhere else?"

"We have lost a lot of people," the woman answered, handing each of them a pen.

Emma walked to the plastic table and began to fill out her form. James did the same. Blake stared at the paper in his hand, particularly the blank space next to the word "family." After a moment, he turned to the soldier and said, "Hey, I don't need this. I don't have any family, and everyone I know is pretty much here. So, yeah, thanks anyway." He pushed the form back into her hand.

The soldier brushed a strand of red hair from her face and gave him a stone-cold frown. "One thing that the last few days have shown me is that more people love us than we realise," she said, and shoved the form back into his hand. "Fill it out."

Blake reluctantly took the form over to the table and popped the lid off the pen. Leaning over the table next to Emma, he filled out his name, his address, and his date of birth. When he arrived at the family section he paused. What the hell was he supposed to write? Orphan? Not applicable? He figured leaving it blank was the best option.

Emma finished her form and peeked over at his. She knew Blake was overthinking it. Quickly, she snatched his form and set it down in front of her. Blake watched curiously as Emma scribbled over his page, but he couldn't see what she was writing. One satisfied hum later, Emma put down her pen and handed the form back to him. Blake cracked half a smile as he read over her neat handwriting. Under the parents' section, Emma had written *Gary Rupert Jones*; under siblings, *James Jost*; and under extended family, she had put *Emma Riley, Lila,* and *William*.

Emma shot Blake a cheeky wink before walking off and handing her completed form to the soldier.

"Thank you. Please remember to see me if you decide to leave. I'll need to sign you out," the soldier explained, sliding the form into her clipboard.

"No problem." Emma quickly reached into her backpack and pulled out the crumpled photograph. "Have you seen this man anywhere?"

The soldier studied it closely. "Has he got grey hair now?" she asked.

Emma's heart fluttered as she replied, "Yes! He does!"

"A cop, right? Tom, I think his name is."

"Yes! Yes! That's him!" Emma jumped in excitement.

The soldier smiled and said, "Sure have! Man's a damn hero. Saved the lives of a few people here. Got a broken leg to show for it, though. He's down in medical, resting up."

"Thank you!" Emma said gratefully, then realised she had no idea where medical was. "Um, where's that exactly?"

"They turned the big supermarket into a hospital," the soldier explained. "Just head left, and go straight down to the end. You can't miss it," she finished, as Blake and James handed their forms to her.

"Thank you again!" Emma said, and darted into the mall at full speed.

"Hey! Wait up!" James called out, but she was already gone.

Emma moved though the mall's wide atrium like she was in the mosh pit at a rock concert. Having perfected the technique at countless music festivals, Emma pushed, shoved, and apologised her way through the sea of grubby faces until she could see a carboard sign reading "Medical" taped over the supermarket's entrance.

James and Blake could only chase Emma like the wake of a boat, squeezing through the gaps she carved in the crowd before they sealed up behind her. "Wait up!" James called out, but the tenacious girl didn't slow a bit. When Emma finally reached the supermarket, she showed her dad's photo to an orderly at the entrance. The man happily directed her inside.

By the time James and Blake arrived at the supermarket, Emma was gone. "Okay, enough running," James said, winded, then leaned on a garbage bin to catch his breath.

"You alright there, buddy?" Blake teased him.

"Shut… up," James groaned. "I did all the pushing."

"If you say so." Blake left his breathless friend to recoup and approached the orderly whom Emma had spoken to. After the man explained that patients with broken bones were being treated at the rear of the store, Blake returned to James and asked, "You good now?"

James wiped the sweat from his forehead and said, "I'm waiting on you."

Upon entering the makeshift medical centre, the pair found that the former supermarket was hardly recognisable. A group of wide timber cabinets that had once displayed an assortment of fresh fruits, vegetables and weekly specials had now been repurposed into a group of beds, each made with a thin layer of foam with a cotton sheet across the top. The do-it-yourself beds were all occupied, leaving many sick and injured lying across the floor. Some slept on towels, sheets and doubled-over tablecloths; some were even lucky enough to get a sleeping bag. The less fortunate, however, had nothing but the cold hard floor to rest on.

Aisles numbered one through fifteen were stripped bare of their respective goods and had their shelving dismantled to make room for the influx of patients seeking treatment. The few aisles that remained were reorganised into food and medical supplies only, with nurses and doctors constantly coming and going as needed.

"Man, look at all these people," James said, his gaze hopping from face to face. Most of them were bruised, bandaged or both. Some were worse.

"There are so many…" Blake trailed off, distracted by the sight of bedridden children who bore some truly horrific injuries. He couldn't help but wonder how many lives he could change if he told someone about the Dreyan spiders' blood. He couldn't, though – not with Drakken out there listening. But, even if he could, he wasn't sure he would.

James and Blake continued towards the rear of the supermarket, careful not to bump into any of the patients or get in the way of the overworked nurses aiding them. "Ma'am, you have to take your pills," a man frustratedly argued with his defiant patient as they passed by.

"You're not going to poison me with those things," the frail woman shouted from her makeshift bed. Blake paused, as there was something familiar about her voice. Judging by the look on James's face, he recognised it, too. The pair stopped and turned back, taking a second to watch as the nurse tried to hand the elderly woman a pair of red pills. "Piss off! I'm not taking your poison," she yelled, smacking the medicine right out of his hand.

James grinned from ear to ear. "Is that who I think it is?"

"No frickin' way." Blake recognised her too. "Old Lady Margret?"

Quickly, the pair pushed through the crowd and made their way to Margret's bedside. The exhausted nurse exhaled several curse words as he crouched down and picked the pills up. He had a solid build, messy short dark hair and an untamed stubbly beard. Blake couldn't help but notice the strong stench of vomit coming from his filthy green scrubs.

"Hey, Marge!" James greeted their former neighbour from the foot of her display-cabinet-turned bed. Blake, too, was overjoyed to see her.

Margret glanced up at the two smiling young men at the foot of her bed. She had a large gash above her right eye, and her left wrist was wrapped in a bandage. Her medical robe had several food stains on it, and her sheets were half hanging off the bed.

The male nurse seemed relieved. "You boys know her?" he asked.

"Ah, sort of. She's our neighbour," James answered.

Margret's ears perked up, then she squinted to get a better look at her guests.

Blake continued to smile. "Hey there, Margret, you remember us?"

Margret quickly slapped the nurse across the arm. "Hand me my glasses, useless twat."

The nurse sighed, reached over to a small table behind him and picked up a pair of thick-framed glasses. "Margret! I've told you before. You can't speak to people like that," he said half-heartedly, handing her the glasses.

Old Lady Margret placed the glasses on the bridge of her nose, and then looked the boys up and down. Blake and James held their big smiles. Margret smiled back, but she didn't hold it. Her smile quickly faded to an angry frown. "You two! You two!" Margret yelled so loudly that she startled everyone nearby. "You stole my car! These two," she said, and pointed at them accusingly, "they stole my car!"

All eyes were now on the boys. "Uh... no we didn't..." James mumbled, next to a sweating but completely speechless Blake.

"Okay, okay! That's enough," the nurse said, as he winked at the boys.

"They did! They stole my car, I tell you," Margret continued.

James turned red before dozens of watchful eyes. "She's kidding. It's the medicine. We wouldn't... from an old lady... probably the medicine."

Blake leaned into his panicking friend and whispered, "Dude, you said you checked her apartment. You said she wasn't home."

"I was in the toilet," Margret carried on. "When I came out, I saw them out my window, stealing my car!"

"I may have forgotten to check the bathroom," James whispered, clenching his teeth.

"I'm gonna kill you," Blake replied, holding his smile for appearance's sake.

To their surprise, and relief, the nurse laughed it off and produced a syringe from a nearby cabinet. "Yes, of course, I'm sure they did. I'm gonna talk to them about it in just a minute," he humoured her, then injected the contents of the syringe into Margret's arm when she wasn't looking.

"They did! They sto—" Margret's speech began to slur and, within seconds, she was out cold, snoring on her pillow.

"Nap time," said the nurse, and threw the syringe into a small medical bin. He looked over at the boys. "Ha, what a crazy old duck, aye? She's losing it."

"Oh, yeah, right, tell us about it," James agreed. "She's losing it, alright."

"Unless you really did steal her car. Ha ha," the nurse chuckled.

Blake and James gave their best fake laugh as the many surrounding eyes continued to stare at them.

The nurse clapped his hands and said, "Just kidding!"

Blake looked at the bandage wrapped around Margret's arm. "What happened to her?"

The nurse removed his rubber gloves and tossed them into the bin. "Some soldiers went searching for anyone who missed the evacuation order and found her knitting in her apartment. When they tried to escort her out, she refused to leave and clocked one of the boys across the jaw – fractured her wrist in two places. The scratch on her head she got here – slight disagreement with a low-hanging branch outside. She'll be fine. Pretty tough for an old girl."

"Yeah," Blake agreed, "she's no pushover."

"Ah, dude," James whispered, "can we please get the hell out of here now?"

Blake glanced at James and quietly said, "What about Margret? Shouldn't we take her with us or something?"

James almost choked. "What? Yeah, sure! That's a great idea! Let's take her with us. Hey, Marge, meet our new friend, Drakken. He's a fifteen-storey-tall, fire-breathing dragon from the stone age. He burned down the whole city, but don't worry; he's lovely now. Blake, are you trying to kill this woman?"

"Fine, you made your point," Blake said, and elbowed him. "Let's go."

"Definitely," James agreed, then realised the nurse was still looking at them. "Okay, so we're going to go find our friends. Take good care of our crazy neighbour. Yeah, thanks. Bye."

"Okay, see you around." Amused, the nurse folded his arms and watched as the pair quickly fled into the crowd. "Weird guys," he thought, as he chuckled to himself.

∽∽∽∽∽∽∽∽∽

Overlooking a wall of empty freezers, Emma found herself standing in the 'Critical Ward'. Mattresses from a nearby bedding store were spread around the area and occupied by dozens of people with broken bones or similar injuries. "Excuse me!" Emma grabbed the shoulder of a lady rolling past her in a wheelchair. "Have you seen this man?" she asked, holding the photograph up in front of her wrinkly face. The lady mumbled something incoherently and became immediately distressed. Emma quickly let her go. "I'm sorry. I didn't mean to upset you." The irritated lady babbled a little more then continued on her way with an angry grunt.

"Didn't your father teach you not to talk to strangers?" a familiar voice asked from behind her.

She would have known that voice anywhere. Emma's heart skipped a beat. She spun around, tears rolling down her face. She saw a man on crutches – tall, with grey hair, glassy brown eyes, perfect white teeth, and donning an emotional smile. Thomas Riley.

She had found him.

"Dad!" Emma ran so fast that she almost knocked her father over when she hugged him. Thomas dropped one of his crutches and wrapped his arm around his daughter. A stray tear escaped down his cheek.

Unexpectedly, the lady in the wheelchair began to clap her hands at the sight of the reunited pair, then an older man in a nearby bed quickly joined in. Suddenly, the Critical Ward erupted in applause, cheers and whistles. Emma held on to her father tight. For the many watching, it was a symbol of hope. Blake and James stepped into the crowd and exhaled a deep sigh of relief at the long-awaited reunion.

"He's actually here." Blake couldn't believe it. He then noticed James rubbing his eyes. "Are you crying?"

"No," James said, and turned away. "Something flew into my eye."

Emma let go of her father as the excited crowd began to quiet down. "You look a little rough," she said, checking him over.

Thomas leaned on a crutch under his right arm. His police-issue pants had been cut into shorts, as his left leg was bandaged from the ankle up to the knee. His white T-shirt was grimy, and the left side of his face was bruised extensively above the jaw.

"I thought I had lost you," Thomas said.

Emma wiped away the tears and shook her head. "Dad, I'm so sorry. That last phone call… I was so mean to you. I never meant to be. I'm so sorry. I'm so, so sorry."

"Phone call? Don't be silly." Thomas reached out for her hand. "You have nothing to apologise for. All that matters is that you're okay."

Emma hugged him again. "I can't believe you're actually here," she whispered.

Thomas rubbed her back and rested his chin on her head. "How did you find me?"

"It's a really long story." Emma didn't know what else to say. "I'll explain everything when we get home."

Not wanting to interrupt Emma's moment, Blake turned to James. "I need to find this Captain Edwards guy before he leaves."

"I'll come with you," James insisted. "They could use the catch-up time."

"Hey, Emma," James called out. Emma spun around, her smile stretching from ear to ear. "We're gonna give you some time to catch up. We'll meet you back here."

"Okay," Emma happily agreed. She was clearly a little overwhelmed. "I'll see you guys soon."

Blake and James waved goodbye, then disappeared into the crowd.

Thomas glanced down at his daughter. "So… the two boys…"

Emma smirked at his overprotective nature. "You'll like them," she answered.

26

CROSSROADS

"He just made me feel really uneasy. Maybe it was the tattoo on his face... I don't know. I just didn't like the way he looked at me – or the other girls," the lady explained, and clenched her handbag a little tighter.

Mitch could see how nervous she was. "And when was the last time you saw him?"

The forty-something woman leaned in closer and said quietly, "Last night. He was with two other men. They followed him like a pair of hungry dogs, always whispering to each other. They are definitely up to something."

Mitch had to let her off the hook. She was sweating now. "Okay, thank you for your time," he said.

"I hope you find him. Something's not right about him," the lady declared, then briskly walked off. Mitch looked to Damien, who had just finished questioning several people outside the supermarket.

"Any luck?" Damien asked, seething from frustration.

Mitch shook his head and replied, "Not really. Same story – Guy has a dragon tattoo on his face, likes to watch women. It's definitely our guy, but she hasn't seen him since yesterday."

Damien slung his rifle over his shoulder and added, "Neither has the nurse I spoke to. It's like the arsehole disappeared."

"He has to be here somewhere." Mitch dug into his left pocket and pulled out a packet of Briske Minty Chews. "The captain already checked with the guards. People have come in, but no one has left here in days," he said, then flicked a piece of gum into his mouth.

"Briske Mints? Where did you get those?" Damien asked, holding out an open palm.

"One of the nurses gave them to me. I think she likes me."

"Cleary a sign of the apocalypse," Damien replied, as Mitch dropped a piece of gum in his hand. "Just one?" he asked, looking at the single white tablet.

Mitch stuffed the packet back into his pocket. "Hey, you're lucky to get that! Shit's gonna be worth more than gold, the way things are going around here."

Damien tossed the gum into his mouth, then re-equipped his rifle. "Let's hope the captain had more luck than us."

"Excuse me, guys," a voice called from behind them.

Both soldiers turned around to find two young men approaching them from the supermarket: a tall one with blond hair and a short one with dark hair.

"Do you know where I can find a Captain Edwards?" the blond one asked.

"Who's asking?" Damien barked, raising a suspicious eyebrow.

"Sorry. I'm Blake, and this is my friend, James. I have information for Colonel Henrickson. I was told Captain Edwards could help me get it to him."

"What information?" Mitch asked.

"Sorry, I really need to speak to the colonel himself."

Damien shrugged and said, "Well, too bad, mate, you're speaking to us."

"Screw these guys, man," James said, as he tapped Blake on the shoulder. "Let's ask someone else."

"No," Blake said, reading the soldiers' stubborn faces, "these guys definitely know where he is."

"One more time, and I'll speak slowly for you," Damien said. "What… information?"

Blake returned the condescending tone. "Captain Edwards."

"If you're not willing to co-operate," Mitch intervened, pulling Damien back a few steps, "then no one cares what bullshit you wanna talk about. So, piss off. Is that clear enough for you?"

"You have no idea how important this is."

"Oh, we're sure it is," Damien said with a snicker. Then he and Mitch turned and began to walk into the crowd.

"Dickheads," James said, watching as the soldiers moved further away.

"I know what the dragon is!" Blake yelled.

Mitch and Damien stopped in their tracks and slowly turned around. "Oh, that's clever," Damien mocked him. "It has wings, breathes fire and looks like a lizard. You know what, now that you mention it, it does look like a dragon."

"Hey, maybe these guys will understand sign language better," James said, as he raised his middle fingers at the unhelpful soldiers.

"Cute," Mitch brushed it off. "Trust me. Whatever you guys think you know about that thing, we already know." He turned around and continued to walk away.

"Its name is Drakken. It belongs to a race known as the Dreyan, speaks shitty English, sleeps underground for a couple thousand years and, oh yeah, it wants world peace."

Mitch didn't take another step.

"It spoke to you?" Damien spun around with a stunned expression.

"Yeah," Blake said, "that's what I'm trying to tell you."

"And it wants peace?" Mitch checked he had heard that right.

"Yeah, well, sort of."

Damien walked over to Blake and looked deeply into his eyes, "Listen, Blondie, there is a great medical team in the supermarket behind you. I suggest you go in there and ask them to flush out whatever crack you smoked this morning, okay? Thanks for your assistance."

Damien and Mitch laughed and joked between themselves as they left Blake and James standing in stunned silence.

"Well, that went well," James said, as he watched the two soldiers vanish into the crowd.

"The hell with this!" Undeterred, and a little pissed off, Blake charged into the mall's mosh pit after them.

"Shoulda stayed with Emma," James groaned, then reluctantly went after his friend.

∞∞∞∞∞∞∞∞∞

Outside the Robina Mall entrance, Lorcan and Amanda had spent the last twenty minutes questioning people about the man with the dragon tattoo. No one had seen him since the previous day. Amanda leaned on the metal handrail overlooking the flat murky pond. "Maybe Gabriel is gone. He could have snuck out," she said, gazing at the sun's reflection on the water. Lorcan was too busy contemplating his next move to respond. "Maybe it's time we locate Doctor Tate? Henrickson won't like it if we take too long."

Lorcan continued to ignore her. "There are only a few exits out of the building. Each of them is patrolled by armed guards. He couldn't have snuck out. He is still here. Somewhere. We need to keep looking."

"Okay," Amanda said. She knew when there was no point in arguing with him.

"Captain!"

Lorcan turned to see Mitch and Damien approaching through the car-cluttered lawn. "What have you got for me?" he asked them.

"Nothing. It's the same everywhere," Mitch reported. "No one has seen this guy since yesterday."

"That's the story we got out here, too," Amanda added.

Damien stopped next to a small tree. "So, what now?" he asked, sticking his gum to one of its branches.

"We keep looking," Lorcan answered.

"Captain Edwards!" a voice carried across the gardens.

Squad Seven turned their attention to the Robina Mall entrance. Lorcan didn't recognise the pair jogging towards him, but somehow, they knew his name.

"I need to speak with you!" Blake shouted, rushing through the maze of police cars and military vehicles before arriving at the large pond, with James trailing not far behind.

"Not this guy again," Damien muttered, as he quickly intercepted Blake with a firm hand on his chest, blocking the path to the captain. "That's far enough."

"Man, what is your problem?" Blake tried to sidestep around him, but Damien shoved him back. "Captain Edwards! I need to speak to you!" Lorcan just stared at the young man with curiosity. "Captain! It's important!"

"I'm going to count to ten, and you're going to leave," Damien warned Blake, shoving him back again.

"Ignore him, cap. He's nuts," Mitch whispered into Lorcan's ear. "He claims he's been talking to the monster."

"Is that right?" Lorcan replied, watching as Damien continued to usher the stranger back.

Tired of being shoved, Blake snapped and pushed Damien back. "Touch me again, arsehole!"

"Hey, dipshits," James shouted, moving to his friend's side, "you should really listen to him!"

"Captain," Blake added, "we can stop all of this. But I need your help. Please hear me out."

"Piss off, kid," Damien barked, then went to push Blake back again.

"I said don't touch me!" Blake clenched his fist and gave the soldier a meaty right hook to the cheek, sending Damien staggering back.

Lorcan sprang into action. Charging past Damien, he snatched the young man by his throat and began to choke him. "Who the hell do you think you are? You wanna hit my men, tough guy? We're out here risking our lives to protect punks like you." Lorcan's massive hands effortlessly squeezed the air from Blake's lungs.

With a flimsy fist clenched, James darted at Lorcan. Mitch immediately locked his rifle onto him. "Freeze!" he ordered.

James froze, then reluctantly raised his hands.

Blake's face was beginning to turn blue.

"Captain, stop," Amanda shouted, genuinely fearing for the young man's life.

Lorcan stared into Blake's brown eyes as he gasped for air. "You wanted my attention, and now you have it. Speak."

"The... monster... wants to... help us..." Blake could feel himself losing consciousness. Lorcan released his grip. Blake fell to the ground, desperately gasping for air as James dropped his hands and rushed to his side.

"I don't know what you are playing at, but you need to take a good look around," Lorcan said, and pointed to the line of people waiting for food and water. "I haven't got time for cute fantasies."

James gently lifted Blake to his feet. "I can prove it. The dragon, it will come to me... But I can't do it here," Blake said, rubbing his throat.

"Well, that's convenient." Lorcan glared at him and said, "So, you can call it to you... but not right now?"

"If I do it here, everyone will panic. I'm not lying to you. Do you seriously think I'd be standing here if this was some kind of game?"

Lorcan was already tired of the young man's antics. He didn't have time for them. He could see the only way to get rid of him was to call his bluff. "Do it anyway," he insisted.

"What?" Blake said hesitantly.

Lorcan took a step closer and said, "Do it anyway. Prove it. Right here, right now. Go on."

Blake looked around. He saw the line of hungry people waiting for soup, the children still playing soccer with the young soldier, and the dozens of exhausted faces waiting for medical treatment. He turned back to the captain and asked, "Please, can we go somewhere else?"

Lorcan unslung his rifle and walked towards the pond. "Just as I thought. I have shit to do today and don't have time for this," he said, signalling Mitch, Damien and Amanda to move out. "Seven, let's go! We've got people to find!"

Blake didn't know if the dragon would even come. "Drakken, do not harm anyone... even if they shoot at you," he said, then looked up to the sky. "I need your help."

Lorcan and Damien rejoined Mitch and Amanda at the pond's edge when a horrible roar crackled from behind the clouds. Squad Seven raised their rifles to the sky, but they were too slow. Drakken slammed down into the large body of water behind them, sending a murky wave crashing over the squad.

"Move!" Mitch barked, as he darted to his right and took cover behind a parked car. Damien yanked Amanda away and pulled her behind a police van on the left. Lorcan didn't move. He just stared at Blake with disbelief. Blake stared back. Slowly, Lorcan turned around and faced the massive dragon standing in the water.

Gunfire erupted as panic swept over the Robina Mall gardens. Terrified people, swarming the area from all directions, stampeded inside through the mall's main entrance. Mitch, Damien and a dozen other soldiers barraged the monster with automatic fire. Blake and James dropped to the ground as bullets zipped past them. Drakken didn't flinch. Standing high on his back legs, he stretched out his massive wings and let out a ferocious roar as bullets ricocheted off his thick scales like stones against steel.

"Stop shooting! Stop shooting!" Blake yelled from the ground. It was no use. No one could hear him. A dozen soldiers closed in, unloading every bullet they could into the towering dragon.

"Drakken, go! Get out of here!" Blake screamed.

The dragon effortlessly launched into the sky like a rocket, sending another wave of murky water crashing over the pond's edge. All gunfire ceased. Unsure of what had just happened, confused soldiers looked to each other for answers. Mitch, Damien and Amanda emerged from behind their cover, unable to take their eyes off the two young men lying in the grass. James and Blake rose to their feet, brushing the dirt off their clothes.

Damien raised his rifle and made for Blake.

Mitch quickly intervened and blocked his squad mate. "Do you really think that's a good idea?" He pushed Damien's rifle towards the ground and put a comforting hand on his shoulder. "Relax."

"Bet you feel like a dickhead now," James shouted to the pair of soldiers.

Lorcan walked over to Blake and quickly sized him up. "Who are you?"

"I'll tell you everything," Blake coughed, still rubbing his strangled throat, "but you need to take me to Colonel Henrickson."

Lorcan nodded and said, "Alright. Just you. Your friend doesn't get to tag along."

"Fine," Blake agreed.

"Ah, hello?" James scoffed. "Bullshit! That's not fine! He doesn't go anywhere without me."

Lorcan ignored him. "Those are the terms. Take it or leave it."

"We'll take it." Blake turned to James and handed him the keys to the four-wheel drive. "Dude, it's fine. I need you to take Emma and her dad back to their farm anyway. I'll meet you guys back there. Trust me, I can handle this."

"Okay. Just be careful," James said, as he reluctantly put the keys in his pocket.

Captain Edwards and his squad then escorted Blake to a high-tech military vehicle parked on the far side of the gardens.

"This doesn't feel right," James thought, watching the vehicle leave the gardens in a hurry.

〰〰〰〰〰〰

Emma was assisting her father to a chair when screams of hysteria and panic echoed throughout the Robina Mall. The sound of heavy footsteps and desperate cries filled the air. No sooner had Emma helped her father to his feet than a tidal wave of frightened people poured into the supermarket from every perceivable angle. Nurses and volunteers scrambled to get the sick and elderly off the ground as the endless mob stampeded through the empty checkouts and leapt over counters to get inside.

"Everybody out! The monster is here!" a soldier yelled, as he sprinted past Emma with a pair of bolt cutters in his hand. "Quick! This way." He stopped at the back wall and clamped the cutters around a heavy chain wrapped over the handle of an emergency exit door. With a loud rattle, the chain fell to the ground. The flustered soldier began calling out to anyone who would listen and waved them to the exit.

"Blake…" Emma turned pale. Why had Drakken come? Had the monster turned on them?

"Em, we've got to go! We're gonna get trampled," Thomas said, as he reached for his crutches. But they were knocked to the ground by a fleeing patient and then trampled by an onslaught of evacuating people.

Quickly, Emma grabbed her father's arm and rested it over her shoulder. "Dad, I have to find my friends," she said.

Thomas hobbled with her towards the emergency exit. "We will find them outside. Come on! We have to move!"

"Let me help you, mate," a man said, stopping to help them.

"Thank you," Emma said, as the stranger lifted Thomas's arm from her shoulder and placed it over his own. Snatching her backpack off the table, she followed the man as he assisted her father to the exit. The scruffy-looking stranger was the last type of person she would have expected to help. His long silver hair was tied in a ponytail, his blue jeans had rips and stains all over, and his muscular arms were barely contained by his black T-shirt.

Emma followed them through the darkness of the emergency exit's hallway. "Thank you. I could never have carried him on my own," she said, as terrified people continued to overtake them.

"No worries, baby girl," the man said, as he glanced over his shoulder and smiled, but Emma couldn't make out his face in the dark. They continued down the hall towards the sunlit exit. Emma felt a shove from someone passing by, but for some reason it stung like a bee sting. She glanced down to see a man's hand removing an empty syringe from her arm. Her body began to feel heavy. She stumbled, then turned back to see a shadowy silhouette reaching for her.

"Dad…" Emma tried to call out. Her legs gave way. The man scooped her up from behind and carried her in his arms. She could barely lift her head but did so long enough to see her father unconscious and slumped against the other man's shoulder. A third shadowy stranger ran up and helped carry Thomas into an adjacent hallway. Emma tried to scream, but no sound came out. Her eyelids closed. Everything went black.

27

MONSTERS AND MEN

After spending four hours searching the Robina Mall for Emma and Thomas, James came to one obvious conclusion: they bailed on him. He stayed to listen to the soldiers' roll call after they settled the crowd down. The only people not present were Blake, Emma, her dad and three guys he had never heard of. Angry and annoyed that Emma would leave the refuge centre without saying a word, James fired up the four-wheel drive and left the Robina Mall in his rearview mirror, all the while rehearsing his "how could you be so inconsiderate" speech.

James followed the road the same way they had come, while going over the last few hours in his mind. He had looked everywhere. There was no way he could have missed them.

Speeding down the ramp, he floored it onto the desolate M1 highway, enjoying the symphony of the V8 echoing off the concrete walls, though he'd never admit this to Blake. After putting several kilometres behind him, James slowed down for the next exit when he spotted something unusual at the side of the road. Or was it *someone*? He pulled the car over and unbuckled his seatbelt. Sure enough, there was a man's body in the emergency lane. James opened his door and climbed out. The man was lying on his side with a small pool of blood around his head, which had soaked his grey hair red.

"Hello? You alive there?" James called out, and walked over to the body, noticing the man's bandaged leg before he rolled him over. "Holy shit!" James jumped back. He knew him. It was Thomas Riley. He hunched down and placed his head against Thomas's chest. He was still breathing – but only just.

"Emma?" James spun around but couldn't see any other bodies lying on the road. Something was seriously wrong. A deep pit formed in his stomach. James rushed over to the four-wheel drive and opened the tail gate before returning to Thomas. Reaching under his armpits, he lifted Thomas up from the ground and dragged him over to the rear of the car. After a mental count to three, James heaved Emma's father into the rear compartment and slammed the tailgate shut – then crashed to the ground in an exhausted slump.

James suddenly felt ill. How did this happen? What had happened to Emma? The last person to see her was clinging to life in the back of Will's car. All he could hope for now was that Gary, Will and Lila would know what to do next.

〰〰〰〰〰〰

Blake squinted as the blurry light swayed back and forth above him, which was all he could make out through the black sack covering his head. Captain Edwards had gifted him with this, the moment he had climbed into their vehicle at the Robina Mall, explaining that it was necessary to keep the location of their base a secret. Blake thought it a rather pointless precaution as Drakken could track all their scents, should he decide to. But Captain Edwards didn't know that, and from what Blake could tell, neither did the rest of the military.

After a half-hour drive across town, Blake had been escorted into a room, cuffed to a chair and left there. That was hours ago, and he wondered why no one had come to see him, given the importance of the situation.

The screech of an iron door was followed by the clap of approaching footsteps, causing Blake to straighten his posture. He went to scratch his nose, which itched like crazy from the black sack covering his face, but the restraint of the handcuffs brought a quick end to that idea.

The footsteps continued to move around until they stopped somewhere behind his chair. Blake tried to see the mystery person. He turned left, then right, but couldn't make anything out through the cloth. Suddenly the sack was lifted off his head.

Thousands of dust particles twinkled under a swinging lightbulb as Blake peered around the dark room. Captain Edwards emerged from the shadows, holding the empty sack in his hand, but before Blake could ask what was going on, another man appeared and stood under the light. Judging from his uniform, the man was a decorated officer. His short black hair was neatly combed; however, his jaw was showing early signs of a beard.

"My name is Samuel Henrickson. I am a colonel in the Australian army." The colonel pulled a folder from under his arm and flicked it open. "Blake Daniels, twenty-four years old, dropped out of high school, multiple driving offences and licence disqualifications. Had a promising career in motorsports but opted for life as a courier driver instead. Orphan. Only a few known friends, and my personal favourite," he said, as he slammed the folder shut, "can control dragons."

"I don't control anything," Blake calmly replied.

Lorcan had no idea what to make of the young man either, so he backed up against the wall and gave the colonel the room.

Henrickson was pacing back and forth. "But the dragon came to you when you called it?"

"Yes," Blake said, but he knew how it sounded. "That's why I'm here. We can stop all of this. I just need your help. You need to call the prime minister or someone high up."

Doubt filled Henrickson's face. "Well, that's a very noble proposal. But let's start from the beginning. Tell me, why did it come to you?"

"It's gonna sound crazy," Blake warned him. "It was dumb luck. He watched me save a spider."

Henrickson found that amusing. "I'm sorry. Did you say, save a spider? You mean the bug, right? A 'spider' spider?" He glanced at Lorcan with a contemptuous grin. However, Lorcan wasn't as eager to write the young man off; he had made that mistake at the Robina refuge centre.

"It's true," Blake insisted. "That's the reason he came to me."

"And why would it care about a spider?"

"Well, you see, to us, a spider isn't all that significant, but to his kind, all life is equal. Which is why this is happening."

"How do you know this?" Henrickson asked.

"Because he told me," Blake answered.

"It spoke to you?" Henrickson couldn't believe his ears. "English? It speaks English?" He laughed at the notion. "Can you explain to me how it speaks English? Can it speak Chinese, too?"

"I think you mean Mandarin, colonel," Blake remarked, aware that nothing he had said up to this point was being taken seriously.

Henrickson stopped pacing, clenched his fist and punched Blake across the face. Lorcan flinched, surprised by the colonel's sudden aggression. Henrickson leaned over Blake, who was bleeding from the mouth, and whispered, "I don't think you realise the predicament you're in."

Blake spat blood on the floor. "I don't know how it can talk! Okay?" he said, trying to ignore the ringing in his ears. "Listen to me. Drakken wants to give our kind a chance! That's why I came here. I need to speak to the government, the prime minister, someone who can handle this. They need to know what is happening out there!"

"Is that what it told you?" Henrickson flicked his folder open again and pulled out several surveillance photographs. "Brisbane." He held the picture up to Blake's face: the smouldering ruins of a levelled city. "Canberra." The next photo was of Parliament House. There was nothing left – just fire, smoke and rubble. "The prime minister was inside. Guess we can't call him." Henrickson dropped the picture on Blake's lap. "Sydney." The image showed the famous Sydney Harbour Bridge completely melted in half, collapsing into the water below. A thick smog filled the sky above the Opera House, which was engulfed in blue flames. Henrickson tossed the remaining photos on the ground. "Adelaide, Melbourne, Perth, Darwin. All gone. Does this look like a species searching for peace to you?"

Blake stared at the images lying by his feet. He felt hollow. How did this happen so fast? Why hadn't Drakken told him about the other cities?

Henrickson closed his folder. "The death toll is well into the millions. There is no one left to call. Your fire-breathing buddy is playing you."

Blake felt sick.

Lorcan was just as shocked as Blake was. The colonel had told everyone under his command that the Gold Coast was the only major city to have been hit. If the prime minister had been killed and Canberra was now gone, then who was commanding the military? Who was Henrickson reporting to?

The colonel crouched down and grabbed Blake's bloodied chin. "How do we kill it?" he asked, squeezing tightly.

Blake looked into his eyes. "I don't think you can. You have already tried. Drakken is a Guardian. They're the leaders of their species, the strongest of them – or something like that. The rest of the Dreyan will be here soon, and they believe humanity has destroyed their home. If you attack Drakken, you may destroy any chance we have of proving we can co-exist. They will exterminate us, colonel."

Henrickson's grip tightened around Blake's jaw. "Here is what we are going to do. You're going to tell me and Captain Edwards here everything that happened to you from the moment the city was attacked to how you ended up sitting right here." He let go of Blake's face and produced a large hunting knife from his pocket. "And if I think you're lying to me, then this is going to get very painful for you."

Staring at the razor-sharp blade, Blake nervously agreed. "Okay, but you might wanna get a chair."

〰〰〰〰〰〰

Stones sprayed out from the four-wheel drive's rubber tyres as James sped down the Riley Farm's gravel driveway. He could only hope that the constant banging coming from behind the rear seats wasn't Thomas's head, which he had wrapped with rags he'd found in the glove compartment to slow the bleeding.

James slammed the brakes, bringing the car to a dusty halt near the front deck. Will and Gary were busy hammering a large sheet of timber over what used to be the lounge room window. Hearing the car behind them, they both stopped what they were doing and turned around, but not before Lila burst out the front door with a broom in her hand.

"Where are Emma and Blake?" she asked nervously.

Gary rushed over to the four-wheel drive. "Boy, where are the others? Where is Blake?"

James didn't answer him. Instead, he got out of the car and ran to the rear tailgate. "Get over here and give me a hand!"

Lila and Will jumped down from the deck and hurried to assist.

"Will, help me with him," James popped open the tailgate.

"Help... who?" Will asked, then immediately noticed the unconscious person in the back seat. "Who the hell is that?"

"Emma's dad," Lila answered. "Emma showed me his photo before she left."

"I found him on the side of the road. Be careful with him." James leaned in and grabbed Thomas's legs, minding the bandage around his left calf. Will slid his hands under the man's shoulders, and together the pair gently lifted Thomas out of the vehicle and carried him towards the house.

"I'll get a mattress," Gary said, and jogged ahead, making sure the way was clear before disappearing inside. By the time they got Thomas into the house, Gary had a mattress ready on the lounge room floor. James and Will gently lowered Emma's father onto it.

"I need to take a look at him." Gary shoved between them and crouched beside Thomas. "He's taken a bad hit to the head. It doesn't look good."

"I know. He was barely breathing when I found him," James said.

Lila was rattled, partly because of Thomas and partly because James still hadn't explained where Blake and Emma were. "We have to do something. We can't just let him die."

"Wait here," Will said, then rushed into the kitchen.

"He has lost a lot of blood. Unless you have a miracle," Gary said, shaking his head, "there is nothing else we can do, darlin'."

"Actually," Will said, as he re-entered the room holding a familiar jar of neon-green goo, "I might have your miracle right here."

James's eyes widened as he asked, "Where the hell did you get that?"

"I went to the neighbour's house after you guys left this morning. Figured we might need it if one of us gets hurt." Will kneeled next to Thomas and began to unscrew the lid.

"Man, I hope this works." James didn't want to admit it, but he wanted to hug Will at that moment.

Will lifted James's home-made bandage and applied the green substance to the wound on Thomas's head. He then turned his attention to Thomas's broken leg. "Well, this is the last of it anyway. Hope this guy is worth it."

"It's Emma's father, hun," Lila assured him. "He is worth it."

"Let's hope so." Will unwrapped the dirty bandage and massaged what was left in the jar over Thomas's calf.

"I need him to wake up fast." James seemed shaken. "He's the only one who knows what happened to Emma."

"What do you mean? *Happened* to her?" Gary stood up, worry smeared across his face. "Boy, you better tell us everything – right now."

"Okay," James agreed. All eyes were now on him.

〰〰〰〰〰

"And that's how I got here." Blake concluded his account of recent events for the colonel but opted to leave out the fact that the giant reptilian spiders had super-healing blood.

The colonel twirled the knife in his hand as he mentally digested Blake's story. "So where is Drakken now?" he eventually asked.

Blake shook his head and said, "I don't know."

Lorcan stood against the wall, mentally repeating the story to himself. It was quite a lot to take in, even for him. Yet, despite how insane it all sounded, he believed it. All of it.

Henrickson, however, wasn't convinced. "Are you familiar with Stockholm syndrome?" he asked Blake. "It's when a captive falls under the influence of his captor. It's very real – the natural survival instinct of an untrained mind."

Blake groaned and said, "That's not what this is."

"Oh, really?" the colonel replied. "Classic cases demonstrate that captives can feel protective of their captors; some idolise them, fall in love even. It's the overwhelming fear, the feeling of powerlessness – knowing that you could be killed at any moment and there is nothing you can do to stop it." Henrickson began pacing again. "No one could blame you. That thing is terrifying. Who knows what it would have done if you had refused its demands? I get it." He stopped pacing, crouched down and put a hand on Blake's shoulder. "We can protect you. You're safe here."

Blake looked the colonel squarely in the eye and stated, "I don't need your protection. I need your help."

"Actually, we need *your* help," Henrickson said, and dropped the knife on the ground. "I believe that you could be the key to taking this monster down. That is, if you're willing to step up and be a hero for all the people we've lost." The colonel pulled a set of keys from his pocket, reached over and unlocked both sets of handcuffs. Blake immediately rubbed his wrists. "So, what do you say? Care to help us here?" he asked, smiling, offering the young man a hand up.

Blake knew that smile was about to fade. "Colonel, please, you need to listen to me! If you attack Drakken, you will destroy our only chance at fixing this."

"No, you listen to me!" Henrickson raised his voice as he grabbed Blake by his shirt collar. "I want you to take a long hard look at this!" He then removed a photo from his jacket pocket and held it up. The photo was of a pretty woman with strawberry blonde hair and two young girls. "Gracie was thirteen years old. Bia was seven. Do you see these faces?" He gripped Blake by his hair and yanked his head back. "That bastard burned my children! It murdered my wife! And you... you have the audacity to come here and ask me to help it?"

"I'm not defending what it's done. I'm not," Blake replied, but couldn't take his eyes off the picture. "Colonel, I'm sorry. I'm trying to stop this, too."

"I don't want your sympathy." The colonel let go and stepped away to compose himself. "We will fight these monsters and send every single one of them back to the ground they came from." He straightened his jacket, then turned back to Blake. "I will not aid the monster that slaughtered my family."

"I... don't..." Blake knew then that no matter what he said, the colonel was never going to help him. He didn't blame him. Blake glanced over at Lorcan, who was mostly hidden in shadow, by the wall.

"You see, Mr Daniels, a key to winning any war is to cut off the enemy's lines of communication." Henrickson kneeled and picked the hunting knife up from the ground. "You've made your allegiances clear enough. Unfortunately, I can't have you running around, feeding that thing more information."

"Colonel?" Blake went to stand up, but Henrickson quickly slammed his forehead, sending him crashing backwards over the chair.

"You're a damn coward," Henrickson said, watching as the young man clutched his bleeding face. "How could you turn your back on everyone? You disgust me." The colonel put a foot on Blake's chest and ran his fingers along the edge of the knife.

"Sam! What are you doing?" Lorcan moved to intervene.

The colonel raised his hand. "Stand down, captain! That's an order!"

Lorcan hesitated. Surely this was a scare tactic.

"Colonel, please!" Blake raised his hands in surrender. "You don't need to do this!"

A swift kick from Henrickson's boot sent blood spraying from his captive's mouth. "I'm sorry, but we have enough monsters running around out there." He then lowered the knife to Blake's chest and said, "I can't have you helping them."

"Sam, don't!" Lorcan lunged for the colonel, but before he could reach him, gunfire erupted outside. Henrickson hesitated, feeling the floor tremble under his shoes. Lorcan froze. Dust fell from the ceiling. The lightbulb dimmed to black.

"Captain Edwards?" Henrickson couldn't see a thing.

With a resounding *crack*, sunlight filled the room as Drakken's massive claws tore the concrete ceiling from the grey brick walls.

Blake kicked, then shoved the distracted colonel off him, sending Henrickson to the ground and the knife bouncing from his hand. Lorcan covered his head and took cover by the rear wall as crumpled bullets rained down from above, each one flattened after ricocheting off the dragon's thick scales. Concrete dust filled the room. Drakken slammed his hand to the ground, crushing two brick walls and the iron door beneath it. Lorcan moved back but wasn't scared; he knew why the monster was there.

"Come," Drakken roared, opening his reptilian hand. Blake scrambled to his feet and leapt into the creature's massive palm; the scales felt like stone against his skin.

Choking on the filthy air, Henrickson rolled onto his back and stared at his enemy. The dragon's fiery eyes glowed through the haze. "Somebody, kill that thing!" he screamed in a rage. Drakken closed his fist around Blake and lifted him out of the room. "Shoot it! Goddammit!"

Feeling a sudden rush of vertigo, Blake tried not to vomit as he peeked through a gap in the dragon's scaly fingers. "Castra Dam?" He couldn't believe where he was. Dozens of frantic soldiers were converging on the dam wall, unloading every weapon they had upon them. Henrickson and Lorcan watched as the dragon rose over them and stretched out its wings.

"Would you like me to eradicate these humans? They pose a threat to our cause." Drakken's booming voice echoed over the base.

"What? No!" Blake shouted from the monster's enclosed fist. "No killing! Don't hurt anyone!"

"Very well." With a flap of his wings, Drakken launched into the air.

"Oh crap, oh crap, oh crap!" The G-force slammed Blake to his hands and knees. "You could have warned me," he cried out, feeling his ears pop under the sudden pressure change.

Drakken cut through the clouds, twisting, turning and barrel-rolling across the sky while Blake bounced inside the dragon's fist like a rubber ball.

"Hey, cut that out!" Blake cried out. Drakken slowed down and levelled out, allowing Blake to roll over and orientate himself upright. "Oh, man," Blake said in awe, as he saw slithers of blue sky between the dragon's fingers, "how high are we?"

"Can you breathe?" Drakken asked, soaring over a strong updraft.

"Yeah."

"Then not too high."

Blake rested his back against the dragon's scaly palm. "Thanks, you know, for saving me. Why *did you* save me?"

"You saved the spider," Drakken answered.

"Right, the spider," Blake said. "Henrickson isn't going to help us. But I'm guessing you heard everything."

"I killed his family," Drakken said bluntly.

"Yeah," Blake could feel the dragon beginning to descend, "you did. Does that even bother you?"

"No."

"I feel sick. Can we stop somewhere?"

"Yes." Drakken then nosedived at what felt like warp speed.

"Whoa! Slowly!" Blake scrambled for something to grab on to, but the dragon came to a sudden halt, and he rolled out of the dragon's open palm onto a rocky cliff edge.

"Thanks," he said, as he coughed up a bloody mix of saliva and vomit. After clearing his throat, Blake sat back in the dirt and found himself overlooking a vast valley, a beautiful palette of brown rock faces, green treetops and a tall waterfall that gushed over a nearby mountainside.

"That's quite a view," Blake said, catching his breath. "I never knew there were places like this so close to home." Drakken folded his wings onto his back and lowered himself down on all fours, his mountainous shadow looming over the valley.

"There was a girl – Amy," Blake said quietly. "When you attacked the city, I tried to save her. Her mother asked me to. I tried. But I couldn't. I let her down. I let her mother down.

And now I'm helping you, the one that killed her. What kind of person does that make me?" He looked at Drakken with teary eyes, but the dragon just looked away. "I understand why Henrickson won't help us. I need you to know that I can't forgive you for what you've done."

Drakken kept his gaze on the valley. "Your forgiveness is not a requirement for our success."

"Good," Blake nodded, wiping his eyes. "We should probably get going."

〰〰〰〰〰〰

Sitting along the edge of the deck where the handrail used to be, Will and James continued to discuss their increasingly limited options. "So basically, we're helpless until Blake gets back or Emma's dad wakes up," Will said, then took a drink from his water bottle.

"Yeah, pretty much," James replied. "Don't worry. Blake will make it back."

Will looked at him doubtfully and said, "I don't know about that. I don't have the same faith in that guy that you do – or that Lila does."

"Oh," James snickered, "is that why you guys are fighting?"

"Who said we were fighting?"

"Are you serious? It's obvious. Ever since we bandaged Thomas up, she has barely spoken to you."

Will glanced down at his shorts pocket. He could feel the ring box pressing against his leg. "It doesn't matter. She'll get over it."

James huffed, "Well, that's healthy."

Will took another sip of his water, then said, "My job is to keep Lila safe. That's all I was trying to do."

"Hey, I'm not judging," James said, as he put his hand up in surrender. "Just saying, maybe you should stick with me for a while. Angry woman… she might cut your man bun off or something."

Will screwed the lid on his water bottle and replied, "Do you ever shut up?"

"Not very often, no."

"Didn't think so."

"Who the hell are you two?" a voice interrupted them.

James and Will turned around to see Thomas standing on the deck outside the front doorway. They leapt to their feet.

"Where is my daughter?" Thomas asked, clearly disorientated. "Where is Emma?"

"Actually," James swallowed the lump in his throat, "we were hoping you could tell us."

28

A FALLEN ANGEL

James and Will helped Thomas onto the leather recliner.
"And that's the last thing you remember?" Gary asked.

"I heard her call out my name," Thomas answered, sweat pouring down his face. "Then someone stabbed a syringe into my arm. I don't remember anything after that. How could I let this happen?" He went to stand up again but fell back into the chair. "I need to go back! I have to find her!"

"You need to rest," Lila said, returning from the kitchen and handing Thomas a glass of water.

James and Will looked at each other nervously, then James said, "Blake and I saw one of the nurses use a sedative on our neighbour. Whoever knocked you guys out must have got their hands on some, too."

"Drakken can find her," Lila said, "but we need to find Blake."

"Who's Drakken? How can he find Emma?" Thomas asked, then gulped down his water.

"The same way we found you," Lila answered him, then turned to Gary, Will and James. "If Blake can get it to track Emma the same way it tracked the people at the refuge centre, then we can find her."

"Track them?" Thomas was more confused than ever. "What are you talking about? What did you use to find me?"

"The creature that attacked the city," Gary answered bluntly, "led us to you at the refuge centre. It can track scents for miles."

"That fire-breathing dinosaur? How?" Thomas asked, grasping for anything that would help make sense of the conversation.

"Listen, Tom," Gary stopped him. "It's a long story. We have a lot to catch you up on. We'll explain the big dinosaur, and we'll explain how we healed your leg. But right now, we need to find your daughter."

"But—" Thomas caught the next word before it escaped his mouth, and conceded in silence.

"Right. But there is one problem," Will interrupted. "No one knows where Blake is or where they took him."

No sooner had Will finished speaking than the house rattled from an earthquake-like impact. "That's got to be Drakken!" James ran out the front door with Lila, Gary and Will close behind. The group, to their relief, found Drakken standing over the driveway.

Thomas staggered out after them. "It's here… my God."

The dragon lowered its hand to the ground and opened its fist. A dizzy Blake stumbled out, collapsed, then vomited all over the gravel driveway.

"That's disgusting," James cringed, stepping down off the deck.

Gary was the first to notice the bloodied state of Blake's face. "What the hell did you do to him?" he cried, and quickly rushed to Blake's aid.

"It wasn't Drakken." Blake coughed and sluggishly rose from the ground with Gary's assistance. "The colonel; he wouldn't listen."

"*They* did this to you?" James couldn't believe it. "They are supposed to be the good guys!"

Wiping his mouth, Blake tried to ignore the world spinning around him. "I told Henrickson everything. He won't help. They were gonna kill me. Drakken... saved my life... wait..." Blake paused, realising their concern wasn't just for him. He looked at the group – Will, Lila, Gary, James. He looked over to the doorway. Thomas was here, too. "Where's Emma?" he asked.

"We don't know," James said guiltily. "Someone took her."

Blake became rigid as he asked, "What do you mean 'someone took her'? From where?"

"The refuge centre. After you left, I went back to find her. Everyone had been evacuated to the carpark once Drakken showed up. I looked for hours... thought I had lost them in the chaos somehow." James looked back over his shoulder at Thomas, who was warily staring up at the dragon. "I found her dad nearly dead on the highway." His face filled with sorrow as he turned back to Blake. "Someone has taken her. I'm sorry, dude."

Thomas stumbled off the deck and pushed past the others. "I don't know who you are, what the hell is going on with that monster, or how I'm able to walk on this leg, but these people tell me that you can save my daughter. I'm begging you. Please find her. Bring her home."

Blake's eyes lingered on the man's heartbroken ones, then he nodded and said, "I will. I promise."

"Be careful, kid," Gary warned.

Blake turned to Drakken. "Do you have her scent?"

Drakken lowered himself on all fours, his powerful arms crushing the earth on either side of the driveway. "You need rest," he responded in his usual growl. "We have much to do. One life should not delay saving the many."

"One life? Finding her is the only thing that matters right now." Blake wasn't negotiating. "You said *every life* matters. *You* said that! We *are* going to get her."

"Very well." Drakken opened his massive claws. "I have her scent."

Blake climbed onto his palm, then took one last look at the others. "I'll bring her home."

Drakken closed his fist with Blake inside and, once again, spread out his massive wings. With a loud crack, the dragon propelled himself into the sky as the group watched from the ground below.

"I still don't trust that thing," Will said, as the monster disappeared behind the clouds.

Lila ignored him. Instead, she reached over and grabbed Thomas's hand. "They'll find her," she said, offering Emma's father what little reassurance she could.

"One thing's for sure," Gary said, as he turned to the others, "the bastard that took her won't see this coming."

〰〰〰〰〰〰

Emma's eyelids felt like bricks. Everything was blurry. Feebly lifting her head, she strained to construct the room beyond the dim smudges. She moved to wipe her eyes but couldn't lift her arms: three leather belts were fastened around her wrists and chest, binding her to the cheap office chair she sat on. The smudges began to sharpen. Empty beer bottles and a few shards of broken glass covered the metal table next to her, and the stench of cigarette smoke wafted from an overflowing ashtray.

"Hello?" she croaked.

Muffled rock and roll music blared from a nearby room. Emma's head rolled back. Cobwebs stretched between steel rafters and a rusted iron roof. Her mind flashed back to the sting of the syringe stabbing into her arm. "Dad?" Panic quickly replaced drowsiness. *Where am I?* Her body stiffened. *Concrete floors, bleak walls and roller doors – a warehouse or factory maybe?* "Dad, are you here?"

"Daddy isn't home, beautiful," a gravelly voice replied. "Finally awake, I see," a man said, as he walked around from behind her and made his way to the metal table. Aged somewhere in his fifties, the man was quite tall, and muscular but ratty. His black boots were untied, his jeans were filthy, and judging from the ingrained dirt across his bare muscular torso, he hadn't showered in quite some time. His silver ponytail was grimy and frayed, whilst his goatee was spreading across his jaw like an untamed weed.

"You?" Emma recognised him right away. "You were the one who helped carry my dad."

"Well," the man said, and grinned, a cigarette pegged between his teeth, "I wouldn't go that far."

"Where is my dad?" Emma asked, still groggy.

The man exhaled smoke from his nostrils and crushed the cigarette against the ashtray. "Questions, questions..." He turned and faced her, revealing a dragon tattoo that snaked down the left side of his face. "You are a pretty one," he said, taking a long gander at Emma's legs. "Yes, you are."

"What do you want?" she demanded, struggling against her constraints.

The man grinned. "There is no point in trying to shake loose. Those belts are leather. You're just going to hurt yourself." He grabbed a half-empty bottle of beer from the table and chugged it down, his eyes never leaving hers.

Emma continued to squirm in her seat. "Who are you?"

"Gabriel Miller," the man said, then tossed the beer bottle over her head, resulting in a loud crash somewhere behind her. "But you can call me whatever you like."

Emma thrashed around in her chair. "How about 'creep'? 'Arsehole'? 'Pathetic old man'?"

Gabriel's grin grew larger. "I like a woman that can talk dirty," he replied, as he pulled out another cigarette and struck a match.

Emma fought her restraints once more, and after a moment of pointless struggle, she shouted, "Where is my father?"

"The old guy? Exceptional jawline? Found a nice photo of you two in your bag. He looked pretty good, back in his day."

"Where is he?" she yelled again.

"We dumped him on the highway somewhere. Probably lizard food by now." Gabriel took a long drag of his cigarette and crouched down in front of Emma, sliding his hands over her thighs up to the denim of her shorts. "Now, little lady, we are going to be friends. How painful that friendship is will be up to you," he said, blowing smoke over her face.

She stared squarely into his eyes and said, "Go fuck yourself."

Gabriel grabbed Emma by the jaw and squeezed his dirty fingers into her face. "You know something, you remind me of this bitch I met at a bar once. She was a rude little slut, too." He then struck her with a heavy backhand. Emma's head flung back, her ears ringing as everything went hazy again.

Somewhere in the warehouse, the rock and roll music momentarily blared through an open door before becoming muffled by its closing. Soon after, two men emerged from a shadowy corner and joined Gabriel by the table. Both had short dark hair and wore jeans and black T-shirts; one man was noticeably older than the other.

"Come to watch the show, boys?" Gabriel said, handing each of them a half-drunk beer from the table. The pair clinked bottles and gestured to the girl strapped to the chair.

"Is that her?" the older of the two men asked.

"Yeah, that's her," the younger one answered. "I used to follow her online. She's so hot."

"Well, you're gonna have to wait your turn." Gabriel returned his attention to the girl strapped to the chair. "Now, where was I?"

Blood trickled out of Emma's nose as she slowly raised her head. "My dad is a cop. When he finds you…"

"What will he do?" Gabriel mocked, then heaved another right hook across her face. Blood sprayed from Emma's mouth as her head snapped to the side, causing the chair to almost topple over. "Go on. Tell me what your daddy is going to do to me." Red saliva trickled down Emma's chin as she drifted in and out of consciousness. "Darlin', do you see this?" Gabriel took the cigarette out of his mouth, yanked her ponytail back and pressed his forehead to hers. "This God – this right here," he whispered, running his finger down the tattoo on his face, "I brought him here, you see. He set me free. He set all of us free. Brought the world back to how it should be – survival of the fittest. Where a man can take what he wants without rules, without judgement. And I *will* take it. And you're gonna *like* it." He then pressed the lit cigarette into Emma's right leg and held their heads together as she screamed horrifically into his ear.

The other two men watched with enthusiasm, joyfully clinking their beers together as her cries for help echoed off the iron ceiling.

Once the ember faded, Gabriel flicked the crumpled cigarette and let go of Emma's hair. "Now, where was I?" he said, and stood up. "That's right… you women! You all want equal rights, equal pay – all that new-age bullshit. My mother was not equal, and my father made sure she knew it, too. Smart man my father was. He used to tell me: if someone can't beat you in a fist fight, then they're no *equal*." He righteously glanced at the men behind him. "Am I right, boys?"

"Damn right!" The pair toasted the notion before sipping their drinks again.

Emma coughed, and drops of blood splattered over her knees. "You're sick," she said, wheezing.

"Hey, Gabe," the younger man interrupted, "seeing as I spotted her at the refuge centre, and I knew who she was, I reckon I should get first dibs on her," he said smugly.

The wheels in Gabriel's mind were turning. He paused, then turned to face the young man. "You wanna go first?" He seemed to think on it, then walked over to him. "Okay," he said, stopping mere inches from the twenty-something's face. "But, what did I just talk about?"

"Huh?" The young man looked confused, and it was clear that the man beside him wasn't about to get involved. Before he could answer, Gabriel unleashed a flurry of punches into his stomach, sending his beer bottle smashing on the concrete floor as he fell to knees, winded and gasping.

"Tell me!" Gabriel reefed the young man's face to the ground, pressing it into the jagged shards of the broken bottle. The young man let out an agonising scream. "Do lions let their pack eat first? No! They fucking don't! Everybody waits for the king of the jungle to have his feast, then the rest get whatever scraps he leaves."

"Please stop!" the young man begged. "Dad! Help!"

The older man – *his father* – didn't say a word, which brought an even bigger grin to Gabriel's face.

"You see that, Danny?" Gabriel whispered. "Your daddy knows his place. Interrupt me again and I'll kill you. Understand?"

"Y-yes!" Danny stammered. "I understand."

"Good," Gabriel said. He pulled the young man up by his hair. "Now go clean yourself up. We've got company," he said, brushing the dirt off Danny's shirt. "Fix your face too, will ya?" Several pieces of broken glass were protruding from the young man's right cheek.

"Yes, sir." Danny was shaking. So was his father.

"Right," Gabriel said, as he focused back on Emma, "sorry about that." Then he walked over to the metal table. "You see Paul over there? He understands the order of things; he understands respect. But his son, Danny… young buck's still figuring it out."

Emma watched as Paul carefully began removing the glass from his son's face.

"Anyway, enough about them," Gabriel said, as he crouched in front of Emma again. "You know, you have perfect skin. So tanned…" He danced his finger around the fresh cigarette burn on her right leg. "You're incredibly beautiful. You must take good care of yourself," he said, then began stroking her leg with the tips of his fingers.

Emma tearfully watched as his hand moved up her thigh. "My friend will come for me, and when he gets here, you're gonna wish you had never touched me."

"Is that right?" Gabriel's fingers found the denim of her shorts. "You think he'll be rough with me?" he mocked, then leaned in and whispered in Emma's ear. "I hope so."

"I will be!" Emma suddenly jerked to the side and thrust her forehead into the bridge of Gabriel's nose.

"You fuckin' little bitch!" Gabriel cried, and staggered backward, clutching his face with both hands as blood poured through his fingers.

"That's for putting your hands on me, you fuckin' creep!" Emma shouted, her head still reeling with pain.

Gabriel lowered his hands. His nose was broken, and blood was gushing into his mouth. Paul and Danny were like statues. Gabriel glared at them; they both took several steps back. "That was a good hit. Gotta admit, didn't think you had it in ya." Gabriel stared at Emma for a moment, his rage brewing. And, as if his timer had suddenly gone off, he charged at her with clenched fists.

Paul and Danny watched like cowards as Gabriel took to Emma's face like a punching bag. She screamed for help at first, but her screams didn't last long. When Emma's body went limp, the leather belts kept her upright. By the time Gabriel was finished, he could hardly lift his arms, and Emma was hardly recognisable.

"No one is coming for you, darlin'," Gabriel said, as he pulled a handkerchief from his back pocket. Emma's motionless body sat slumped in the chair, the leather belts dripping with blood, as Gabriel wiped his knuckles clean. "She's all yours now, Danny," he said, throwing the handkerchief on the floor.

29

THE SAVIOUR

Sitting on a small wooden chair beside Emma's bed, a defeated and emotionally drained Lila stared aimlessly through the broken window at the creek outside. Damaged furniture, scattered clothes and splintered timber were spread throughout the room, while the door to the hall hung by a single hinge and was creaking in the breeze. Overwhelmed by all the things that had happened – Emma going missing, Drakken recruiting Blake, and Will constantly fighting with her, to list a few – Lila decided to escape upstairs and take a moment for herself.

Gary, unfortunately, had never been good at reading a situation and soon entered the room with two cups of warm tea in hand. "Damn, this place looks terrible. What a mess!" he said, taking a good look around. "Those darn snake things really got the jump on us, didn't they?"

"They sure did," Lila replied, as she straightened her posture and quickly dabbed her eyes with a tissue.

"Thought you could probably use some company," Gary said, with a heartfelt smile. "It's been a long day." He kicked a broken piece of timber across the floor and made his way to the foot of the bed. "Oh, and I'm gonna fix that later," he said, and pointed to the window frame without glass. A strong breeze was blowing through it and running amok with Lila's blonde bob.

"Oh, you don't have to. Will said he's gonna fix it after they finish talking to Thomas." Lila reached out and took one of the cups from him. "Thanks. This is really nice."

"No problem, kiddo," Gary said, and winked as he took a seat on the edge of the mattress. "How ya holding up?"

"I honestly don't know." Lila tucked a strand of hair behind her ear. "Everything feels so surreal. It's like a bad dream."

"I hear ya," Gary agreed, "and there's not a drop of liquor left in the house."

The joke fell flat on Lila. She didn't even smirk, but after a moment of reflection she asked, "Do you think Blake will get Emma back?"

Gary paused before answering the question… maybe a little too long. Eventually, he smiled at Lila and said, "Blake went missing once – years ago – when he was a boy. He grew up in foster care, you see. I didn't care for the people he was living with much; that woman saw him more like a government paycheque than her kid. I tried to adopt him, but my drinking – story for another time. Anyway, one day, the little bugger rode his bike to the river and didn't come home. Ended up missing for two days!"

"What? What happened?" Lila asked, eager for any distraction.

Gary chuckled as he replied, "Well, the police searched along the bike track and found his backpack and his push bike, but little Blake was nowhere to be seen. They thought he'd been kidnapped or something. Anyhow, the next afternoon, some teenager working at a gas station called them and said the missing kid had just showed up there. And that the kid was holding a dog but wouldn't let anyone near it. It was little Blake, alright."

"Really?" Lila was genuinely intrigued now. "Where did the dog come from?"

"No one knows. But, turns out Blake saw this stray pup floating down the river, fighting against the current. So, he dropped his bike and backpack and jumped in after it." Gary let out a big laugh. "Damn current was so strong, though; it swept the two of them away. Wound up a couple of miles down the river! But little Blake held onto that dog the whole way, till they both washed up on shore."

"Wow!" Lila giggled. "He's lucky he didn't drown!"

"Blake spent two days carrying that starving dog through the woods. He didn't eat once and was damn near dehydrated, but that didn't stop him. Carried that flee-ridden pup through the forest until he found that gas station. Police said he wouldn't let go of the bloody thing until someone fed it. When I got there, he made me take the dog to the vet while they rushed him to the hospital. Even at that age, the kid was telling me what to do! Vet cost me a fortune, too, though I never told him that."

"So, what happened to the dog?"

"They let Blake keep him – at my place. No way that ratty woman would allow it at her house. I had to get my carpets flea-bombed twice! I tell ya, Blake loved that damned dog, though. Named him Ben. Those two were practically inseparable until Ben passed away a few years back."

Lila took a long pause then said, "He wouldn't let go of the dog." She smiled, then took another sip of her tea.

Gary couldn't hide the proud expression on his face. "That kid will never quit, and that's one thing you can always count on. I don't know where Emma is, or who has her, but I know that Blake won't stop until he finds her. And if that dragon – or whatever it is – really wants to stop all this nonsense, then he picked the right man for the job."

"You really believe in him, don't you?" Lila admired his faith.

"I do," Gary nodded. "He's the best man I know." He then chuckled and added, "I'd damn well never tell him, though."

Lila glanced at the overgrown trees by the creek and said, "I hope you're right."

"Don't worry. I am." Gary groaned at his aching back as he stood up from the bed. "You'll see, darlin'. You'll see. Anyway, I'll leave you be. Enjoy the tea," he said, and quietly left Lila to her thoughts and exited the room before she could thank him again.

God, I hope he's right. Lila stared at Emma's empty bed. *Please be right.*

〰〰〰〰〰〰

Sunlight poured through the open door, casting Blake's tall shadow far into the dank and grimy warehouse. There wasn't much to the place – a dusty concrete floor, steel rafters supporting a hole-riddled iron roof, and some empty racks mounted on the grey brick walls. Blake edged his way through the darkness, watching every step as he carefully avoided making any noise. There was light ahead, coming from a skylight above, and an echo of several men bickering – or were they laughing? Following the noisy trail, he quickly came upon three men gathered at a metal table. One was smoking and drinking, while another was tending to the third man's bloodied face. There seemed to be a fourth person sitting on a chair behind them, but Blake's view was obscured by the other three.

"Who is that?" Paul asked, noticing Blake's shadowy figure over Danny's shoulder.

Gabriel stepped away from the table, his freshly lit cigarette dangling from his mouth under his split nose. "No use hiding back there! We can see you plain as day."

"Where is she?" Blake asked angrily. He was done hiding anyway. He emerged from the shadows with clenched fists and gritted teeth. "Where the fuck is she?"

Paul moved to intercept him, but Blake swung a weighty right hook across the man's face and sent him crashing to the floor.

"Hot damn!" Gabriel beamed, watching as Danny rushed to help his father up from the floor. "I like this guy!" Blake walked over and stopped mere inches from Gabriel's face. "Oh yeah, you got that fury in your eye, don't ya."

Blake stared at Gabriel's demonic grin. "I know you have her. Where is Emma?"

"Oh, calm down. You must be the boyfriend." Gabriel winked as he said, "Well, I got some bad news for ya. I got a little *handsy* with your girl." He stepped to the side and revealed Emma's lifeless body bound to the chair behind him. "My bad."

"Oh no..." Blake felt his insides flutter, then felt so heavy he couldn't move. "What have you done? What have you done to her?"

Gabriel soaked it all in. The sight of a man's face going from furious to grief-stricken was delightful. "Don't worry. She liked it. Well, I did at least."

Blake tried to breathe but couldn't. "What did you... do? No... please no..." He struggled to stand.

Gabriel puffed on his cigarette and studied Blake's bruised and beaten face. "You're not looking too hot yourself there, mate."

He glanced over at Danny and Paul, then gestured for them to come over. The pair quickly pounced and restrained Blake's arms behind his back, dragging him away from Emma's body. Blake hardly fought back. His devastated eyes never left the girl bound to the chair. Gabriel waved a hand over Blake's face, which quickly brought the young man's attention back to him.

"You're gonna pay!" Blake screamed and began thrashing around, but Danny and Paul had both his arms firmly secured. "You son of a bitch! You'll pay!"

Gabriel smirked, then rested his cigarette on the table before turning back to Blake. "Did you think that you could just waltz in here alone, like some action hero, kick our arses and save the fuckin' princess?" he laughed, then swung a punch deep into Blake's stomach.

Blake's legs buckled as he hunched over in pain, coughing. "I didn't... come..."

"What?" Gabriel asked, indulging himself. "What? I didn't quite catch that."

Danny pulled Blake's head up to meet Gabriel's. "What did you say, tough guy?"

Blake coughed once more, then sputtered, "I didn't... come alone."

"How the hell did this guy bloody find us, anyway?" Paul asked, just as a violent chorus of screeching iron reverberated from above. Sunlight poured into the warehouse; the steel rafters and metal roofing were torn from the walls like the lid from a tin can.

Stunned, Danny and Paul fell back, their eyes fixed above them as Drakken's massive head eclipsed the sun and cast them all in shadow once again. Blake made straight for Emma and began unclasping the leather belts binding her. Gabriel stood in wonderment and gazed up at the dragon's fiery eyes and pulsing orange skin. "You are here," he rejoiced, stretching his arms to the sky.

Blake lifted Emma's limp body with his arms and rested her head against his shoulder.

"Don't you see, boys? My God has come for me!" Gabriel closed his eyes and felt the intense heat from the creature's jaws.

"Actually, arsehole," Blake interrupted, "he's here for her." Gabriel opened his eyes to see Blake standing by the chair with Emma in his arms.

"What?" Gabriel asked incredulously as Drakken's massive hand swung down and swatted him across the room, along with Paul and Danny. The three hit the far brick wall with a bone-crunching snap.

Drakken opened his fist over the floor. Blake stepped onto it and carefully lowered himself down in the middle of the dragon's palm. Caressing Emma's head, he surveyed the brutality that had been unleashed upon her face. "We're too late…"

"She is not yet lost. Her heart still beats," Drakken growled, "though she will not make it through the night."

"She's alive?" Blake listened carefully. She was breathing – barely. "Get us home."

Drakken's fingers closed over them, and gently the dragon lifted off the ground with a swift flap of its wings. Soon the warehouse was nothing but a speck among the countless rooftops below.

30

THE ENEMY OF MY ENEMY

After being greeted by a uniformed soldier guarding the door, Lorcan entered the dam's recommissioned museum room to find its various glass cabinets, replica models and information boards covered in white sheets. An oval-shaped table was now the centrepiece of Henrickson's new war room with the man himself and an unknown female civilian standing at opposite ends, awaiting his arrival.

"Ah, Captain Edwards," the colonel was eager to begin. "This is Doctor Diane Tate, the scientist you and your team failed to retrieve from the Robina refuge centre this morning. Luckily, one of our supply teams was able to bring her here a short time ago."

In her forties, Diane Tate had a sleek bald head and a pair of thick-framed glasses that magnified her dazzling hazel eyes. She was dressed neatly in a pressed pantsuit that covered her slender frame. "Nice to meet you, captain. Sorry we missed each other at Robina, but from what I hear, you boys have had quite the day."

"You could say that." Lorcan politely shook the doctor's hand and noticed several scabby cuts and an angry bruise across her wrist. He then took his place at the side of the table between her and the colonel.

"Since the initial attack, Doctor Tate and her team have been studying the creatures from a secure facility several clicks west of here," Henrickson explained. "Her team was conducting a field trip when they were attacked by one of the monsters just south of the border. It's a miracle she is here, captain, so pay attention to what the doctor has to say."

"Right then. Let's begin," Doctor Tate said, as she spread several photographs on the table. "These, gentlemen, are some of the creatures our teams have encountered over the past week." Lorcan immediately recognised several of them. One image showed the dragon-like monster – or Drakken, as Blake had called it – breathing fire into a Surfers Paradise street. The next showed a giant snake with a bony frill around its neck, just like the serpent he had watched through the gas station window. The next photograph, however, was of something he hadn't seen yet. At first glance, it could have been mistaken for a sea urchin, but according to the notes scribbled across the bottom of the image, it was some type of beetle. The round tennis ball-sized creature was covered in long pointy spikes. There were no visible eyes, antennae or legs that he could see. It was just a spiky black ball. Lorcan didn't know of any insect like it. A spider-like creature was next. The dome-shaped shell at the centre of eight armoured legs matched the description of a creature that Blake had mentioned during his interrogation. The final image was of the same towering black dragon that Lorcan and his team had encountered during their mission in Broadbeach. He immediately thought of the survivors, the ones he could have saved – should have saved.

"At first glance, these animals seem distinctly different; they vary in size, shape and behaviour patterns. If it weren't for their simultaneous arrival, we might never have managed to connect the dots." Doctor Tate pointed to the images of Drakken and the black dragon and explained, "You see, while these two seemingly have the most in common, we have discovered that all of these creatures share something incredibly unique."

"What is that, exactly?" Henrickson asked.

"Their biological structure, sir," Doctor Tate answered. "To put it simply, the way their bodies consume energy. None of these creatures eat. Not like we do, anyway. Instead, their bodies consume thermal energy. Their organs turn heat into the nutrients their bodies require."

"You mean heat from the sun?" Lorcan asked, as he studied the images on the table.

"No, not the sun, but the earth's core – or so we believe. You see, their bodies function like rechargeable batteries. During their hibernation, they burrow deep into the earth's core for extensive periods of time to absorb heat from the earth's core. When they eventually resurface, they do so with all the energy they need to function," the doctor explained.

"How long?" Henrickson asked.

"Pardon, sir?"

"How long, doctor, before they need to return underground? To recharge, as you called it?"

Doctor Tate flinched with uncertainty. "We need to run more tests, but our current estimation is near a thousand years, colonel."

"Shit." Lorcan cursed before turning to the colonel. "That's what Blake said."

"A thousand years? That's not possible," Henrickson said, refuting the doctor's claim. He leaned over and pressed a finger on Drakken's photograph. "You're telling me that this thing won't sleep for another thousand years?"

Doctor Tate nodded and replied, "Give or take a hundred years, yes, sir."

"Jesus," Henrickson mumbled, and stressfully stoked his stubble.

"You see, colonel, these monsters are very old. We have already managed to link several of them to various periods in history. In the year two hundred and forty-seven BCE, Chinese Emperor Liu Bang declared to his people that he was conceived by a dragon."

"You can't be serious," Henrickson said.

"The story was that the emperor's mother hid under a bridge during a fierce lightning storm. When her husband found her she was naked, with a serpent-like dragon hovering over her."

"Seriously, doc? Knocked up by a dragon?" Lorcan interrupted. "You can't tell me you actually believe that."

"No, captain, we don't believe the fairy tales of ancient Chinese emperors. However, there is some truth in most fiction. Lui Bang's description of the creature that hovered above his mother fits the description of this animal precisely," Doctor Tate remarked, as she pointed to the image of the snake-like creature. "This monster is ferocious. Hidden within its long body are eight retractable legs and a pair of bladed arms. When extended, those legs are capable of splitting into fan-like wings. In full flight, this creature bears an uncanny resemblance to the mythological Chinese dragon," she explained, pulling out an old Chinese textbook from a bag next to her feet. She opened it and slid it to the middle of the table.

Lorcan and Henrickson glanced at the old book. Neither could read it, but several drawings of Chinese dragons lent a certain credibility to the doctor's claims.

"Well, I'll be," Henrickson mumbled to himself.

"Or perhaps you both would prefer something more local." Doctor Tate dropped a second book on the table: *Studies of the Dreamtime.* She flicked the book open to a marked page. "I give you the aboriginal rainbow serpent. Look familiar?" The book showed a long snake with various colours emanating from its body.

"Doctor, are you clutching at straws here?" Henrickson asked doubtfully, as he studied the primitive illustrations.

"You tell me, colonel. Those retractable wings I mentioned, well, these creatures display a variety of changing colour patterns as they move through the air. One witness even described the monster as a *slithering rainbow.*"

Lorcan didn't know what to make of it all, but it was clear that the doctor was confident in her research. "What about this one?" he pointed to the image of Drakken.

"Ah, the monster that levelled Surfers Paradise." Diane slid the photo to the middle of the table. "The Anglo Saxons told stories of two warring dragons – a white one and a red one. The battle was said to have been so fierce that Britain was left a barren, scorched wasteland after the white dragon emerged victorious. My team and I have discovered numerous connections across history that seemingly refer to the same white dragon. Gentlemen, we believe that this monster here may be the very creature from which *all* dragon mythology in Europe originated."

"It's more of a sandy white, really. Some parts are grey," the colonel muttered.

"Well, thank you, colonel," Doctor Tate politely humoured Henrickson's pointless observation. "We have taken that into account."

"Ah, yes, of course," the embarrassed colonel said, and cleared his throat.

"What about the other one?" Lorcan asked, sliding the photograph of the black dragon closer.

Doctor Tate shrugged. "Honestly, we don't know much about it. Four wings, two tails, over fifteen storeys tall, highly agile, and it breathes a blue flame that's so hot you'd turn to ash before you even realised it had touched you. This monster should be your top priority. It single-handedly wiped out most of the east coast. Starting with Sydney, approximately twelve hours after Surfers Paradise was hit, it then burned every major town and city along the eastern shoreline. Our last reported sighting was here in the ruins of Broadbeach, but you already knew that, captain. Honestly, I find it a miracle that your team survived that encounter a few days ago."

"Not the word I'd use," Lorcan responded.

"Thanks for the history lesson, doctor, but I have a question." Henrickson held up the photo of the serpent. "You claim these creatures don't eat, yet I have received numerous reports of these things dicing people up and devouring them. Your theory must be incorrect."

"It's no theory, colonel, I assure you. But you are right, and your guess is as good as mine. I've personally cut one open in the lab. They have no stomach or intestines, just a series of cavities that they use to store their victims' remains. However, we don't know to what end. But we are certain that it is not for digestion.

"I see…" Henrickson trailed off, deep in thought, staring silently at the images on the table.

"So, what do you make of all this, doctor?" Lorcan asked, eager to hear some form of conclusion.

Doctor Tate removed her glasses and began cleaning the lenses with her sleeve. "Honestly, captain, I'm not sure. These attacks are too organised to be coincidental. The large dragons have burnt almost every major city in the country. The smaller serpents seem to kill anyone they miss, and these spider things have spread throughout the ruins, leaving all vegetation growing at an unprecedented rate. But they are elusive, and we have not yet managed to capture one to see how they do this. But if I had to guess, "invasion" is the only word that comes to mind. It's as if they are systematically taking over the country."

"I'd say you're pretty accurate," Lorcan agreed. "Your theory matches everything Blake—"

"Captain!" Colonel Henrickson quickly interjected. "That does not concern Doctor Tate."

"Sir, everything the doctor has told us falls in line with the information Blake provided," Lorcan argued. "He told us exactly why the Dreyan were doing this."

"The Dreyan?" Doctor Tate asked. She clearly hadn't heard that name before.

"Captain, that's enough!" The colonel raised his voice as he slammed his hands on the table. "I know what Blake said!" Henrickson took a moment to compose himself, then turned to the doctor and said, "Doctor Tate, thank you for the information. You have been a great help."

But Doctor Tate was now scrambling for her own answers. "Colonel, who is Blake? What are Dreyan? Sir, what is the captain talking about?"

Henrickson ignored her and waved over the uniformed soldier by the door. "Private, please take the doctor back to her tent. That will be all I need."

"But, colonel," Doctor Tate protested, "I can help you!"

"That will be all for today, thank you." Henrickson declined her offer as the young private quickly escorted Doctor Tate out of the room. The colonel frustratedly turned to Lorcan. "Captain, you and I don't see eye to eye, but I've put up with it. You don't agree with the way I do things – that much is clear.

But I need soldiers, *not* rebels. I need men who follow orders willingly. I need your trust."

Lorcan's frustration was also at the breaking point. "With respect, sir, you speak to me of trust. But tell me, colonel, who is giving you orders? Canberra is gone; our government is gone. Do the men even know? Are you planning to tell them that *you are* the top of the food chain, colonel?"

Henrickson thought about his answer for a moment, which caught Lorcan a little off guard. He then looked the captain squarely in the eyes and said, "The men and women under my command are good soldiers. They are loyal. They respect the chain of command. I am their colonel. Sometimes in war, it's the top of that chain that gets hit first. So, yes, our leadership is gone, but it is up to the rest of the chain to carry out the duties of the fallen. This, captain, is something that you have clearly forgotten."

Lorcan didn't completely disagree, but he wasn't about to let his point go. "The men and women who serve under you have a right to know. Damn it, colonel! They had families in those cites!"

"That's right, captain, they did," Henrickson shouted, having had enough of Lorcan's insubordination. "And I know that pain, captain. I know the agony of losing your family. I know how that pain can cripple a man," he continued, then took a deep long breath to calm himself. "We are at war now, and I need soldiers who have something to fight for. The country needs soldiers who are focused, formidable. Not grieving ones, not broken ones. I will break the news when the time is right."

"Well, tell me one thing, colonel. Are you broken?"

Henrickson arched his shoulders back and straightened his posture. "We all are, captain," he answered, then slid a white folder across the table.

"What's this?" Lorcan asked.

"Squad Seven's next assignment."

Lorcan picked the folder up and opened it. Inside were several aerial photographs of what appeared to be a large country property. "What kind of assignment?"

"When Blake and his associates entered the Robina refuge centre, they each filled out identification forms. We have tracked them to a property owned by a Thomas Riley. These are the last images we were able to obtain before we lost contact with our satellites.

"Our satellites are down?"

Henrickson nodded. "We are rapidly losing resources, captain. Communications, ordnance, transportation, men, women – we're down to what we have here. Make no mistake, these monsters are winning this fight. Which is why this mission is critical. One of Blake's companions left the refuge centre shortly after you extracted him. We believe this location is where he and the dragon have likely fled to. Your team is to locate Blake, and his associates, and eliminate them."

Closing the folder, Lorcan stared at his commanding officer with disbelief. "Sam, they're just kids."

"Captain Edwards, don't be naive!" Henrickson pointed to the photo of Drakken on the table. "This thing may be the biggest threat to humanity we have ever seen. We cannot have people helping these monsters."

"With all due respect, sir, Blake came to us for help. I don't believe he poses a threat."

Henrickson laughed dismissively. "That monster walking around killed a quarter of a million people in a single day. Blake made his choice. We should have put him down when we had the chance."

Lorcan dropped the folder on the table. "Colonel, think this through. That monster could have burned this whole place to the ground this morning. It could have killed us all. Instead, it took Blake and left. Why do that? *Why*? If it intended to destroy us, it would have. Sir, I really think he was telling us the truth. There may be a chance to stop all this."

Henrickson picked up the surveillance photo of Drakken and crumpled it in his hand. "I will not make peace with the thing that burned my wife and children alive. Is that clear?" Lorcan didn't say another word. After all, what could he say? "But, don't worry, captain. We will stop it. All of it. War is never easy. That's why they invented soldiers. We do the hard things that most people can't bring themselves to do."

"I thought it was to protect our people," Lorcan remarked.

"Not all of them," Henrickson replied, picking the white folder up and shoving it into Lorcan's hand. "You have your orders, Edwards. Like I said, I need soldiers, not rebels. You deploy at dawn. Get some rest. You will need it."

Reluctantly, Lorcan took the folder and headed towards the door.

"Oh, and captain," Henrickson added, "if you disobey my orders again, I will put you in a hole so dark that you will never see light again. Am I clear?"

Lorcan ignored the colonel's threat and left the room.

Angry and frustrated, Lorcan navigated the busy hallway and headed for the offices that Samantha, Jack and Mindy had been recovering in. The small window in the door to Samantha's room showed that no lights were on inside. Lorcan turned the handle and opened the door. Flicking the light switch on, he found himself staring into an empty room – no medical equipment, no food trays or flowers – just an empty bed and rumpled sheets where Samantha had been resting.

Lorcan stepped out of the room and opened the door to the next office. It was empty – no toys, no nurse, no Mindy.

"Jack?" Lorcan called, as he rushed to the next door over and opened it. All the children's toys had been put away neatly, and the furniture was now stacked against the wall. No Jack. Looking around, a familiar stuffed green dinosaur caught his eye on the window seat. Lorcan walked over and picked it up. A piece of paper had been taped to the dinosaur's back. He pulled it off and flipped the paper over. "For the Army Man" was written in crayon.

"He left that for you," a woman's voice said from the doorway.

Lorcan turned around to see the same nurse who had been taking care of Jack standing behind him. "Where are they?"

"Gone. Colonel Henrickson had all medical treatments moved to a government facility. He said we couldn't treat them here – that we didn't have the resources. He's right, though. Samantha needs around-the-clock medical attention. She has severe head trauma."

"Where?"

"I'm not sure," the nurse answered cautiously. "The facility was not disclosed. The colonel said it was secure, though; a safer place for the children."

Lorcan stuffed Jack's toy in his left thigh pocket and zipped it up. "Nowhere is safe anymore," he muttered, passing the nurse as he left the room.

The sun was setting over the mountains as Lorcan exited the main building and made his way towards the dam wall. He felt utterly lost. The organised chaos of a military base had always felt like home, but for the first time in his twenty-year career, it felt foreign. Men and women walked back and forth, carrying out their assignments, each one a cog in the well-oiled war machine.

How could Henrickson have sent Samantha and her kids away like that? And where did he send them? Lorcan didn't know of any facility nearby that was suitable. And then the colonel had ordered him to assassinate Blake and everyone with him. Had the death of the colonel's family tipped the man over the edge? Or was it Lorcan who had finally lost his nerve?

Pushing the thoughts to the back of his mind, he arrived at the top of the dam wall and stood by the railing. The sunset was beautiful, painting the dam's lake with a reddish hue as two ducks swooped down and landed in the water.

"Never picked you for the sunset-watching type, captain." Amanda's English accent was hard to mistake.

"It's peaceful here. No one disturbs you." Lorcan didn't bother to greet her.

"Subtle hint taken, but I don't care." Amanda joined him at the railing and watched the ducks swim across the lake. "So, I take it you've heard that Henrickson shipped Samantha and the kids to a government facility?"

"Nurse said she needs around-the-clock treatment."

"Captain? Are you actually okay with this?" Amanda turned to him. "Henrickson didn't even tell us!"

Lorcan kept his gaze on the water. "He's a colonel. He doesn't have to tell us anything."

"Don't," Amanda scoffed at him. "Don't pretend that they don't mean something to you. I know you're just as worried about them as I am."

"What do you want from me?" He reluctantly faced her and said, "There is nothing to say. They're gone, and that's that."

"Captain, I've asked everyone," she said sternly. "No one can tell me if their chopper even arrived at the facility. That's why I've come to you. We need to go after them."

"And how do you propose we do that?" Lorcan laughed at her ignorance. "We don't even know where they are."

"I do," Amanda said, and pulled a torn piece of paper from her pocket. "I told the colonel that I wanted out of here. It seems my usefulness has reached its end. He was more than happy to send me to the same facility tomorrow. These are the coordinates," she said, offering the paper to him.

"I can't," Lorcan declined, pushing her hand away. "I can't just leave, Amanda. Seven was just given a new assignment."

"So I've heard." Amanda moved away from the railing with a disgusted scowl. "You're being sent to assassinate a group of innocent people because Samuel Henrickson can't see anything past the death of his own family." She could see the surprise written on Lorcan's face. After all, he had only just found out about the mission himself. "That's right! I know what he's making you do. I saw the assignment sitting on the colonel's desk when I asked him about Samantha."

"Orders are orders."

"Don't say that! I know you don't really believe that. You are soldiers, not murderers!"

Lorcan turned back to the water and continued to watch the ducks.

Amanda snatched a stone from the pavement and pegged it in the water, scaring the ducks away in a fit of quacks and squawks.

"Hey," Lorcan growled at her, "what the hell did the ducks do?"

"Orders are orders? Since when?" Amanda's demeanour quickly softened. "Don't do this. Please, captain, don't kill those people for him. The army, the colonel – they don't own you."

"Yes, actually, they do." Lorcan turned away again as he said, "I'm still a soldier."

"No, captain," Amanda shook her head, "you're a coward. Now, I'm leaving tomorrow, first thing in the morning. A supply chopper is going to take me to that facility. If you find your soul between now and then, I suggest you get on that chopper and come with me." She turned and gazed at the countless olive-green military tents filling the carpark. "Henrickson is right about one thing. The world has changed. There are enough monsters out there, captain. Don't become one of them." She folded the paper and forced it into Lorcan's hand. "If you truly don't care about them, then why is that dinosaur in your pocket again?"

Lorcan looked down and found his thigh pocket half-un-zipped; Jack's green dinosaur was sticking out a little. Before he could say a word, Amanda walked away and uttered, "Good day, captain. May God have mercy on your soul."

Lorcan watched until she was lost amongst the olive-green tents, then turned back to the fading sunset and the silhouettes of two scared ducks that had flown further into the distance. He wished he could trade places with them.

31

WHAT WE LIVE FOR

A light fog emanating from the forest rolled over the creek and slowly consumed the Riley Farm in a damp, moonlit haze.

With her face pressed to the kitchen window, Lila anxiously watched the trees for any sign of movement. "Come on. They should be back by now," she said nervously.

"They'll be back. Don't worry," Gary said, lifting a flat timber board over the broken window above the sink. "Just gonna bang a few nails in. Hope you don't mind."

"I don't mind," Lila replied and turned to him, filled with worry. "Emma doesn't look good. I don't know what we're gonna do if they come back empty-handed."

"I'm not gonna lie to ya, darlin'," Gary answered. He placed a nail on the timber but hesitated to hammer it in. "She's in bad shape. Blake and Tom haven't left her side. She's still breathing, but she's getting weaker. I don't know what else we can do."

"And the dragon… Drakken, I mean. It can't help us?"

"I don't know how it can. Those big spiders are untraceable, apparently. But even if we could find one, ain't a person here that feels okay about dicing one up – especially Emma."

"Will would," Lila said, disapprovingly.

Gary quickly hammered the nail in with three swift strikes, then turned back to Lila. "You don't mean that."

"I do." Lila folded her arms and glanced back out the window. "He's different now. Or maybe I just never really knew him before."

Gary rested the hammer on the bench and joined Lila by the window. "I don't really know Will like you do. I mean, I never really talk to the guy, but one thing I can tell you is that nothing he has done since this all started has been for his own wellbeing. It's been for yours. Now, I know that you two need to sort through some things, but give him a chance. He might surprise you. Love isn't always easy, but it's always worth it."

Lila donned a pleasantly surprised smirk and said, "Wow! That was quite deep."

"Hah, to be honest, I got the line about love from an old movie. But it's still a valid point," Gary said with a wink, then returned to boarding up the broken window.

Out of the corner of her eye, Lila noticed something moving in the woods – two familiar silhouettes. "They're back!" she cheered. Will and James emerged from the woods, stone-hopped across the creek and sprinted for the house. Lila unlocked the back door and rushed outside. "Took you long enough! Did you find it?"

Will walked up to the deck, breathing heavily. "Well, James took forever."

James hunched behind him to catch his breath. "It's seriously dark in there. I had to search the whole house properly."

"Oh, right, "Will quipped, "so that's why you looked in the oven?"

"Shut up," James said, as he leaned against the rail. "You don't understand. Those muffins were delicious."

"So, did you find any?" Lila asked again.

"No," James shook his head, "I don't think she had any left. To be honest, I'm not surprised; they were amazing muffins."

"Not the muffins, James!" Lila snapped "Did you find any spider blood?"

James quickly shut up, but Will's sorry expression said it all. "We searched everywhere. The jars in the shed were smashed on the ground. Must have happened when they were attacked by the shriekers. Like I said before, we used the last jar on Thomas."

Folding her arms in defeat, Lila went back inside and prompted the others to follow her. "So, what do we do now?"

Gary shut the door as the group formed a circle around the repaired kitchen table.

"Well, we could try to find another spider," Will suggested.

"Are you crazy?" James asked, as he raised his hands in the air. "We are not doing that! Oh, and Drakken can probably hear you out there."

Lila was equally disgusted by the idea and by the fact that her earlier assumption about Will had been correct. He would do it. "You wanna cut one of those things up and use its blood to heal Emma? After she risked her life to set one free? Do you really think she would ever be okay with that? She would never forgive us!"

"Who cares!" Will scoffed. "It would save her life!"

For the first time ever, Lila slapped Will across his face. "You just don't get it, do you?"

"Lila?" Will rubbed his cheek in disbelief as his girlfriend burst into tears and left the room.

"Way to go, Man Bun," James remarked, shaking his head in disapproval.

Not one for awkward situations, Gary stepped away from the table and headed for the doorway. "Ah, listen, I'm gonna go check on the kid while y'all take a minute," he said, before heading upstairs.

James took a seat at the table and turned to Will, who was still rubbing his cheek. "So..." he began.

Will ignored him and quietly exited the room.

Letting out a loud sigh, James leaned back in his seat, gazed around at the empty kitchen and muttered, "Go team."

~~~~~~~~~~~

Listening to the chirping crickets outside, Blake sat silently at Emma's bedside. He hadn't moved for hours, unable to take his eyes off the unrecognisable face resting on the pillow. The longer he stayed with Emma, the guiltier he felt; he should never have left her alone. Blake glanced over at Emma's father, Thomas, who was snoring in a fold-out chair at the foot of the bed. He hadn't left her side either, but the exhausted man had been through a lot. He had found his daughter, only to almost lose her again. Not to mention trying to comprehend fire-breathing monsters and the fact that his broken leg had been healed by a mysterious animal's blood – blood that could have been used to save his daughter's life. The guilt alone was enough to knock the man out cold.

Leaning back in his chair, Blake turned his attention to the ceiling; it was easier to look at than the purple-and-black swelling that had overtaken Emma's face. Gary quietly entered the room and immediately noticed Thomas snoring in his seat. Blake didn't bother to check who had come in.

"The boys just got back," Gary informed him, approaching the bed. "They couldn't find any more of that magic blood stuff. Will used the last of it on sleeping beauty here."

Blake kept his eyes on the ceiling as he said, "The man's been through a lot. He needs the rest."

"How's she doing?" Gary asked.

"Her breathing is getting weaker." Blake finally looked at him. "Had to check her pulse a few times."

"At least she's home now, I suppose. Thanks to you, kid."

"Thanks to Drakken, you mean," Blake said. "If it wasn't for him, we would never have found her."

Gary reached over and abruptly tilted Blake's head back. "The swelling is starting to go down," he said, observing Blake's own black eye and split lip.

Blake yanked Gary's hand off his head and turned back to Emma. "Thomas said she's in some sort of coma state – that she'll probably go in her sleep tonight."

"Well," Gary exhaled, "he's a worried dad. Let's see how she goes. She's a tough girl." Blake didn't say anything, so Gary chose his next words carefully. "You know, kid, I can't imagine what you're feeling right now. I mean, between the giant gecko outside and Emma here. It's a lot. Just want you to know we can talk about it, you know, whenever you're ready."

Blake didn't react.

"Okay then, I'll give you some time." Gary took the hint and made his way to the door.

"I don't know what to say," Blake said softly. "Emma might die in this bed, and I freed the only thing that could have saved her. Those people next door, too. I got them killed. This is all my fault. Will was right."

Gary came back and put a reassuring hand on Blake's shoulder. "I don't know Emma that well, but in the short time I have known her, I learned how strong-willed she is. When you two freed that spider thing, you both did it believing it was right. I know she wouldn't take it back, not for a second."

"Yeah, maybe," Blake said sombrely. "There's something else. Something I haven't told anyone yet."

"What is it?"

"Henrickson. He told me that most of the country has been destroyed. I saw the photos. All the major cities are gone. The Dreyan are already taking over. James has probably lost his family. How do I tell him that?"

Gary felt his whole body go numb. The news shook him to the core. "Already? But it's only been…" All the faces he had encountered during his fifty-two years flickered through his mind. He wondered how many of them still lived.

"Gary," Blake said, reading the shock on the man's face, "I have no idea what I'm supposed to do now."

Gary focused back on Blake and said, "Kid, that dragon out there, it may only talk to you, but that doesn't mean that you have to carry this on your own." Gary gestured to Thomas and Emma. "We're a family – all of us. It doesn't matter what brought us together; what matters is that we handle this together. That's what families are for."

Blake nodded. "So, what do I do?"

"Let these guys in – even Will. We all want the same thing here."

"I don't want to let anyone down."

"Then don't keep them out, kid. We'll figure this out together."

〰〰〰〰〰〰

Will opened the bedroom door. Lila was sitting on their bed, patting Milky, who was purring on her lap. "We're lucky we found her," he said, shutting the door behind him.

"Are we, Will?" Lila turned her glassy eyes on him. "Do you actually care?"

"Of course I do!" Will responded. "How could you even say that? What is going on with you? With us?"

Lila avoided looking at him. "I don't recognise you anymore. I really don't." She choked up. "When the others left for Robina, you wanted to run and leave them behind. When Blake freed that spider thing from torture, you said it was *worth* torturing! It's like you only care about yourself!"

"Are you serious?" Will pointed to the door behind him. "If Blake hadn't let that thing go, then Emma wouldn't be upstairs dying in her bed, right now!"

"How dare you!" Lila glared at him. "The only person responsible for Emma's condition is the psychopath who nearly beat her to death!"

Will was about to argue back, but lowered his tone instead. "Fine. But everything I've done was to keep you safe. I'm not worried about myself. I promised your father I'd keep you safe, and that's what I'm trying to do!"

"That's just it!" Lila shook her head and continued to pat Milky. "You don't even know why I'm upset."

"Then tell me," said Will, and walked over and sat on the bed next to her.

Lila stared into his eyes for a moment before she said, "Will, I need you to understand something. I believe that *what* we live for is more important than how long we live. Call me silly, call me naive, but I mean it. That's why I do those quirky things, you know? I collect the plants, raise money for the wildlife shelter, lecture you on global warming. That's why I spent time with that crazy old man living down the street from us!"

"You know, I wondered about you two," Will joked.

"Shut up. He has no family," Lila said, and nudged him with her shoulder. "My point is: I don't do these things to be nice. I do them because I believe it is important. I know this is going to bother you, but I really believe in what Blake is trying to do. He is trying to stop this from happening everywhere else, and I want to help him do that. I have spent my whole life observing people's mistakes – our selfishness, and our ignorance of our own behaviour. This is my chance. I want to stand up for what I believe is right. I used to believe that you did, too."

"You know I do." Will reached out for her hand, but she pulled it away. "I've been trying to keep you safe. I would do anything for you; you know that."

"That's the thing. I don't want you to do it for me," Lila said, but her eyes revealed her heartache. "The world is bigger than me, Will. It's bigger than us. The man I love would never agree with torturing an innocent animal, no matter what its blood could do."

"Lila… I…" Will could feel her slipping away.

Lila felt it, too. "I know what I stand for. What do you stand for, Will? I need you to figure it out."

Will paused for a moment, then stood up and made his way to the door. "You are my world. It will never be bigger than you – not for me." He left the room and quietly shut the door behind him.

Lila listened to his footsteps fade away as she quietly wept on the bed. Running her fingers through Milky's white fur, she wondered how she and Will had ended up so far apart. It was never supposed to end like this; not for them, and not like this.

~~~~~~~~~~

Cold air whistled between the timber boards covering Emma's broken bedroom window. Blake stared out between the gaps but could only see moonlight reflecting off the creek. Thomas was still sound asleep and had just begun snoring again. Blake envied him. He, too, was exhausted, but his mind wasn't about to let him rest. He found himself riding an endless loop of unanswerable questions. He wondered about his home and if it was still standing. If Luther, Andy, or his boss, Kimmy, were still alive, or if he would ever know what had happened to any of them.

Suddenly, the gaps in the timber boards turned black, and the creek was gone. Blake stood up and moved away from the window; something was on the other side. He went to wake Thomas, but before he could reach him, the timber plank flew across the room, narrowly missing Blake's head before slamming into the opposite wall.

A groggy and disorientated Thomas leapt out of his chair. "What the hell was that?"

"I don't know," Blake replied, and directed him to the window. Something scurried out of sight. "There is something out there."

Another board fell from the window frame with a loud crash, revealing a round silhouette surrounded by a haze of foggy moonlight.

"We need to get Emma out of here," Thomas said urgently.

Blake could almost make out the shape. It was big. Not a shrieker, though. Several shadowy legs slowly began to reach through the window. "Grab Emma," he shouted.

Thomas rushed for his daughter, but the mystery monster quickly clambered through the window frame and blocked him. Hundreds of small eyes seemed to appear and disappear as the creature climbed onto Emma's bed and stood over the comatose girl. Blake noticed that the two-metre-high shadow seemed to be dragging five of its eight legs behind it. They were also significantly shorter than the others.

"Quick! Grab something!" Thomas quickly snatched a timber board from the ground.

"Wait!" Blake noticed a green shimmer across the creature's dome-shaped head. "I know what it is."

"I don't care what it is," Thomas said, and raised the plank to strike, but Blake quickly knocked it out of his hands. "What are you doing? We've got to get her out of here!"

"Look!" Blake pointed to something metallic around the monster's leg – a shackle. "You see that?"

"See what?"

Blake grabbed Thomas by the shoulders. "Listen to me. Whatever happens, I need you to trust me. I think it's here to help her."

"What? How?" Thomas argued.

"Trust me. Please."

Letting out a soft hum, the spider extended its long purple tongue from under its body and began feeling over the blankets. Thomas nervously took a step forward, but Blake stopped him with a hand on his chest. "Trust me."

The spider's tongue quickly found Emma's beaten face.

"What the hell is going on up here?" Will shouted as he, Gary and James burst into the room and startled the creature.

"Stop!" Blake raised a hand. "Don't come any closer!"

"Um, dude?" James whispered, staring at the monster standing over Emma. "Is that what I think it is?"

The creature latched its tongue onto Emma's cheek, jerking the unconscious girl upright before she fell back onto the pillow and stopped breathing.

"Emma?" Thomas cried out. "It's killing her!"

"No! Wait!" Blake put himself between Thomas and the monster. "Please trust me. She'll be okay."

James, Gary and Will swapped uncertain glances.

"Okay." Thomas relaxed his stance, then reluctantly moved back.

The monster hummed again; it almost sounded happy. The long purple tongue detached from Emma's cheek, leaving strands of saliva hanging from the girl's face. Slowly, the tall spider-like creature stepped off the bed and headed back to the window. The five men watched in silence. With another loud hum, the spider climbed outside and disappeared into the moonlight.

"Well, that was terrifying," James said, swallowing the lump in his throat.

Emma suddenly sat up in a flurry of gasps and coughs.

Gary, James and Will almost jumped out of their skins. "Jee-zus, she's awake," Gary cried, and clenched his chest in fright.

"Emma!" Thomas rushed to his daughter's side.

Blake slumped against the wall, staring at her through glassy eyes. "Can't believe it," he mumbled, exhaling an emotional breath.

"How did you know it was gonna help her?" James asked.

Blake smirked, then said proudly, "Because she saved it first."

Thomas tightly clenched his daughter's hand. "How are you feeling?" he asked, watching as the girl's face began to change colour.

"Where are we?" Emma groaned. "I can't feel my face."

"At home." Thomas smiled tearfully.

Gary subtly tapped James and Will on the shoulder. "Let's give them a minute."

Quietly, they all left the room.

As Emma went to speak, everything came flooding back – the needle in her arm, the warehouse, Gabriel. She looked at her father. "Dad, how did you find me?"

"Blake found you," Thomas answered, "with the dragon. They brought you back."

"Where is Blake?"

"He's right here." Thomas turned around, but Blake was no longer in the room.

∿∿∿∿∿∿∿∿∿∿

Blake exited the house and headed for the burnt field. There, standing on his hind legs, was Drakken, with his snout raised to the sky. "So how about a heads-up next time one of your giant spider buddies comes to visit," Blake said, as he approached.

Drakken closed his eyes and sniffed the air. "The Ovachi have no scent. They absorb the scent of their surroundings and expel it as their own."

Blake came to a burnt stump and stopped. "So that's why you can't track them?"

"They are the children of Grannus. They are as elusive as they are powerful."

"So… no, basically." Blake brushed some ash off the stump and sat on it. "Well, it sure gave us a fright."

Drakken inhaled deeply and growled. "They seek to harm no being. They are healers."

"Did you know it would come for Emma?" Blake had to ask. "Did you know it would help her?"

"No."

"So why did it?"

Drakken exhaled through his nostrils, keeping his snout to the sky. "The Ovachi only preserve what is of value to the earth. That is their role. It must have found value in her life."

"Well, it was right," Blake said, but couldn't help but wonder what the dragon was doing. "So, do you just stand there and sniff the air all night?"

Drakken opened his eyes and lowered his head. "I am observing."

"Observing what?" Blake asked.

"Everything."

"So, you can tell what's going on out there just by smelling the air?"

"Yes."

"Can you tell what everything is just by its smell? Like, could you smell the difference between me and James? I mean, even, if we were miles away?"

"Yes," Drakken growled. "The human you call James has a strong scent. He would be easy to identify."

Blake chuckled a little and said, "You're not the first to say that."

"Once I am familiar with a scent, then I can track it across great distances."

"Okay, what about things you have never encountered up close? You can smell them, but you don't know what they are?"

"Correct."

"Interesting," Blake remarked, leaned back on his arms and gazed up at the stars. They were beautiful; twinkling like Christmas lights. He found himself unusually comfortable in Drakken's company, but he couldn't tell if he trusted the creature or if he was just too numb to care anymore.

"I have another question. If those serpents are part of your kind, then why did you kill them? I mean, I'm grateful that you saved us last night, but why not just ask them to stop?"

Drakken let out a frustrated growl. "They are the Reanoi, a vicious Dreyan species that cares not for the earth or its survival. They are rebellious beings and cannot be trusted. The Reanoi build their hives underground and hunt at night. They contain their prey within their bodies and return them to the burrow."

"To eat them, right?"

"No. Each burrow has a mother – a master of the hive. For the mother to bear offspring, she must consume high amounts of organic life. The Reanoi must be constantly monitored. Their species can spread at an alarming rate. A long time ago, Alarak culled their species, much like he intends to do with your own."

"If they're so dangerous, then why didn't Alarak wipe them out?"

"He sought to, but much like your own kind, they also fall under my protection. All living things have a right to live. I negotiated a cull to reduce their numbers and vowed to keep them in order."

Blake couldn't help but wonder if humanity was destined for the same fate. Instead of asking, he opted for another question that had been lingering in his mind. "How is it you can speak, anyway?"

Drakken gazed down upon him once more. "Adopting new languages is not a trait exclusive to humans, although your species' arrogance would have you believe so. As a Guardian, I am required to communicate with all beings."

"You can talk to everything? That's kind of awesome, actually."

Having finished his observations, Drakken lowered himself onto all fours with a ground-shaking thud. "I also have questions."

"Shoot," Blake said, intrigued as to what they might be.

"You and I have a grand task ahead: to prevent the extermination of your kind and unify our species."

"Pretty big words for a dude that just started speaking English." Blake thought he'd test out some humour, but Drakken didn't react. "Sorry, bad joke. Carry on."

"We have great work ahead, yet your focus is the protection of the individual instead of the greater species. I can't decide if this is humanity's weakness or its strength. What do you believe?"

Blake exhaled and replied, "It's both. I don't think I ever really understood this until right now. You see, all these people here... most of them are strangers. Yet here they are, sticking together, keeping each other safe from something they don't understand. I mean, we don't all agree or get along at times, but no matter what has happened, we have stuck together. Even with you standing outside their window. I didn't get the whole family thing. This is kinda my first one. But I get it now. I get why people fight for this."

Drakken took a moment to process what Blake had told him, then said, "I thought emotion to be a defect of your kind. That it created a distracted species – one with no focus, no greater insight. Perhaps I was mistaken. Perhaps it enhances your resolve."

"You want my advice?" Blake asked, hopped off the stump and brushed the dirt off his backside. "If you really want to understand humanity, then get to know us. Talk to the people here. Get to know them. Get to know the species that you are trying to protect."

"This may not be wise. I killed many of your kind," Drakken replied.

Blake nodded, "Yeah, you did, and they will never forgive you for that. But today, you found Thomas, you saved Emma's life, and you saved my life. If *we* are going to stop all this, we need to do it together. Give it a shot; talk to them." Drakken went silent and seemed to be considering his suggestion, but Blake wasn't quite sure. "Anyway, I'm going to try and get some sleep. Think about what I said."

32

THE ARMY MAN

As the sun peeked over the horizon in an array of red and yellow, Lorcan once again found himself atop the dam wall, staring out at the distant ruins of Surfers Paradise. He'd been standing at that railing for an hour now, unable to peel his eyes away from the devastated city.

Today was going to be a hard day. He knew that they wouldn't understand his choice. He wasn't sure if he understood it. He wondered what David would have said – what advice he would have given him. Lorcan felt the warmth of the rising sun on his face; it was the only warmth he had felt that morning. Everything else was cold.

The low howl of a helicopter winding its rotors quickly drew his attention to the carpark. The Castra Dam base was alive with activity. Soldiers swarmed between the countless olive-green tents as they went about their usual morning duties. A large clearing in the middle of the tents housed two military helicopters; one of them was being prepped for take-off. A small group of military personal, civilians and medical staff were gathered around the aircraft.

"Everybody, line up!" A young male soldier pushed through the crowd and slid the chopper's side door open. Slowly, the group began shuffling into the helicopter.

Carrying a bag over her shoulder and a briefcase in her hand, Amanda exited the main building and immediately looked towards the dam wall. She knew he'd be there. Lorcan turned away and focused back on the view. Amanda muttered something to herself, straightened her jacket and made for the chopper.

Lorcan wanted to go with her. He wanted to check on Jack, but he couldn't. He had to handle the situation with Blake and the dragon. It was too important to walk away from. At least, that's what he told himself.

"Captain!" Damien's voice came from behind him. "Wombat's ready to roll, sir."

"Roger," Lorcan answered. He reached into his pocket and took out the piece of paper Amanda had given him the previous day. Something else was jotted on the back. The words "You always have a choice" were written in neat handwriting. Lorcan grunted. He hadn't noticed it before. He folded the paper up and stuffed it into the pocket with Jack's toy.

"Ready to go hunting, sir?" Damien asked.

Lorcan glanced back. Amanda was being assisted into the chopper by the young soldier. "Yeah, let's move out." A moment later, the helicopter lifted off and flew high over the dam wall toward the mountains.

"Sir?" Damien tapped his captain on the shoulder. "Big man? You okay?"

Lorcan nodded and said, "Let's get this over with." The pair walked the length of the dam wall until they found Mitch at the end, with the ATV-X's engine running.

"Where's Civi?" Mitch asked.

"She left," Lorcan answered bluntly.

Damien stopped. "What? Why?"

Lorcan could see that he was a little hurt. "This life. It's not for her."

"Good," Damien said, as he slammed his fist into the touchpad, "I didn't wanna babysit anyway." The Wombat's side door retracted. He climbed into the rear cabin and took a seat.

"Oh, come on now, puddin'," Mitch said, as he leaned inside and pinched Damien's cheek. "Don't worry. I'll talk in a sexy English accent and give you a big wet kiss!"

"Shut up, arsehole." Damien shoved him out of the vehicle and hit the touchpad. The door slid closed.

"He's so sensitive," Mitch chuckled. "Guess you're riding up front with me, cap."

"Actually, I'm driving today." Lorcan walked around to the front of the Wombat and climbed into the driver's seat.

Mitch opened the passenger door. "You sure you can drive this thing?" he asked, hopping into his seat. Lorcan ignored him. "Guess so." Mitch settled in and pushed the intercom button on the dash. "How about you, Princess? You got your seatbelt on back there?"

"Yeah, your wife is doing it up right now," Damien's voice crackled through the speaker.

Lorcan put the Wombat in gear and sped down the winding access road. Mitch could see the captain was distracted but decided not to ask about it, choosing to gaze out the window instead. Flourishing trees and wavy grass had reclaimed large portions of the narrow two-lane road, causing the Wombat to bump and shudder over protruding tree roots and broken pavement.

"World's gone crazy, captain. Just look at all this," Mitch said, watching the dense vegetation pass by. "The colonel says that some spider is making it grow like that." Lorcan kept his eyes on the road. "Now we have this Blake kid working for that dragon thing. It's a shame we gotta put him down like this. I don't know how he could do it, you know? Turn against his own people like that, after everything that monster did."

"That's Henrickson talking," Lorcan muttered.

"You don't agree with the colonel?" Mitch asked with a smirk. "No shocker there."

Lorcan glanced at his passenger then looked back to the road. "Tell me something. That monster could have levelled the whole dam, but it didn't. Why? It just grabbed Blake and left. It doesn't make sense."

Mitch thought to himself for a moment. "So, what's your theory, captain?"

"Blake was telling the truth."

"Really, cap? You can't be serious. You think that giant lizard had a change of heart because some guy didn't step on a spider?" Mitch shook his head in disbelief. "Captain, I'm sorry, but I don't buy it. You don't just go and kill thousands of people then suddenly decide, oh, I don't know, maybe I was wrong."

Lorcan shifted gear and asked, "Why not? Isn't that what people do? Isn't that what we've *always* done?"

"I don't know, maybe." Mitch shrugged. "Well, it's too late for Blake now. We have our orders." Lorcan, unsurprisingly, didn't respond. Mitch turned to his captain, choosing his next few words cautiously. "You know, Henrickson told me about David."

"That's not what this is about," Lorcan replied bluntly.

"Really? Are you sure? Because this empathy for Blake seems very familiar to me. A soldier, in the middle of a gunfight, disobeys a direct order and abandons his squad to save some kids caught in the crossfire. The soldier saves the boys but is shot and killed before he can return to his squad. After a formal inquiry, his captain is found unfit to lead and is therefore demoted indefinitely."

"That's not why I was demoted."

"You were demoted because David didn't respect your authority." Mitch added, "He disobeyed your order, got himself killed, and your career died with him."

Lorcan glared at Mitch. "Those kids lived. But I'd pick your next words very carefully if I were you."

"Captain, all I'm saying is, this is your second chance. Henrickson has given you the chance to lead again. Don't mess it up for yourself. This Blake kid poses a serious threat. Don't confuse this situation with the one that David faced. Those kids were innocent. Blake is not."

"Hey, so I've got a question back here," Damien interrupted through the intercom.

Mitch leaned over and pushed the button. "What is it? We're kinda in the middle of something here."

"Oh, my apologies, milady. I didn't realise you two were in the middle of something. I was just foolishly wondering if we had a plan. You know, for the giant dragon that is guarding the people we have been sent to take out."

Mitch shook his head and pushed the intercom again. "Somebody didn't read the brief, did they?"

"Um, no."

"We stay low and survey the area from a distance. You two won't even have to get your hands dirty today. This is my turf; a sniper's mission. We can't fight the big guy, so we take them out from a distance. By the time the monster realises what's happened, we will be long gone."

"What if that thing tracks us?"

"Henrickson doesn't think it can. He thinks Blake made it up to intimidate us."

"He thinks?" Damien's alarmed voice spluttered.

"The colonel needs every man he can get right now. He wouldn't send us if he wasn't sure it would work."

"You've got more faith in the colonel than me, sniper boy."

"Look, man, I don't like this either, but we've got our orders. Let's just get this done and we can go home." Mitch took his hand off the intercom and fell back into his seat.

"Roger that."

Mitch looked at Lorcan and asked, "You with me on this, captain?"

Lorcan glanced at him, then focused back on the road. "Yeah... Yeah, I'm with you."

Mitch pulled a photograph of his family from his chest pocket. "I know Henrickson can be difficult, but the colonel... he lost his girls. I can't imagine how he feels. I'd be lost without my angels." He ran his finger over the photo. "We have to fight these monsters, captain. I need to make sure my family has a future. Henrickson's girls had that future stolen from them, you know? He was a father, too; a husband. He will never stop fighting for his girls now, just like I can't stop fighting for mine." He lifted the photo up for Lorcan to see.

Mitch's wife was beautiful, with long black hair and a white smile. She was holding their twin baby girls, one in each arm.

"You have a beautiful family," Lorcan said quietly.

"Thanks, cap." Mitch kissed the picture before putting it back in his pocket.

The Wombat's engine echoed over the quiet valley. The high-tech machine handled the spaghetti-like road as if it were a modern-day sports car. The three remaining members of Squad Seven sat in silence for the remainder of the journey. It was easier. There wasn't much else to say at this point. They had their mission.

A short while later, Lorcan turned into a narrow gravel driveway. Mitch looked out through the dusty windshield. There was an old abandoned farmhouse ahead. The front door flapped in the wind, several windows were broken, and two cars were parked out the front – their windshields shattered and their bonnets caved in.

"Looks like those serpents have come through here," Mitch said, gripping his rifle tight. A barn on the right had collapsed in a heap of timber, next to an overturned tractor. "According to the brief, from the barn we should be able to see Riley's property over the valley."

Lorcan brought the Wombat to a stop at the end of the driveway, grabbed his stowed rifle and engaged the intercom. "Damien, you take point. Watch your six; we don't know what's out here."

"Roger that!" Damien cocked his rifle and hit the touchpad. The rear side door retracted. He exited the vehicle and quickly checked his surroundings through the sights of his rifle.

"Falling in!" Mitch hopped out and dropped into position alongside Damien.

Scattered leaves and twigs littered the ground as the pair cautiously approached the house. It was uncomfortably quiet.

"Clear out front," Damien reported over the com channel.

"Hold it," Mitch said and halted, noticing something unusual. The collapsed barn to the right of the house seemed closer than it had in the surveillance photos. The timber panels were a light brown, too, but Mitch clearly remembered that the barn in the images was a deep red.

"What is it?" Damien asked.

"Something's not right." Mitch looked around. "This isn't the right house." At that moment something cold and metallic pressed against the back of his head. He shivered; there was no mistaking a gun barrel.

Damien snapped around, but flinched at what he saw. "Why?"

Lorcan stood at Mitch's back, holding a rifle to their squad mate's head. "Drop your guns. Both of you."

"Captain! What the fuck are you doing?" Damien eased his finger off the trigger and lowered his weapon.

"Drop it, or I'll put a bullet in him," Lorcan said calmly.

"Okay! Okay!" Damien complied and dropped his rifle on the ground, then kicked it past Lorcan's boots.

Mitch begrudgingly tossed his weapon toward the house. "Why are you doing this?" he asked, raising his hands in surrender.

"Get in the back." Lorcan directed them to the open side door of the Wombat. Mitch and Damien marched back to the ATV-X with their hands up.

"Captain! Don't do this." Mitch tried to reason with him. "These people are working with a monster! We're soldiers. If Command says we take 'em out, we take 'em out. It's our job."

Damien remained silent. His face was a mix of shock, rage and betrayal.

"Get in." Lorcan shoved the two soldiers into the rear cabin of the Wombat.

Mitch sat against the wall. "Captain, for your sake, don't do this! Henrickson will hunt you down."

"I know." Lorcan stepped back from the door, keeping his rifle aimed at the two men.

"Captain! *We* will hunt you down!" Mitch angrily shouted.

"I know."

Damien angrily slouched into a seat and uttered, "I always knew you were a coward, Edwards."

Lorcan reached for the exterior touchpad. "When I shut this door, the Wombat will go into survival lockdown mode. Nothing will be able to get in, and you will not be able to get out. I have disabled the weapons and communications system.

There is water and food for three days in the rations cabinet. The oxygen system is on, too. Should be enough until the colonel finds you."

Damien didn't break eye contact as he said, "When we get out of here, I'm going to kill you for this."

Lorcan scowled at him and replied, "When you get out of here, don't come for Blake or the others. Stay as far away as you can. That's my only warning." He hit the touchpad, and the door snapped shut.

The sound of Mitch kicking the armoured door of the ATV-X was like a constant drum. Lorcan picked the two rifles up from the dirt and leaned them up against the Wombat. Reaching into his pocket, he pulled out a piece of paper that had been cut from a road map. The Riley Farm was circled in red. After plotting the quickest route, he slung his rifle over his shoulder and made his way down the driveway, leaving Squad Seven – and his career – behind him.

"Captain! Don't be stupid!" Mitch continued to kick against the door.

A low hum sang from the vents as the Wombat's air filtration system switched on. Damien checked the surveillance screens. The words "Lockdown Engaged" began flashing on each display.

"He's not our captain anymore," Damien grunted, then slid back against the wall.

"Guess not." An exhausted Mitch slumped down next to him.

"Three days, huh?"

"That's what he said."

Damien sighed. "Knew I shoulda taken a piss before we left."

"Shit."

"Probably shoulda taken that too."

33

A MOMENT IN THE SUN

Birds chirped from rustling trees, the country air was crisp, and the sky couldn't be any brighter. At least that's what James was thinking when he strolled onto the front deck with a steaming cup of green tea and a renewed sense of enthusiasm. Miracles could happen – Emma was alive.

"GOOD MORNING!"

James squealed, spilling warm tea over his freshly washed blue T-shirt. "What the hell?" His heart was trying to escape through his ribcage. He staggered back and found Drakken's scaly head lurching over him. "Dude! You scared the crap out of me!"

"GOOD MORNING!" the dragon repeated.

"Yeah, yeah, good morning." James surveyed the wet patch on his shirt. "Do you have any idea how long it takes to get a shirt washed in this house?"

"No."

"Wait," James paused. "Why are you talking to me? I thought you were only talking to Blake? You know, 'cause he's so great and all that."

Drakken backed away from the house, his massive tail swinging behind him as sunlight shimmered over his sandy scales. "I must learn more about your species. When I convene with the other Guardians, I will require an extensive knowledge and understanding in order to convince them to spare humanity."

James flicked the dripping tea from his fingers as he said, "Well, first thing you need to learn is – everyone can hear you! Your voice is like a damn megaphone! Do you know what that is?"

Drakken fell silent.

"No, of course you don't. Well, my point is, we're going to wake everybody up, so let's go over there," James said, as he led the dragon to a clearing in the burnt field. Drakken's colossal footsteps were cracking the dry ground as they went. James found a fallen log and sat down with the remainder of his tea. Drakken, careful not to step too close to James, circled around and faced him.

"Okay," James cleared his throat, "the thing you really need to know about us is: women. Seriously. Chicks are like a Rubik's Cube. You've heard of people figuring them out, but you've never actually done it yourself – know what I mean? You see, us men are logical creatures, but women are the greatest mystery the world has ever known! You Dreyans ain't got nothing on them, buddy."

"I do not understand," Drakken growled, listening intently to James's every word.

"Exactly! That's the point! Seriously, scientists will uncover the meaning of life before they figure out what women really want."

Drakken thought for a moment, then said, "Perhaps the reason human males don't understand the female species is because they lack the required intelligence?"

James spat the last of his tea over his lap. "Have you been talking to Lila this morning?"

"No."

"Trust me," James continued, "no one can understand them. It's like that string theory crap. Do you know how many girls complain that they can't meet a nice guy, then when one comes along and asks them out, they laugh at his silk vest."

Drakken didn't hesitate this time. "I think your chances of obtaining a female mate are significantly lower among your current social group. You are a beta male. My observations indicate that the females of your species are predominantly attracted to alpha males."

James's jaw dropped. "Whoa! Hold up! I don't know where you got your facts from, buddy. *I am* an alpha male. Don't let my height fool you. You're an alpha predator, and I got Emma away from you on Chevron Island. Do you know why?"

"I deemed you too insignificant to pursue?" Drakken replied.

"No, and rude! We got away because my alpha male instincts kicked in." James added, "You clearly have a lot to learn about humans."

"Hey, James," Lila called out. James and Drakken both turned. Lila was watching them from the deck, still wearing her pyjamas. "You okay out there?"

"Yeah." James casually waved her off. "All good here."

Lila looked at him with a curious smirk. She was surprised to see James and Drakken talking. "You *sure* you're okay?"

"GOOD MORNING," Drakken greeted her.

"Shh. Don't be weird," James hushed him. "Yeah, I'm all good. Just teaching Drakken some stuff about alpha males. He's gotta learn, right? This big guy, he isn't even scary. Ha, you just gotta look him in the eye and he'll talk to you. No big deal."

"Right." Lila paused. Even James could see the confused expression on her face. "Yeah, okay, well, be careful," she shouted, then went back inside the house.

"See," James turned back to Drakken, "she totally knows I'm an alpha."

"She just called you strange," the dragon replied.

"What?" James had forgotten about Drakken's super-hearing abilities. "You heard her say that?"

～～～～～～～～

Dressed in shorts and his usual white T-shirt, Blake followed Gary out of the kitchen, passing Lila as she came through the front door. "You might wanna check on your friend," she said, before heading up the staircase.

Blake and Gary looked at each other with puzzled faces. "Who?" they both asked, but Lila was already upstairs and out of sight.

Gary pushed the front door open. "Damn. It's still sticking," he said, running his hand down the door's edge. "I'll have to sand it back some more."

"At least we have a front door again," Blake said, and followed him outside. Feeling the heat, Gary donned his wide-brimmed hat and crouched to look over his handiwork. Blake strolled to the edge of the deck and stood at the broken railing. "What is he doing?" he asked, noticing James and Drakken in the blackened field.

"Say what?" Gary pried his attention away from the door and went to see what Blake was looking at. "Well, that can't be good." The pair found themselves watching James, evidently on some sort of rant, pacing back and forth as Drakken's head tracked him like a spectator at a tennis match. "There's something wrong with that kid."

"I told Drakken to start talking to everyone," Blake said sheepishly.

"Oh, you did, did you?"

"Yeah…"

Gary gulped and said, "Never thought I'd say this, but should we save the dragon?"

"Ah, yeah," Blake agreed. "that might be a good idea."

Gary and Blake made their way across the driveway and into the field. Both couldn't help but wonder what on earth James and Drakken could be talking about. "Good morning," Blake shouted, as they approached. James froze in mid-step, then turned to greet them.

"GOOD MORNING," Drakken eagerly replied.

Gary removed his hat and gazed up at the towering creature. "Did it just say good morning?"

"Yeah," James replied, "it's kinda his new catch phrase."

"So," Blake couldn't wait to ask, "what are you talking about?"

"I am communicating with this James," Drakken answered first. "He is displeased with my assessment of him as a beta male among your social circle. I believe this is why he cannot attract a female mate that he desires."

Gary and Blake both burst out laughing.

James's nostrils flared. "Hey, shut up! Don't you Dreyans have a bro code? You don't tell them that!"

"So, wait," Blake said, as he struggled to contain his laughter, "let me get this straight. A dragon, an actual real dragon, speaks to you, and the first thing you talk about is your women problems?"

"Beta male!" Gary chuckled even louder. "The best!"

James was simmering. "Hey, bite me! He's a better listener than you two." He then turned his frustration to Drakken and asked, "Do you see what you've done?"

The monster said nothing but seemed to be observing the group's behaviour.

Reining in the last of his hysteria, Gary pulled himself together and said, "Okay, Romeo, I need a hand planting the last of these seeds."

"Where?" James asked, rolling his eyes at Blake who was sitting on a log, trying not to laugh.

Gary pointed to a patch of green near the creek bed on the far side of the yard. "The last piece of grass that barbeque breath, here, didn't burn."

"Fine," James sighed in defeat, "but if you tell me another dirty story from back in the day, I'm going to vomit in your hat."

"You love my stories," Gary said, putting his arm around James, who immediately removed it from his shoulder. The pair walked off towards the barn, still bickering between themselves.

"I see you took my advice," Blake said, still laughing a little.

"Yes." Drakken didn't get the humour, though. "The James – he is irrational, not logical. I don't understand his thoughts."

"I heard that." James's voice carried over the yard.

Blake reached down and picked up James's empty teacup. "Well, don't beat yourself up. He's not an easy one to understand."

"I must leave," Drakken said abruptly.

"Leave? Why?"

"Alarak – I must seek him out. I must inform him of what I have learned before he eradicates more of your kind."

"Shouldn't I come with you? Isn't that what you wanted me for?"

Drakken rose onto his back legs and stretched out his wings. "This is not the time. I fear that if Alarak sees you, he will be angered. I must first calm him. He is the Guardian of Balance; he cares for this earth. Alarak will see the value in humanity after we have conversed."

Blake moved back, trying to keep sight of Drakken's head high above. "What if he doesn't? What if he doesn't agree?"

"Take caution in my absence. There are no Dreyan in the area, but I will not be here to protect you." Without warning, the dragon launched into the sky like a rocket. Blake shielded his face as a cloud of dust and leaves exploded across the field.

"We'll be…" Blake spat a dead leaf out of his mouth, "fine." He brushed the dirt off his white T-shirt. "Might need to work on those goodbyes, though."

〜〜〜〜〜〜〜〜〜

Emma and Thomas sat opposite one another at the kitchen table with two steaming cups of tea. Thomas couldn't take his eyes off Emma's miraculously healed face. "Are you sure you feel okay?" he asked her for the fourth time in five minutes.

"Dad, I told you – I'm okay," she assured him.

"Em, you were nearly killed. When Blake carried you inside—"

"Dad, enough, please!" Emma snapped, but instantly regretted it. She pushed her teacup to the side and reached across the table, taking her father's hand. "Listen, I know how scary that must have been for you. I'm sorry. I don't mean to be rude. It's just, everyone is looking at me like I'm fragile or something. Except Blake – he hasn't said a word to me."

"No one thinks you're fragile, Em," Thomas said endearingly.

"Thanks, Dad."

Eager to lighten the mood, Thomas said, "You missed out, you know?"

Emma was hesitant to ask. "On what?"

"On seeing my face when I woke up here," Thomas grinned. "The house was in pieces, there were holes in the walls, the windows were smashed to bits, and I had all these strangers walking around in my clothes!"

"Yeah, I wish I had seen that, actually." Emma couldn't help but smile a little. "You'll get used to everyone, Dad."

Thomas raised an eyebrow humorously and said, "Em, Gary didn't have pants on twenty minutes ago, and I just saw that James kid arguing with a dragon in our yard." Emma let out a small laugh; the frazzled look on her father's face was too much. Thomas was just happy to finally see her smile. "I haven't seen you like that in a long time," he said. "You have your mother's smile. Do you know that?"

Emma reached over the table and grabbed his hand again. "Actually, I was hoping we could go visit her."

"Of course," Thomas replied, surprised by his daughter's request. She'd never wanted to before. "Absolutely."

"Great. Let's go now." Feeling a little emotional, Emma stood up, grabbed a tea towel from the table and blew her nose into it.

Thomas reeled with disgust. "Em? Yuck!"

"Sorry, Dad. We're out of tissues."

"Right. Well, let's just be grateful that we still have toilet paper." Thomas got up from the table and escorted his daughter to the back door. "Shall we?"

"After you," Emma replied, as she tossed the tea towel in the dustbin and followed her father outside.

The pair made their way across the lawn towards the creek. At the water's edge, Emma slipped her sneakers off and hopped through the shallow water. Thomas kicked off his flip-flops and did the same. The dense overgrown forest now felt very foreign to him. Instead of dead branches and dry grass, dozens of butterflies fluttered between green leaves and colourful flowers. "This is beautiful," Thomas said, taking it all in. "Your mother always loved coming out here. I wish she was here to see it like this."

"Me too." Emma took his hand and said, "Come on. The grass is covering the path, so watch your step." Emma led her father along a trail of large flat stones, which were barely visible through the thick jungle-like flora. She could also feel the air growing thicker and damper, the deeper they went.

Thomas was in awe. Even the once dirty brown rocks were now covered in a lime-green moss. "Gary said that all this happened in less than an hour."

"Yep," Emma said, brushing a vine to the side.

"And it was a big spider thing like the one that healed you? They hung from the trees and after they left, everything grew like this?"

"Yeah, except there were like, hundreds of them."

Thomas was trying to wrap his head around it all. "And the boys used the blood from one of them to heal me?"

"That's right." Emma glanced over her shoulder at him. "Sounds crazy, I know."

"Gary said you set one free. Rodney had it chained up?"

Emma wasn't sure if she heard disapproval in his voice. "It was innocent, Dad, and I would do it again." She turned around and looked at her father. "The price was too high."

"Fair enough," Thomas said respectfully. "I'm not judging you. I'm proud of you."

Emma smiled and said, "I don't know if you've ever told me that before."

"Well," Thomas added, "I should have."

"Thank you," Emma said.

A short time later, the pair reached a narrow gap between two trees with a wide clearing on the other side. "Come on, it's just up here," Emma said. Thomas parted two branches and peeked beyond them. A single citrus tree stood tall in the centre, its green leaves beautifully contrasting with the countless perfect oranges hanging from its branches.

"Wow, it's gotten so big!" Emma squeezed through the gap and approached the tall tree.

"Sure has," Thomas agreed, pulling a small knife from his pocket as he walked over and kneeled before its trunk. He then began slicing through the long blades of grass near the foot of the tree. Emma stood behind him and waited. A minute passed by. Thomas tossed the strands of grass to the side to reveal a small grey headstone with a gold plaque. *Kathleen Riley* was engraved on the plaque. "Hi, baby," he said smiling.

"I can't remember the last time I was out here," Emma admitted. "I've been so angry at her. I don't know if I'll ever get past what she did to you, Dad."

Thomas's eyes lingered on the headstone for a while. "When I met your mother, Em, I told her I was going to be a writer. Seriously, don't laugh. I did. I used to write stories for your mother all the time. She loved them, too. Used to keep them in a gold tin box under our bed. Sometimes, we'd stay up late and talk about how I could write from home – how we could spend each day together. After a while, we hit a tough time financially. Nothing I had written was getting picked up, and we couldn't survive on your mother's wage alone. So, that's when I joined the army. The work was guaranteed, and the benefits were good. Your mother wasn't happy about it. She didn't like the long times apart. I told her it would only be temporary – just until we got back on our feet."

"I've never heard this before." Emma quickly realised how little she knew about her parents' lives before she was born.

"Yeah, well, a few years turned into twenty," Thomas continued. "During that time, we had you, and your mother became a married woman who raised a child almost completely on her own. Hardly the life I promised her, Em. I was deployed on four tours overseas. Don't get me wrong; I thought of you girls every day. But I forgot about what was most important – actually being there."

"Dad, it's okay." Emma could see the pain in her father's eyes.

"I missed birthdays, your first steps, your first word. Your mother, she did it all. And she never complained once." Thomas glanced back at his wife's headstone. "The man she had an affair with – the man in the car with her – he was a real writer. He wrote children's books and raised money for charity. He was the man I told her I would be; the one she originally fell in love with. As much as I hate to admit it, he was the man she deserved. He was there for her when she needed him."

"Dad, are you okay?"

"Em, I know your mother never got to give us her side of the story, but please know this. Your mother didn't do this to me. I did this to her." Thomas struggled to get the next words out. "I can't stand seeing you mad at her. It breaks my heart, Em. She gave everything to us. She made a mistake, but this was never her fault."

"Dad," Emma clutched his hand and whispered, "I'm sorry."

"God, I miss her so much," Thomas said, and burst into tears.

"Dad?" Emma held her father as he wept on her shoulder. "It's okay. I love you, Dad. I miss her, too."

∞∞∞∞∞∞∞∞∞

With his knees caked in dirt, Gary patted the soil over another planted seed and wiped the sweat from his face. The day was beginning to warm up, which had already sent James into his usual cycle of whining and cursing. "Why does Blake get to go inside with the others while we slave away out here?" he complained, thrusting his shovel into the dirt a few metres ahead.

"Stop complaining and keep digging," Gary said, as he dropped a few seeds into the next hole.

"So, do you think the magic mojo those spiders left behind will work on these seeds, too? 'Cause I hate to say it, old man, but we aren't exactly farmers." James tossed another heap of dirt to the side.

"I hope so," Gary replied and stood up, fanning himself with his hat. He was about to ask James if he wanted to take a break when something cold pressed up against the back of his head.

"Don't move, old man."

Gary didn't recognise the voice, just the cocking of the gun.

"Why don't we raid a fast-food joint? That crap lasts forever. Be easier than planting this…" James's voice trailed off. "Hey? Are you even listening to me?" he asked, then turned around and dropped the shovel immediately. "Don't shoot! Please don't…"

〜〜〜〜〜〜〜〜

Sitting quietly by the creek, Will rolled the shiny engagement ring around his palm. It hadn't left his side since that fateful Saturday morning, and yet, he had managed to keep it a secret from everyone. With his jeans rolled up, he put his feet in the water; the current felt soothing between his toes. The sunlight glistened off the gold, reminding him of the last time he had studied the ring. Will wondered if Lila would have said yes that day. There was no way she would now. He couldn't help but wonder if she still loved him at all. Had he really changed? Had he shown her his true colours? Had he shown himself?

"Help!" A dire cry for help bellowed from the other side of the house. It was one of the girls. "Will!"

"What the…?" Will sprung to his feet, putting the ring back in the box as he started to run across the lawn. "This better not be another spider."

"Will! Blake! Someone! Help!" It was Lila's voice, and now she was screaming.

Will sprinted as fast as his bare feet could take him, and as he reached the front yard, Blake also charged out the front door to see what the commotion was about. There, on the deck, Lila stood trembling at the broken railing as she stared out at the driveway. Gary and James were on their knees in the gravel, facing the ground. But it was the dishevelled man holding a black handgun to James's head that robbed Blake's face of all colour.

"Who is he?" Will didn't recognise him.

"Oh no." Blake did.

"Who are you?" Lila cried. "What do you want?"

The man winked at her. "My name is Gabriel, darlin'. What's your name?" His left eye was completely bloodshot, while his face was blackened with bruises. Gabriel's singlet and denim jeans were also torn all over, doing little to hide the matching bruises over his body.

"He's the one who kidnapped Emma," Blake said, cautiously stepping off the deck.

"Ah, here he is," Gabriel cackled. "Here comes the hero boy."

"What do you want?" Blake asked, stopping a few feet from Gary and James.

"You know what I want."

"You're not taking Emma."

"The girl? That bitch is *still* kicking? Must be losing my touch," Gabriel said, scratching an itch on his head with the barrel of his gun. "Nah, I don't want her. She was just a toy. Besides, she didn't look too good yesterday."

"Then what *do* you want?" Blake asked again.

Will moved back slowly, hoping to sneak out of Gabriel's line of sight.

Gabriel snapped the gun to the left and fired. Lila squealed. The bullet hit the dirt by Will's foot. "Move again and I put the next one in your head."

"Okay, nobody's moving. Calm down," Blake pleaded with him. "Just tell me what you want."

Drawn to Lila's calls for help, Thomas and Emma came skidding around the corner in a flustered panic. "Was that a—? Oh no." Emma's face fell. "Dad, that's him!"

"Who?" Thomas quickly put his daughter behind him.

"Well, would you look at that?" Gabriel beamed. "There's my angel. Hey, baby," he paused. "Wow, your face. That is… interesting."

"You son of a bitch!" Thomas exploded. "You think you can hit my daughter!"

"Calm down," Will intervened, keeping the angry father at bay.

Gabriel seemed to be enjoying himself. "Found Daddy, too, I see. Didn't die on the side of the road after all. Good for you, pops!" He aimed the gun at Thomas and said, "You three, get over here. Stand next to hero boy." Will, Thomas and Emma raised their hands and joined Blake on the driveway. "You, the cute blonde, get down here, too," he ordered.

Lila did what he asked.

"Ah, very nice indeed," Gabriel said, as he looked Lila up and down, licking his lips. "You boys have been very spoiled. One of every flavour."

Will put himself between Lila and Gabriel, but the gunman didn't seem to care.

"What do you want?" Thomas asked.

"Shut it." Gabriel shoved the gun into the back of James's neck. "This is between me and the hero here!"

James was quivering, and tears rolled down his face as the barrel pressed hard into his skin.

Gary, still facing the gravelly floor, whispered to him, "It's gonna be okay."

Blake couldn't take his eyes off the gun. "Okay, you got it. This is between us. Let them go, and we can sort this out. Just us."

"Let them go?" Gabriel exploded into a fit of rage. "You come into my house and steal my shit! Now, you wanna play nice?" He ran a finger along the tattoo on his face, although it was difficult to make out amid the bruising. "You stole a *God* from me!"

"God?" Blake suddenly remembered Gabriel surrendering himself to Drakken back at the warehouse. "You thought he'd come for *you*..."

"You used him against me! My own fucking conjuration!" Gabriel turned the gun on Blake and shouted, "He is here because of me. My prayers brought him here. But you, you turned him against me!"

"I'm sorry," Blake said, surrendering. "Please, just calm down. We can talk about it. We can sort this out."

Gabriel lowered the gun and snickered, "You're right, hero. When you're right, you're fucking right." He pressed the gun back into James's head. "You know, you didn't leave us in good shape yesterday. I mean, I've got a few broken ribs– a couple of fractures here and there. But Paul and Danny, oh boy, that giant backhand really messed them up. Broke every bone in their body. But, lucky for them, I'm a nice guy. I took care of them. Two bullets – one, two." Gabriel's smile waned. "When I woke up in that warehouse, I felt a little emotional – a little defeated, you know? But then I remembered that I pinched this cute photograph from my angel there," Gabriel said, and pulled a crumpled photo from his pocket – the same picture that Emma had taken to the refuge centre. "It's a good photo of you two. Dark hair suited you, pops. Had an address on the back, a date, and both your names. It's good to keep track of your memories, isn't it?" Gabriel flicked the photograph into the air. The picture swirled around until it landed on the gravel in front of James.

"You still haven't told me what you want." Blake needed to keep him talking. He'd been whispering Drakken's name, hoping the dragon might be close enough to hear him.

"So, tell me," Gabriel said to Blake as he gripped Gary by his hair and yanked his head back, "how do *you* have control of *my* monster?"

"Whoa, relax. I don't control him. He just trusts me. That's all."

Gabriel ripped a clump of hair from Gary's head, causing the man to cry out in pain. "Bullshit! That was *my* fucking dragon! He freed *me*! What did you do? Was it a prayer? A spell? What the fuck did you do?"

"A prayer? *Spell*?" Blake repeated. "No, nothing like that."

"Don't lie to me!" Gabriel was seething.

"I'm not lying to you. Listen. Drakken can talk. He came to me, asked for my help. We are trying to fix things, put things back the way they were. Please, just calm down."

"So, you're telling me," Gabriel began to twitch, "you take my monster, and now you want to put the world back the way it was?"

"I didn't take anything from you," Blake said. "Look, I'm sorry. Please just put the gun down. We can go inside and talk."

"I don't wanna talk to you, hero. I wanna talk to him. Now."

"He's not here. I don't know when he'll be back. Come inside. You can wait for him."

Gabriel reached down and heaved Gary's head upright. "He will come to you, hero boy. So, bring him to me. Now."

"Okay, okay," Blake conceded, hoping to calm him. "Drakken, I need you. Right now!"

Gabriel sneered. "Say it louder."

"Drakken! Please! Help us!"

"Scream, hero!"

"Drakken!" Blake cried out as loud as he could. "Please help!" But the sky remained clear.

Gary closed his eyes as he felt the gun press firmly against the top of his head.

"Again." Gabriel was revelling in Blake's despair. "Come on, hero."

Blake, red-faced and desperate, started to beg, "He can't hear me! He's too far away! Please, come inside. He will be back! We can work this out! Please!"

The rest of the group could only watch in harrowing silence.

"I said fucking scream!"

"Drakken! Please help me!" Blake wailed. Drakken didn't come. Blake looked Gabriel in the eyes and tearily pleaded, "I am begging you. Please don't."

Gabriel cocked his gun.

Blake plunged to his knees and cried, "No! He's my father! Please!"

"It's okay, son," Gary said, comforting him with a weeping smile. "I'm proud of you, kid."

Gabriel scowled at the sentiment. "Hero." He pulled the trigger.

Birds fled from nearby trees as the gunshot rang across the sky. Everybody screamed. James opened his eyes. Blood saturated Emma's photograph. Thomas and Will quickly turned Lila and Emma away, shielding them from the horrific scene.

"I fuckin' hate liars," Gabriel said, as he released Gary's hair. The body slumped to the ground, leaving James to stare into Gary's hollow gaze.

"No!" Blake collapsed, then crawled to Gary's side. "No, please." He clutched Gary's lifeless hand and begged for a miracle he knew would never come. "No... no..."

"This is your fault, hero. Now, call that fuckin' dragon here. I'm not asking again," Gabriel said, as he grabbed James by the hair and pressed the blistering gun barrel into his neck once more. "A bullet through the throat is so much worse. Choking on your own blood isn't a quick death. You got ten seconds, hero."

"You psychopath!" James cried, as he thrashed around in Gabriel's grip. "Go fuck yourself!"

Gabriel grinned and said, "Oh, I like this one. He's a fighter!"

"Stop!" Emma shrieked desperately. "Please!"

"Please don't," Blake pleaded with him. "Drakken, if you can hear me, I need you right now!"

Gabriel checked the sky. Still nothing. "Three."

"No! Please, just wait!"

"Two."

"Please, don't!"

"One."

"Drakken!"

The second gunshot was as deafening as the first.

Will and Thomas clutched Lila and Emma tightly as blood trickled between the gravel stones of the Riley Farm's driveway.

James opened his eyes. "What?" He quickly checked himself for a bullet wound. Nothing. "How?" The black handgun dropped next to Gary's body with a heavy thud.

"James?" Blake slowly rose to his knees.

But it was Gabriel who was clenching a hole in his chest, blood gushing through his fingers. "How?" he coughed, then staggered to the ground.

James scrambled over to Blake, who pulled his friend into a hug before helping him to his feet. The pair looked towards the driveway. A lone soldier strolled towards them with a smoking pistol and a rifle slung over his back. Blake recognised him right away. Thomas, Will, Lila and Emma opened their eyes and watched in astonishment as the mysterious soldier veered towards the gunman bleeding out on the ground.

"You?" Gabriel tried to chuckle as the blood gurgled in his throat. The soldier's shadow loomed over him. "How's the bitch? And her fu...'en kids... I should... killed you."

"You should have." Lorcan pointed his gun at Gabriel's right knee and pulled the trigger. Gabriel howled in agony. "That's for the man you just killed." Lorcan then shot his left knee and said, "For Barry and Samantha."

"Fu...ck ...you."

Lorcan watched Gabriel quiver in agony then fired two more rounds into the man's crotch. "That was for all the women." A cry of anguish echoed over the valley.

Gabriel looked up, choking on his own blood, but still grinning as he asked, "This… one… for… you, soldier boy?"

"No." Lorcan raised the pistol to the dragon tattoo. "This is for the kids." He emptied the rest of the clip.

34

THE LAST CIGAR

"We're lucky you came when you did," Thomas said, when he and Lorcan were alone in the forest.

Gabriel's limp body flopped over the tall grass as Lorcan rolled it over with the heel of his boot. "Wasn't soon enough."

Thomas stared at the blood seeping into the ground and said, "I don't think any of them will shake this off easily."

"They're gonna have to," Lorcan said. Leaving the body behind, the pair turned around and began making their way out of the forest. "The colonel has put a target on their heads. We need to move out as soon as we can."

Thomas ducked under a twisted branch and several vines. "They need some time to grieve."

Lorcan empathised, but couldn't agree. "Henrickson has lost all satellite imagery and communication. He still thinks the dragon is here. This is our window to move."

"And go where, exactly?"

"Inland, maybe. The further from the coast we are, the better."

"And what about Gary? They won't leave without giving him a proper burial."

"They don't have the time."

Thomas was sceptical. "I don't know Blake that well, but from what Emma has said, Gary was like a father to him. Trust me. You won't win that argument."

Lorcan followed him out of the forest, and they stopped by the creek bed. "Okay. We bury the old man, but then we gotta move. I didn't risk all this to have Blake get himself killed."

"I'll talk to him," Thomas agreed. "Just give him some time. It's been a rough day – for all of them."

~~~~~~~~~~~~~

The shovel resonated with a sharp clang as Blake struck an obstinate rock in the ground for the third time. Tipping a minuscule mound of dirt onto the pile next to him, he found himself staring into the hole he had dug. It was small and shallow, quite a way from the size he needed.

Blake turned his bloodshot eyes to the mattress resting on the ground near Houdini. Thomas had dragged it out of the barn earlier. Gary's body rested on it, the white sheet covering his face now soaked red. Blake's shaky fingers could barely grip the shovel. He focused on the hole and lifted his arm. It weighed a ton. Blake thrust the shovel down, striking the same rock – again.

"Do you have a moment?" Thomas appeared from behind Houdini. "I don't mean to interrupt."

Blake stabbed the shovel into the softer ground and let it stand there. "I'd rather be alone."

"I know, I'll be quick," Thomas said, and walked around to the other side of the hole, keeping Blake's attention away from the mattress. "I spoke to Emma earlier; she's a total mess. But we were thinking, if it's okay with you, well, we'd be honoured if we could bury Gary by the orange tree in the woods. It's beautiful. My wife Kathleen, Emma's mother, is buried there. I thought it would be nice. You two could visit them together, maybe. If you wanted, I mean."

Blake knew this was a massive gesture, but couldn't look Thomas in the eye. If he did, he thought he would completely fall apart. "Yeah, okay. Thanks."

"Okay, great. It's settled," Thomas said quietly. "For what it's worth, I'm really sorry for your loss."

Blake ignored the sentiment. "Where is this orange tree?" he asked instead.

"I'll show you," Thomas said, as he pulled the shovel from the ground. "Come with me."

Thomas guided Blake through the overgrown forest until they reached the large clearing. Blake was taken aback by the impressive citrus tree. It was perfect – not a single brown leaf or discolouration in the fruit – just green with a touch of orange, almost as if someone had painted it. "Emma never mentioned this place," he said, astounded.

Thomas hung back, giving Blake plenty of space to look around. "Emma would come out here with her mother when she was little. They'd play, throw tea parties... all that stuff. Kathy loved oranges, so one day they planted this tree together. Of course, it was only about half this size before those things came through here, but it was always a beautiful tree. After my wife died, Emma never came out here again. I'd try to get her to visit, but... well, you know how stubborn Em can be."

Only then did Blake notice the headstone at the foot of the tree. *Kathleen Riley*, it read.

Thomas walked over with the shovel in hand and stood at Blake's side. "She'll keep him good company, I promise."

Blake's eyes lingered on the headstone for a while, then he nodded with appreciation. "Thank you."

"I'll take care of everything. You go clean up; take some time for yourself. When we're ready, I'll come get you."

~~~~~~~~~~~~

Lorcan had never been able to handle grieving people well. It was the fragility in their eyes, the hopelessness in their gaze; it unnerved him. Borrowing a chair from the kitchen, he took a position on the house's rear deck where he had a wide view of the forest and the surrounding yard, but more importantly, where he'd be clear of the "emotional hot zone." Moths fluttered by and crickets chirped as dusk claimed the valley.

Lorcan wondered how Mitch and Damien were faring in the Wombat, and if Henrickson had gotten word of his betrayal yet. He wondered if Amanda was now with Jack, Mindy and Samantha. He wondered if they were safe, and if he should have gone with her. Lorcan reached into his pocket and took out Jack's dinosaur, noticing how grubby the toy had become. He licked his thumb and wiped some dirt from the dinosaur's nose.

"You coming?" Will interrupted, stepping out through the back door.

"Nah," Lorcan declined. "It's not my place. I'll keep an eye out here."

"Okay." Will gestured to the kitchen door, saying, "There's tea and water inside if you want some. It's pretty much all we have these days."

"I'm good. Thanks."

Will started to walk away but hesitated at the first step. "Hey, listen, with everything that's been going on, we didn't… thanks for saving James… and the rest of us."

"It's okay." Lorcan turned away. "I'm sorry I wasn't there sooner." He didn't handle thankful people well, either.

Will left the soldier to his solitude and made for the creek.

〰〰〰〰〰〰〰

Emma placed the final candle at the base of the orange tree, and the flame twitched in the gentle breeze. A dozen lit candles now circled a small wooden box that contained Gary's last cigar. Emma stepped back and rejoined the others. Alongside her mother's headstone, a patch of disturbed dirt marked Gary's final resting place. Thomas placed a firm hand on her back; he could tell she was struggling. They all were. Lila could barely breathe between her own convulsions. Will held her close, but it did little to comfort her. Emma glanced over at James, who stood staring at the mound of dirt in complete silence. He hadn't spoken a word since it happened. Everyone knew that being held hostage must have been terrifying, so no one had bothered him all afternoon. It could just as easily have been James buried there. It could have been any of them.

Emma glanced toward the end of the clearing, but the gap in the trees remained dark; no light or lantern approached. Thomas had informed Blake that Gary had been buried and everyone was gathering to say goodbye. He hadn't come. Blake and Emma had barely exchanged two words since he had brought her back from that warehouse yesterday. She hadn't even thanked him yet. Now, she didn't know if he'd ever look at her the same way. After all, if he hadn't saved her, Gary would still be here.

Thomas produced a small black bible from his coat and stepped forward. He wasn't particularly religious, but hoped that a bible reading would convey a certain respect for the man they had lost. Facing the candlelit orange tree, he began reading a passage aloud.

~~~~~~~~~~~~~~~

Outside the barn, Blake ran his hands over Houdini's worn steering wheel and slammed the door shut. The air inside reeked of gasoline. He slumped back into the bucket seat and saw the distant flicker of candlelight in the dark forest; everyone was gathered at the orange tree. He couldn't bring himself to go. To stand there like it wasn't his fault. How could he face them? He rested his head against the wheel and wept. Why didn't he tell Drakken to kill Gabriel at the warehouse? How could he have been so stupid? So naive? So blind? Gary would still be alive right now. He almost got James killed, too. Just like he got all the people at Patrice and Rodney's farm killed.

Blake raised his head and noticed a wooden plank leaning up against the barn wall. Gary had left it there that morning. Running his fingers along the door trimming, he found the handle and pulled it. The door popped open. Blake climbed out of his seat and staggered over to the barn. He picked up the plank and carried it back to the car, stopping at the driver's side door.

"How could I be so stupid?" he shouted, swinging the plank into Houdini's windshield. The glass cracked. He swung again and again. The windshield exploded over the seats. "He trusted me!" He lifted the plank over his head, then smashed the driver's side mirror clean off. "He didn't deserve this." Blake made his way around the car, beating dents into every panel. "This is all my fault." Eventually, he couldn't lift his arm. Blake slumped back against the car and dropped the plank by his side. "I'm so sorry, Gary. Man, I'm so sorry."

Gary would have clipped him around the ears for losing his temper like that. It didn't matter now. Blake had overheard that Henrickson's soldiers were coming to kill him. He hoped they did.

~~~~~~~~~~~

A short time later, Thomas, Emma and Lorcan convened in the kitchen to discuss Colonel Henrickson's assassination order. "The colonel is down to under fifty men and women," Lorcan said. "The only qualified marksman capable of taking the shot is Private Mitchel Kay. He was a member of my squad. Unknown to Henrickson, Private Kay is currently locked down in a secluded location. However, I'll bet the colonel has already sent a search party."

"We have no choice. We need to leave," Emma concluded. "They could show up here at any time."

"And go where?" Thomas asked. "We still have no idea what else is out there."

"I have co-ordinates to a medical facility further inland – a military one," Lorcan suggested. "It will be well guarded, so you will be safe there."

"Military?" Emma scoffed. "Aren't they the ones who are coming to kill us? Not to mention, didn't you just turn your back on them? Can't imagine we'll be welcomed with open arms."

"Henrickson is running his own operation now. He has limited resources. With the rest of the country down, it's unlikely that anyone will know who you are—"

"What?" Emma cut in. "The rest of the *country* is down? You mean like the phone lines?"

Lorcan hesitated, as he was surprised by her shock. "Blake… he didn't tell you?"

"No…" Emma trailed off. "We haven't… spoken…"

"The country. What happened here. It happened everywhere."

"But…" Emma couldn't fathom it. "But…"

Thomas eagerly moved the conversation forward. "This facility. What happens to *you* if we go there?"

"Let me deal with that," Lorcan dismissed his concern.

"Well, at least that's some sort of plan," Thomas said, trying to keep some morale up.

"You can all stay. I'm leaving." The group turned to find a dishevelled Blake standing in the kitchen doorway. "We are not superheroes. This is real. Trained soldiers are coming to kill anyone associated with me. I'm turning myself in. Henrickson wants me. I won't let anyone else die because of my choices."

Lorcan folded his muscular arms and gave a disapproving glare. "The colonel will shoot you on sight. You understand that? Drakken killed his wife and both his daughters. He will not show you any mercy."

Blake didn't waver. "I know exactly what Drakken did. The colonel can do what he wants. I've made my decision."

"That's not your decision to make!" Emma marched over to him and cried, "We don't abandon each other!"

"Are you kidding me?" Blake scowled at her. "I chose to help Drakken. Me! It's barely been two days and my stupidity – my fucked-up sense of right and wrong – cost Gary his life. It cost your neighbours their lives. Not to mention all the people they were trying to help. How many more people do I need to get killed before you wake up and listen to me?"

"How dare you!" Emma slapped him – hard. "I know how much pain you're in right now. I know what Gary meant to you. But how dare you cheapen everything like that! You also *saved* my life. Your *stupidity*, your *fucked-up morality*, also stopped Drakken from killing even more innocent people. That includes everyone in this house. Gary believed in you.

More than anyone! He died because a psychopath walked in here and shot him. But if you need to blame anyone, blame me. It was my photo that led Gabriel here."

Blake's cheek throbbed, along with the rest of the bruises on his face. "I don't blame you," he said, looking into her eyes, "but he's still dead. And I can't let that happen to anyone else." Blake clutched his backpack's strap and calmly exited through the front door, leaving Emma standing in the kitchen doorway as the click of the latch reverberated through the quiet house.

"We can't just let him leave," she said, turning back to Lorcan and Thomas, eyes welling with tears.

"Em," Thomas said gently, "it's not up to us."

Lorcan grunted, grabbed his rifle from the bench and left the kitchen through the back door.

◇◇◇◇◇◇◇◇◇◇◇◇

Moonlight shone over every dent in Houdini's beaten panels as Blake made his way through the grass towards the barn. The crunch of dry twigs under his sneakers was loud enough to drown out the countless chirping crickets but couldn't quash the guilty racket filling his every thought. He had to leave. No two ways about it.

Reaching his car, Blake opened Houdini's passenger door and tossed his backpack onto the seat.

"I can't stop seeing his face," a voice said softly.

Blake shut the car door and found James sitting on the ground with his back against the barn wall. "What are you doing out here?"

James tearily glanced at the driveway in the distance, where Gabriel had held him. "I see his face when I close my eyes. It's all I see."

"Gabriel's?" Blake asked.

"Gary's," James said, as he tucked his knees into his chest and fiddled with the grass by his shoes. "When Gabriel was yelling at you, Gary whispered to me. Said it would all be okay. I keep replaying that moment in my head."

"Man," Blake said, as he walked over and took a seat next to him against the barn wall, "I'm so sorry. I haven't even asked you how you're doing. That must have been scary as hell."

"It's okay. I'm getting used to being scared," James sniffed, and wiped his nose on his wrist. "I overheard that Lorcan guy say that the rest of the country was destroyed, too."

Blake's head dropped. "Yeah, Henrickson showed me the photos. I was waiting to find the right time to tell everyone, but—"

"Shit kinda got out of hand real quick," James finished his sentence. "To be honest, I expected it. It makes sense, right? Why no one came to help us here."

"Yeah," Blake rested his back against the timber, "makes sense."

"Dude," James fixed his gaze on the battered race car for a moment, then said, "I don't know where you're planning to go – probably somewhere stupid, I'm guessing – but I lost Gary today, and probably my family before that. I'm not gonna fight with you. I'm sure Emma has already beaten me to it. But I'm asking you, selfishly; don't leave me here alone. Don't make me lose a brother as well."

Blake drew a deep breath, but eventually said, "The colonel won't stop. He'll keep coming until he kills me, Drakken, and anyone helping us."

"I know. We'll figure it out," James said, "but I can't do this alone."

Blake stared at the broken shell of a man who was his best friend. They had been together since he could remember. Even when Blake had moved to different foster homes, James had always found a way to be there. James was the one constant in his life – the only family he had left.

Blake sighed, then smirked half-heartedly. "You really can't live without me, can you?"

"Pfft! Please," James said, and cringed. "I just don't wanna be stuck with Will when his monthly cycle kicks in."

"Fair call."

For a short while, the pair sat in silence, revelling in the thousands of stars sparkling over the expansive night sky. Curiously, James started to notice something, so he squinted harder. "Is it just me, or are some of the stars disappearing?"

Blake saw it, too. The black was expanding or the stars were vanishing. "What is that?"

Before either one could react, a monstrous silhouette crashed into the field behind Houdini, an orange light flickering through its scaly body.

"Holy shit!" Blake yelped, feeling the shock wave blast through them.

"Oh, yeah," James said, as he stood up. Slightly disoriented, he steadied himself against the barn wall. "I think I just crapped myself."

"Hello," Drakken growled, his wings folding up behind his back.

"You know, I'm never gonna get used to that," James muttered.

"Where have you been?" Blake barked, moving away from the barn to get a better look at the towering dragon. "I called for you!"

"I heard no call. I was far from these parts. Alarak and I have had much discussion." Drakken lowered himself onto all fours and shook his body like a restless dog. "He will await Grannus's counsel before culling anymore of your kind."

Blake softened and said, "Well, that's good, right?"

Drakken suddenly snarled. "Why is this human here?"

Blake and James spun around to see Lorcan standing behind them, rifle in hand. "Surprised?" Lorcan remarked.

"No," Drakken growled, "I picked up your scent upon my return."

"It's okay," Blake said reassuringly. "He's here to help. He saved us."

Drakken pressed his snout to the ground. "He saved you… from the dangerous man… the one that took the female." He raised his head toward the forest and continued, "His body rests in the trees. The Gary did not survive the encounter. The earth is retaking him now."

"Quite the playback," Lorcan said curiously. "You get all that from sniffing the ground?"

"Yes," Drakken answered.

"So, the other dragon," James started, "he's gonna stop killing people now, right?"

"For now. Alarak has agreed."

Lorcan kept a little more distance between himself and the dragon than the other two, and never lifted his finger off the trigger. Gradually, he began to feel more at ease around the gargantuan reptile. "This Alarak. He got black scales, four wings, a couple of tails, breathes blue fire?"

"Yes," Drakken replied.

"Shit," Lorcan cursed. "My squad ran into that thing a few days ago. He's quite the arsehole. Brought down a building while we were still in it. Killed a bunch of civilians, too. Kinda reminds me of you, actually."

"That's enough," Blake cut in, then turned to Drakken. "Listen, there are some people coming to kill us – the soldiers from the dam. I need time to figure out what our next move is.

I need you to do that sniffing thing. Keep an eye out. If anyone or anything moves in this direction, you need to warn us."

"Agreed." Drakken rose onto his hind legs and began his watch.

Admittedly, Lorcan couldn't help but gape at the dragon's incredible size. As he followed Blake and James back to the house, he wondered how on earth anyone could fight such a beast. Hopefully, soon, no one would have to.

∞∞∞∞∞∞∞∞

Ironically, upon hearing the news of Drakken's return, the exhausted and emotionally drained occupants of the Riley Farm slept soundly for the remainder of the night – everyone except Lorcan, who perched himself between Gary's red truck and the yellow four-wheel drive so that he could observe the dragon's behaviour. Other than the odd snort, tail reposition or leg scratch, Drakken never wavered. The dragon monitored the scents till the sun peeked over the horizon. Admittedly, Lorcan found it somewhat fascinating to watch; there was so much beneath the surface of the creature he had pegged as being no different than a murderous and instinctive animal.

During the early hours of the morning, Will found himself pacing the hallway in his boxer shorts. Lila was once again crying at the end of their bed, and he had no idea how to comfort her. Having left to fetch her a glass of water from the kitchen, he was now hesitating to return to the room. The last forty-eight hours had been brutal, but the sudden loss of Gary had brought with it a dim reality check. What if Lila had died instead? What if Gabriel had taken her hostage, instead of Gary or James?

"What are you doing out there?" Lila could hear him outside the door.

"Nothing," Will answered, and quickly entered the room, shutting the door behind him. "I was just thinking."

"About Gary?" Lila asked. Will handed her the glass of water.

"Sort of. I was just thinking that if I had lost you, then…" Will didn't have the words. "Well, I don't know what I'd do."

Lila drank from her glass then looked up at him. "You want to leave, don't you?"

"No. That's not what this is about." Will picked his jeans up from the floor and slid them on, feeling the ring box as he zipped them up. "You said to me that I needed to figure out what I stand for. My answer hasn't changed. It's you. But I realised that *you* means I need to stand for what makes you who you are. I need to support you in every way I can. Even if it scares me – which it does."

Lila was caught a little off guard. "So, you don't wanna leave the group?"

"No. I know how much you believe in stopping all this. It doesn't mean I'll always agree with Blake, but I believe in you, Lila. And I still believe in us."

"I believe in us, too," Lila said tearily. "I'm sorry. I know this has been hard on you, too." She went to hug him, but Will stopped her and got on one knee instead. "What are you doing?"

"I was going to ask you this, the day everything started. I guess I've been waiting for the right time since then. Will reached into his pocket and took out the blue ring box. "But now I realise that our time is so precious, and I don't want to wait anymore. You don't have to say yes, but I just want you to know how much I love you."

"Will?" Lila gasped, as he opened the box and revealed the glistening diamond ring inside.

"Lila Joy, you've given my life more purpose than you'll ever know. All I want to do is spend the rest of it loving you, and watering your countless plants. Will you marry me?"

"Yes. Yes, I will marry you!"

Will gently slid the ring on her finger.

Lila yanked him up from the floor and kissed him passionately.

Will embraced his new fiancée and, for the first time in a long time, the world happily faded away.

35

TO LOVE AND TO HOLD

Lorcan and Blake tossed the last of the packed bags onto the rear seats of Will's four-wheel drive. There were six bags total, full of clothes, toiletries and what little food they had left. It was nearly 11:00 am, and all that remained now was to rally the group together, get in the cars and put the Riley Farm in the rearview mirror.

"That's the last of it," Blake said, satisfied.

"Good," Lorcan muttered, shutting the car's tailgate. "Wheels up in ten."

Being quite tall, Blake had never felt small, but standing next to Lorcan – who was not only his height, but also had more muscles than seemed anatomically possible – he felt slightly emasculated, especially since Lorcan had removed his fatigues jacket and had opted for a black singlet to cope with the heat. He even caught Emma admiring the man's biceps at one point, though he didn't dare mention it. The pair hadn't spoken since he had walked out on her in the kitchen last night.

One thing Blake did notice, though, was the 'R.I.P. David' tattoo on Lorcan's back, peeking out from under the black fabric. "So, who was David?" he asked bluntly.

Lorcan glanced over his shoulder, then donned an annoyed expression. "He was family," he begrudgingly answered.

"A soldier?" Blake didn't care that the man seemed reluctant to talk about it.

"Yeah," Lorcan glared at him. "Any other questions?"

"How'd he die?"

Lorcan shook his head and asked, "You trying to push me?"

Blake leaned back against Gary's truck and said, "Just asking. Sorry, I'm new to this whole social interaction thing. It used to just be me, James and Gary."

Lorcan folded his arms and rested back against the four-wheel drive, annoyance gradually fading from his expression. "David died on my last tour, a few years ago. He was under my command during a mission in the Middle East. We got caught in a firefight with the local militia that had us outmanned five to one. Bullets were flying everywhere. Somehow, a few children got caught in the middle of it. They were on a bus, and their driver had been killed. Private David Nelson disobeyed my direct order and abandoned our squad. David fought his way to the bus and killed four insurgents, to get those kids. He got them out and stashed them in a nearby shopfront. They were safe. We held our position as David made his way back to us. He never made it. Killed by some punk with a shotgun from an apartment building window. My squad took out the shooter and retrieved David's body. We brought him home. When I returned to base, Command conducted a formal investigation. I was found unfit for leadership and demoted."

"They pinned his death on you?" Blake asked.

Lorcan grunted and replied, "That, and they deemed it inappropriate that I was sleeping with him."

"Oh, shit. Sorry," Blake apologised. "So, you two were—"

"Like I said," Lorcan interrupted. "We were family."

"Hey, you two," James called out, leaning out the front door. "Come inside. The others wanna see you."

Lorcan and Blake followed James inside and into the kitchen. There, gathered around the dining table, Thomas, Emma, Will and Lila were chatting among themselves, seemingly excited about something.

"Here they are!" Emma greeted them cheerfully, which made James, Lorcan and Blake suspicious.

"Okay," James said carefully, "what's going on in here?"

"Well," Lila started, smiling at Will next to her, "we're engaged!" She lifted her hand, flaunting the sparkling diamond ring on her finger.

"W-what?" Blake stammered. "Congratulations!"

"How?" James couldn't clear the confused look from his face. "How the hell did you get time to shop for a ring?"

"Oh, I snuck out yesterday," Will remarked.

"He's kidding." Lila joyfully waved him off. "He had it the whole time."

"Oh," James frowned, "so, all those times you kept feeling in your pocket, you weren't just happy to see me?"

"Sorry, mate," Will draped his arm over Lila's shoulder and kissed the top of her head, "only this one keeps my hands in my pockets."

"Eww, gross," Lila elbowed him, then slid out from under his arm. "Actually, we wanted to ask you all something." Her gaze panned over all the faces in the room. "We thought, seeing as we've been through so much here, maybe, before we leave, we could get married here? I know it won't be legal or whatever."

"Yes!" Emma didn't hesitate.

Blake and Lorcan, however, did. "Em," Blake started, "Henrickson... he..."

"Drakken is back," Emma argued. "If Henrickson comes, we'll know before he even gets close. Besides, it won't take long."

Lila clutched Will's hand once more. "Blake, it would mean a lot to us. We'll be quick. I promise."

Blake couldn't help but admire the buoyancy in Lila's eyes. They could all use a little of that right now. "Okay," he caved, "let's get you guys married."

"Thank you! We'll be quick! I promise."

Lorcan wasn't so easily swayed, but he could see this wasn't an argument that he was going to win. He hung back near the entrance and watched as the group began congratulating Will and Lila one at a time. Once everyone had made their rounds, Thomas whispered something in Emma's ear, then the pair escorted Lila out of the kitchen and the three hurried upstairs like children on Christmas morning.

∽∽∽∽∽∽∽∽

Upstairs in the master bedroom, Thomas dragged a tattered cardboard box out from under his bedframe and lifted it onto the mattress. Emma and Lila were bursting with anticipation – especially Lila, who had no idea what she was about to be shown. Opening the old box, Thomas reached in and lifted a wedding dress into the air.

Lila gasped. "That's beautiful."

Thomas moved the box aside and laid the dress on the bed. "It was my wife's dress," he said proudly. "I'd never seen anyone look so beautiful. It was a good day."

"So," Emma faced Lila and grasped the bride-to-be's hands, "Dad and I were wondering if you'd like to wear it?"

Lila nervously clutched her beaded necklace. "I… couldn't. That's your mother's."

"Kathy would have loved for you to wear it," Thomas reassured her. "And, after everything you and Will have done for Emma, it would be my pleasure, too."

"I don't know what to say," Lila whispered, her smile widening. "Thank you so much!"

Emma embraced her in a warm hug. "You and Will saved my life in that supermarket. I never got to thank you properly. Besides, it's your wedding day! You will look gorgeous in it."

"You're making me cry," Lila said in Emma's ear.

"Don't say that," Emma said, as she let her go and wiped her own eyes. "Now, look – I'm crying!"

Both girls began to giggle at their own embarrassment.

Thomas cleared his throat and turned away, seemingly to tend to the box on the bed.

"Dad?" Emma grinned curiously and asked, "Dad, are you crying, too?"

"Don't be silly," Thomas said, as he picked up the box and quickly walked to the doorway, not even glancing their way. "I'll leave you ladies be." He hurried out of the room, slamming the door behind him.

"Aww, cute," Lila said with a smile, then she and Emma broke into a fit of laughter.

∞∞∞∞∞∞∞∞

An hour later, Will anxiously stood at the bathroom mirror, dressed in one of Thomas's tuxedos, quietly reciting his vows – which was going terribly.

There was a gentle knock on the door, then it swung open. "Oh, shit. Sorry, man. Thought no one was in here." Blake, also dressed in a black suit, clumsily grasped for the handle as he went to leave.

"Hey, wait." Will stopped him. "I need to talk to you."

"Okay, sure." Blake stepped back into the bathroom and closed the door. "What's up?" he asked, unsure if had the energy for another argument with Will.

"So, listen," Will started, avoiding direct eye contact, "I know we haven't always got along. But I don't really have any mates here. Actually, I don't really have mates anywhere. But I was wondering if you'd be my best man?"

"Me?" Blake almost fell over. "Wow! You're really desperate, aren't you?"

"Hah, yep," Will agreed sheepishly. "Guess you could say that. It was either you or James, so…"

"Yeah, you made the right call," Blake said, then offered a handshake. "I'd be honoured."

"Thanks," Will said appreciatively, shaking his hand.

Whistling a casual tune, James barged through the bathroom door without so much as a knock. His face seized awkwardly. Will and Blake looked like deer caught in the headlights. "Hey," James said, a suspicious frown on his face.

"Hey," Will replied.

"'Sup?" Blake added.

"On your wedding day, William." James shook his head disapprovingly. "Does Lila know about you two?"

"You're just jealous," Blake said, as he shoved him out of the way and left the bathroom, much to James's amusement.

James then studied Will's tuxedo for a moment before giving him a thumbs up. "Not bad, Man Bun. Not bad at all."

"Thanks," Will replied.

"Everyone's ready except you, Emma and the bride," James informed him. "And, boy, if you lose that race, then—"

"Get out."

"Yeah, okay, I'll go now. Outside." James skulked out of the room, closing the door behind him.

～～～～～～～～

While Lorcan opted to stand guard from the house's front deck and Drakken continued his watch from the burnt field, Blake, James and Will gathered by the creek before a backdrop of vibrant green trees and crystal blue water. Thomas had lent each of the boys a suit, which they pulled off rather nicely, though they were cooking under the afternoon sun. Will didn't care, though; he had been picturing this day for years.

"I'm just saying – would definitely pick me," James said confidently.

"There is no way! I am taller and bigger than you, and I have the dreamy blond hair," Blake disagreed. "People love blond hair!"

"Chicks! People love blonde *chicks*," James replied. "You're tall and lanky, like a blond streetlamp, except there's nothing bright upstairs and you never stand still. It's all about dark and handsome when it comes to dudes – which is me all over!"

"Thought it was *tall*, dark, and handsome."

"Whatever, man," James said, and straightened his tie. "I got two out of three. Let's just agree: it would be me."

Tired of overhearing them bicker, Will decided to interrupt. "Are you two seriously arguing about who Emma would pick?"

"What? Emma? No!" James and Blake scoffed unanimously. "Lorcan."

"Oh." Will withdrew his interruption, stewed for a moment, then said, "You two are out of your minds. He'd definitely pick me."

Blake and James were about to dispute Will's claim when the clap of the back door closing carried across the yard. The three spun around to see Thomas and Emma escorting the beautiful bride towards them. Thomas looked particularly dapper; his chiselled jawline was freshly shaven and his short grey hair parted to one side. Blake, however, couldn't take his eyes off Emma, who looked stunning in her elegant black cocktail dress with her curled ponytail draped over her left shoulder.

"A wedding dress? How did she?" Will gasped, mesmerised by his gorgeous bride.

Lila's straight blonde hair bounced over her pale freckled shoulders with each cheerful stride. Will could tell she was trying not to fall over, which made his smile grow even bigger. As beautiful as it was, the sparkling wedding dress couldn't compete with Lila's pearly white smile, and Will loved that smile – more than anything.

Lila reached for her fiancé's hand and threaded her fingers between his. "Hi," she said lovingly, gazing happily into his eyes.

"Hi," Will said, and kissed her hand. "You look just… wow."

"Thank you. You look so handsome."

As the bride and groom settled in, Blake and Emma shuffled into position opposite one another. It didn't take long before Emma's brown eyes made contact with Blake's, where they remained until embarrassment caused them both to glance the other way. "Nice suit," Emma said, breaking the ice.

"Thanks," Blake replied, feeling a little awkward. "Your dad picked it, actually."

"Well, it's the man that makes the suit – or so they say."

"Right." Blake couldn't tell if he was blushing or not. He was. "You look beautiful."

"Thank you," Emma said, brushing a strand of hair over her ear. "Knew I bought this dress for some reason."

Standing between Blake and Thomas, James let out an obnoxious sigh. "Don't everyone tell me how great I look, all at once!" But Emma and Blake were too busy complimenting one another to take any notice.

Thomas, who was holding Milky in one arm, did notice. He leaned close to James's ear and whispered, "Your fly is open."

"What? Oh shit!" James's face reddened. He quickly fixed himself up, then sneezed heavily. "Did you have to bring the cat?" he winced, wiping his dripping nose on his jacket sleeve, which Thomas pretended not to see.

Thomas ignored him and moved over to the bride and groom, who were happily locked in a loving trance. "Shall we?" he asked. The pair anxiously agreed, so Thomas faced the group and began. "Normally, someone would thank friends and family for gathering today, but I can't do that. We have no friends here today. Only family. Now, someone might say that this wedding is not official – that it is not binding under the law. Well, I can tell you that no signed piece of paper makes for a proper marriage. Love, commitment, honesty and trust are the only marital laws that matter. Will and Lila have this in abundance. Which is why we are all so grateful to share this special moment with both of you." Thomas smiled at the bride, who was already tearing up. "I understand that you both would like to say your own vows."

"Yes, I'll go first," Lila quickly jumped in, resulting in a resounding chuckle from her audience.

"Okay," Thomas humoured her, "you first."

Lila relaxed her shoulders, steadied her breathing, then focused on Will. "William Duncan West, there are so many things I want to say to you, but seeing as time is of the essence, I'll try to stick to the important stuff. Never has anyone stood by my side the way you have. You stood by me when I brought a stray kitten into our house, when I converted our lounge room into a greenhouse while you were at work, and you didn't even get that mad when I turned your old acoustic guitar into a flower pot for my sunflowers." Lila paused as the group chuckled at that one. "You have run headfirst into danger for me. And even when we struggled, you never gave up on me. Not once. I promise I will never give up on you. You and Milky, this little family, is my world. We are so lucky. I love you, William. I always will." Lila, smiling through happy tears, finished to a round of cheers, whistles and applause.

Will smiled back at her, then cleared his throat. "Ethel Lila Joy, you have given my life a sense of purpose that I had never thought was possible. The compassion and care you show to every person you meet, the love you show every living thing you find, no matter what it is – you even water the weeds. And the constant drive you have to always do the right thing. You have shown me what selflessness *truly* is, and for that I'll always be grateful to you. I don't know if I'll ever be able to reach the bar that you set so high, but I know that I'll spend the rest of my life trying for you. You make me a better man. You are the love of my life, and I'll always be here to fill your watering can and take care of any stray cats lucky enough to find you. I love you."

Lila stared at him adoringly. "I love you, too."

"Well said." Thomas commended the happy couple, then delivered the only words they wanted to hear. "By the power you have entrusted to me, I now pronounce you husband and wife."

Blake, James, Emma and Thomas cheered in celebration as Will and Lila shared their first kiss as husband and wife.

James slinked in between Emma and Blake. "Did you guys know her first name was *Ethel*?" he whispered jokingly.

Lila pulled her lips away from Will's and shot James a threatening grin. "Don't you start! I *hate* that name."

"Sorry, Ethel," James teased. "Won't happen again."

"Good," she said, and smiled, then focused her attention back on her husband.

James turned back to Blake and Emma but caught a glimpse of something unusual over their shoulders. At the far end of the yard, Drakken seemed unsettled, casting the house and most of the grounds in a looming shadow as he began surveying the sky. "Hey, dude." James tapped Blake on the shoulder. "What is he doing?"

Blake became rigid, then pushed past Emma to get a better look. "I think he's found something," he said, watching the dragon's wings unfold.

Feeling the warmth of the sun disappear, Thomas, Lila and Will turned to see Drakken propel himself into the sky and vanish above the clouds. "Where is he going?" Lila asked, clutching Will's hand nervously.

Blake shielded his eyes but couldn't see the dragon anywhere, just white clouds and a dozen flocking birds. He noticed Lorcan coming around the side of the house, his rifle ready and cautiously aimed toward the sky. He didn't seem to know what was happening either.

"Wait, I see something," Emma shouted, then pointed to the left of where Drakken had disappeared. A streak of orange and blue flashed behind the clouds, then Drakken plunged through the cottony layers in a blaze of blue fire, spiralling back towards earth with a smoky trail billowing from his spiny back.

"Oh no!" Blake paled and took another step forward.

Emma's heart raced. "What just happened?"

The group could only watch as the building-sized dragon corkscrewed over their heads and plummeted into the forest like a meteor. A tidal wave of tree branches, dirt and stone resulted from the impact, blasting the whole group off their feet and sending them tumbling across the grass.

"Everybody okay?" Thomas called out, still holding the restless cat as dust enveloped the area.

"Yep, okay over here," James said, spitting dirt from his mouth.

Struggling to see through the haze, Emma coughed heavily but managed to answer, "I'm okay!"

"We're okay, too," Lila said, as she and Will brushed themselves off and sat up. "What happened to him?"

A fierce roar crackled high above. Blake didn't recognise it. He picked himself up from the ground, then assisted Emma, who had a bleeding gash on her forehead. Before he could ask if she was okay, Lorcan's grizzly voice carried across the yard: "Look out!" The pair peered up to see another massive dragon break through the clouds.

"Alarak," Blake stammered.

The black dragon swooped down and blasted a stream of blue fire over the front yard. The flames cut through the earth like a laser and melted Gary's truck and Will's four-wheel drive into the gravel like bubbling hot butter. Blake couldn't see Lorcan anymore. The monster curved through the air like a jet, using its four wings to adjust its pitch and speed while its two long tails swiftly changed its direction.

"My God," Thomas said, horrified by the sight of the grotesque creature.

Alarak slammed down on the far side of the yard with an earthquaking *crack*. Everyone froze. The dragon snapped its alligator-like jaws and stood tall. It was taller than Drakken, but far leaner. Blue light surged between the glossy black scales covering the monster's nightmarish frame. Its long bony arms stretched to the ground with four sickle-like claws curling out of its fingertips. Blue fire burned around its pupils, and a line of jagged horns, crowning the ridge of its spine, divided two sets of bat-like wings before splitting off at the pair of flailing tails.

The earth began to shake again. Blake turned back to the forest where a familiar orange glow began refracting through the dust cloud.

"Run! Now!" Drakken growled, as he rose out of the crater with an inferno raging throughout his body.

Alarak readied himself, jaws open and claws twitching. A moment passed, then Drakken leapt over the house and tackled the towering black dragon to the ground. Power pylons snapped like twigs, chunks of road flipped into the air, and the white timber fence lining the street disintegrated under the mass of the two tussling monsters.

"We gotta move!" Blake barked, as a stray beam of fire obliterated a section of forest nearby.

"This way," Thomas yelled, sprinting for the barn, with Emma and James behind him.

Will, Blake and Lila followed, the latter lifting her wedding dress up so that she wouldn't trip.

The whopping crack of Drakken's muscular tail colliding with Alarak's jaw brought the group to a skidding halt. The black dragon sailed across the yard, narrowly missing Houdini's roof before hurtling through the barn like it was made of tissue paper.

"Come on! This way!" James shouted, sprinting back in the other direction before veering left towards the road. Emma and Thomas were close behind, but Will hung back, helping Lila as she struggled to run in her dress. As they neared the house, Will quickly yanked Blake towards him as searing blue fire blasted past their faces and left a flaming wall between them and the others.

"Quick!" Will turned back to the creek. "Back this way!" He clutched Lila's hand and the three sprinted along the creek towards the overgrown tree line.

Letting out a ferocious roar, the two dragons launched into an aerial wrestling match, unleashing a barrage of blue and orange fire upon the sky. James, Emma and Thomas rounded the corner to find Lorcan crouched behind Gary's melted truck, firing his rifle at the duelling monsters.

"Hey," James called out to him. Lorcan ceased fire and checked over his shoulder. "You know, I've got a slingshot inside if you need some backup."

Lorcan grunted at his ineffective rifle. "Shut up. Out of ammo anyway." He tossed the gun aside and jogged over to the others.

"We need to get out of here," Thomas said, still holding Milky in his arms.

Emma agreed, then looked around for Will, Blake and Lila. "Wait. Where are the others?"

"I don't know. Shit!" James cursed. "We must have got separated!"

High in the sky above, Drakken took a mighty swipe at Alarak with his massive claws. However, the black dragon was too quick and thrust backward before unleashing a scorching blue inferno into his chest. Drakken let out an agonising howl as his scales melted under the flames. Swooping right, he retaliated with molten hot steam that engulfed Alarak's face. The four-winged dragon wailed horrifically as its left eye was burned out of its socket. In a desperate move, Alarak dug its claws into Drakken's torso and, with a powerful flap of its four wings, propelled them toward the ground like a building-sized missile.

Thomas, Lorcan, James and Emma could do nothing but flee as the two dragons plummeted straight into the Riley farmhouse. An explosion of timber decking, steel beams and shattered roof tiles scattered in every direction. With a deep groan, Alarak rose out of the crater and snarled victoriously at Drakken, who was pinned beneath his bony foot. Drakken's eyes ignited, but before he could blast his opponent once more, Alarak flung him from the crater with a swift flick of its leg.

Lila ran ahead, leading Will and Blake along the bank. "Where are the others?" she yelled, keeping her dress up around her knees as she carefully navigated the rocky terrain.

"Don't know! Just keep running!" Blake felt the ground tremble as another wave of debris sprayed overhead.

"Head into the forest!" Will called out from the back.

"Okay," Lila replied, "but we need to find the oth—"

Blake saw nothing but grey scales and dirt as the earth erupted in his face. The force was enough to send him and Will hurtling back into the stony creek. His head hit a large boulder, but somehow, he hardly felt it. Water and blood gushed into his mouth. He choked and sputtered, then crawled out of the creek and up onto the bank. "Will? Lila?" he coughed, tasting more blood than water.

The ground shook again. Blake rolled over. Will was standing at the crater's edge where Drakken lay motionless. Will fell to his knees. The dragon sluggishly began to move.

"Will?" Blake reeled with pain, now feeling the bulging welt on the back of his head.

Orange light flickered between Drakken's scales, and the dragon climbed to its feet. Growling furiously, he then launched himself at Alarak, not even noticing Will or Blake beside him.

Will didn't move. He stared into the crater as the creek poured in over the edge. A bloodied wedding dress rested at the centre. Water dripped from his hair while his knees sank deeper into the mud. "Lila?" he called, then feebly tried to stand.

"Will!" Blake struggled to get up. "Will, don't go in there!"

Will stumbled down the incline till he tripped and fell to the muddy ground. He lifted his head; he could see Lila's hand only metres from his face. "Honey?" he crawled towards her, pain surging through every part of his body. He reached for her arm but fell short, his palm instead clasping something in the dirt – a mangled diamond ring. "Lila?" he called out.

"You don't need to see this!" Blake suddenly wrapped his arms around Will and fought to drag him away. "Not like this, Will. You don't wanna see her like this."

"Get off me!" Will struggled in Blake's grip before breaking free. The pair tumbled back to the ground with a splash. Water continued to fill the crater. Will sat up and opened his hand; the ring was caked in mud. "This is all your fault," he sobbed, then clutched the ring tight. "If she hadn't listened to you... if I had just taken her away..."

"I'm so sorry, Will," Blake wept, struggling to stand. When he eventually did stand, Will met him with a weighty punch that sent Blake straight back into the mud. He choked on the filthy water, then slowly rolled over to find Will standing over him with clenched fists.

"This is all your fault!" Will screamed, tears rolling down his muddy face as he belted Blake in the stomach with a vicious kick. "We should never have come here! I should have left you in that mall." He kicked him again and again until the sight of blood dripping from his own hand caused him to falter. Will opened his fist; more blood trickled out. The diamond ring was still in his palm. He'd been clenching it so tight that the ring had cut into his skin.

Clutching his beaten stomach, Blake wheezed and gasped for breath and tried to keep his head above the water.

Earthquake-like tremors and criss-crossing streaks of blue and orange continued to play out in the background. Will didn't even notice anymore. He walked over to Lila, removed his torn tuxedo jacket and gently placed it over her body. "I failed you, honey." Will's eyes lingered on the ring for several seconds, then he carelessly tossed it to Blake. It bounced off his shoulder and rolled into the water.

By the time Blake could get up again, Will was nowhere to be seen. There was just a trail of footprints leading from the crater toward the forest. "Will?" he called out, but nobody answered. Will was gone.

∞∞∞∞∞∞∞∞

Following Lorcan's lead, Emma, James and Thomas fled down the road, trying to put as much distance between them and the two raging titans as possible. As they rounded the bend near Rodney and Patrice's farm, a small convoy of military vehicles came barrelling down the road. Lorcan recognised the first one right away. The ATV-X wasn't easily mistaken. He reached for his pistol but found nothing but an empty holster. "Shit," he cursed. He must have dropped it.

James and Emma swapped a nervous glance, then Emma said, "They'll help us, right?"

Thomas looked at her doubtfully as the vehicles quickly surrounded them.

"Everybody stay calm," Lorcan said quietly.

Soldiers poured out of the vehicle with drawn weapons. The ATV-X's rear door retracted. Mitch and Damien stepped out and immediately locked eyes with Lorcan.

"Cap," Mitch nodded, then slammed the butt of his rifle into Lorcan's mouth.

"Are you crazy?' Emma shrieked. "The dragons are right there! Shoot them!"

Damien gave Lorcan a backhand of his own, then looked at Emma, saying, "Let them kill each other. We're not here for them. Where is the dragon kid – Blake, or whatever his name is?"

"He's dead," Emma answered quickly, earning a distrustful smirk from Mitch.

"Is that right?" Mitch asked, as he moved closer to her.

"You stay away from her," Thomas barked, but was immediately restrained by the surrounding soldiers.

Emma didn't flinch. "You can go check for yourself. Why do you think they're fighting?"

Mitch backed away, certain that the girl couldn't be trusted. It didn't matter, though. He had what he needed. "Let's go."

"Some soldiers you are," James muttered.

Damien leaned in next to James's ear and whispered, "Give me a reason to shoot you."

"Mitch, Damien!" Lorcan shouted, then wiped the blood from his mouth. "Just let these people go. Goddammit! Don't let Henrickson—"

Mitch struck him again. "Say another word, and I *will* shoot you." He then gestured to the rear cabin of the Wombat. "Load them in the back. Double-time."

The soldiers followed their orders. Placing each of them in handcuffs, they then herded Emma, James, Thomas and Lorcan into the rear cabin of the ATV-X. "Yuk!" James squirmed as Damien shoved him into his seat. "Why does it smell like piss in here?"

"Just shut up," Damien barked, clutching his rifle. He slammed the touchpad and closed the rear door. "You sure about this?" Damien asked, walking over to Mitch.

Mitch hesitated to answer, then said, "No. But the colonel is."

"What if the colonel is wrong?"

"Then we are all dead anyway," Mitch replied, as the pair watched the dragons tear at one another in the distance.

"We better go," Damien said nervously, "before it notices."

"Yeah, I think you're right. Move out!" Mitch ordered.

~~~~~~~~~~~~~

"James? Emma?" Blake staggered out of the crater and found he no longer recognised his surroundings. Debris from the Riley farmhouse lay scattered over sections of scorched earth while a thick black smog spread over the sky. Clutching his ribs, many of which were broken, Blake watched as Drakken's massive body slammed limply into the ground ahead of him.

"Run," Drakken croaked.

Alarak pounced onto the dragon's back, thrusting his sickle-like claws deep into his flesh. Drakken let out a harrowing roar. The black dragon was about to strike again when it caught a glimpse of Blake watching from the far end of the yard. Retracting its claws from Drakken's back, Alarak started toward Blake, limberly crawling like a stalking lion.

Blake didn't try to run. There was nowhere to go; nowhere he could hide, even if he wanted to. He stood his ground as the dragon's enormous shadow draped over him. A blue inferno raged in Alarak's remaining eye. "It doesn't have to be this way," Blake said softly.

"Yes... it... does," Alarak hissed, then opened its gaping jaws.

Blake could feel the heat across his skin. The dragon arched its back then lunged, but the bladed tips of Drakken's tail impaled its chest, sending its fiery breath streaking into the sky. Alarak howled in agony as Drakken's long tail lifted the black dragon off the ground. No matter how much Alarak flailed its tails or swiped over its shoulders, it couldn't break free.

Fire surged through Drakken's battered scales as he rose from the ground and unleashed hell upon the black dragon. Alarak roared in pain as its scales were burned from its bony skull.

"You betrayed your word. You are no Guardian," Drakken growled. Then, with his thorn-covered arms, he dug his claws into Alarak's neck and ripped it from its body. Tossing the dragon's severed head to one side, he swung his tail around and flung the limp torso across the yard, sending it crashing into the woods.

"Shit." Blake could hardly breathe. "You okay?' he asked, noticing that most of Drakken's body was gouged, charred and burned.

"I will heal," Drakken said, shaking himself off.

"Lila… she was…" Blake could hardly say it.

"I know. I am sorry for your friend."

"Where are the others?" Blake asked, looking around. "Did they get away? Please tell me they got away."

Drakken raised his snout to the air. "They have been taken."

"Taken?" Blake questioned, then the obvious dawned on him. "Henrickson."

"Yes. The man you sought for help. He has them."

"We have to get them back," Blake said desperately. "I know this isn't our great task or whatever, but please, I'll do anything you ask. Just help me get them back first."

Drakken lowered his hand to the ground and opened his claws. "I will help you. But tell me, human, are you prepared to do what is necessary?"

Blake staggered onto the dragon's rock-like palm. "Yes, I can't lose anyone else. I'll do whatever it takes."

36

THE DRAGON'S REIGN

As the sun finally sank behind the mountains, several tall spotlights flickered to life with a low buzz, illuminating the Castra Dam carpark like a football stadium. Blake stood before an endless number of deserted olive-green tents, but he couldn't help noticing the four military trucks he passed at the gate. Their engines were still ticking. Even though the dam seemed unoccupied, he knew he wasn't alone.

He moved through the tents quietly, and when he neared the ramp leading to the dam wall, the patter of cantering boots brought him to a halt. Suddenly, the spotlights snapped onto his position, and two dozen combat-ready soldiers emerged from various dark places.

"Hands up!" one soldier barked.

"We have him, sir," another radioed in.

Blake complied and kept his hands high. Four armed soldiers then escorted him up the ramp and to the dam wall. The remaining troops hung back, switching their rifle's torch lights on to scan their surroundings for any signs of a giant dragon. Blake noticed the corner of the maintenance building was missing its roof – the interrogation room that Drakken had rescued him from.

When he arrived at the centre of the dam wall, Blake found Henrickson standing by the same high-tech vehicle that had taken him from the Robina refuge centre – the Wombat, or so the soldiers had called it. At the colonel's side were two other men he recognised from that day: Lorcan's former squad mates, though Blake couldn't remember their names.

"Mr Daniels," Henrickson greeted him. "You don't look too good," he added, surveying the state of Blake's shredded clothes and beaten face.

"People keep telling me that," Blake reluctantly humoured him.

"I wasn't expecting you to come alone." Henrickson glanced past Blake's shoulder at the soldiers searching through the grounds. "So, where is it?"

"Dead," Blake replied. "The black one killed it."

Henrickson massaged his fingers over his unkempt stubble. "Dead, you say?" He looked doubtful.

"Where are my friends?"

"Your friends?" Henrickson mocked. "You mean the treasonous pricks that want to help that monster?" He nodded to one of the soldiers standing guard.

Mitch then opened the vehicle's armoured door and leaned in. "Everyone out. Slowly," he barked, removing his pistol from its holster.

Thomas was the first out. His hair was rumpled, and his suit was filthy, but he seemed okay – as did Milky. Emma followed her father shortly afterwards. "Don't touch me," she snarled at Mitch, who went to assist her as she struggled to move in her black cocktail dress and handcuffs.

"Hurry up in there," Damien shouted, as he moved up alongside Mitch and reached into the cabin.

"Get your hands off me, Ginger Kong." James kicked and thrashed as Damien dragged him out of the vehicle by his ankles.

Blake and Emma briefly locked eyes, but the colonel quickly brought the attention back to himself by producing a handgun from his jacket's inner pocket.

"Now," Henrickson said, as he cocked the gun, "you have a choice. Tell me where that dragon is, and I might let them go."

"I told you. It's dead."

"That's a shame," Henrickson snapped back, and fired a round into James's leg.

James screamed, dropped to the pavement and keeled over in agony.

"You bastard!" Emma shrieked. With her cuffed hands, she quickly kneeled and applied pressure to James's wound.

"Colonel, please stop," Blake pleaded, feeling an unnerving sense of déjà vu.

"Colonel?" Damien was stunned. He crouched next to Emma and adjusted her hands over the bullet hole. "Keep the pressure here."

"The next one is in his head," Henrickson said coldly. "So, I'll ask again. Where is the dragon?"

"Okay, I'll tell you," Blake yielded, "but I don't understand. You know you can't kill it, so why even find it?"

The colonel lowered the gun and pridefully straightened his posture. "Because I *will* kill it. I will hit it with everything I've got or die trying. I will not let that thing get away with murdering thousands – something you seem to be quite content with."

"I'm not content," Blake replied carefully. "I'm just trying to stop this from happening to more people. Drakken wants to help us do that."

Henrickson turned his pistol on Blake. "Don't say that fucking thing's name."

"I'm sorry." Blake instinctively stepped back but collided with the four armed soldiers standing behind him. "It's the truth, colonel. He knows what he did to us, but now, he's trying to help us, and we could use the help, colonel. I could use *your* help."

Henrickson began to laugh. "Wow! That thing really has done a number on you, hasn't it?" He reached back and aimed the gun at Emma, who was still tending to James's wound.

"Stop!" Thomas squirmed, but Mitch had him firmly restrained.

"Colonel?" Mitch interrupted, feeling more uneasy with each passing second. Surely Henrickson wouldn't go through with it?

"Wait!" Blake cut in. "The dragon is here," he said, urging the colonel to lower his weapon.

Henrickson looked up at the night sky. "Where?" he asked mockingly, then spun around in a circle. "I don't see it."

"I'll show you. But please, don't shoot."

"Show me," Henrickson demanded, "or I'll shoot all of them."

"Drakken," Blake said cautiously, "remember what we talked about."

Steam began to rise from the dam's moonlit lake. Henrickson moved over to the railing. The water was starting to boil. Blake heard the armed soldiers behind him shuffle back. Bubbles popped and crackled as the black water began to strobe with an orange glow.

"Oh, shit," Mitch cursed to himself.

Drakken's massive head broke the surface; his reptilian eyes were a blazing inferno as the lake poured out between his teeth. The dragon rose over the dam wall, water gushing off its spiny back and flat snout as three glowing gills closed along the side of its neck.

"Open fire!" the colonel barked, staggering back to see the whole creature.

Suddenly the base erupted into chaos. Bullets, rockets and missiles sliced through the night like fireworks. Drakken vanished behind an onslaught of fireballs and streaking gunfire. The blasts were close enough to send everyone atop the dam wall toppling to the ground. Mitch and Damien quickly lifted James into the Wombat for cover, then helped Emma and Thomas get in after him. The two soldiers shut the Wombat's armoured door, and opened fire on the dragon.

Blake rolled onto his back. He could only watch as the evolving explosions completely consumed Drakken. Almost every weapon in the base had been discharged by the time the colonel ordered, "Cease fire!"

Castra Dam was plunged into silence. Balls of fire dissipated into thick smoke over the lake. Henrickson anxiously waited for the smog to clear, but an all-too-familiar orange glow began to pulse behind the haze. "No. How?" The air parted, revealing an unscathed Drakken still towering over the water. "No!" Henrickson fired three pointless rounds into the dragon's torso. The bullets crumpled against his thick scales.

"Colonel, look!" Blake climbed to his feet and pointed at the dragon. "He's not fighting back. He's not here to hurt anyone. We are going to stop all this. Please! I only came for my friends. Just let them go."

Henrickson's shoulders slumped and he said, "Get them out."

Mitch opened the Wombat's rear door and waved everyone out. This time Lorcan was the first to disembark. Blake hadn't realised he'd been in there the whole time. Both Lorcan's wrists were bleeding from the tight handcuffs. Emma and Thomas assisted James out, who looked increasingly pale and was now shivering.

"Get him a medic," Damien ordered one of the four soldiers near Blake.

"No," Henrickson barked, "cancel that order."

"Sir," Damien said, gesturing at James, "he will bleed out."

Henrickson didn't answer him, leaving everyone in uncertain silence. Eventually, the emotional colonel lifted his gaze to the dragon in the lake. "You… you took everything from me! You murdered my children, my wife. So many children, so many people!"

"Colonel," Blake started, "We—"

"Don't!" Henrickson distraughtly shouted. "I may not be able to kill this monster. But I can take everything from you, just like it took everything from me." He raised his gun and pointed it at Emma.

"Whoa!" Damien and Mitch moved to her side. "Colonel, don't do this," Mitch pleaded.

"Colonel, stop!" Blake desperately cried.

"Please, don't," Emma begged for her life. "I don't want to die."

Thomas quickly put himself between his daughter and the colonel.

Henrickson struggled to keep the gun steady. "It killed my babies."

"Sam! Please!" Mitch pleaded. "This isn't you. Don't kill her. She's just a girl. They're all just trying to make sense of this, just like we are. Please, sir, think of Bia. Think of Gracie. The man behind me is the girl's father. Don't take her from him the way your girls were taken from you."

Henrickson stared at Mitch with glassy eyes. "It killed them."

"Yes, sir, I know," Mitch said calmly. "But this isn't the way. Please. Let these people go. We can get through this."

Henrickson loosened his grip on the pistol and stumbled back. "Everybody stand down," he ordered, then hopelessly fell to his knees.

Mitch quickly tended to the colonel while Damien unlocked each prisoner's handcuffs and called a medic for James. Lorcan, assisted by the four soldiers, quickly helped James from the dam wall and down the ramp, where a doctor was waiting for him.

Thomas, still holding the cat, hugged Emma with his free arm and whispered, "It's okay. You're safe. It's over now. You're okay, Em." He then walked the shaken girl past Blake and down the ramp towards James and another pair of medics.

"You did the right thing, colonel," Damien said softly, joining Mitch at Henrickson's side as he wept on the concrete floor.

Blake could only watch them. His whole body was numb. He'd lost Lila. Gary, too. And Amy. He'd lost so many. He glanced over at James and Emma who were being tended to by medical personnel in the carpark. He'd almost lost them, too. They'd almost paid the price for his choices, just like Gary had. He couldn't bear the thought of it. They were his family now.

Blake continued to watch Henrickson; the man was completely broken. He knew what that kind of pain could do to a man. After all, the colonel had been only one trigger pull away from taking everything from him. That kind of pain was relentless, unforgiving even. Blake knew that.

"You'll come for them, won't you?" Blake said softly.

"Huh?" Mitch paused, and he noticed Blake was shaking. "You okay, mate?"

Henrickson wiped his eyes and feebly looked up.

"What did the kid say?" Damien asked, with a supportive hand on the colonel's back.

"You'll change your mind." Blake stared helplessly into Samuel Henrickson's devastated gaze. "You'll come for them. Like he did. You'll kill them, just like he did. I can't lose them."

"What? Mate, it's okay. Everything is okay now," Mitch said, confused, then turned his attention to the dragon standing over the lake, its eyes flaring. He leapt to his feet. "No! Stop!"

Drakken arched his back.

"Wait!" But Mitch realised too late.

Drakken unleashed a stream of fire upon Castra Dam's wall, consuming Mitch, Damien and Samuel Henrickson in the furious blaze.

Down at the medical tent, the fiery glow swept over the night sky. James shoved the doctor attending to him back, and turned towards the towering dragon. "Oh no. What has he done?"

"Blake!" Emma barged through Lorcan and Thomas to get out of the medical tent. Ash trickled over the dam wall as smog billowed into the night. "Oh, God! No!" She sprinted for the ramp. "Blake?"

"What happened?" Lorcan asked one of the doctors, but the doctor was in shock. He and Thomas ducked out to see cracks spreading across the concrete structure. "Oh, shit! We gotta move," he wailed. "Everybody out!"

Thomas quickly lifted James to his feet and helped him hobble out of the tent. "I need to find Emma," he shouted to Lorcan.

"She's fine," Lorcan assured him. "She went after Blake. She's probably the safest one here!" This did little to reassure the worried father.

The remaining soldiers and military personnel scattered like ants, fleeing in whatever trucks and vehicles they could find.

Emma reached the top of the dam wall where she found scorched concrete and rising smoke. Blake was there, too, on his knees, cradling his face. "Blake! Are you okay?" she called out, rushing to his side.

"What did I just do?" Blake lowered his hands; he was a mess. "I killed them."

"What?" Emma lingered on that thought for a moment, then said, "Listen. We can work this out. But we need to go. The wall is about to come down!"

"I couldn't let them. The colonel, he would have come for us, just like Gabriel."

Emma grabbed Blake by his shoulders and tried to lift him to his feet. She couldn't, and he was too delirious to help himself. She looked to Drakken, who was already watching her. "If you really care about him, then help me!"

The dragon growled and moved through the water towards her, which put even more stress on the crumbling wall. "Hold onto something," Drakken said, and thrust his claws under the very concrete she and Blake were standing on, then tore it from the wall itself. With a flap of his wings, Drakken ascended out of the water, resulting in a terrified scream from Emma as their concrete island rose into the air.

She clutched Blake's hand and steadied herself as Drakken flew them high above Castra Dam.

The view was unexpectedly breathtaking. Instead of a plethora of orange-and-white streetlights, Emma saw little more than black, and a single light shining brightly in the distance. She stared at it. Someone else was out there. She then noticed another one a little further to her right, then another a bit further than that. Emma slowly rose to her feet and gazed at the dozens of lights still glittering in the distance. For every twinkling glow she saw, a glimmer of hope shone back at her.

With a deafening crash, the dam wall split open then completely collapsed, unleashing over three hundred thousand megalitres of water into the valley. Emma tightly wove her fingers between Blake's, listening as the tidal wave consumed the sea of military tents and gushed into the wilderness. Blake barely flinched and seemed to be in a state of shock. Drakken passed the surrounding tree line and descended over a nearby access road. James, Thomas and Lorcan were already there with several surviving soldiers and medical personnel.

Drakken carefully touched down and placed the concrete slab on the road. Emma climbed off and ran to her father, who embraced her in a warm hug. Lorcan hung back, still reeling from the sudden loss of Damien, Mitch and Henrickson.

With a blood-soaked bandage wrapped around his leg, James hobbled over to Blake who sat silently on the chunk of dam wall. "Hey, dude, you okay? What happened?"

"Lila," Blake mumbled incoherently. "She died."

"What?" James turned back to Emma. The colour drained from her face.

"We were running... they were fighting... and she... Will just left..." Blake gradually rose to his feet but could hardly stand straight.

"Dude, listen to me!" James reached up for his friend and offered his hand. "This isn't your fault. We're in this together."

Blake tried to speak, but his gaze just lingered helplessly. "I'm sorry... I have to go... I have to save us... I need to stop *all* of this." He stumbled backward off the concrete and fell into Drakken's open palm.

"Dude, you're not thinking clearly!" James painfully climbed onto the slab as the dragon's claws began to close over his friend. "No! Don't you *dare* take him," James shouted at Drakken. "Open your fucking hand right now!"

He glanced back at Emma who was watching helplessly by her father's side.

Drakken's wings unfolded and stretched out, blocking the moonlight.

"Blake, wait!" Emma cried, then left her father behind as she desperately rushed to the dragon's closed fist.

Blake could hear her on the other side. "I'm sorry," he said softly, slumping back against the thick scales. Her voice brought tears to his eyes. "I have to go... to protect you... all of you."

"Don't go," Emma begged him, resting her head against the dragon's scaly hand. "Please don't go."

"I'm sorry. I have to fix this."

"Blake! Don't go!" Emma begged, but the dragon's hand lifted up from the ground. "Blake, please!"

Drakken flapped his wings and launched into the night sky, leaving Emma and James watching from the street below until they could see nothing but stars and moonlight filtering through the clouds.

EPILOGUE

After recovering the battered ATV-X from a flooded ditch in the valley, Lorcan parted ways with James, Thomas and Emma and set out on his own mission: the return of a certain green dinosaur to its rightful owner. Like Lorcan himself, the ATV- X had seen better days. Its roof-mounted turret had been torn off during the ride off the Castra Dam wall, and the armoured door on the right-hand side was now melted into the chassis itself, thanks to Drakken's fiery breath.

Long streaks of dry grime and dirt covered the Wombat's cracked windshield. Lorcan lowered his newly requisitioned sunglasses over his eyes and quickly referred to his map. There was a fork in the road ahead. Once he noted the correct road to take, he tossed the map to the side and glanced at the green stuffed toy on the seat beside him. Jack's dinosaur rested atop the note that Amanda had given him. "You always have a choice," it read. Co-ordinates to the facility where the Marsh family had been taken were scribbled on the other side. They were the same co-ordinates he had circled on his map.

As the Wombat curved around the next bend, Lorcan spotted something he didn't expect to see at the side of a country dirt road – three people with their thumbs raised, hoping to hitch a ride. Easing on the brake, he slowed to a crawl and noted one was a woman, probably in her forties, and the others were a teenage girl and her younger sister, probably six or seven years of age. He pulled up alongside them and wound down the passenger window. "You three need a ride?" he asked.

The woman's face was quite beaten, and her strawberry blonde hair, tattered. "Yes, please! Are you military?"

"Yes, ma'am," Lorcan replied, as he pulled the latch on the door and pushed it open. "There's only room for one in the front. Plenty of room in the back, though." He hit a button on the dash, and the rear sliding door retracted.

The woman turned her attention to her weary daughters. "Bia, you hop in the back with your sister. Mummy's gonna ride up front with the nice man."

"Are you sure?" the teenage girl questioned her mother. "We don't even know him."

"Gracie, I just need you to trust me," the woman said, helping her youngest into the rear cabin. "Get in the back with your sister. This man is military. He might know where your father is."

"Bia… Gracie…" Lorcan sunk back in his seat, repeating their names to himself. "It can't be."

"Sorry about that," the woman said, climbing into her seat and shutting her door. "You know how kids can be."

"Lisa." Lorcan studied her face, then stared at her with disbelief as the recovered driver's licence flashed through his mind. "You…You're Lisa Henrickson."

The woman went to clip in her seatbelt but froze at the sound of her name. "Do you know my husband?" She turned to Lorcan with hopeful eyes.

〰〰〰〰〰〰

Feeling the wet sand squish between their toes, Emma, James and Thomas stood side by side as another wave crashed over their feet. Each held a single yellow sunflower in their hand – Lila's favourite.

"She loved the beach," Emma said softly.

James smiled. "She loved everything."

"You two ready?" Thomas asked.

Emma nodded, then peered into the water. "You will always be our friend, our family, our sister. We love you, Lila."

James gently tossed his flower into the water, saying, "Miss you already."

Thomas carefully placed his down and watched as the rip whisked the yellow flower out to sea.

Emma struggled to let her flower go.

Thomas rested his hand on top of hers. "It's okay, Em," he told her.

Emma wiped away another tear. "I just miss her so much."

"I know you do, honey," Thomas said, and gently opened his daughter's fingers and watched the yellow flower fall into the water. The sunflower's petals soaked into the ocean as it rolled over countless waves and gradually drifted out to sea.

"I'm proud of you, Em," Thomas said quietly, then clutched his daughter's hand tight.

Respectfully, James quietly wandered down the shore to give them some much-needed space. He soon found himself staring down the beach and couldn't help but wonder what would come next. The ruins of Surfers Paradise glowed with a golden shine under the morning sun. James smirked, for even now, after everything, the city still seemed like paradise.

A swooping winged shadow suddenly crossed over the sand. Emma let go of her father's hand and spun around to see a flock of seagulls flying overhead.

"Just birds, Em," Thomas said softly. "Don't worry. We'll find him."

"We have to," Emma said. "I can't let him do this on his own. He needs us." She gazed at the devastated city. "He'll need his family."

〜〜〜〜〜〜〜〜〜

Blake tightened the screw on the bonnet latch and dropped the hood. It clicked shut – finally. Thankfully, the deserted gas station had every tool he needed to fix Houdini up. Wiping the sweat from his face, he sat on the bonnet and rested back on his hands. It was only morning, but it felt like an oven outside.

"Why fix the machine?" Drakken questioned him.

Blake watched as the dragon landed in the street outside the gas station. "It's important to me. Gary worked hard on this thing. We both did, actually." He ran his hand over the bonnet, then stood up and walked onto the road. "Besides, every time I fly with you, I end up vomiting all over the place." Blake blocked the sun from his eyes and gazed up at the dragon. "Did you find them?" he asked.

"Yes," Drakken answered in his usual growling tone. "She is seeking you."

"Did she see you?"

"No."

"Okay," Blake said, then glanced back at his car, "and you're sure that you can't locate Will?"

"I cannot detect his scent; it is likely he has perished."

"Somehow, I doubt it." Blake reached into his pocket and pulled out Lila's engagement ring. He'd fished it out of the water before crawling out of the crater. "And what about Grannus? What if he doesn't agree to help us?"

Drakken lowered himself on all fours, his claws tearing into the pavement. "Then a dark fate will befall your species. But do not fret. He is the wisest of all beings. I trust his counsel. He will see as I do."

"I hope you're right."

Drakken growled, "As do I, human."

Blake drew a deep breath and said, "Guess we've got work to do."

"Very well. I will follow your lead." Drakken opened his massive wings and launched into the sky, shattering the road beneath in the process.

"Okay then," Blake said, as he climbed into his car and fired up the engine. Houdini howled to life. Shifting into first, he dropped the clutch, flattened the accelerator and took off down the road. Drakken's winged shadow glided over the Gold Coast Highway as Blake wove Houdini through the devastated traffic and left paradise in his rearview mirror.

With each fork in the road he passed, Blake questioned whether the path he had chosen was the right one. For he knew that with every coming choice, there would be consequences; with every life, there would be death; and when one reign came to an end, another would soon begin.